Teddy sauntered a little closer to the shadows she lurked in so he wouldn't have to speak so loudly. "Should you not be dancing?"

"This was my only empty set. You saw that when you looked at my card."

"Did I?"

"I assumed that was why you followed me out now."

"I was warm, and I didn't follow you," he promised. He couldn't see her clearly in the shadows, so he took another step that way. "Why are you out here alone?"

"I was warm, too," she laughed softly.

No one inside seemed to be looking in this direction, so Teddy took another step, and then another, until he stood in the shadows with Eugenia. He could see her face better now. Eugenia was grinning at him and, yes, quite alone and lovely by moonlight.

He grinned, too. "So, I am not interrupting a romantic rendezvous?"

Eugenia lifted her chin. "That depends on what you say next, sir."

HEATHER BOYD

USAT BESTSELLING AUTHOR

PLEASURES OF THE NIGHT

Distinguished Rogues

16

The characters and events portrayed in this book are fictitious. Any similarity to real persons, living or dead, is purely coincidental and not intended by the author.

PLEASURES OF THE NIGHT © 2021 by Heather Boyd
ISBN: 978-1-925239-80-5
Editing by Kelli Collins

All rights reserved. No part of this book may be reproduced in any form by any electronic or mechanical means—except in the case of brief quotations embodied in critical articles or reviews—without written permission of the author.

Chapter One

May 1816
London

"Why are you deferring to Sylvia at home? It is not as if she's becoming royalty," Eugenia Hillcrest complained to her youngest cousin as they entered Wharton House, the Marquess of Wharton's grand London mansion in Cavendish Square, after a night of rubbing shoulders with the cream of society.

"Close enough," Aurora noted as she passed off her shawl and reticule to a hovering servant. "Sylvia is to marry one of the most eligible bachelors and popular lords in society. Everyone had been trying to catch his eye until our cousin seduced him."

"She did not seduce him," Eugenia hissed and then moderated her tone down to a whisper. "They fell in love in the best way. Secretly."

"I still cannot believe she didn't say a word to warn us of the blossoming romance, and she should have given us time to prepare for all this," Aurora said, casting a glance up at the vaulted ceiling, where a pastoral scene had recently been painted. Gilt and mirrors, too, as far as the eye could see. "I thought we had a pact to share everything."

Eugenia had thought so, too. But Sylvia had deceived them both, meeting secretly with a marquess for weeks before they'd both borne witness to the most startling marriage proposal from Lord Wharton. Although annoyed with Sylvia, Eugenia could understand why she had kept her silence about the affair. There were some situations in a woman's life that were impossible to explain properly, especially when one's heart was deeply involved.

The Marquess of Wharton was quite the catch, but he had flaws, too. The first being, he was extremely high-handed. They would never have imagined such a powerful man might be drawn to their dear but poor cousin. But he was utterly besotted with Sylvia. She was glad Wharton had done the honorable thing in the end and proposed a partnership of love and trust.

It helped that Sylvia loved Wharton to distraction, too, and had declared him her perfect match in every way that mattered. Wharton's respect for Sylvia's opinions, even when they were the opposite of his own, had made it easier for Eugenia to accept the match in the end. With Sylvia's marriage into an important family, though, Aurora and Eugenia were both under the continual scrutiny of the unforgiving *ton* forevermore.

And members of the *ton* were easily provoked to spiteful tattling. Even women of her age, seven and twenty, came in for censure for misbehavior, real or imagined, all the time. It was fortunate she had no expectation of making a match herself, but she did worry about spoiling her younger cousin's chances by putting a foot wrong.

A hard rap on the door sounded behind them, and the butler sprang into action to admit a dozen titled gentlemen, wives, and bachelors who had been invited to follow them home. Lord Wharton liked to entertain.

"Ooh, look. More company for tea," Aurora crooned in obvious delight.

Actual tea at this hour of the night tended to be in short supply for Wharton's impromptu parties, but spirits and wine were always plentiful and far more popular.

Eugenia glanced over her shoulder as a pair of late stragglers were admitted. Mr. Thaddeus Berringer, a dark-haired gentleman she'd admired from afar for a while, and Lord Sullivan, a former client of the Hillcrest Academy, strode into the chamber and looked about them, smiling.

Eugenia uttered a happy sigh.

The attendance of the Duke of Exeter's heir would make the evening more enjoyable for her. Good-looking men were meant to be appreciated from all angles and from top to firm-muscled bottom.

She leaned toward her cousin. "Lord Sullivan is here."

Aurora made an unhappy sound but did not turn to see. She had never hidden the fact that she thought little of Lord Sullivan.

Eugenia sighed. "Why can you not be kinder to our former client?"

"I have my reasons," she said loftily.

Sullivan was a nice man. Wealthy. Softly spoken when in the company of ladies. He had not been keen to marry the last time they had met, although he was being pressured by his family. She shrugged away her curiosity about Lord Sullivan's arrival or situation. They were no longer in the business of helping gentlemen prepare to find a bride. Sylvia's engagement had made continuing their work impossible.

She resumed her discreet admiration of Mr. Berringer. "Do you think Exeter's heir has a mistress yet? There is any number of ladies I know trying to catch his eye."

"All the ladies I know who have tried have been soundly rebuffed," Aurora confided.

That made Eugenia even more curious about him. It was no hardship to imagine he could have his pick of lovers. "Married or other?"

"Married," Aurora said with a heavy sigh. "It seems our Mr. Berringer has a severe dislike of becoming an adulterer, and he avoids marriage-minded spinsters, too."

"Society is overrun with both." She chuckled. "Widows will be overjoyed if they figure out they have the best chance of becoming a duchess one day. But I like him all the more for his restraint when it comes to avoiding married women," Eugenia murmured. "I dislike the idea of anyone coming between a couple, even if they are poorly matched."

"Do not disregard the appeal of illicit love," Aurora warned.

"He's a man. He'll find someone willing, I'm sure," she said with a decidedly wicked laugh.

He might, too.

Thaddeus Berringer was handsome, of sober habits so far, and a duke's heir. It was widely reported that the Duke of Exeter had settled funds and property on his heir last year. There would be no limit to the vices and scandals he might indulge in one day, if he had the money and the company of wicked friends. He had little influence yet, though, and did not appear overly ambitious. Everyone gossiped over the tiniest details about his days. She had heard he'd left Town two weeks ago, and everyone speculated that there'd been a falling out in the family.

Utterly unfounded, most likely. She had borne witness to the Duke of Exeter and Thaddeus Berringer laughing together with pleasing frequency.

But debutants constantly followed him around ballrooms, hoping to be noticed and singled out for attention. Little was known of his reputation with the ladies at all, which was likely why she found him fascinating.

If he turned out to be as predictable as all other lords in society, Thaddeus Berringer would align himself with a woman of fortune and family in an attempt to gain power and influence over society, even before he became a duke.

They flowed along with everyone else to the drawing room as conversation sprang up between guests. Aurora and Eugenia were largely ignored. They had neither fortune nor fame. Although Sylvia looked their way with an expression of longing, they knew better than to believe she would join them tonight. Wharton talked of politics a great deal at these sorts of things, or he flattered Sylvia outrageously. Neither Eugenia nor Aurora enjoyed such talk for too long, but Sylvia hung on his every word —as it should be.

Besides, there were other topics that interested Eugenia and Aurora, which could entertain them for hours. Their favorite subject would shock prudish members of the *ton*.

Eugenia drew her younger cousin along, circling those

gathered. She leaned close to Aurora to whisper, "Who would you have?"

"Tonight…" Aurora pursed her lips briefly, a small smile emerging as they strolled about the chamber considering the choices before them. "I think I should like tall, dark and," her eyes lit up, "mysterious."

Eugenia scanned the crowd again. Tall, dark, and handsome was in plentiful supply. Mr. Berringer was present, and Eugenia's interest had become sadly fixed of late on him—the unobtainable man. But then a new man caught her eye—a stranger to Wharton's late-night gatherings who seemed to match Aurora's description. "I wonder who he could be?"

"Who cares who he is. It's what he can do for a lady that is the real question."

Eugenia hid a smile and discreetly observed the fellow, from the top of his perfectly tousled dark hair to the nicely formed bulge in his black satin breeches. "He seems quite well turned out. Meyer?"

"No, he wears a Weston creation, I believe." Aurora made an approving sound as she twisted a lock of hair around her gloved fingers. "Delightfully fitted garments, one and all. I swear I can estimate his measurements even from here. I wonder if our cousin has the time to introduce us."

Sylvia had her back to them and was laughing in Lord Wharton's company.

"Patience, cousin. Anticipation is half the reward." And it did not do to appear too eager at these sorts of gatherings. Some gentlemen took exception to women they considered forward, and all men gossiped as well as women. If they put a toe out of line, they could find themselves on the outs very quickly with this persnickety set. That might impact Sylvia's standing in society, too.

Aurora pouted. "But am I not deserving of a reward as enticing as he appears to be?"

"Rewards might have to wait until Sylvia is actually married, and we can be ourselves again," Eugenia said, reminding Aurora of their mutual decision to be on their best behavior. Eugenia appreciated a well-proportioned man as much as Aurora did. But the way they had pursued pleasure before Sylvia's engagement was markedly different to how they could do so now.

There were many delights Eugenia had forbidden herself. Dalliances with anyone connected to the Marquess of Wharton's family were a risky venture. She might talk of hope of seduction, but that was as far as she dared imagine for now. And since they mingled almost exclusively with Wharton's set of friends, opportunities for trysts were virtually nonexistent.

A woman joined the mystery man, capturing his arm and full attention. She clung to the man with a proprietary air, so it seemed clear he belonged to some lucky woman. A wife?

Aurora sighed sadly. "Sometimes wondering is more enjoyable than discovering the truth that a man might be married already."

"Indeed, it is." She flashed a conciliatory smile in Aurora's direction. "We can still observe and imagine."

"Indeed, we will, cousin," Aurora promised.

A call rang for everyone to move along to another room where refreshments had been laid out, and they followed with the masses again into the long gallery. After Wharton and Sylvia's engagement had become common knowledge, they had all been pressed to come and live under Wharton's not unsubstantial roof. Not for his benefit but for his mother's health and happiness. Lizzy, the Marchioness of Wharton was still recovering from her breast surgery and remained in a delicate state of health in her chambers upstairs.

They had come along with Sylvia to cheer up the marchioness, distract her from the pain if they could. Neither task was easy, but none of them minded very much. Out of the three of them, Sylvia was most often in her future mama's company. The marchioness had a dry wit Eugenia found compatible with her own, and she didn't mind feeding the older lady harmless tidbits of gossip discovered during their outings.

But their new lives were not confined to sitting by the

marchioness' bedside every day. They had been invited to make themselves at home. Sixteen bedchambers, a ballroom, a vast library, a dining room, and a long gallery were now their playground. They were to enjoy themselves at any of Wharton's impromptu gatherings as if they were family already, too. They could drink and entertain their friends as much as they liked.

Until the marchioness' strength returned, the wedding ceremony had been delayed indefinitely, so they lived in wait for that happy day to come.

Eugenia smiled, knowing her evening was likely bound to be long, but the view always pleasurable. The opulence of the marquess' home had been startling at first, but she'd grown accustomed to gilt everything, and even being introduced to members of the king's family, too. The marquess and his mother kept a large circle of acquaintances from all walks of society, and close friends tended to drop by at all hours.

However, despite Eugenia's love of conversation, she was often relegated to the sidelines due to circumstances beyond her control. First, she was a woman, considered by society as dependent on Wharton's charity because of Sylvia's future elevation to marchioness.

Second, she was considered a bluestocking sort of woman. She had been the driving force behind the Hillcrest Academy— managing the accounting and negotiations for their little enterprise. No one seemed quite sure what to make of their ties to trade. But she had been told that an unmarried cousin of a future marchioness could not possibly earn her own way in the world without facing criticism from all quarters. The Hillcrest Academy was no more.

And third, unfortunately, the best conversations tended to be led by the very same irritating creatures who constantly overlooked that she was more educated than the wealthy debutants they circled. They only asked exceedingly naive debutants of fortune their opinion on any number of topics they could never have knowledge or experience of at their tender ages.

Eugenia possessed a brain and the will to use it. She refused to become a sheep—following nose to tail because she was expected to be like every other lady. She was more intelligent than most debutants and unimpressed by what was considered popular.

As expected, Wharton swept Sylvia into another political debate, leaving Eugenia and Aurora to their own devices as usual.

"There they go," Aurora grumbled. "Forgetting us again."

Eugenia sometimes preferred it that way. An hour with Wharton pontificating on what society needed to do, or stand for, tended to give her a sore head.

Little groups sprang up immediately; gentlemen with their wives and friends attracted most of the bachelors for the present moment. "Would you care for a breath of fresh air, cousin?"

"Yes, indeed I would."

Arm in arm, they sauntered away from all to the quiet end of the long gallery, where a grouping of chairs had been placed beside a window they could open a crack to let in some night air. Eugenia positioned herself directly in the cool draft and signaled to a footman. "Tea, please, Mr. Bloom."

"I've already had it sent for, Miss Hillcrest," he said with a tilt of his ginger head.

"You are a treasure," she enthused, pleased with the new footman's thoughtfulness. "He'll do well if he keeps this up," she whispered to Aurora when he was gone.

Aurora smiled. "I think he is trying to impress you."

"He's the new man below-stairs hoping to make a good impression on all of us to advance his career. If he pleases me, he probably hopes I'll put in a good word for him with the future marchioness." She shrugged, having already made such a recommendation for him to Sylvia a few days ago. "Besides, we're entirely predictable. We always end an evening sipping tea in our corner."

"How terrible to be so predictable."

"We're likely the only ones who are."

They remained on the edge of the crowd in the long gallery, sipping their tea when it came. Happy with their own company and confidences. Though not technically correct for them to remain apart from everyone, they resisted society's rules as often as they could, especially here. Wharton had tried to insist they should have a chaperone when they had first moved under his roof. However, he'd quickly changed his mind when Sylvia had suggested she needed a chaperone now, too.

"Look at them," Aurora whispered.

Eugenia studied the end of the room, where their cousin stood encircled in her future husband's arms. It was a quick embrace, laced with much laughter and tenderness. At home, Wharton could barely keep his hands from his future bride. A chaperone would undoubtedly have gotten in his way.

Eugenia glanced down at her empty teacup and then put it aside. "Still very much in love."

"I hope that never changes," Aurora whispered.

"I'm sure it won't." Eugenia inched closer to her cousin and fluffed out the skirts of her favorite plum-colored gown. She usually favored dark colors, though her family tried to lure her into white or brighter hues. She held on to her individuality as hard as she could. "When two people love each other in that fashion, nothing but death will keep them apart."

"Are you sure?"

She nodded slowly and smiled. "I knew a woman once who proved my point. As a young woman, she was utterly swept off her feet by a man she knew but half a day. She married him by banns a month later and had just one blissful night in his arms as his wife, before he left her."

"This doesn't seem a happy story," Aurora chided.

"It's not, I suppose. When word reached her of his death, she cried for weeks. Bereft and facing a future alone, she could have fallen down and never gotten up again. But that brief love comforts her to this very day. Love, true love, never really dies for the one left behind."

Aurora frowned. "Why did he leave her?"

"She begged him not to," Eugenia swallowed the lump that had suddenly sprung to her throat. Partings were never easy. "He had a mother who waited for his return far away. He was supposed to break the news of his marriage gently, since his mother's health was delicate, and then return to Hastings. But he drowned before he even reached his mother to tell her."

"How sad for both of them. Did they ever meet? The mother and new widow?"

"No. Unfortunately, the lady had been left with insufficient funds. She never did seek out her husband's final resting place to mourn. She wanted to go so very badly, but…"

"What happened to her? The widow. Have you kept in touch with her?"

Eugenia nodded. "She's content. She lives with her cousins."

"Just like us," Eugenia noted.

"Yes, exactly like us." Eugenia didn't like to imagine how her life might have gone on if not for the love and support of her cousins. Together, they had started a new and more exciting life than she'd dreamed.

"I'm glad she had a family to support her," Aurora whispered.

Aurora and Sylvia could never understand how much Eugenia had needed them in her life. "I am, too."

Aurora sighed. "I can't wait to fall in love like them, your friend and Sylvia, I mean."

"You'll be next, I'm sure," Eugenia promised. She ran her eye over the visitors to Wharton House. They were the same men they'd known for almost a year. None had expressed interest in courting Aurora, and Eugenia was disappointed by that. She'd always thought Aurora, being the youngest, would be the first of them to marry, if a marriage was in the cards for any. Aurora was the prettiest and most bubbly of personality, too. Sylvia the most agreeable, while also being the most stubborn.

What society thought of herself, Eugenia had no idea…but she hoped they didn't ever inquire too deeply into her past.

Chapter Two

IF MINGLING with society could always mean a night spent in a private home, devoid of matchmakers seeking to tempt him, Teddy would be entirely happy with his new life. Two years ago, his circumstances had been very simple. He'd spent his early mornings mucking out stalls at a posting house stables; occasionally served ale to weary farmers on Sunday evenings, who spoke mostly of the chance of rain or praised the cook's fine stew. No one had cared about his opinion there. No one had reason to curry his favor…because his connection to the Duke of Exeter had been a closely guarded secret at that time.

And he'd been happy with that life, until family concerns had taken precedence over his desire for obscurity and set him down in the heart of London's social whirl. And that had made him a target for everyone with a daughter, niece, or widowed sister of a certain age to marry off.

Every word he said now, every smile he bestowed, was considered, pondered, and reflected upon by those who claimed to know what he wanted. Recognition seemed to be the greatest disadvantage of being a duke's heir, after the loss of his liberty, and of course, the memory of the taste of Cook's stew had long since grown dim.

Teddy circulated the Marquess of Wharton's long gallery at the end of another endless evening on the Town, his mind half on what he overheard tonight and the rest contemplating a future of more of this. He was a bachelor still, and a bachelor he'd remain for some time. For this season, at least, or perhaps even longer yet.

He was only just six and twenty. Much too young to need a wife.

Wharton's long gallery was filled with the cream of society, as it was on so many nights. These were the people his cousin Sinclair, the Duke of Exeter, claimed he must mingle with and get to know. Lords and ladies, some already fast friends, and a few unknowns to be introduced to as the night wore on. There were spinsters and widows too, but he made sure not to single any out for particular attention.

As usual, the Hillcrest cousins were included in their number, despite them not being married or engaged or even in the center of things. There were three Hillcrests. Until recently, they had all engaged in a business, offering advice to gentlemen in search of a bride. Not matchmaking them, he believed, but helping to make them over into a more appealing version of themselves, or so he'd heard. A finishing school for gentlemen. Dance practice, love letter writing, courtship offerings.

He had a long acquaintance with one of the Miss Hillcrests, through the Duchess of Exeter's friendship with her, and the other two only by association as a consequence of attending the same events.

Sylvia Hillcrest, the duchess' friend, recently become engaged to the Marquess of Wharton. She smiled his way but remained close to her betrothed. Once upon a time, he might have considered she could be a very good friend of his—and perhaps more could have come of their association. But with her engagement, any particular interest he'd had in her welfare or future ended. He did not pursue engaged women, or married ones either. That way led to strife.

He would much rather pursue a woman with no impediments, when he eventually did.

Giving up on Miss Sylvia Hillcrest had been easier than he'd first thought it might be. Teddy could only conclude that the feelings he'd held for her had not run very deep. He wished her happy with Wharton, but he was not heartbroken as many seemed to suspect.

The other Hillcrest women sat apart from everyone. He envied them their seclusion over there on the far side of the chamber with their cups of tea. They always seemed content with their own company, while he was frequently bored to death with his.

But this was his life now, waiting for something to be given him to do. Although he had money to invest and a home to furnish one day, thanks to his cousin's—the Duke of Exeter's—generosity, not much else appealed in Town. Gambling didn't interest him in the slightest, nor did whoring—a popular pastime of bachelors in the circles he moved in now. He'd come very late to riding, and ownership of horseflesh and breeding them interested him only in that it mattered to Exeter. There was always the hunt, but it was the wrong time of year for the chase.

Which left him stranded in London for the season in search of any amusement that didn't result in his imminent marriage.

"I'm going to have another crack," Lord Scarsdale muttered at his side.

Teddy looked at Scarsdale, startled, and then around the room, until he spotted a popular widow. "How many times will you suffer the rebuff before giving up on her?"

Scarsdale, a young man with the temperament of an overeager puppy, rubbed his hands together briskly. "As many times as needed until Miss Hillcrest gives in to temptation."

"Miss Hillcrest? I thought you were speaking of your infatuation with Lady Parry," Teddy whispered. Lady Parry welcomed pursuit, and engaged in them, too. Teddy had been the recipient of her overtures already, but he'd known of Scarsdale's interest and had politely declined.

"My interest ended when I saw her kissing Lord Molesworth last night," Scarsdale complained.

Teddy blinked. "He's married."

Scarsdale scowled. "Deeper pockets than mine, too."

"So, you've decided to court a spinster instead?"

Scarsdale snorted. "Are you mad?"

"Not that I can tell," Teddy answered, but he thought that

Scarsdale might be. Flirting with spinsters was risky, almost always ending in a marriage. But pursuing a close connection of Wharton's might just shorten one's life, too. "Which Miss Hillcrest has caught your fancy?"

"The younger, of course. She's more my type than the older," Scarsdale said with an exaggerated wiggle of his brows.

Teddy had sensed no particular interest in Scarsdale from the lady in question. Miss Aurora Hillcrest had flirted with Teddy, not that he encouraged her or wanted her to. "What is your type? Uninterested?"

"Oh, she's interested," Scarsdale smirked. "You know why they sit away from us, don't you?"

"I thought it because they preferred tea to late-night political debate."

"They remain apart, night after night, discussing *us*. Men."

Teddy laughed at that. "There is no law against it. Most unmarried ladies probably do that a great deal. How else would they know who to encourage and the scoundrels to avoid?"

Scarsdale turned to him slowly, one brow raised. "Debating our attributes without leaving clothes on us?"

Teddy laughed again. "Come now. Surely that cannot be the case."

"I tell you, none of them are as prim as they appear. For example, you only have to consider that Wharton is marrying one of them. The other pair must be just like her. I poured out my heart to them in a series of interviews, only to later overhear a shockingly personal discussion about a fellow they'd just met with. I bet they talked of me that way, too, after I left. Discussing my size and proportions like they did him, as if they were in the market for a man to warm their beds. Well, I plan to make it clear I am available for closer inspection."

"You should not have been eavesdropping on a private conversation," Teddy chided, knowing his complaint would fall on deaf ears. Men spoke of women that same way all the time in private. While perhaps scandalous, he didn't understand why Scarsdale was in high alt over the women talking about men that way, too. But any suggestion that the Hillcrests were fast could only lead to gossip that would harm all their reputations. And Wharton would not care for that. "Let me wish you a hearty congratulations on your upcoming marriage."

Scarsdale smiled. "I've no need for a wife, though don't tell them that."

"Why?"

"I pretended an ailment to get my foot in the door," he confessed. "Wanted to see what all the fuss was about."

Teddy stepped closer to Scarsdale and lowered his voice, so it didn't carry. "Meddle with any of the Hillcrest ladies in any way now, and you'll have to answer to Wharton. He treats them as family already. I warn you to leave them alone."

Teddy glanced at the pair of ladies now and hoped Scarsdale listened to him for a change.

Aurora Hillcrest, Scarsdale's new infatuation, was a bright woman. Open and exuberant and rather fun, the few times he'd engaged in any prolonged conversation with her. She was undoubtedly the favorite in the family. Both Sylvia and Eugenia tended to promote their cousin for notice of any gentleman they met over themselves. He wouldn't like to see any lady embroiled in a scandal.

Scarsdale tugged down his waistcoat. "I tell you they're not as they seem—and I'll prove it to you."

Teddy glanced at Scarsdale in annoyance. "What good will that do?"

"Wait and see." Scarsdale tilted his head a certain way and strutted off in their direction.

Teddy raked a hand through his dark hair, exasperated by Scarsdale's plans to make trouble where none ought to exist. What did it matter if women had opinions about the gentlemen they met, or imagined them naked, too? Women could study Teddy all they liked, so long as none wanted to marry him.

Teddy turned to view the Hillcrest cousins again. Aurora was already being engaged in conversation with Scarsdale, but the elder, Eugenia, was being ignored.

He'd spoken with Eugenia Hillcrest a few times when he'd called upon her cousin, Sylvia, before Sylvia had become engaged. What he remembered of Eugenia was that she seemed a polite if reserved woman, someone who had seemed straightforward around men, blunt almost.

Fearing that Scarsdale's interest in Aurora would seem too obvious to others, he felt he had no choice but to join them to at least even the numbers.

Teddy approached and bowed. "Good evening, ladies."

"Surely it must be almost morning, sir," Eugenia answered with a welcoming smile. "Please do join us."

"Yes, do join us," Aurora gushed, clearly too happy to have more company. She even patted the space beside her.

After careful consideration, Teddy sat down beside Eugenia instead. He would do nothing to encourage the young woman. He would direct his attention to the older cousin, who had never once flirted with him. "How are you bearing up?" he asked of Eugenia.

"I shall be very happy to go to bed, but I do not think it will be for a while yet." She twirled her feet in circles in front of her.

"Footsore?"

"Not really. My feet have pins and needles, a dreadful sign that I might be growing older. But do not worry about me." She smiled quickly. "We haven't seen you in society for a while. Where have you been hiding of late?"

"We heard you went away," Aurora said, pouting as she moved her chair closer, farther away from Scarsdale, he noticed. "And you didn't even say goodbye."

Teddy ignored Aurora's pout. "I spent some time by the sea on the duke's business, as I conducted an inspection of one of his grace's properties there. Boundary fences, kitchen gardens. Orchards. Very dull by comparison to a night in London," he promised.

Teddy had wanted to escape from society, actually, though he wouldn't mention that fact out loud here. It hadn't all been work. He'd finished his business in two days and then spent what remained of a week in joyful isolation to celebrate his birthday. The sea views had been spectacular from his large empty bed each morning as he woke to a day of nothing much to do but read and take long walks.

But he'd found he soon tired of that long-wished-for escape from society and returned late yesterday afternoon to London, where his cousin had immediately complained he'd been gone too long.

He'd missed the company of Sinclair, and his wife Kitty, too.

"I wish I could visit the sea," Aurora gushed. "You were so lucky to grow up in a port town, Eugenia. Nothing ever happened in my village. We must go back one day soon so you can show us where you grew up."

"Must we?" Eugenia grimaced. "I could do without the long days of travel being thrown about in a carriage to reach the coast. Besides, we cannot possibly leave the marchioness' side until she's completely well, you know that."

"It's something to look forward to still," Aurora countered. "Maybe she'd like to visit the sea, too. I wonder if Wharton has a seaside property somewhere on the coast. I must remember to ask him or Sylvia later."

"We might all go to the sea together one day, but likely it will be some other year," Eugenia said firmly, waving aside the topic with one elegant sweep of her hand.

Aurora seemed not to be finished planning for the future, though it was clear that Eugenia was tired of the topic. "We could visit Hastings and your old friend there, as well."

Eugenia shrugged. "She doesn't live in Hastings anymore, but I could put flowers on my brother's grave if we went back."

Aurora sighed heavily. "I wish we'd lived closer growing up. Just imagine the mischief we'd have gotten into together."

Teddy glanced at Eugenia, full of curiosity. "I thought you lived with Sylvia in Marlow before you came to London?"

"No. Sylvia was born in Marlow. Aurora, in a village not even on the map."

He guessed he'd never really known much about the Hillcrest

women after all. He'd thought they'd been close their entire lives, but it must only be a recent development. "And how is the adventure going, might I ask?"

Eugenia darted a glance down the long gallery to where her cousin stood. "Quite a bit differently than we first dreamed it might."

Teddy chuckled. He was sure Sylvia hadn't planned to one day become a marchioness in the beginning, either. "That sounds like my life. I can never tell what will happen next."

"Poor Mr. Berringer. Life is not supposed to be predictable." Eugenia glanced sideways at him. "But I suppose for you, it's a different story altogether. Everyone must quiz you to find out if the Duchess of Exeter is showing any sign of increasing, so I will not bore you by doing the same."

"They do, and she's not."

Eugenia smiled. "She and Exeter are happy, and that is all that matters, yes?"

"I couldn't agree more," he said, relaxing a bit more. Some acquaintances would hint that he must be champing at the bit to inherit Sinclair's title and lands. The duke's late marriage to Kitty had surprised everyone, himself included. But he was happy about it. Few understood the depths of his affection for his older cousin, and his pleasure at seeing Sinclair reunited with the woman he'd loved long ago and thought lost to him.

"A marriage with love like that is the ideal every couple should aspire to," Aurora declared passionately, leaning a little more in his direction. "Isn't that true, Mr. Berringer?"

He kept his eyes on her face and refused to let them fall to her chest where, he suspected, her bosom was on inappropriate display now. "Indeed."

Beside him, Eugenia smothered a laugh.

Scarsdale, who'd been silent during their exchange, shuffled his chair closer to Aurora's now. "Are you to attend the Sanderson route tomorrow night? I'm a much sought-after dance partner," Scarsdale boasted. "You'd do well to give me your dance card to sign now, before I'm snapped up by your competition."

"Sir, you are sadly misinformed," Aurora murmured, sitting up again but casting a cheeky smile toward Teddy. "I have no competition!"

Teddy laughed heartily at her claim. Aurora's humor was one of her best features. They could possibly be friends one day, he suspected. If she ever stopped flirting with him, that was. "Quite true."

Scarsdale, though, continued to try to charm his way onto Aurora's dance card for the route and any balls beyond. The younger Hillcrest cousin was frequently seen on the dance floor while the older, more serious Eugenia often was not. It was rude of Scarsdale to single out the young cousin for attention and ignore the elder, who, in Teddy's opinion, was just as worthy of a good time.

"I should be happy to dance with both of you," Teddy promised.

Aurora smiled her thanks, but Scarsdale continued his barrage, claiming to be the superior dance partner and warned that Teddy had two left feet.

Teddy shook his head. "Scarsdale, you speak nonsense." And if this was how Scarsdale planned to capture Miss Aurora Hillcrest's interest, he was going about it all wrong, too.

Lord Sullivan strolled over then and joined in with Scarsdale and Aurora Hillcrest, commenting on the prowess of their friends on the dance floor.

"Might I give you a compliment, sir?" Eugenia whispered out the side of her mouth. At his nod, she whispered, "You dance very well, sir."

Teddy smiled. They had not danced with each other, but he'd seen her dance once, and clearly, she'd been watching him dance to have formed any opinion. "Thank you," he whispered back, turning toward her slightly. He placed his arm on the back of their chaise and rested his chin on his fist. "You do not dance very often. Why is that?"

A brief wince flashed over her face, and her gaze flickered toward her cousin for a moment.

Eugenia Hillcrest was an attractive woman, easygoing in nature and good company tonight. She should have been chosen to dance with any night, at any ball. She'd never stomped on any toes of her partners that he knew of.

"Tell me," he pressed.

She considered him for a moment and then shrugged. "Because men are fools who think women want nothing more than to be married."

"I don't follow. Weren't we talking of dancing, not marriage?"

"Dancing is considered by society to be the first step toward matrimony—the beginning of any courtship. So, I do not often dance because… Well, for many obvious reasons that I shouldn't need to spell out for you." Eugenia heaved a heavy sigh. "I have the same expectations as many gentlemen do."

That was definitely a complaint against his sex. He wasn't offended but found his interest and curiosity were unexpectedly increasing to hear more of her thoughts. "What might those desires amount to, if it is not an expectation of marriage?"

She studied him for a long moment. "The occasional flirtation or stolen kiss is always pleasant."

Teddy nearly choked. *This* from a spinster. He was on dangerous ground now. "You don't say?"

She nodded slowly, a tiny smile tilting her lips up at the corners.

Eugenia Hillcrest was enjoying his shock. *Cheeky minx.* And clearly, she was not as reserved as he'd first thought. "Pray continue," he murmured, although he checked that the others were well engaging in debate first.

"It seems to me that if a lady openly shows enjoyment of either of those things—kissing and flirting—and not a marriage, she's considered odd and, of course, fast. Gentlemen reinforce society's rules and only seek out young, well-dowered women from good families for dancing and consideration to be wives, but widows and wives for dalliances."

Teddy straightened. "I'll take no part in adultery."

Eugenia nodded approvingly. "A commendable moral stand in a society that thrives on sin and vice."

Teddy nodded. He'd not imagined Eugenia would be so aware of the failings of so many in society. But perhaps in her former business, she'd been exposed to the frequent disappointments and regrets of her clients. And clearly, she was not just talking of her own experience, but the situations of other ladies not married, too. "So, you feel older spinsters unable to marry, through no fault of their own, are excluded from enjoying the season fully because men can either marry you or cause your ruin."

"Ridiculous, isn't it?" She shrugged. "Our friends often lament the lack of excitement in their lives as they remain in the company of largely unnecessary chaperones."

"It should not be that way."

"Sadly, it is so for a great many wildflowers, incorrectly labeled a *wallflower* because they sit on the sidelines due to a lack of dowry. Relegated to watch all the fun simply for the lack of youth or exalted connections, too. The nights passed in boredom for lack of excitement is criminal. My young cousin is better at putting herself forward than most, and dances often, but after a while, for the rest of us, it becomes harder to hope for a little harmless excitement of any other kind. There are only so many times you can be amused by some scoundrel spiking the punch with rum."

Teddy laughed as he regarded Eugenia Hillcrest. He'd overlooked a great many unwed ladies for all the reasons she'd just complained of. Yet those ladies—wallflowers, he'd labeled them—might have been as bored as he'd been, but he'd never sensed it. And he really should have paid more attention to Eugenia Hillcrest—a wildflower keen to kick up her heels.

"I see now why you were so highly regarded by the gentlemen who speak of their visit to the academy. You make us open our eyes and see the world from the other side."

"It is the same view."

"So it is." He glanced across at Aurora Hillcrest, whose

attention Scarsdale and Sullivan were still monopolizing, to be sure his next words might not be noticed. "I should also very much like to continue our conversations concerning the needs of a particular wildflower one evening soon. Might I claim your first dance tomorrow night?"

Eugenia Hillcrest regarded him a long moment. So long that he feared he'd mistaken the nature of her interest in him. He was quite willing to flirt and kiss spinsters, provided they understood he would not seek to ruin *or* marry them.

Eventually, she inclined her head. "It would be an honor to dance with you tomorrow night."

"We could talk more then, too, about your desire for *other* amusements," he offered. He normally avoided spinsters, but he'd make an exception for Eugenia tomorrow night.

"I would like to talk more about fulfilling your desires as well," she murmured. "In private."

He did his best to keep a straight face, but he wanted to laugh out loud. The best flirtations were the ones kept private, after all, and almost always totally unplanned.

Chapter Three

EUGENIA WOKE and stretched and became instantly aware that she was not alone. "There are twelve unused bedchambers in this mansion. Why are you both in mine?"

"Well, you don't come to mine anymore," Sylvia complained.

"That is because the chances of finding a marquess in your bed are so very great." Eugenia raised her head, grinning. Her cousins were gathered around her, still in their nightclothes, and both seemed wide awake. "What time is it?"

"A little after one in the afternoon."

"Only just past the middle of the day!" She collapsed back upon her pillow. "Could we not have slept till it was almost time for dinner? The bags under my eyes will have bags under them again."

"We're tired, too," Sylvia promised.

Eugenia sat up immediately and slid her sleeping cap from her hair, allowing it to tumble down over her shoulders and back as she studied her cousins' faces. Since coming to live under Wharton's roof to be of help with the marchioness, they all kept very odd hours. Sleep time was precious and usually guarded well. "What has happened to the marchioness overnight?"

"Nothing has changed for her, but Aurora couldn't sleep."

Relief swept over Eugenia. It was known that the marchioness' health fluctuated depending on the day, and sometimes the hour, too. But the news that Aurora couldn't sleep was disconcerting. "You sleep like the dead unless you have a man on her mind."

"I do, but it's not the usual," Aurora said and then sighed. "I wish it were as uncomplicated as lusting after the unobtainable."

Eugenia narrowed her eyes. "Scarsdale? Or is it Sullivan again?"

"Scarsdale," Aurora whispered. "I don't like that he's singled me out for attention, even here."

"Perhaps he loves you," Sylvia said with a hopeful expression.

"Love is not what is on his mind," Aurora warned. "All of last, he kept hinting at things a proper lady ought not to understand. Even Lord Sullivan caught his meaning, and you both know how dense he can be."

Eugenia had missed that last night. Her attention had been too fixed on Mr. Berringer and his distracting nearness. "Did Scarsdale make overtures toward having you?"

"No, but it's in his eyes. I fear he's become infatuated. That's why we woke you. I hoped I had imagined it."

"I'm sorry to say I was distracted by Mr. Berringer's conversation last night and heard nothing that gave me alarm."

"Yes, you did seem more entertained than I was," Aurora noted. "I had to rely on Lord Sullivan's tedious conversation about his family to offer a reprieve from Scarsdale."

"I could ask Wharton to warn him off," Sylvia offered.

"I'd rather not go that far yet. The man is his friend."

"And frequently visiting my betrothed here," Sylvia reminded her. "If you've not encouraged Scarsdale, and you don't use Wharton to keep him at bay, what else can you do to drive him away from your side? You can't resort to unladylike behavior here. Lord Sullivan won't always be around to curb any scandalous conversation."

"I don't know what I can do, but it must be something, and soon," Aurora shivered. "Last night, I couldn't shake the feeling that he was waiting to pounce on me. Thank heavens Mr. Berringer offered to see Scarsdale home when the evening came to an end. The look in his eyes as he kissed the back of my hand in farewell haunted my dreams and made sleep impossible."

Eugenia climbed from her warm bed, pulled on her robe, and then went to her cousin. Aurora sat at the very end, hugging her knees now. Clearly more than a little unnerved. She was the beauty of the family and was no stranger to lustful men devouring her with their eyes. But she really must be frightened if she dreamed of a man she didn't want. Eugenia embraced her. "We'll stay together. I won't let him corner you again. Where you go, I go now, too."

Aurora hugged her back, then smiled up at her. "Thank you."

"You'll have me as well," Sylvia reminded them.

"But you're busy with the marchioness so much and…"

"Scarsdale visits at any hour," Eugenia murmured, rubbing her cousin's back when she shivered. "He could easily corner her in the morning room alone."

"A pity you cannot always carry a parasol in the house in case you need to beat him with it," Sylvia suggested with a frustrated laugh. "Oh—if we had our own servants, she might never be surprised by scoundrels."

Eugenia nodded slowly. "What is on our agenda for today?"

"A meal with Lizzy, and fittings."

"Fittings?" Both Eugenia and Aurora said, startled.

"The marchioness insists you both need a new wardrobe. A modiste will come here, and she plans to help with the selection," Sylvia said with a wince of apology.

The marchioness, Lizzy, had a great many opinions, most of which had only been imposed upon Sylvia until now. But lately, she'd been commenting on the quality and style of Eugenia's gowns, and Aurora's, too.

"Apparently, we are not acceptably dressed, cousin," Eugenia said to Aurora, pulling a face in the hope of making her laugh.

"At least fittings and discussion of fashion will keep all men at arm's length for today," Aurora murmured, leaning back against Eugenia.

It was the days after, at the frequent late-night parties to come, where Scarsdale might seek out their cousin again. If only they did have their own servants in the house. A footman wasn't much of a deterrent for a libertine with sufficient coin to bribe them away on an errand, but they did have their uses. They could fetch one of them, or the marquess even, to put a stop to any importuning going on.

They really did need their own loyal servants again. Eugenia regretted allowing their few former employees to be pensioned off by Wharton upon their move into his home.

She gave Aurora one last squeeze, thinking hard about their options. So many of the decisions they'd made and taken for granted were no longer in their control. She could protest, but she'd lost more battles than she cared to recall since moving here. Was it only a month ago that they'd all moved in? It was starting to feel much longer.

"She means well," Sylvia promised, appealing to Eugenia not to make a fuss over the new gowns the marchioness wanted her to have. "She wants you both to be seen as the equal of everyone you meet."

Aurora fiddled with her nightgown. "It is kind of her to worry about us, given her poor health."

"We're merely a distraction from the pain," Eugenia noted, turning to her wash basin and making a sour expression. "Please thank her, but do tell her I couldn't possibly need another gown."

Sylvia sighed. "Why must you always be difficult and try to thwart her plans?"

"Because a lively debate means more to her than gracious acceptance. She thinks of her own mortality less when she faces my opposition."

"You're evil," Aurora whispered.

"It does no good to coddle the sick," Eugenia said. "I cannot sit about patting her hand or wringing mine, hoping for a swift recovery for her. She wants only Sylvia for a confidant, anyway."

Spending funds on them was shamefully wasteful, but the marchioness would have her way in the end, no doubt. Appearing to refuse at first made Eugenia feel better, though, and gave the marchioness something of a challenge.

After throwing water on her face and patting her skin dry, she moved to the mirror. Her dark hair was in disarray now, but her skin was flawless. And although her eyes felt sandy and dry, she looked well enough to be seen.

When she turned back to her cousins, she found that Aurora had crawled up the bed to lie her head upon her pillows. It had not been uncommon for them to share their beds before coming to live here, but not since. Aurora yawned widely and shut her eyes. Eugenia pulled a sheet over Aurora's shoulders and heard a mumbled thanks before her cousin became still.

She and Sylvia moved away to sit by the fire. "She must be truly worried."

Sylvia nodded. "I really would like to have a word with Wharton about Scarsdale's attentions to our cousin, but she made me promise not to. I don't want to break my word to her."

"She refused *you*, but I made no such promise," Eugenia said. "If the need arises, I'll tell him to control his friend."

"Thank you." Sylvia breathed a sigh of relief. "This is all so very strange still, isn't it? Not really being our home. We cannot order the servants not to admit a man we don't entirely trust."

"It is." Sylvia was helping the marchioness run the household because she was too weak to do it alone. Aurora and Eugenia had very little to do besides arranging flowers occasionally.

"I do miss living in Albemarle Street. Our independence was a casualty of accepting Wharton's proposal. I miss the home we shared, but not the creaking floorboards there."

Eugenia chuckled. "I actually miss that. I could always tell which one of you was moving through the house. Now, I don't hear anything, and you constantly catch me by surprise while I'm sleeping."

"You did seem very deeply asleep. Were you dreaming?"

"Not last night. Not for a while, actually." She glanced at Sylvia. "I can guess what and who *you* probably dreamed of."

"Falling flat on my face in front of Princess Caroline." Sylvia sighed. "Things are so complicated now, aren't they?"

They were indeed. But Sylvia was in love and loved in return, and that was good. As for Aurora's situation, Eugenia would watch and act if need be. "Would you change who you love?"

"No." Sylvia sighed. "If I didn't love him, I don't know that I would have loved anyone."

"Not even Mr. Berringer?" Eugenia teased in a whisper. For a while, Eugenia had suspected a partiality on Berringer's part toward Sylvia. But that had vanished the moment the engagement was announced. He did not call upon them anymore, but he did call on Wharton, as many gentlemen and lords of the *ton* appeared to do on a regular basis.

"I never felt that way about him, although you tease that I did. I wish him well, though. He's a fine man and deserves the best life has to offer."

Eugenia chewed on her lip a moment. "So, you wouldn't mind if some other woman snatches him up?"

"Of course, I would not. As long as it is what he wants, too. I could not bear the idea of any of our male acquaintances, or our former clients, forced to marry someone they did not love."

"But that's the way of things in society."

"Not for everyone. Not for us." Sylvia looked up at Eugenia. "Promise me you'll only marry for love."

Eugenia swallowed the lump that had formed in her throat. "Only love could ever compel me."

Sylvia sighed. "I think it will be a long time before I am a wife."

"Do you regret your promise to delay the wedding until the marchioness heals, to give her something to live for?"

"Sometimes. She's so very weak. I hoped she might improve quicker than this."

Eugenia caught her hand. Sylvia had come to love the marchioness as if she was her own mother. If she died, Sylvia would grieve most heartily. But the marchioness was strong-willed. Despite the frequent setbacks, Eugenia couldn't imagine them losing Lizzy now. "If she's survived this much, I think you can count on her planning your wedding—as she's threatened to do."

"I hope so," Sylvia whispered. "The thought of not having her support is terrifying. She tells me that my first ball as marchioness will most likely be attended by the Prince Regent himself."

"How ghastly." Eugenia shuddered. The Prince Regent was known to terrify most experienced hostesses. Eugenia nudged her cousin. "You'd better go. I'm sure there are a dozen things you're meant to do for the marchioness today."

"Yes, there are, unfortunately." She sighed. "I miss the carefree days we had at the academy."

"I miss them more." Eugenia winked. The academy, for all its limited success, had been their project. Their means of earning an income meant for their old age. It hadn't exactly been carefree for Eugenia. She'd had a great many tasks to do every day, but she'd enjoyed the challenge. They had lost any hope of busyness the day Sylvia had convinced them all to move here.

Sylvia disappeared, and Eugenia turned toward the bed. Aurora was sleeping soundly now. It would be Aurora who married next, if Eugenia had her way. Eugenia was determined that her darling younger cousin marry a man worthy of her— and it would not be the man intent on seducing her for the fun of it.

Eugenia dressed herself in a morning gown, styled her hair herself, and then slipped out of her chamber, leaving Aurora to sleep in her bed.

At this hour, the atmosphere of the house was subdued, and no visitors were hopefully expected for some hours yet. Maids and footmen trotted in and out of bedchambers, remaking beds, emptying chamber pots, resetting fires for the evening.

She informed the upper maid not to disturb her chamber, since her cousin was sleeping there, and then her ear caught a criticism leveled at Mr. Bloom—the new footman.

"You've got to work faster," a shrill upstairs maid complained to him. "No, for heaven's sake. Not that way around."

Eugenia drew closer and watched as the maid gave the new man a dressing down in front of the other giggling maids. Mr. Bloom was younger than most servants in the house and was taking the criticism to heart, she could see. His face was growing quite pink from embarrassment—poor fellow.

She cleared her throat. "Do keep your voice down. My cousin is sleeping still."

"Beg pardon, Miss Hillcrest. I'm sorry you had to hear that," the maid said, but she scowled at Mr. Bloom, who apologized profusely, though he'd not been making any noise.

Eugenia regarded the servants and noticed the maids stepping away from Mr. Bloom to gather near the more experienced maid.

Clearly, Mr. Bloom was on the outs with them all. Perhaps she'd found the one man in the household who might serve their needs and not tattle to the others, if given the right incentive. "Mr. Bloom, would you be so kind as to have tea brought to the parlor downstairs for me?"

"I can do that for you," the upstairs maid offered.

"No. Mr. Bloom is the one I want," Eugenia said, growing annoyed with the bossy maid now for the suggestion.

"Right away, Miss Hillcrest," he said as he came forward. "Will you want sandwiches, too?"

"Yes, in half an hour, I should think." She thought a moment. "If you could also supply me with today's news sheet to read as well, I'd be most appreciative."

He nodded. "Any particular one?"

"*The Times* will do for a start." Wharton read *The Times* each day. She'd asked for her own copy, but the marquess had failed to arrange it yet.

"I'll do my best." The fellow rushed off to do her bidding, and all the maids sighed with apparent relief.

Eugenia narrowed her eyes on the head maid as she snorted. "What seems to be the problem?"

"The housekeeper likes things a certain way, and, well, he's so slow. I've had to hurry him along all morning. He's set me back, and I'll be scolded for his mistakes."

"Hmm. Well, he's new to the house, and young. I'm sure he'll learn as he goes."

"If he lasts that long," the head maid whispered under her breath, but Eugenia heard her, and the maids as they snickered.

Eugenia pursed her lips. "Get back to your duties, all of you."

Nobody became good at anything overnight. Perhaps she *could* appropriate Mr. Bloom's services. She pasted a smile on her face and continued downstairs.

Mr. Bloom was waiting in the chilly parlor, paper in hand. "Lord Wharton asked me to say that he'd like it back when you're done with it."

"Well, then," she murmured. "You'd better find yourself a chair."

"Beg pardon, Miss Hillcrest. Did I understand that you want me to wait here with you?"

"Indeed, I think you must. I'm not going to spend every morning returning the paper to Lord Wharton when I'm done reading it."

She perched on a chair positioned at the middle of the table and spread the large paper out. "Did you arrange my tea to be delivered here?"

"Yes, miss."

"Very good." She looked across the room at the fire. "I've a mind to spend the day here with my cousin, instead of the larger drawing room. Would you stir up the fire, please?"

Mr. Bloom sprang to life, rushing about as if she was in danger of freezing at any moment. "Slowly does it, Mr. Bloom. A good fire cannot be rushed."

"Beg pardon, miss, but they say I'm too slow at my duties."

Eugenia regarded him evenly. "You'll hear no complaints from me about your service, and I'll be sure to pass that along to any in the house who might disparage your attention to detail."

Mr. Bloom grinned. A little encouragement went a long way toward ensuring the future loyalty of any servant. When he was done with her fire, she sent him back upstairs to wait outside her door for when Aurora woke again, so he could escort her here. There would be no chance of Scarsdale surprising Aurora today if she had a loyal servant by her side at all times.

Chapter Four

Leadership did not come naturally to Teddy, but he would take charge for a good cause. "Gentlemen, you each have your lists. Pay no attention to the order of names and go find your first partner."

Scarsdale groaned. "Why are we doing this again?"

"Because we gentleman have a duty to provide the ladies with an enjoyable evening. *All* the ladies, not just the ones in want of a husband or a lover."

"Surely you're not saying these women do not wish for matrimony," the young Duke of Brandestock asked in a shocked tone as he studied the names on his list.

"Of course, I'm not saying that. Brandestock, have you stuffed wool in your ears again? These ladies are overlooked and bored," he told them all. "Just as bored as we often are at these sorts of things. Go make someone smile. Don't compromise any one of them."

Each list contained a different set of six spinsters' names. The recipients were chosen at random. Teddy would play no part in matchmaking. As Eugenia had claimed, not everyone wanted to marry, but dancing and good company were universally acceptable and desired by all.

At that moment, he heard the announcement that the first set would commence shortly. He smoothed his hair and started back into the ballroom behind his friends, urging them to fan out and seek partners. Admittedly, some were skeptical of his plan for their evening; others had outright refused to consider joining in and walked away. But there were a few who had easily seen the value of Teddy's suggestion and were willing to play along.

His first dance partner of the night was Eugenia Hillcrest, but she wasn't on his list. Her name was on a few other men's lists, though, and because he was last to return to the ballroom, he had to fight his way through them to claim his already reserved first dance.

She seemed a little bewildered by her sudden popularity but appeared grateful to take his hand.

"Excuse me, gentlemen," she apologized with a regretful smile.

They stepped aside, leaving a clear space around Eugenia. But after a few steps, she glanced down at her dance card with a perplexed expression.

"What is wrong?"

"Nothing now, but I...forgive me. I thought you had not come tonight," she confided. "Lord Wallingham was trying to convince me to scratch out your name and replace it with his."

Teddy turned and wagged a finger at Wallingham, who was pretending innocence a few feet away. "I was just in the garden talking with him."

He caught sight of the dance card in her hand, pleased to see so many of his friends had sought her out for a set so quickly. "Any dances left free tonight?"

"I cannot account for it. I have just one left."

"Ah, well. Perhaps someone will come along later to claim that last one, so you can say you danced all night."

He held out his hand and swept her away to the dance floor. As they waited to begin, Eugenia began to crane her neck every which way, waving to her friends in similar situations upon the dance floor, each waiting to dance with one of the most popular bachelors of the season.

Left on the sidelines for this set were all the heiresses and more popular, well-connected debutants—and they did not look pleased about it at all.

Suddenly, Eugenia swung around and looked at him, eyes wide. "You did this."

Teddy held in a grin, shaking his head to deny any responsibility. "I've no idea what you mean."

"You did," she protested. "I know it."

He looked at her and smiled at her stunned expression. Eugenia wore a gown in an extremely dark shade of red, which was quite different from all the other wallflowers gathered around them, in their prim white muslins and pastel silks. The color suited her, he thought. She stood out in a sea of sameness. The wildflower amongst the wallflowers. "I assume you are pleased, whoever arranged it."

"You knew I would be." She gaped. "I never imagined you would listen so well."

"I suspect if we put our heads together more often, we might continue a mutually beneficial partnership in other areas too," he suggested, flirting because she had all but promised she wasn't expecting a proposal.

Teddy had a long, dull future ahead of him, waiting for an inheritance he was in no hurry to receive. Arranging for his bored friends to dance with equally bored wallflowers and wildflowers like Eugenia was perhaps one of the most satisfying things he'd done this month.

She frowned, though. "My cousin Aurora has a great many ideas in that direction."

"I'd rather hear yours," he promised. Aurora was all very well to laugh with, but Eugenia…he only now suspected she might be more to his taste.

Teddy had been thinking of Eugenia all day. It was odd that he'd only just noticed her when he'd known of her existence for almost a year.

And then he had no time left for contemplation. He was swept off his feet by Eugenia's enthusiasm and skill on the dance floor.

They danced well together, getting lost in the music and the steps along with everyone else, but always aware of their commitment to each other for the dance. And when other dancers lost their way, they merely laughed and dodged around them to continue on. For Teddy, it was one of the most enjoyable half hours of his life, seeing Eugenia and those other ladies dance and smile and be appreciated, and for his friends to seem to be having a good time, too.

He turned Eugenia around and around as the set ended and smiled down into her upturned face. There was a look of warm appreciation in her amber eyes that affected him from head to toe. When they finally stopped spinning, he was almost sorry to let her go.

Regretfully, Teddy guided Eugenia back to her cousin Sylvia and bowed over her hand. "Thank you for the dance. You dance very well, too," he whispered for her ears alone.

Before she could respond with more than a smile, she was snatched up by Lord Wallingham to be his next partner.

Teddy took himself off to find his next woman to dance with but looked over his shoulder once just as Eugenia took the floor with Wallingham. She did not look bored at all, and that was all he wanted.

His next dance partner proved elusive at first. When he finally found Miss Charlotte Waters to ask her to dance, they were too late to join the current set forming. Charlotte Waters was someone he'd met before, so securing an introduction was unnecessary. She usually sat with the chaperones and tended to sway to whatever tune was being played, which normally made her easy to spot from any angle.

Tonight, she was seated on the edge of a smaller than the usual group of spinsters. A dozen heads whipped around to stare at him as he neared. Her eyes widened as he smiled. "Miss Waters, might I have the pleasure of the next set?"

Charlotte spluttered and stammered but eventually found her voice. "Of course, sir. How kind of you to think of me."

"I should have long before now, too," he confessed, apologetic. Charlotte was very nice. A wallflower of longstanding, though. Her parents were acquaintances of Exeter's and something of an odd pair. Historians with an interest in far-flung places—and not in seeing their daughter make a match. Charlotte had been away from London last year, which explained her continued spinsterhood. She, like everyone else, deserved an enjoyable evening.

"That is quite all right, sir. You're here now."

By rights, Teddy did not need to remain by her side between asking and the dancing. However, he discovered the wallflower's location had an almost unobstructed view of the dance floor. He moved slightly to one side and watched Eugenia and Wallingham twirl about.

A throat cleared. "Do you mind if I stand with you, sir?"

Teddy smiled at Miss Waters' timid question. "Of course not."

She beamed and looked around the room, unconsciously swinging her skirts about her legs. "It's a pretty evening, isn't it?"

"It is," he murmured. "Pretty loud at times, too."

Miss Waters laughed behind her hand. "Oh, yes indeed. I think the orchestra is determined to be heard in all corners of the chamber, and the guests are equally determined to talk over the music."

He looked down at her. "Are you suggesting society is made up of windbags?"

Charlotte put both her hands over her mouth as she laughed heartily. "Perhaps I did. Are you going to deny it?"

"No." Teddy grinned. "Miss Waters, you are very amusing."

"My last companion would not agree with you," she confessed.

"I don't believe I had the pleasure of meeting her," he noted, looking about for a new one. No one seemed to be looking upon him and Charlotte with any great excitement.

"She did not believe in frivolity of any kind, which I think made gentlemen flee to the other side of the room."

He looked about them. "Where is your chaperone or your parents tonight?"

"They, ah…they are in the library, I expect."

"Ah," he said, feeling sympathy for the girl. From what he'd heard, Miss Waters had raised herself. Her parents were not particularly interested in what their daughter did.

At last, Eugenia and Wallingham paused and bowed to each other, signaling the end of their set. "Shall we be ready to take our places?"

Miss Waters blushed and nodded enthusiastically. They drew stares and hushed whispers before they even reached the dance floor. A pair of heiresses standing with Lady Fuller glared daggers at Charlotte as he skirted around them.

"She must have forced him to dance with her," Lady Fuller assured the heiresses all too loudly.

Teddy reached for Charlotte's hand and placed it upon his sleeve, just to annoy the woman.

Charlotte's eyes were round by the time they took their places. "You chose a wallflower over an heiress?"

He smiled down at Charlotte. "Yes, I did indeed."

Charlotte beamed and patted her blushing cheeks. "I'll never forget the look on their faces for as long as I live. Thank you."

"My pleasure."

Their dance was a waltz. Charlotte was very good, but the difference in height and length of leg meant she had to tilt her head up unnaturally to look at him, and he had to shorten his stride considerably. He also found he had a clear view down her tiny bodice as she bounced along in his arms. By the end of their dance, he felt his face must be flaming. It seemed indecent to see so much of Miss Waters' figure than he had a right to, even if it was by accident.

As he was walking with Miss Waters from the floor, an acquaintance approached and asked for an introduction so he might ask Charlotte to dance with him, too. This particular acquaintance hadn't been part of Teddy's scheme, and his interest in Charlotte seemed quite genuine. Teddy performed the introductions and gladly excused himself so that Charlotte and her new admirer might speak without him towering over the pair.

And since the ballroom had become stuffy, and he was feeling overly warm from his exertions on the dance floor, he stepped out of the first set of open doors he found for a bit of fresh air to cool himself with.

"Why did you do it?"

Teddy spun around at the unexpected question.

Eugenia Hillcrest stood in the shadows, watching him, her back to the wall. She appeared to be quite alone.

Mindful of stepping unwittingly into a marriage trap or scandal, Teddy remained at a distance in the light. "You got me thinking about all the things I never do anymore."

"Such as?"

He shrugged. "Before I came to London, I would have danced every dance with any woman in want of a partner. Now I'm a duke's heir, I've become more reserved than I once was."

"So, you did this for yourself?"

"Isn't everything we do at some point self-serving?"

"Not always," she murmured.

Teddy leaned against the balustrade, keeping an eye on the guests inside in case any thought to join him. But no one appeared to notice he was outside and apparently alone, yet. He hoped it stayed that way. "No one will be hurt, no one imposed upon, I swear."

"You recruited your friends to dance with wallflowers?"

"Who better to ask than friends?"

She hmphed. "Who better indeed. Thank you."

"My pleasure."

He sauntered a little closer to the shadows she lurked in so he wouldn't have to speak so loudly. "Should you not be dancing?"

"This was my only empty set. You saw that when you looked at my card."

"Did I?"

"I assumed that was why you followed me out now."

"I was warm, and I didn't follow you," he promised. He couldn't see her clearly in the shadows, so he took another step that way. "Why are you out here alone?"

"I was warm, too," she laughed softly.

No one inside seemed to be looking in this direction, so Teddy took another step, and then another, until he stood in the shadows with Eugenia. He could see her face better now. Eugenia was grinning at him and, yes, quite alone and lovely by moonlight.

He grinned, too. "So, I am not interrupting a romantic rendezvous?"

She lifted her chin. "That depends on what you say next, sir."

Teddy approached her slowly. "Am I wrong to assume you might like the attention of a bachelor unwilling to marry you?"

Eugenia turned to glance into the ballroom, where they could just see the dancers promenade through the sheer curtain. "You've made a lot of ladies very happy tonight."

Teddy moved to stand behind her. His attention was not on the dancers but upon her slender neck. What had she said? Kisses could be stolen without uttering a marriage proposal. He hoped that was true…because he was tempted. "Might I do something that may please one more lady tonight?"

She turned her head toward him a little. "You could try."

He dropped his lips to the skin of her neck and nibbled a little on the softness he found there.

Although Eugenia gasped, she didn't dart away. In fact, she tilted her head to allow him better access.

But he couldn't linger too long in the shadows with her. She might be missed. He might be, too. Reluctantly, he raised his head after all too brief a tasting of her soft, warm skin.

"That was lovely," she whispered.

"All stolen kisses are meant to be," he whispered, and then he placed his hands lightly on her upper arms. He wished he wasn't wearing gloves so he could feel how soft her skin might be with his hands, too. Reluctantly, he withdrew them as well.

She turned to look at him. "Feel free to do that again, sir. At any time," she told him in a husky tone that hinted at desire, carefully banked.

He might have fanned the flame of that desire if their

location had been different. More private. As it was, he was restrained by concern for her reputation.

But there could and might be other nights in the future where they could meet again. "I might be tempted, but you'll never know when I want to be wicked," he teased, then stepped back. He'd lingered out here too long, but he'd done as intended. A dance, a stolen kiss, and that was enough to be going on with. "I do hope the rest of your evening is as enjoyable, Eugenia."

"Doubtful, unless there's another handsome bachelor I can lure into the shadows." She grinned. "Sir, before you go, I have an impertinent question to ask of you?"

"You can ask me anything."

She cocked her head to one side. "Do you have any particular interest in my cousin?"

Teddy shook his head. "None. It's not my way to hunger for a lady who belongs to another."

"I meant my other cousin."

"Nor her, either. Besides, I think she has another admirer."

Eugenia approached him. "Your friend Scarsdale's attentions to Aurora are entirely unwanted."

Teddy nodded, unsurprised. "I'm interested in *you*."

He grazed her cheek with one finger and then quickly slipped back into the ballroom, none the wiser that he'd misbehaved.

He found Scarsdale loitering around Aurora Hillcrest and, mindful of Eugenia's comment, headed in that direction. He liked Aurora purely as a friend. Scarsdale knew of her hesitation and yet continued a pursuit. It wasn't right.

Teddy inserted himself between them.

"I thought you were dancing," Scarsdale complained.

"The music has stopped," he answered, smiling down at Aurora. "How are you enjoying your evening?"

"Better, now that you're here."

That wasn't a flirtation. It was relief. He leaned toward Scarsdale. "Would you see if you can spot a footman with a tray of champagne, Scarsdale?"

While Scarsdale's back was turned, Aurora slipped away.

When Scarsdale finally turned back, two glasses of champagne in hand, he began speaking almost immediately. "I say, Miss Hillcrest, how about we have another drink together, and then we'll take a turn…" He looked around, his expression stunned. "*Devil take it!* She's gone? Oh, a merry dance she's leading me on tonight."

Teddy took the glass meant for Aurora as Scarsdale started craning his neck in search of the missing Hillcrest cousin.

"She's long gone," Teddy warned him.

"Where?"

"Anywhere you are not, I expect."

Scarsdale huffed.

"If you continue to harass the chit, Wharton will notice and put you in your place," Teddy warned him yet again.

"He wouldn't lay a hand on me. I'm his best friend."

Teddy shook his head. "I wouldn't be too sure if he discovers you're bothering an unwilling woman. Neither would I be, either." Not that he expected his disapproval carried much weight. But Wharton…he was a man few wished to cross—even his friends.

Scarsdale frowned. "I just can't figure her out."

"Forget her and go find another lady to dance with. There are plenty more ladies keen for an enjoyable night. Consult the list I gave you and see if I'm proved right in the end."

Scarsdale grumbled some more under his breath but consulted his list at last. "Yes, Miss Waters probably hasn't been asked yet."

"Last seen on the dance floor with Wallingham," Teddy noted.

"Really?"

"Yes. Really."

Scarsdale scoffed as if he didn't believe it and then hurried off looking for her. At least Teddy hoped so.

"Thank you," Aurora whispered, suddenly reappearing at his side again, her hand patting his arm in thanks.

"You're very welcome," Teddy said with a wry smile. "If he's any more of a bother, do let me know, and I'll take him aside."

She beamed. "I hope it will not be necessary for you to thrash him on my account, but thank you for the offer."

"I didn't—"

Aurora started to laugh. "I'm pulling your leg, sir."

Eugenia returned, her face flushed as she strolled beside Lord Hurlston, laughing. She met his gaze, and then hers slipped down to where Aurora clung to his arm still. Her lips pursed in resignation.

Teddy handed Aurora the champagne that had been meant for her all along and put some distance between them. "I'm afraid, as much as I'd prefer to remain in your exceptional company, ladies, I'm off to find a new dance partner. Excuse me."

"Oh, too bad," Hurlston added hastily, casting an admiring glance at both Eugenia and Aurora Hillcrest before engaging the latter in conversation.

Teddy brushed his hand against Eugenia's where it hung loosely by her side, as he shuffled around her and Hurlston. He'd promised to have no interest in Eugenia's cousin, and he certainly did not. Aurora was nice enough, but he was much more attracted to Eugenia. Which was unexpected.

Perhaps it was merely her invitation to steal a kiss without consequences that had caused him to view her in a completely different light. There were not too many spinsters who would offer a bachelor such an unlooked-for boon, especially one destined for a duke's title.

But it was a boon he would not exploit to her detriment.

He chose not to dance for the next set so he could keep a watchful eye on Scarsdale's behavior. He was pleased to see the man had taken his second warning to heart and steered clear of the Hillcrest cousins entirely. Innocent or not, every woman deserved to feel safe in the company of friends and family.

Eugenia caught his eye later in the night. He discovered her watching him with a tiny smile twitching her lips. He winked at her and discovered the experience of knowing he was being admired from afar was rather fun.

Eugenia smothered a laugh and immediately turned to whisper something in her cousin's ear. He hoped it was about him.

Chapter Five

"I TELL YOU, it was the most exciting and exhausting night of my life," Miss Charlotte Waters declared, looking around at everyone to see if any agreed with her. "I could barely get my slippers on my feet this morning. They hurt so much."

Aurora, Miss Harriet Long, and Miss Seraphine Draven agreed to have the same problem this morning, and it was all thanks to a dozen or so distinguished rogues asking them to dance.

Today's smiles had all stemmed from Thaddeus Berringer's unexpected kindness toward wallflowers. "I agree. I haven't danced so much in years. I had one dance free all night. Just one."

Charlotte glanced toward the door. "I danced with Lord Brandestock, and we all know how top-lofty he can be."

"And my older sister only danced half the dances on offer, and she was overlooked by every man who danced with me," Seraphine whispered. "You should have heard her complain to Mama this morning about me. She felt insulted because I danced when she was not asked."

"Perhaps, now she's had a taste of life as a wallflower, she might give her long-suffering suitors an answer soon," Charlotte murmured dryly, earning a chuckle. "She's beautiful but not as clever as you. It's about time that was made apparent to others."

Miss Draven blushed at the praise.

The competition was rife among heiresses and beauties for all the best titles and the men who came with them. Even between siblings, the rivalry was fierce for a husband with a superior rank.

Eugenia fervently hoped that Aurora wouldn't be put out that

Thaddeus Berringer was now flirting with her. She was still rather startled he was interested in her at all. He could have pursued anyone in society. She pushed the memory of his lips on her neck firmly away, but she would think of him later—as she had when she'd awoken that morning. "I'm sorry to say my cousin Sylvia won't be joining us today."

"The marchioness?"

Aurora nodded. "We hope she will be able to join us later."

"I wish there was something we could do for the marchioness," Charlotte whispered.

"Your best wishes are enough for now," Eugenia promised as Mr. Bloom set down a large tray with a teapot and cups and saucers for all. A maid accompanied him today and deposited small cakes and tiny sandwiches onto the low table they sat around. "Thank you, Mary. You may go. Mr. Bloom, could you stoke the fire and then shut the doors and remain there to ensure our privacy remains undisturbed."

"Yes, Miss Hillcrest."

Seraphine seemed interested in the young man, but she was about *all* young men with a pulse and a trim figure.

When Mr. Bloom was gone, Eugenia fetched a bottle of sweet sherry from a nearby sideboard. Their friends preferred sherry sometimes to sipping tea exclusively with luncheon, and, with Mr. Bloom at the door, there was no one to stumble in and catch them partaking.

Once everyone had a beverage of their choice to sip, Eugenia filled a plate with sandwiches for herself, feeling famished. "Well, now we're alone, do feel free to take those slippers off your tired feet," Eugenia offered. "Put your feet up, too. There are plenty of footstools."

A few slippers landed with a dull thump on the thick and expensive rug.

Harriet Long took a quick sip of her sherry, nodding approvingly. "I had no idea Lord Pinner even remembered we were acquainted until he asked me to dance last night. He asked after my family, too, which was very kind."

"Well, something about you caught his eye last night," Aurora declared. "This is good news for you, and for all of us."

Eugenia didn't want any misunderstandings, though, and cleared her throat. After the joy of last night's dancing frenzy, it had struck her that expectations might have been risen in these ladies because they didn't know the truth yet. She didn't want them to get their hopes up, only to have them dashed when the dance partners of last night failed to seek them out again in the future. "Ladies, I have a confession."

All eyes fixed upon her.

"Last night, those men were encouraged to seek you out to dance, but not out of any consideration of a future romance."

"Speak plainly, Eugenia," Aurora complained.

She swallowed. "A few nights ago, I mentioned in passing to a male acquaintance of ours that not every unmarried lady expects a marriage proposal along with an invitation to dance. I said that we are often relegated to the sidelines and bored, and he confessed to the same. The gentleman—on his own, I must stress —decided to enliven all our evenings. He arranged for his friends to dance with all of us for one night. I had no idea until it was happening."

Harriet laughed. "Which gentleman arranged it?"

"I'd rather not say," Eugenia said, wincing. "It might make him uncomfortable."

"Oh, please. Spare us the concern for a gentleman's tender feelings," Harriet complained. "I think we all knew last night was a rare treat. None of us really believe the young Duke of Brandestock isn't going to marry a diamond of the first water that his mother hasn't already chosen for him."

Eugenia considered keeping the secret, but what was the harm, really? "Oh, very well. It was Mr. Thaddeus Berringer's doing."

Harriet giggled. "Oh, *him*."

"What does that mean?"

"Well, Thaddeus Berringer is just gorgeous, and now we find out he's also kind to wallflowers, too. All the more reason he deserves our endless admiration, even if he's so far out of our reach."

"He did not refer to any of you as wallflowers," she insisted.

"He could refer to me any way he likes, and I wouldn't complain," Harriet mused. "Such broad shoulders."

"His dark eyes give me chills," Seraphine murmured.

"His sense of humor," Eugenia added, determined not to be so shallow that she only focused on his good looks.

"Such a tight derrière," Charlotte added with a fiery blush, burying her nose in her teacup. "Or so it seems from my low height."

The room erupted into fits of giggles. "Oh, Miss Waters, how terribly corrupted you've become," Aurora declared.

Charlotte sighed and looked around at everyone. "It's the company I've been keeping. Brazen hussies, every single one."

"Few believe wallflowers should even possess vivid imaginations like ours," Harriet warned.

"That is their loss, not ours."

"Well, we must think of something to keep ourselves amused at those endlessly dull gatherings." Aurora placed her hands on her lap. "Shall we get down to business?"

Eugenia found her notebook and opened it. "Yes. Yes. Let us bring the meeting to order."

Aurora glanced over Eugenia's shoulder to read from the notebook. "The first order of business is, as always, the collection plate."

She went to fetch it and set it in the center of the table. Reticules flew open around the chamber then. Harriet was the first to toss out a handful of coins. "I won a little money at cards so I can repay my earlier loan."

"I need enough for a new hat," Seraphine murmured, claiming a few coins from the plate and counting out only what she felt was required. "My dog ate my last straw hat."

Eugenia clucked her tongue. "How that hound needs a muzzle."

"I know, but when he looks at me with those big brown eyes,

I cannot help but forgive him for any indiscretion," Seraphine declared mournfully.

"Eugenia, please make a note that Seraphine must not be permitted to consider a marriage to a man with warm brown eyes," Charlotte murmured. "She'd never win any argument."

"I like brown eyes on a man," Seraphine mumbled, but everyone erupted into laughter again.

"You like all men," Aurora argued. "The color of their eye has nothing to do with your taste whatsoever."

Eugenia made a note of the additions and subtractions, crossing out a debt that had stood for several weeks for Harriet. "Congratulations on your win, Harriet."

Even though the ladies had come together by chance only recently, Eugenia hoped they might always be friends. They were good women. *Wildflowers* all, but having no luck on the marriage mart yet. They offered each other moral support and advice and the occasional loan, too, so they could keep up appearances when their quarterly allowances failed to appear or when a guardian was unreasonable, as happened in Miss Draven's case. Miss Waters was their only almost-heiress of any great expectation, but un-courted still, and she had generously promised to cover any small debts out of the goodness of her heart. Now, a few months into their friendship, the pot was largely self-sustaining.

"New business?"

"The Newtons are hosting a small ball tonight, and although I have an invitation, I am again without a chaperone."

"Will your parents not employ a provide one for you?"

"My last chaperone was my third this season—and they still think she was my first. I don't know where I'm going wrong, but they all seem to desert me for a better situation." Charlotte winced. "So, I am in need of someone to keep me company tonight at short notice. My parents will attend too, they promised, but they'll likely spend the evening poring over Lord Newton's collection of books in the library, like they always do. I would appreciate someone to talk to tonight."

Harriet raised her hand. "Even if we do not dance, I would be proud to sit among the wallflowers with you."

"Thank you. My carriage will collect you at seven, and we can have dinner together with my parents before crossing the square to Lord and Lady Newton's home."

Eugenia smiled, proud of the way their friends supported each other. A far cry from the behavior of heiresses in society, who'd sooner trip each other than offer the hand of help or friendship. "Any other new business?"

Seraphine shook her head as did the others.

She glanced down at her book, wishing there was more to this meeting than she'd written down. "I suppose if there is no other business, we can close off the book for today."

"Yes, that would be best."

"Can we please go back to discussing the gentlemen we danced with last night," Harriet begged, tucking her feet up under her on the settee.

A round of heavy sighs echoed through the chamber. Postures relaxed as teacups were refilled with more sherry.

"I swear Lord Brandestock tickled me when we danced," Charlotte admitted.

"Lord Pinner told me my gown was quite pretty," Harriet confessed. "But I caught him looking down my bodice."

"Lucky you," Aurora grumbled. "Lord Brandestock kept talking about his boring new horse when we danced. We share the same name, apparently, and he kept talking about riding her, a mare, into a lather. I'm not even certain *he* realized what he was implying."

"He never does."

Charlotte sighed. "How many of us danced with Mr. Berringer?"

"We all did, I think," Eugenia said, glancing around and receiving nods of confirmation.

"He is so tall and smells divine. Didn't you think so?"

Eugenia shivered, remembering not only his scent but his lips on her neck and his fingers spreading lightly on her upper arms. She had been much too affected to forget him easily. "Yes."

Aurora sighed. "Did he call on everyone this morning?"

"He did, though very early, and I was not able to receive him. He left a bunch of tulips with the butler who brought them to me in my room," Charlotte murmured. "Of course, my mother ruined the moment by coming to my room for the first time in a month and sneezed all over them *and* me."

"Poor Charlotte…"

Thaddeus had sent a bunch of wildflowers to Eugenia early that morning, too, with a note begging her forgiveness for not delivering them personally. The duke apparently had need of him elsewhere. But he'd found the time to do his duty and send flowers to his other dance partners.

"Well, it doesn't matter that Mother ruined the moment. I have danced with several of the most eligible bachelors of the *ton* this week. All of them in the same night," she said, preening. "Mr. Berringer chose me over an heiress. The man has excellent taste in dance partners and friends, if I may say so."

Eugenia smiled to herself, thinking of him. She had her wildflowers and a stolen kiss upon her neck, which was ten times more pleasing than a public display of preference for conversation or a dance. They would never know the delights of having Thaddeus Berringer's hot breath teasing their throats. But Eugenia did. It was all she had wanted from him last night. And perhaps next time, if there was one, she might arrange a longer meeting…and a longer kiss somewhere else, too.

Chapter Six

TEDDY THOUGHT of any gathering of his closest friends, consisting of five lords—Hurlston, Pinner, Scarsdale, Wallingham, and Brandestock—and two wealthy misters, Luther Newington and himself, as The Company of Distinguished Rogues. When they were gathered together in Town at the same time, Teddy sometimes had to pinch himself to remember that he belonged among them.

Each man had a connection to an exalted title and years to wait before taking up that mantle, just as he did.

Of all of them, though, his eventual elevation to the title of duke would be the most unexpected rise of all. The rest had been groomed for the job since birth and had the advantage of knowing everyone important to know. However, none teased him for his ignorance. He stood up from his chair at the dining table in Exeter House, where he'd been entertaining his friends for the last hour, and called for order. "Thank you, one and all, for your help last night."

"Our pleasure," most murmured.

"It wasn't all bad," Lord Pinner joked. "None of us ended up married."

"That is a good thing. Quite a flattering reaction, I must say, from what I heard," Lord Hurlston claimed. "I had no idea you'd create such a stir or gain so much praise with your little scheme."

"The idea was not to flatter ourselves but *them*, Hurlston," Teddy clarified.

Lord Hurlston had not participated in the wider scheme, being already committed to a betrothal of longstanding.

"Yes, of course, but still. One cannot help but reflect that *certain* ladies have taken our attention for granted in the past months. That was not the case last night when you were all dancing with your wallflowers. I found your efforts to look beyond the diamonds deeply satisfying from where I stood, too. The sour and confused looks upon the faces of the heiresses were utterly priceless," he said, laughing.

Teddy poured himself a drink. "How does everyone feel about continuing?"

"I'm all for it." Pinner cast his smile around the table. "I'm sure I speak for everyone gathered here tonight."

"Not for me," Scarsdale protested. "I've better use for my time than having wallflowers stomp on my toes."

"Perhaps if you didn't drink so much, you could prevent yourself from offending women with every word out of your mouth," Hurlston suggested in an uncharacteristically firm tone as he glowered at Scarsdale.

"Women who wear low-cut gowns should not complain when a man notices she's about to fall out of it." Scarsdale folded his arms over his chest, defiantly glaring at Hurlston.

Hurlston cleared his throat. "Any woman who's been on the marriage mart on and off for three years deserves your kindness. The low level of the neckline is no doubt a deliberate decision to hurry things along."

Teddy had a feeling they were discussing Miss Waters and her ample charms.

Scarsdale shrugged. "Makes sense for her to be a bit reckless, but she can't complain if it is noticed."

"Women don't want to remain wallflowers all their lives. They know any marriage is better than none."

Teddy disagreed with that. He wouldn't like Miss Waters to settle for a poor marriage if there was a better one to be made.

"All too true," Luther Newington murmured and then winced. "As much as I would like to join you again, I have a situation I must not set aside indefinitely."

The man had been hunting a bride for a while, long before Teddy had hatched his scheme to alleviate their boredom. It wouldn't do for him to become distracted by another woman when he almost had the heiress he desperately needed to restore his family fortunes on the hook.

"That is understandable." Teddy addressed the others. "Perhaps the simplest way to go is to pass your current list to the man standing next to you who wants to participate. We don't want to give rise to any false expectations among the ladies you're partnering by paying them too much attention."

His suggestion was met with agreement, and everyone exchanged lists, except for Scarsdale.

"It's too late to attend the Fellowship ball at short notice. But I hope to see you all at Somerton's in a few days after that."

Scarsdale handed him his list. "All yours, my friend."

"Thank you." Teddy looked down at his two lists. That was probably more women than he could handle in one night.

Lord Hurlston drew close and plucked Scarsdale's list from his hand. "I'll take care of these ladies for you, shall I?"

That relieved Teddy, but... "What about your betrothed? I thought you said your dancing days were behind you because of her."

"At this point in our betrothal, I highly doubt my Elizabeth will care if I'm seen escorting other women about on the dance floor. There's no danger she will cry off if I appear to be enjoying the season without her."

"Not when one day she'll become a duchess."

"Precisely. She knows what's good for her family and what can be overlooked. If I have too much fun without her, it's entirely her own fault. She promised to spend the season in London and hasn't come." Hurlston suddenly laughed. "Besides, I've missed dancing with pretty ladies in low-cut bodices. Though I'm not foolish like Scarsdale to say anything about it and risk a set down."

"Or the bruised toes." Teddy chuckled and slapped his friend on the back. "Thank you."

Teddy's friends fell to discussing their wallflower lists, but a tap at the door drew his attention. "Forgive the intrusion, Mr.

Berringer, but His Grace seeks a moment of your time in his study."

Teddy quickly got to his feet. "Hurlston, if you'd be so kind as to look after everyone in my absence. I will return as soon as I can."

"It would be an honor," Hurlston promised. "Now, whose glass needs tending and who wants a cigar," he called, taking charge of refreshments. "Berringer is always too slow at this business, isn't he, but he's young, and he'll learn one day," Hurlston teased, likely knowing Teddy was still in earshot.

Teddy made his way through the dimly lit and empty public rooms to the smaller chamber the duke used as his study. He knocked before entering, but still found the duke and duchess in each other's arms as they stood before the fire.

"Forgive the interruption, cousins," he murmured, bowing to give them a moment more of privacy. "They said you wanted to see me."

The duke and duchess parted with a laugh. "Good evening, Teddy. Sorry to have dragged you away from your dinner companions."

"Think nothing of it."

"Kitty and I need to make a trip and wondered if you wished to join us."

"Is something the matter?"

"Lord Baxter and his wife have invited us to spend a few days in the country."

Teddy thought about it. "Fishing?"

"Among other things," Sinclair said evasively.

Teddy peered at him. "Doesn't he have a daughter?"

"A pair. Only one twin is in need of a husband," the duchess murmured.

"That is beside the point. Baxter is one of my oldest friends," Sinclair explained. "I think it was very kind of him to invite you, too. You can have no complaints about the daughters not being pretty enough. They take after their mother, and both have pretty manners."

"If that is all you can say to recommend them, then my answer is I'd rather not go," Teddy replied, exasperated by his cousin's determination to pair him off. "I'd truly rather not spend a few days in a strange manor house trying not to be surprised by two young women with pretty manners, who may be so desperate for a husband that they might jump out of a closet or find a way into my guest room…like the *last* time we stayed at one of your oldest friends' estates."

"He has a point, Sinclair," the duchess murmured. "He was looking very ragged indeed before we left that last house party."

The duke's face fell. "They're not at all like those other girls."

"They're all that way, Sinclair," the duchess said, laughing. "How many times did you tell me you found unexpected visitors in your chambers during the years before you married me?"

"Too many to count," he said, looking sour at being reminded. "I just want to help him find someone suitable to love."

"Admirable," Teddy promised, "but I think I'd prefer to manage that on my own."

The duchess laughed softly. "I tried to warn you he likely wouldn't come."

"I know," Sinclair said with a sigh and then reached for his duchess' hand. "You're far more practical than I."

"It's not hard to be more, my love," she teased.

The duke laughed, too, and then turned to Teddy. "What will you do while we're away?"

Teddy thought of his scheme, and of Eugenia, too. He was even more reluctant to leave London just at the moment things were starting to get interesting. "I'll find something."

"Very well," the duke said, approaching him. "We're leaving in the morning. Do try to have fun while we're away."

"I'll do my best," Teddy promised, embracing his cousin briefly. He would miss Sinclair and Kitty, but they'd be back before he knew it. He turned for the duchess and kissed the back of her hand. "Keep him out of trouble for me."

"I always try," she promised as she turned for the door.

Exeter put his arm over Teddy's shoulders as soon as she was gone. "So, tell me, how goes the bride hunt, really?"

Teddy groaned. "It's not. You know that."

"You can't blame me for hoping someone has caught your eye this season," the duke said. "Love is the best thing that ever happened to me."

The duke, not yet a year married, gushed about the benefits of a wife nonstop. It might have something to do with being parted from Kitty for so many years before they found each other again. Sinclair was happy and insisted Teddy be the same.

"And I'm sure it will be for me, too. Eventually. One day. But not today. Not tomorrow and likely not next month, either." Teddy laughed. "Maybe I'll fall in love, and maybe I won't. It's out of my hands, and yours too, I might add."

Teddy had no aversion to love or marriage, so long it was with the right woman, and she was *his* choice, not a duty he owed to the family.

"It would be a nice surprise if you did. I'd rest easier knowing you had someone to look after you."

Teddy quickly changed the subject before the duke became maudlin about his age again. It had gotten worse since he started wearing glasses for reading. "When will you return?"

"Not for two weeks, I imagine. I thought since you're not coming with us that I might see if I can convince Kitty to visit Hastings for a few days."

"I'll have the servants organize a welcome home dinner after you return."

The duke smiled. "Don't spend all your time thinking about us. You should be out there dazzling the ladies."

Dazzling one, perhaps. Eugenia Hillcrest intrigued him. A mix of proper and wanton, rolled up in one elegant, underrated package. Scarsdale had been right about the Hillcrests; there was something different about them.

And with the duke out of Town for two weeks, Teddy would have quite a bit more time to devote to exploring the other curves of Eugenia's body...and perhaps kissing those tempting and wise lips, too. But the first order of business was deciding how best to get her alone so he could ask if he might touch her again—repeatedly, if she was agreeable. He was fairly confident she would be, but it was never a good idea to assume anything when it came to a woman's desires.

"Enjoy your trip together," he murmured to his cousin before he was released to head back to his friends. Wallingham, Newington and Brandestock had left to attend an entertainment together, and the remaining three had decided, as luck would have it, to go out together.

Their destination—the Marquess of Wharton's Cavendish Square home, where Eugenia just happened to live now.

Teddy climbed into Hurlston's carriage and sat beside Scarsdale.

"I'm surprised you could join us," Scarsdale muttered. "Doesn't the duke need you?"

"Not tonight," he admitted. He would keep the news about Sinclair departing London to himself for a while. The last time he announced the duke's departure, he ended up hosting a three-day dinner for his new friends. He had other plans for his time than drinking.

"Oh, well, that suits us very well indeed," Hurlston claimed. "Four is always better company than three."

"But *the three rogues* rolls off the tongue better," Scarsdale argued.

Teddy reached for the latch on the door and started to rise from his seat, despite the fact that the carriage had already started moving. "I can get out here," he offered.

Pinner pushed him back to his seat. "You're one of us now."

"Never to escape," Hurlston warned. "Besides, it's eight rogues, if you count Sullivan and I think we must. He's not as buttoned up as he first seemed."

Teddy did not mind their insistence on adding Sullivan. He did not know him at all well yet, but he would eventually, if he spent more time with the man. There were worse companions to be found in London, or a man might have none at all and be an outcast.

It had surprised him how quickly these three fellows, in particular, had rallied around when he'd become known as Exeter's heir. He was fairly sure his cousin might have had something to do with their initial approach, though he had no doubts of the sincerity of their continued goodwill and wise counsel since.

They were honest men, struggling like himself with challenges in life that few others had to consider. They watched each other's backs but always with an eye to protecting their dukes, too. Like him, most were fond of the one who currently held the title they would eventually inherit. Only Pinner was on the outs with his duke—and all because of a woman.

They reached Wharton's home quicker than he'd expected, and he was rushed along and through the front door before he had time to even consider what he might say when he saw Eugenia tonight.

And she was the first person he saw, coming down the stairs in response to their noisy arrival.

A hot flush of color swept up his face. *Lust*. She looked rather fetching tonight in a dark blue gown, her hair swept back in a loose chignon.

"Gentlemen, to what do we owe the pleasure," she called out, laughing.

"Boredom, Miss Hillcrest. We come in search of amusement and to amuse," Hurlston promised.

Her gaze collided with Teddy's, and she seemed to wink. Though, from this distance, he couldn't be sure it had been meant just for him alone. "I'll let the others know," she promised before grabbing hold of her skirts and rushing back upstairs, flashing him a tiny bit of slender, stocking-clad ankle and calf.

But it was enough to make him eagerly desire her swift return.

Teddy fought to curb his anticipation as he followed his friends into Wharton's library and found a chair for himself to sit upon with a good view of the door. The others helped themselves to spirits and then spread out around the room, waiting for the family to join them.

Wharton appeared first, flustered. "Don't you have better things to do than make so much noise?"

"Our apologies," Pinner said. "Our intentions were pure of heart. We came to keep you company for the evening."

Wharton tossed the evening paper at Pinner and then poured himself a drink. "How generous of you."

Teddy shifted uncomfortably in his chair. "Have we interrupted a tête-à-tête with your betrothed?"

Wharton's smile was smug as he swung about to sit in his usual chair. "You're too late arriving for that."

Pinner chuckled and looked at them all. "Perhaps there's some merit to settling down, like our friend is about to do."

"I cannot see why anyone should delay," Wharton began, then stopped and cocked his head to one side as his betrothed and her two cousins waltzed into the room, followed by a footman.

Teddy stood and bowed, as did the others in the room.

"Gentlemen, such pretty manners," Sylvia Hillcrest said in praise of them. "The marchioness sends her warmest welcome but regrets that she cannot come down to keep you all under control."

Hurlston placed his hand over his heart. "Please convey our hope that Lady Wharton will be well enough to join us in the near future. We are bereft without her familiar and frequent gentle scolding's."

Wharton gave up his chair to Sylvia, and her cousins sat side by side on the chaise opposite Teddy. Eugenia smiled at everyone, then her eyes finally met his again.

There was such a keen light to them tonight—as much anticipation as he felt or hoped to see in her. A secret thrill that he felt to the depths of his soul stirred just because they sat in the same room again.

From that one look from her, he decided she would want to

see him in private. But in this setting, he couldn't hope to broach such a scandalous invitation. He would have to bide his time until it was safe to speak of his desires.

Aurora Hillcrest was pressed to play the pianoforte, previously hidden behind a set of sliding doors at the far end of the chamber behind him. Teddy decided to move to sit on the chaise beside Eugenia, so he would have a better view of the performance and be nearer to her.

Eugenia, alas, abruptly followed Aurora to the instrument to help select music, just as he was sitting down.

Pinner went to join them at the pianoforte and offered to turn the pages for Aurora.

Eugenia returned, and as she passed him, her skirts dragged heavily across his legs before she claimed the empty seat at his side and Aurora began to play.

After checking no one was really paying attention to anything but the beginning performance, he set his hand down on the seat between them. His pleasure in the night soared when Eugenia's small hand fluttered above his. He heard her sigh as he captured her fingers to squeeze them. But she withdrew from him almost immediately.

No one in the room was looking at anyone but Aurora Hillcrest now.

"Their graces will leave Town tomorrow," he confided in a whisper. "I don't expect them back for a while."

"I'm sure you'll miss them," she murmured.

"I will, and I won't," he confessed. "I will have a lot more time on my hands."

"However will you fill the hours?"

Teddy checked to see that the occupants were still preoccupied with Aurora's performance. "With you, if you will allow."

"I would."

Teddy allowed himself a small smile of triumph. "Did you hear that the duke gifted me a house not far from your old abode?"

A frown marred her brow. "I do recall hearing that, but I'm afraid I don't remember exactly where it is."

"Clifford Street. Number seven."

"I know the street but not well. Does your home, by chance, have a blue front door?"

"Indeed, it does. It stands empty, but it's high time I considered doing something with it."

"Will you live there?"

"That is an option," he confessed. "The duke has preferred me to live with him, and I prefer to know what he's up to too. But soon, I should think about setting up my own household."

"Do you have servants?"

"Not anymore. But never fear, the house is guarded by kindly neighbors' servants, so it is safe from squatters and the like. There's nothing there worth stealing other than the woodwork staircase and glass windowpanes."

"A fortune indeed in certain circles," she reminded him. "It sounds like a house in desperate need of visiting."

"Yes, and I suspect now is a perfect time. Perhaps I'll go there tomorrow."

"At what time?"

"In the morning."

She shook her head. "Mornings are all well and good, but it is the afternoon's light that should be considered first before any redecoration begins."

They were not really discussing any renovation plans but a time for a meeting and perhaps a tryst. He wet his lips. "From luncheon on then. I shall arrive around noon with a picnic basket for my lunch and survey the house from top to bottom as the light changes. I should be there for hours, I imagine."

Eugenia's fingers stole back to tangle with his. "Would the front door be locked?"

"Not after I enter. I'll leave it closed but unlatched in anticipation of my very first visitor."

Eugenia withdrew her hand as the music died away, and everyone started talking and looking around. They clapped along with everyone else, and then Eugenia laughed quietly. "Oh, tomorrow seems like an eternity away."

"I hope tomorrow, when it arrives, can fulfill your heart's every desire," he whispered.

For an answer, she only smiled before she was drawn away again by her cousins.

Teddy sat back, watching with satisfaction as she moved about from guest to guest for the remainder of the evening, smiling and partaking of wine and good company. Mingling as easily as if she'd always been part of society.

And every now and then, her gaze met his, and his anticipation for tomorrow only grew.

But he'd done it. He'd arranged a tryst with a spinster as unwilling to marry as he, and it had been easier than he'd ever dreamed. All that was left to do was get himself ready for tomorrow, secure a picnic basket, and wait for as long as it took so he could spend an afternoon with a willing and perhaps wanton lady with no fear of interruption.

Chapter Seven

WHEN EUGENIA HAD COME to London to live with her cousins, she'd never imagined she might want to sneak out of the house they shared. She checked the hall for lurkers and then stepped out before shutting her bedchamber door as quietly as she could. The servants should have moved on to another floor by this hour. Her cousins' doors were closed still, which she hoped meant they were still abed and sleeping. She might just be able to leave Wharton House today without them even knowing she was going.

Lord Wharton had already driven away in his carriage for an important meeting.

She was currently unsupervised, and Thaddeus Berringer was waiting for her.

She managed three steps down the carpeted rug before Aurora's door burst open.

"Where are you going?" Aurora squawked, much too loudly for Eugenia's liking.

Eugenia turned and quickly padded back down the hall to her cousin's chamber door. "Shh, do you want to wake everyone able to sleep?"

Aurora winced and stepped back into the privacy of her bedchamber, ushering Eugenia in with her. Aurora was still in her nightgown. "Honestly, I forgot."

Eugenia followed but remained close to the door. "Well, you should try to remember."

Aurora climbed back into her bed. "I'm sorry. It won't happen again. Where are you going at this hour?" And then her eyes widened as she stared at the clock on her mantel. Aurora threw herself back out of bed and rushed to her dressing screen. "Oh, no! I'm supposed to be at Lady Bisley's in half an hour. You have to help me dress."

"Call a maid or send a note round."

"A maid will take too long, and Lady Bisley promised me a glimpse of her love letters, too."

"What love letters?"

Aurora's head appeared above the dressing screen. "Old ones. It seems the darling lady once had a string of beaus wrapped around her dainty finger after she was made a widow. Such a surprise."

"She never remarried," Eugenia murmured.

"With all the attention she hinted she received, Lady Bisley might never have found the time for another husband. Some of her lovers were quite important men." Aurora disappeared behind the screen again.

Eugenia smiled. "Good for her. No one is too old or too young to take a lover."

"Can you help me, please?" Aurora begged as she reappeared wearing a sheer chemise now. "If I wait for a maid to come up, I might never see them. Besides, at this hour, they're all helping reposition the marchioness in her bed."

Eugenia had hoped to slip away unnoticed, but since that was no longer possible, she agreed to assist her cousin for the sake of peace and no questions. "Of course."

Eugenia set aside her reticule and reached for the stays that Aurora had tossed onto her bed. She helped Aurora into them, binding her breasts firmly the way she preferred. "Breathe out now."

Eugenia tightened and tied off the strings of her stays and then found a petticoat to throw over her head. The gown Aurora chose was a sunny yellow muslin gown, heavily embroidered with green and white thread—a project that had occupied her time last winter and drew the notice of many whenever she wore it now.

Eugenia buttoned her up and then followed her to the

dressing table when she sat. Aurora was definitely the beauty of the family, with lovely thick hair, flawless skin, a straight nose, and perfect rosebud lips. The number of times gentlemen had become mesmerized by her mouth when Aurora spoke could not be counted.

Eugenia was familiar with arranging Aurora's hair, and twisted and pinned it into a pretty style for the daytime visit she was about to make. "How did you get her agreement to show you the letters? You were with her all of last winter, and she said nothing of them then, did she?"

"She hinted at their existence early on in our acquaintance, but I thought she was teasing me. I think it was also her way to keep me coming back to visit her for the next juicy tidbit. Visiting her was something I had intended to do anyway, though. But I let her play her little games. It amuses her."

"As long as you still want to go," Eugenia murmured.

"Of course I want to go. Molly is great fun. She knows all sorts of scandalous tidbits about the older ladies of the *ton*. I occasionally whisper some to the marchioness, with Molly's permission, and it makes her laugh."

Eugenia grinned. "Too much laughter is not good for the marchioness. Be careful what you tell her, so she doesn't hurt herself. But that sort of knowledge could be useful one day when you marry your duke."

Aurora rolled her eyes. "The last thing I will ever do is marry an English lord. I'll marry the man, and it won't matter what his status in society might be."

"A title can come in handy," Eugenia suggested.

"Not for my needs," Aurora vowed as she fitted a simple chain and pendant around her throat. "Perfect. We make a great team as usual."

Eugenia clucked her tongue. "You wouldn't need me if you'd just remember to make your appointments later in the day."

"I will always need you," Aurora promised, rising to hug her. "Now, I'd better go." She kissed Eugenia's cheek. "Enjoy your day."

"And yours. Remember to take Mr. Bloom with you."

"I will." Aurora rushed out and down the hallway. By the time Eugenia reached the entrance hall, Aurora was just being driven off in the carriage Eugenia had called up for herself.

"Oh, curse her," Eugenia cried softly. "That was my carriage!"

The butler winced. "Miss Aurora begs your forgiveness for taking your carriage and promises to send it back for you straight away."

Lady Bisley *did* live too far away for a walking visit, so taking a carriage had been absolutely necessary. Eugenia's professed errand was just as far away though. "Could you hail me a hack, please? I really must be on my way."

The butler rushed outside to hail a hack, and once inside the hired conveyance, Eugenia gave the driver her old address. She tapped her finger on her knee, fighting impatience to reach her destination and then go on to the next.

Eugenia let herself into her old home and looked around with a sigh of relief for the privacy and familiar furnishings surrounding her. There were no servants here now, and the place was cold enough to make her shiver. But her few furnishings remained, pieces that had no right to be moved into Lord Wharton's grand mansion. She placed her hand on her lovely desk, an item too large to move easily and now with no purpose at all. She left a handprint behind in the dust.

They would never sit around this desk again in conversation with nervous bachelors or reluctant widowers, about to embark on the trials of searching for a bride on the marriage mart.

She missed being needed, but at least today, she had a lot to look forward to.

Eugenia turned away from the desk and made her way downstairs to the servants' quarters, toward the rear of the property, and stepped into the tiny yard. The small plot of garden she'd once cultivated had been taken over by neighbors, eager to use the fertile garden beds for themselves to feed their families. She strode past rows of beets and climbing beans, regretful that she couldn't stay out in the sun and tend the plants herself.

She slipped out into the rear alleyway, looking left and right.

Despite the warmth of the sun, she pulled her hood over her hair and hurried north, passing no one as she went. This area was always well kept, and she'd considered it a safe means of egress when she was in a hurry and on foot. She rushed across Old Bond Street between the passing carriages and slipped along to Clifford Street without seeing anyone of her acquaintance. From there, it was a very short walk to where Thaddeus Berringer was waiting.

She approached number seven and the blue-painted door he'd described. Heart in her throat, she walked as calmly as she could up the short flight of stairs, grasped, and turned the handle.

As promised, the door had been left unlocked for her.

Eugenia slipped inside and closed the door behind her as if what she was doing was perfectly normal. She flicked the hood from her head and looked left and right.

The rooms nearest her were huge and empty. No rugs. No chairs at all. It reminded her of the home she'd just left, actually.

She reached back to turn the lock. "Mr. Berringer?"

Silence greeted her, but he had hinted he might be anywhere in the four-story dwelling when she arrived. She explored the lowers rooms, calling for him quietly and admiring the aspect of each room. It seemed a huge home, almost too big for a bachelor.

As she returned to the front door, where a beam of light shone from the fanlight window above the entrance, Eugenia noticed her footprints in the dust. She glanced ruefully at the hem of her dark green gown and grimaced. At least she had the excuse of a visit to Albemarle Street to explain the dust if it was noticed upon her return.

There was another set of footprints, much larger, going up the stair treads.

She looked up the staircase. "Thaddeus?"

She heard him before his head appeared over the highest-floor handrail. "You came."

"I said I would."

He smiled. "Come upstairs. No, wait, I'll meet you halfway," he urged as he started down, bounding down two steps at a time to reach her.

Eugenia met him on the first floor, her stomach tumbling with excitement as he smiled. That smile of his did things to her body that few men could match. However, she would do her best to curb her enthusiasm until she was sure of his intent today. Their conversation had been a little cryptic, after all. "Was I invited to receive a tour of the house?"

"If you'd like, I can show you all of it, but there's not a lot to see." He leaned forward and kissed her cheek. "What do you think so far?"

Blushing, she peeked around him. "The place is larger than I imagined."

"The property is actually three narrow homes merged together." Thaddeus offered his arm. "Let me show you the rest."

Eugenia placed her hand upon his sleeve, liking that he wanted to escort her about. "I would never have realized it so big from the outside."

"Surprised me, too." He looked about with a smile full of pride. "But it's mine."

"I'm glad."

"I've been jotting down what I might need to purchase before I can even think of moving in." He showed her a notebook with neat handwriting top to bottom on all pages.

She peeked into another chamber. "I was at Albemarle Street before coming here today, and I must say a home needs people living in it."

"Yes, I had come to that conclusion as well after an hour here."

He led her around the chambers on this floor, making remarks on what he might use it for and the furniture he might like to purchase. Making more notes.

"Aurora would simply love this chamber. Perfect light for her embroidering and for playing music."

An odd smile crossed his lips.

Eugenia chuckled. "When furnishing a home, one would be wise to consider all possible uses. The master's and the future mistress'."

He nodded. "I thought this room might be my study, actually."

"Excellent light for reading and writing, too," she promised him.

"I quite like the window seat. I could stretch out my legs and peek at the carriages that go by as well."

"An excellent way to spend a rainy afternoon." She could almost see him there, book in hand, children playing at his feet, and a wife going over the accounts at their desk.

Eugenia frowned. Where had that thought come from?

She turned away from the front windows and moved deeper into the house. A series of connected rooms were spread across the back. She stopped in the largest, considering its potential use and those nearest it.

"I thought this to be my bedchamber, and the next a sitting room."

"And the third?"

"My future wife's, I suppose, since you say I must consider all possible uses."

Eugenia laughed nervously and poked about that chamber. There was a small connected closet that might do for a lady's dressing room. "A lovely space for the woman of the house."

"It will be once the plumbing I want is installed."

She looked at him in surprise. "Will you install a bath, too? I've heard they've become all the rage, and especially so with the servants."

He inclined his head. "I have grown used to the little luxuries of the duke's household and would want my wife, family, and staff, to have them too."

Eugenia nodded. "With an attitude like that, I'm sure you'll make a wonderful husband one day."

"But not this year," he said quickly.

She was surprised by the insistence in his voice. "I take it you've been pestered about making a marriage before and too often."

He nodded. "I've promised the duke I'll take a wife in a few years. For now, it's definitely my intent to remain a bachelor for this season."

"You'll have your pick of any lady, given the future ahead of you," she murmured. "You are already one of the most well-considered gents about Town."

"Who is my competition?"

"Your friends—Pinner, Wallingham, Scarsdale, and Brandestock."

"Hurlston will be offended that you didn't list him."

She laughed. "Most likely he would be on the list, but he is engaged."

"And I'm happy to let him marry first before me," Thaddeus assured her.

There seemed nowhere to sit in the empty house besides the cold hearth. She turned to look at Thaddeus expectantly. He'd invited her to slip away to visit him here. He'd mentioned a picnic basket. Surely he had it stashed somewhere about…or perhaps it was for after whatever might happen between them took place.

Eugenia walked to him now and boldly placed her hands on his chest. "Lucky me that you are not yet spoken for."

Thaddeus darted in to steal a kiss, then a longer proper one from her that curled her toes in her slippers and left her senses reeling.

Eugenia tangled her arms about his shoulders and head and rose up on her toes to be closer to him. The touch of his body against her breasts fanned the desire for him that never seemed to have subsided since their first flirtation. Thoughts of him making love to her tortured her.

She shamelessly brushed her mons against the hard cock hidden inside his trousers.

He cupped her head and drew back. "There's more to see yet."

He took her hand and pulled her onward and up to the highest floor. They went up as far as the attics, talking and making suggestions for furnishing the house. The attic space was large, but small windows had been set at regular intervals high up, allowing them to see where they were going. Their placement also afforded them a view of the sky above the city, rather than the nearby dreary townhouses.

"I thought this would be more private."

He gestured for Eugenia to walk ahead of him. A pair of thick mattresses appeared to have been placed on the floor, with blankets and pillows strewn over them. The promised picnic basket rested alongside the mattress. It was a cozy lovers' bower he'd made for them for the afternoon.

"Very comfortable."

"Without furniture, even a bed in the house, it was the best I could do at short notice. It is also warmer up here than down below. There's no wood to light the fires, I'm afraid."

"And smoke from a usually dormant chimney might draw attention to the house." She moved closer to the mattresses, removing her cloak as she went. "You know, at night, you would be able to lie up here and see the stars."

Thaddeus took her cloak and hung it from a nail hammered into the doorframe. "I had thought of that, too."

He came to stand behind her, his fingers slowly sliding around her waist, causing her breath to hitch. "Are you hungry?"

She saw no point in hiding what she'd come for. "I am, for your touch."

His hands rose to her breasts, and he cupped them.

Eugenia moaned, leaning back against his chest as he flicked her hardening nipples with his thumbs. And then his lips were on her neck, kissing and nipping her skin the way he'd begun to on a shadowed balcony half a week ago. She stretched back to touch any part of Thaddeus she could reach, though it wasn't easy. He definitely had lovely firm thighs.

Thaddeus' grip tightened on her, and he lifted her up to walk the few remaining steps to his soft bower.

Eugenia kicked off her slippers along the way, her enthusiasm sending them flying far. Thaddeus laughed, and at his urging, she knelt down, shuffling to make room for him to join her. "This reminds me of mornings with my cousins."

He sat cross-legged at her side. "You're close to your cousins."

"Inseparable, at times."

He dug into the basket, producing two glasses and a bottle of dark wine, much to her delight. He poured two glasses and then set the bottle on the floorboards nearby.

He studied her as she sipped. "How did I not see you so clearly before?"

"I did not see you, either."

"Oh, I know you saw me. You and your cousin are always whispering about us men, I hear."

She laughed and didn't deny his suggestion. "A lady must do something to pass the time at all these dull events I'm forced to endure alongside my cousins. London is full of marvels. Some come in the form of a handsome face, broad shoulders, and well-formed rear."

He spluttered and set his glass aside quickly. But he reached over to stroke his fingers along her cheek. "Am I the only one to realize you're not the proper spinster you're pretending to be?"

"This season, yes."

He frowned. "Are you saying you've met with a lover in the past?"

Eugenia sipped her wine, aware that it was almost a criticism from him. "Would you be cross to learn that I have?"

Thaddeus took a moment to answer, then his expression softened. "Did you love him?"

"Heavens, what a question," Eugenia whispered. Yes, she'd loved and lost, but it was none of his business. "I love what a man might do to my senses."

Eugenia had been discreet and satisfied with her brief trysts since coming to London. But her flirtation with Thaddeus was already different from those that had come before him. Thaddeus wasn't so much a stranger as likely a short-term lover she'd see forever. And that was not without potential difficulties down the road when it ended. They could be around each other for years. She would hate there to be awkwardness between them.

"Was that all it was to you?"

She finished her wine and held out her glass to be refilled. "It was a physical release, nothing more."

"I'll not be like them," Thaddeus promised, refilling her glass, then hurrying to catch up by taking a gulp of his. "I'll not use you and cast you aside."

He was sweet to suggest she was special to him already, but it was very unnecessary. "Of course you will."

"Why would I?"

"One, I refuse to become a mistress and I'm not the sort of lady a future duke should pursue to marry. I've no dowry to make me anyone's perfect bride." She swallowed. "Two, I had assumed you were pursing my cousin, but you are in pursuit of pleasure, like me. And three…you don't love me."

"Not yet."

Eugenia laughed softly, amused by him. "For a man determined not to marry this season, you appear to be trying to talk yourself into it."

Thaddeus fell onto his back. "I admit, I admired your cousin, but I was not in love with her. When I learned of her engagement, I wasn't the least bit disappointed."

"I am relieved to hear it."

"My cousin settled money on me right before he married, so that I may live a comfortable life with or without a wife for years. I could marry for love instead of a dowry if I wanted to."

"I'm glad to hear you may choose with your heart and not your pocketbook."

"As am I." He sighed. "There is nothing worse in life than to have no choice."

Eugenia reached out to clasp his hand. "Why did you really bring me here?"

He turned to look at her. "Just for this."

"To talk?"

He nodded. "And to find more moments to steal a kiss from you." He took her glass, set it aside, and pulled her down to rest against his chest. His grin was teasing as he urged her lips toward his. "We went from acquaintances to nearly something more overnight, didn't we? I need the romance, even if you do not care for the notion."

"I didn't say I don't need a little romance in my life, along with your kisses, Thaddeus," she whispered, taking a leap to use his given name.

His lips brushed hers lightly. "Be warned then, Eugenia Hillcrest. I plan to romance kisses from you every chance I get, but I swear I will not marry you."

Any other lady would be hurt by his admission, but she only laughed. "Well, that is a relief. Come here, sir, and kiss me as much as you need."

Chapter Eight

Teddy strode into the sitting room on Duke Street and bowed to Mrs. Sophie Darling, a widow whose recovery and future concerned him greatly. "How are you feeling today, my dear?"

"Improving every day, Mr. Berringer." Sophie Darling remained reclined on a chaise lounge across from where he stood, but not out of any attempt to appear seductive. She was unwell and had been that way since the first day he'd met her. She clutched a handkerchief across her mouth as she coughed and then forced a smile for him. "Please, won't you sit down?"

Teddy perched on the edge of a nearby wooden chair, placed the parcel he'd carried in on his knee, and smiled despite her unenthusiastic welcome. "Your color is a great deal better than the last time I saw you," he noted.

"Is it?" She put her hands to her cheeks, and her lips trembled. "Must be due to the excitement of seeing you again. I expected you last week."

"I was away on the duke's business still, I'm afraid. I have journeyed to the coast and back since I saw you last."

"What an exciting life you lead, sir."

"Yes, I suppose it must seem that way." Sophie hadn't gone much of anywhere since he'd know her. She'd been too ill, too frail to do more. He was glad to see she was improving now, though, and he didn't feel he needed to visit her every week. Earlier in their acquaintance, he'd called every day. But she had a full house of staff now to watch over her and help her care for her children. An apothecary called twice a week with powders for her aching head and syrup for her throat grown raw from coughing.

Teddy had actually met her children first, begging on Bond

Street. His heart had been touched by their sad faces and the hard times that had fallen upon them. He'd taken it upon himself to see to their welfare ever since.

"I hope the children have been behaving and are attending their lessons."

"They have, sir. Master Allan still cannot stop telling his younger brother about your generosity in conveying him to see those tall ships in the navy docks."

"It was my pleasure. I was going there on the duke's business and remembered he had an interest in the service. Thank you for allowing me the privilege of taking him away from you for the day."

He listened carefully now. The children were never usually this quiet when he arrived. The house he leased for Mrs. Darling and her brood was usually full of life and noise. However, today Teddy hadn't heard a peep from anyone besides the butler and softly spoke Sophie since he'd knocked at the front door. "Are the children about? I have a gift for them from my travels."

"I'm afraid not. A good friend has taken them out for the exercise."

"Oh, I am sorry to hear that but glad to know you've finally met one of your neighbors."

"Yes," she said, smiling. "But they will be thrilled to know you remembered them," she hastened to say, stretching out her arms for the parcel on his knee.

Although he'd prefer to have passed it over to the children himself, he gave it up to her. She admired the brown paper, then set it aside. "I will not ask what it is so I can be surprised when they open it. You are so good to them."

Teddy liked the children. He wanted them to know he would always be around. "It's good to be able to help where I can."

"They are growing so fast, I can barely keep up with them," she said with a soft laugh.

"That is what the nursemaids I hired are for," he reminded her. "Rely upon them and safeguard your health, my dear."

Sophie smiled shyly at him. "You always say that. You take

such good care of me, too. Would you care for tea? I think I heard Cook was to bake plum tarts today. I recall you enjoy them."

He sighed heavily. He should not stay too long because she tired too easily. "Not today. I have a great many other errands to run for his grace."

That wasn't strictly true, since the duke was away from London, but it was an excuse he could use that she would easily accept. He'd used it honestly so often before that now she never bothered to ask for specifics.

"Oh, must you leave so soon?"

"I sincerely apologize that I must." He smiled quickly. "But I will return next week, at my usual time, of course."

"I'll count the days until we meet again then, sir."

"Perhaps the children will be here next time, and they can tell me what they thought of my gift today."

She made to rise, but he urged her not to with an outstretched hand. She caught it, though, and squeezed his fingers with her cold ones. "What would have become of us without your kindness to my children?"

"Let us not consider that," he warned. "Good day, madam."

"Sir." She smiled prettily. "I look forward to seeing you again soon."

"As do I." He bowed and walked toward the front door where the butler was waiting. He asked the man to report any change in her health, as he usually did, and headed out to the street, where he found the weather had taken a turn for the worse.

A chill wind blew rain steadily across Duke Street, and he shivered as droplets landed on the back of his neck. He turned up his collar and quickly called up his carriage.

It arrived smartly beside the house, but his men, now wearing waterproof cloaks, looked none too happy about the conditions. "Back to Mayfair," he called.

"Very good, sir," his coachman replied before Teddy jumped inside where it was warm and dry.

Once inside, though, he pondered the future of the widow he

supported again. He had not thought her illness so grave that she would linger for so very many months upon her bed or fainting couch. She often looked pale, except for today. His arrival had perchance caught her unprepared, which of course, it should not have. Whatever the reason behind her improved color, what he'd seen today pleased him enormously. He hoped this meant she was on the mend at last.

Teddy drummed his fingers on his knee, at a loss now for what to do with the afternoon. He had intended to spend an hour or more with the children, watching them play with the collection of seashells he'd found on his holiday by the sea.

He didn't want to return to Grafton House, where he'd only have his own company still. Instead, he instructed his coachman to deliver him to his friend's, Lord Hurlston's, townhouse, hoping he'd be home and available to callers.

He was lucky to catch him just as he was leaving and was invited to go along. Teddy quickly sent his own carriage and men home without him and climbed into Hurlston's larger conveyance. "Where are you bound today?"

"I go in search of amusement, just like you. If all else fails, I hear Lord Sullivan procured a case of very rare French brandy."

"I'd be happy to help him drink it."

"So would everyone, I'm sure," Hurlston claimed. "It's just what the doctor ordered for a depressing rainy afternoon."

"Is everything all right?"

"Of course." Hurlston shrugged. "Just lonely, I suppose."

Teddy pursed his lips, debating the wisdom of asking a question that he wasn't sure he should ask. In the end, he decided to do so anyway. "Can I ask why you're not married yet?"

Hurlston shrugged again. "The time is not right."

"You've been betrothed ten years."

"Five of those before I reached my majority, and for Elizabeth, seven of those where she was a minor."

"So, three years engaged when you were old enough to marry?" He shook his head. "With all the time you've had to know each other before now, surely the time has passed to tie the knot."

"You sound just like my mama," Hurlston complained.

"That's tragic. But I was only curious, not criticizing your decisions." He shrugged. "The duke keeps introducing me to women in want of a husband. I'm growing tired of it."

"Don't think just because I am betrothed that matchmaking ever stops," Hurlston warned. "Believe me, there have been temptations aplenty."

"Have you ever considered breaking the engagement?" He said it quietly, carefully. "I know breaking an engagement is a scandalous thing for a man to do and not without consequences for the lady set aside. But if you are not going to marry Elizabeth soon, might it be better for you to be an actual bachelor?"

"Why on earth would I want to break the engagement?"

"Well, it just seems…" He trailed off, uncertain whether Hurlston's life was any of his business.

"Spit it out, man."

"It seems to me that you don't like her very much." He considered what bothered him most. "When you speak of her, you could be speaking of anyone you might have passed on the street."

Hurlston frowned down at his hands. "I don't dislike Elizabeth."

"You don't love her."

"No. Of course not."

"Why of course not?"

Hurlston drew in a deep breath and looked out the window to where the rain was falling even harder now. "I admire the hell out of you, Berringer, but you see the world, our society, in a completely different fashion than I do. You seem to assume everyone has a choice in when and who they marry, but to me, I see us having no choice at all. You'll eventually marry a woman from a good family, someone the duke approves, and someone capable of running your country estate in your absence—when you have one, that is. You'll do your duty to the family, just like we all must. Sire an heir and a spare, and if love is possible, you'll likely find it outside of marriage."

"That is one way a gentleman might live out his days, I suppose," he admitted.

"It is the truth." Hurlston shrugged. "Elizabeth is a fine woman, from a good family, and is accomplished in all I need her for. I do not need to love her to be a good husband to her. I respect her and look forward to a long and respectful marriage."

Teddy sat back, studying his friend as if he were a stranger. The loveless union Hurlston had just described was something he intended to avoid if he could. He'd not met anyone he'd want to spend all the days of his life with and not even love them. "If all is a duty, then why do you seem sad? What interests do you have in common that made Elizabeth the right choice?"

"Please remember I was young at the time my father arranged the betrothal," Hurlston hastened to explain. "She was our neighbor. We were friends of a sort, I suppose. Elizabeth enjoys all the usual country pursuits. She rides well, shoots straight, my dogs like her, and she is fond of dancing. "

"But not with you," Teddy observed. "If she's keen to become your countess, why isn't she here to dance with you this season?"

Hurlston grimaced. "And marry me. I had hoped to tie the knot at the end of the month, but that seems unlikely now."

Teddy's eyes widened. "You hadn't told me that, or anyone else for that matter."

Hurlston crossed his arms over his chest. "Hardly worth mentioning when she hasn't arrived to set the date."

"What is keeping her away? You're not horrible."

Hurlston glanced out the window. "Oh, thank you so much. I haven't the slightest idea about her delays," he said, his jaw clenching. "She should want to have our wedding over and done with just like I do. My grandfather could die any day. I will require a wife before then to make the transition as seamless as possible," he announced with a trace of impatience.

However, Hurlston was never one to remain ruffled for long.

He relaxed and winced. "I apologize for my grumblings. Elizabeth's excuses vex me."

"Well, honestly, you can be as mad as you like to me. It is a relief to finally hear you speak honestly about the woman you're going to marry. I was starting to think you were happy with the delay."

"Well, it's not all bad. I may still join the bachelors and not have the scolds of a wife to listen to when drunk."

"It would be very dull to be in London and not have you free to join us," Teddy promised. "Very, very dull indeed."

Hurlston turned from the window and met his gaze. "Promise me you will say nothing to anyone about the matter of my betrothal. Particularly my mother or brother. Both are cross enough about the delay as it is. They think I am to blame."

"I wouldn't dream of it." He peered at his friend. "But why do they think it is you holding up the wedding?"

"Because I said it was my doing so they were not cross with Elizabeth. My mother and brother have been cross with me for years, that is expected, but I will not have my future wife finding an excuse to cry off because of their hostility. She has to marry me. She promised."

They had arrived by that time at Lord Sullivan's home, who seemed happy to see them. The brandy, though, was gone. Given as a gift to an uncle for his cellar. Although disappointed to hear the news, Hurlston invited Sullivan to join them in the carriage.

"Where are we bound?"

"To a place where there's always good brandy," Hurlston explained and then said no more.

Teddy and Sullivan exchanged a long glance and then grinned. "Madam Bradshaw's House of Pleasure," they said together.

Hurlston laughed. "We can drink, and if it suits you bachelors, you may leave me to the brandy for the other pleasures to be found there."

Teddy shook his head, and Sullivan did too. "We'll drink

with you," Sullivan announced. "And let's try not to sing this time."

Teddy grinned. "Agreed."

"Berringer can't hold a tune anyway," Hurlston teased.

"Neither can you," Sullivan noted.

"Sad but true," Hurlston said with a regretful sigh. "But we excel in everything else, so that's all right."

Teddy laughed and wisely did not raise the topic of Elizabeth again. He made small talk with Sullivan, who boasted he'd won a fortune in cards the prior night. After deciding to fetch Scarsdale and Pinner, too, Hurlston mused one of them needed to buy a larger conveyance before they made any new friends.

From there, they set out for Madam Bradshaw's to drink and not sing.

"It is a shame Wharton introduced us to this place and now rarely can join us anymore," Hurlston whispered to Teddy when they alighted outside Bradshaw's. "Can he really be as happy to marry as he seems? He hardly looks at another woman now."

"I believe so," Teddy said and then shut up because the proprietress was approaching, and she had sharp ears. Wharton had found his perfect match in Sylvia. Hopefully, Teddy would find his own one day.

Madam Bradshaw greeted them warmly, inquired after their health and needs for the night.

"Purely to stand in the grand surroundings of your establishment and hospitality is all we require," Hurlston promised. "And brandies for all."

Madam Bradshaw clicked her fingers. Immediately, they were each surrounded by a pair of ladies of the night. A blonde and a brunette fussed over Teddy. He allowed the brunette to take his hat and gloves as his friends were treated to the same care.

"I'm so pleased to see you returned, Mr. Berringer," his blonde whispered. "It's been ever so dull tonight."

"Is that so?"

She toyed with a fallen lock of her hair, watching him from

beneath lowered lashes while she did. She suddenly linked her arm with his. "Let's find a nice quiet corner. Just the two of us."

Teddy noticed the brunette had found herself another gentleman to fuss over already. He did not mind she was gone. But the blonde could have gone with her. "We're here for the bandy."

Hurlston strode ahead, his two ladies hanging from his arm and laughing. Two footmen followed him, one carrying a decanter of brandy, the other a tray of glasses.

Teddy followed, leaving the blonde behind.

Hurlston turned into the dining room first, though, where there was always an array of tempting dishes waiting for hungry patrons.

"Are you hungry?" Hurlston asked as he picked up a plate.

"Yes, I suppose I might as well."

"Never drink on an empty stomach," Hurlston warned. "That way leads to the singing of songs we're going to murder."

Teddy picked up a plate and piled it high. "Definitely no singing tonight."

Hurlston chose to sit at the end of the table, and everyone gathered around. He picked up a cutlet and held it up for inspection. "I cannot account for Wharton giving up the place. The food has always been excellent," he said before digging in as if he were starving.

"Perhaps he wouldn't want anyone to think he was patronizing the women here, too," Teddy said, eating at a slower pace. "I cannot imagine Miss Hillcrest would enjoy the spiteful gossip about the possibility."

"Hmm, yes. I suppose that would be hurtful for her."

"Indeed. No one wants to be humiliated by a lover, real or imagined."

Out of the corner of his eye, he noticed Hurlston brush aside another would-be-companion. Not for the first time, either. Hurlston was particular. In fact, Teddy had never known him to have a lover here at Bradshaw's or anywhere. He'd once thought it was because of his betrothal to Elizabeth and being in love with her. Clearly, that was not the case and might never be true.

In every other respect but attention to the ladies, Hurlston was a carefree bachelor with time on his hands like Teddy. Neither of them were happy with their lives. As Hurlston had said, he was lonely, and Teddy thought he might be sometimes, too.

Teddy shrugged. At least he'd found a woman who was interested in dancing with him—and kissing him. He looked forward to his next encounter with Eugenia very much.

Chapter Nine

Eugenia followed along behind her cousin Sylvia and Lord Wharton as they patronized the Bond Street shops on yet another ridiculous spending spree. Lord Wharton opened his purse with alarming regularity for his future bride, spoiling her possibly out of guilt, she suspected, for the delay of their wedding date. Sly touches, inviting glances, were part and parcel of any time spent with the couple, though. Those were things she worked hard to not see. But Eugenia frequently exchanged knowing glances with Aurora and, by mutual agreement, increased the distance between them and the betrothed couple.

Wharton had seemed preoccupied the last few days, but that period of distraction appeared to be at an end. Now all his focus had returned to his bride-to-be. Quite obviously so. They were absorbed in each other in a way few married couples could match.

They paused in front of a shop window, and Wharton leaned down to whisper in Sylvia's ear, causing her to blush.

"We need to get them married soon," Aurora warned. "Before he starts kissing her in public."

"She has done that."

"When? You never told me," Aurora complained.

"At the Fairmont ball just after their engagement was announced. Lady Fairmont couldn't keep her hands to herself. Sylvia smiled sweetly, pulled Wharton close for a kiss until the hostess eventually went off in a huff, never to bother him since."

"What did Wharton do?"

"Laughed and said, 'that's my woman. Fearless to the core'."

"Fearless? Sylvia?"

"I don't blame her for laying claim so boldly. I wouldn't want the man I loved and had just agreed to marry being propositioned right in front of my nose, either."

Wharton turned about and drew Sylvia back with him to speak to them. "Have you shopped enough for one morning?"

"Oh, could we go to just one more shop? Please," Eugenia begged.

"Eugenia is teasing," Sylvia hastened to say. "Aurora and Eugenia would always rather be at home reading a good book."

She smiled. She'd rather be at her *old* home running their former business and helping gentlemen prepare for marriage.

Wharton nodded. "I have an appointment in the afternoon and must return to Wharton House to prepare."

Sylvia looked between them. "Are we all happy to go home?"

"Yes, of course," Eugenia agreed.

They turned to head back to their carriage, and when Sylvia claimed Aurora's arm and fell behind, Eugenia fell into step beside Wharton. She and the marquess didn't really know each other well, and she did not feel he needed to make all the decisions for them all, either. But she respected him and understood his highhanded ways were how he usually took care of his family. He juggled a great many important matters and responsibilities on any given day, but he would learn to share the burdens eventually.

She cleared her throat. "Speaking of reading, my lord. I wonder if you recall a request I made to you some time ago."

Wharton winced. "I do apologize for forgetting to arrange a subscription for you to *The Times*. You are getting it now, I trust?"

"Yes, we are. Thank you. I do appreciate all you do for us." She drew in a breath and let it out slowly. "While we're on the subject of our needs, though, there is one more matter I hoped to speak to you about."

"Oh?"

She smiled, preparing to be her most persuasive. "In coming to live with your mother at Wharton House, we, my cousin and

I, gave up a great many freedoms that we had taken for granted before. We should like, Aurora and I, to have our own footman again."

He nodded to a passing acquaintance as they strolled along, but then he frowned. "You find mine lacking?"

"Gracious, no," Eugenia jumped in quickly. "But Wharton House is not really our home. I know you say it must be, but we will always be guests of yours and then Sylvia's upon your marriage. Your friends come and go at will, and we have occasionally felt unprepared to be *at home* to your visitors. We should like to have a footman of our own in the household who always knows our schedule, and who knows who we will receive or not. They would also keep us informed of who has arrived to visit you, so we do not stumble into a room and overhear a conversation not meant for our ears."

"You do conduct a lot of business at home, my love," Sylvia murmured from behind. "It is not so great an imposition, is it?"

Wharton seemed to chew the matter over for a few minutes. "Who were you hoping to employ?"

"I would have kept on any one of our former staff, were they still available. But I was actually hoping to steal Nigel Bloom from your employ to be our footman." Wharton seemed not to recognize the young footman's name. "New man. Young. Ginger hair. Requested *The Times* from you at my request last Friday."

Wharton nodded but the frown remained. "Why him?"

"He's pleasant, capable, and I've found him trustworthy so far."

"We like him very much," Aurora added. "He is eager to please and hasn't yet become set in his ways."

Sylvia smiled encouragingly at her future spouse.

Wharton nodded slowly to her, then looked around at them all, eyes narrowing with suspicion. "How could I possibly refuse so eloquent and coordinated an argument?"

"We're not arguing. I'll inform the housekeeper today to find a replacement for Mr. Bloom," Sylvia replied. She captured Wharton's hand, brushing her thumb across the back repeatedly, the way Eugenia often did with argumentative men. Usually, they became so distracted by the touch that they forget what they were arguing about. "I promise the change will be no trouble for anyone in the household."

"I'll hope not." Wharton suddenly shook his head and glanced at his bride-to-be. "What of you, my love? Is there anything you need?"

"I am content," Sylvia promised him with a cheeky smile. "All I need is you."

Wharton drew Sylvia to his side, and they returned to the carriage but at a much faster pace. Clearly, Wharton was eager to return home, and Eugenia suspected it had little to do with preparing for any business meeting now.

She was brought up short when they reached the conveyance, though.

Thaddeus Berringer was lounging against it, studying his pocket watch.

"There you are at last," Thaddeus cried as he tucked it away.

Wharton came forward to shake his hand. "Berringer. I didn't think we were meeting today."

"We were not, but I saw your carriage and heard from the grooms that the Hillcrest ladies were with you. I thought I could pay my respects and beg for a boon."

Wharton laughed. "Oh? What sort of boon?"

"I need a lady's opinion on a purchase and hoped I might seek theirs." Thaddeus looked at them all, his gaze never settling upon Eugenia any longer than on the others.

Sylvia spoke first. "I'd be only too happy to render an opinion, sir. What are you buying for the duchess this time?"

"It is something for me. I have decided to furnish a property I own, but I am finding the choices overwhelming." He gestured to a haberdashery shop nearby and raked a hand through his hair. "It should only take a moment."

Aurora pushed forward to claim Thaddeus' arm. "I'd be very happy to render an opinion, too."

Thaddeus nodded slowly and caught Eugenia's eye. "All

opinions would be valued equally. Would you care to assist as well, Miss Hillcrest?"

"Gladly," she promised. She did not move to take his other arm. That hadn't been her habit before they'd kissed, and she was determined not to give away her interest in him. "Lead the way, sir."

He inclined his head, opening a door for Aurora to pass him by. Wharton and Sylvia swept in, arm in arm, and Eugenia followed at the rear.

Thaddeus came up beside her and whispered "carpet," then he moved past her to direct the others deeper into the establishment, pausing to greet the proprietor and his wife.

Eugenia paused, familiarizing herself with the layout of the store again. Cabot's Haberdashery had expanded their shop and offerings during the last winter—adding furniture and carpets to their already substantial catalog. She turned away from the others, exploring the changes on her own.

Cabot had a fine eye, and she saw much that appealed to her. But in her situation, there was nothing she should fall in love with since she had nowhere to put it.

Thaddeus drew near. "Did you survey the carpets yet?"

"Not yet."

"You really should. There's so much more to see in the new rooms on this side."

She inclined her head and went where he directed. The chamber was large, and behind an array of low tables sat dozens of carpet squares littering the floors. She turned right at Thaddeus' subtle suggestion and stopped before a pile of large and thick carpet squares. The top one was done in the Indian style, red and heavily patterned.

Thaddeus' hand caught hers and squeezed. "Tomorrow. In the afternoon again?"

A thrill went through her at the husky tone of his voice. Another afternoon of kissing a handsome rogue was exactly what she needed right now. "I look forward to it."

He released her hand as the others joined them, but no one seemed to notice.

A blue rug beneath the red one caught her eye. She tipped her head toward the pile and smiled at Thaddeus. "Will you help me?"

He rushed forward. "Do you see something you like?"

"Perhaps." She moved to one corner, and he to the other, and together they drew back the heavy upper red square to reveal a beautiful blue rug beneath. The colors were more subtle and elegant than the red. Much more to her taste. "Stunning. Meant to be the focus of any drawing room," she murmured.

"Definitely appealing, but what of this other blue one?" he asked as he pointed to another farther away.

Eugenia followed him across the room and studied his choice, another rectangular and also in blue, but bolder. She nodded. "Stunning as well. But I think this might suit a gentleman's chamber."

"I'm torn now."

Eugenia laughed. "Was it imperative you decide today?"

"Not at all. But I have to start somewhere," he said with a laugh. "I have a pair of candelabras and a fire poker to take with me today. So at least I can light a fire there tomorrow afternoon when my visitor comes."

"At this rate, it could take you a great many afternoon visits to see the house completely furnished, sir."

He seemed to pause. "Was there some other gentleman's house you'd rather visit?"

"Hardly," she whispered. "I thoroughly enjoyed our last meeting."

"Good, because I plan to keep inviting you to visit me," he whispered. "If Wharton wasn't here, I'd ask your opinion on the size of my bed."

Aurora rushed over just then. "How marvelous is Cabot's, and how exciting it must be for you, Mr. Berringer, to be decorating a new house with new things. Though I'm not complaining. It was grateful that Eugenia took care of furnishing our old Albemarle Street townhouse."

"A handsome home it was, too, from what I saw," Thaddeus murmured, glancing toward Eugenia with a question in his eyes.

"Oh, it is still a handsome home," Aurora assured him. "There was simply nowhere to put anything of ours at Lord Wharton's, and she will not consider selling even a single fork yet."

"One day, I might have my own home again," Eugenia replied with a shrug. "I will need something to sit your teacup upon when you and your husband come to call on me with your children."

"I miss your old fainting couch, but don't tell Wharton," Aurora whispered. "He thinks his home superior in every way to the comforts of Albemarle Street."

Thaddeus was studying her closely now. Yes, she could have invited him to meet her at Albemarle Street, instead of going to his empty home and only being able to sit on the floor on blankets. She'd been curious about his new residence, and she hadn't wanted to decline the chance to be shown around. It was clear to see he was proud of his future home, even if it was empty, as he had every right to be.

She fell into step with him as they toured the rest of the business, pointing out new finds. When Aurora moved away from them, he brushed against Eugenia's side.

"I wasn't aware Albemarle was still furnished," he murmured.

"Furnished but not occupied. I cannot bear to part with my own belongings, so they remain where they belong. Wharton has kindly continued the lease on the property. I think he means to make it clear that Sylvia resides under his roof only because the marchioness needs her, and not him. At some point, Aurora and I will return there, likely when the marchioness resumes socializing and the marriage has taken place."

"I only saw two rooms when I visited, a drawing room and the library across the hall. Both were pleasingly arranged and looked comfortable." He grinned down at her. "That is what I hope for, too, so I would welcome any assistance you might offer with my own decoration. What do you say? Will you help me furnish my home?"

"You know, I look about my chamber at Lord Wharton's home and nothing in it really suits my taste, even if everything is first-rate. I think it is easy to display your own possessions, but a great deal harder to do that for a stranger."

Thaddeus inched closer. "We're not truly strangers anymore."

"In all the ways that really matter, we still are," she whispered back.

Thaddeus raked a hand through his hair, making it untidier than ever. "I want to know you."

Eugenia smiled, though she longed to fix his hair for him, so he looked his best. "I would like that, too."

Wharton appeared, a frown on his face again. "Berringer, what are you whispering about to my betrothed's cousin?"

"I am attempting to lure her to my home," Thaddeus answered and then grinned impishly at her. "Solely to take over the chore of decorating from me, I swear."

Wharton shook his head. "Not likely to succeed there, sir. But if you've no other pressing engagements today, would you care to join us for dinner tonight after my meeting? I heard Exeter is from Town for a while. Can't have you at a loose end, unless you've already made plans to go out to Bradshaw's for the evening."

Eugenia frowned, looking up at him. "Bradshaw's?"

She glanced between Wharton and Thaddeus. Thaddeus attended a pleasure house and still found the time to seduce her?

She took a step back, feeling awkward. She'd spend hours with Thaddeus Berringer and all he'd done was kiss and fondle her through her clothes. Eugenia wished she hadn't learned that he was frequenting a pleasure house where more intimate affairs could be paid for.

"It would be a pleasure to join you all," he told Wharton. "Who else is coming?"

"Oh, the usual crowd. I'll expect you at seven, along with all the rest," Wharton confirmed before returning to Sylvia's side.

She stood rooted to the spot, and Thaddeus came closer again. "The food is excellent, the brandy, too, and my friends go to Bradshaw's often."

"I see."

"Do you?"

She looked up at him, and she thought he looked embarrassed. "When were you there last?"

He smiled. "Last night. Hurlston took us all in his carriage. We dined, drank, and did not sing a single bawdy song."

She couldn't help but smile at that. Gentlemen did a lot of singing while drunk. "I cannot imagine you singing any bawdy songs, or Lord Hurlston, for that matter, either."

"It is not a performance meant for a lady's delicate ears," he confessed. "We really do sing rather badly when deep in our cups, I'm afraid."

She nodded and made to pass him by.

Teddy pulled her to a stop. "Eugenia, I swear I haven't been with another woman since you. I wouldn't do that to you."

"I'm happy to hear it." But he could be with anyone he chose, and there wasn't a thing she could do about it. She'd just been surprised today. There was nothing for her to feel upset about, really. He was his own man, and she was her own woman. They could be with anyone they wanted. For right now, she wanted him and no other. That might change one day, but not today. "Meet me in the long gallery at Lord Wharton's after supper."

Since her cousins had started to file out of the shop, she turned to follow them. Thaddeus led her to the carriage, discreetly brushing his fingers against her hand several times, though making it seem accidental. But his fingers squeezing hers very firmly as he helped her in. When he did release her, she was fairly sure he hadn't wanted to.

"Until tonight then," he promised.

"I look forward to it," Eugenia answered, along with everyone else.

Chapter Ten

THE MARQUESS of Wharton had always set a good table, but tonight Teddy's appetites were hardly fulfilled at dinner. And not at all in the drawing room.

There was a certain lady on his mind, just out of reach by the fire. He was still troubled by the obvious disappointment on her face when she'd learned about his attendance at Madam Bradshaw's Pleasure House the previous evening. Many gentlemen kept memberships at such establishments. Married or not. It had seemed to be a requirement for a bachelor about Town.

He hadn't truly given going there a second thought, but clearly, he should have. He didn't have to go the next time he was invited to tag along with friends. He usually only went when his friends were there anyway.

He needed only one woman in his life and bed.

He glanced at his friends. They lingered around Wharton and Hurlston, glasses in hand, discussing agriculture and increasing the profit from their estates. Since Teddy had little knowledge of agriculture, nor possessed a country estate of his own, he wouldn't be expected to contribute much to the conversation.

Out of the corner of his eye, he saw Eugenia rise from her chair. No one else rose, and she moved through the guests until she reached a door uninterrupted.

She suddenly met his gaze and then stepped from the room, leaving the door ajar.

Teddy straightened up, finished his drink, and moved to follow her as discretely as he could. He knew where they were meeting, though it was hardly what he'd call a private enough location for any tryst. But at least he might talk to her and reassure her of his interest if he must.

He made his way out to the hall, pulling the doors to the drawing room shut behind him. Anyone who saw him go would likely assume he was making a call to the privy.

The hall was poorly lit tonight, though it had been brighter when he'd first arrived.

He crossed the hall, slipped back into the empty dining room where the scent of cigar smoke still lingered, and aimed for the far door. He crossed another empty chamber until he reached the entrance to the long gallery.

There, the portraits of Wharton's ancestors peered back at him as he moved as quietly as he could to the end of the chamber, where Eugenia usually sat at night. To his surprise, he discovered a section of the wall was actually a paneled doorway into another small chamber, and it was open tonight.

Since there was no sign of Eugenia in the actual long gallery, he assumed her inside and waiting.

Teddy stepped into the dark chamber, listening for any sign from the lady he sought. He hoped he'd understood her invitation. "Eugenia?"

"I'm here. Pull the panel closed so no one will stumble upon us."

He would not want that. Teddy reached back and did as asked. She was taking a great risk meeting him alone in Lord Wharton's house like this, especially with so many not far away. But he was drawn to Eugenia and willing to take this risk to be near her as often as he could.

Her shape, shadow, was suddenly clear to him across the chamber, now that his eyes had adjusted to the darkness. They were in a small space, a private parlor perhaps. There was a fireplace and chairs. A rug on the floor and books were strewn about. One window was only partially covered by drapes, admitting a sliver of moonlight. It was decorated to suit a lady's taste rather than a man's. He figured this room butted against the dining room wall.

He moved toward Eugenia just as she moved toward him.

"You understood."

"I hoped I had." He stopped not far from her. "This isn't wise."

"Probably not, but I want something from you."

He frowned in question.

"I want a kiss," she whispered.

"More than one, most likely," Teddy said as he reached out to cup her cheek. "I think that can be arranged."

She moved closer, her fingers gripping his waistcoat tight. "But this time, I want a real kiss."

He didn't understand. "What wasn't real about the first, second, or the rest?"

She shook him. "You know."

"No, I don't."

She moved in, and her fingers slid around him, under his waistcoat. "This time, I want you to kiss me like you mean it. Like I'm the only woman in the world for you. The only one you dream of."

"Miss Hillcrest...I think you've misunderstood my intentions."

"I understand perfectly. You should understand mine, too. I don't expect marriage. I don't expect even a tomorrow, or for you to give up other women. I don't want chaste kisses, no matter how nice they were the other day. And here, right now, I need you to kiss me and not hold back that part of yourself that longs to be free. If that is asking too much, I will understand, and you can go back to the party."

Teddy looked down at her. He had not deliberately held any part of himself back from their kisses. He merely thought plundering her mouth like a savage was unnecessary. Tonight though, he could be persuaded to increase their intimacy if she wanted more. "A gentleman shouldn't reveal how much he craves a lady."

"But I know you do anyway. I can see it in your eyes," she whispered. "It's very flattering, considering my competition. I want you that way, too. I want to know you in a way that few do."

He frowned. "You couldn't mean that."

"I do," she promised. "You must feel no obligation or guilt for what we have only just begun, and what will eventually end."

He'd been trying not to read too much into her earlier confession about her lack of innocence, but it was impossible now to pretend. She had experience in passion, and she didn't want to keep him at arm's length.

Teddy took a moment more to consider how to go on with her now. Sneaking off to steal kisses was one thing, but meeting with an experienced and hungry like-minded soul was quite altogether different. A whole host of opportunities presented themselves to his passion-starved body. However, all required careful planning to carry out.

But if she was willing, there were no bounds he couldn't cross with her, provided she kept her word about not demanding a marriage in the end. And if he kept his head, he wouldn't get a child on her. Avoiding a pregnancy was absolutely necessary.

Deep in his heart, he believed her honest. Eugenia was just like him in that way. A seeker of the pleasures of the night and without fear for the future.

All his reasons to hesitate fell away.

Teddy moved closer to her and set his hands on her shoulders. "I felt no guilt when I kissed you, only concern that I might reveal how much I want to strip off your clothes and kiss you everywhere."

Eugenia laughed and fell against him. "I don't believe there'll be time for mutual nakedness tonight."

"A pity," Teddy mused, running his hand down her back to grip her bottom. He squeezed and kneaded her flesh, eliciting a gasp from her lips. His cock begged for freedom from his trousers already. "Will lifting your skirts be enough to satisfying you tonight?"

"Only if you lower your trousers. That's what I want tonight. A good hard joining. Passion with no regrets." Eugenia ran her hands up his chest, and her fingers teased into his hair at the back of his neck. A shiver raced down his spine when she sifted through the strands. "I like how tall and strong you seem."

"I find your deficiency of height equally appealing." Teddy let his fingers slide down the back of her thigh, just barely reaching as far as he'd like to go. He'd have to lift her to align them to make love, or set her down upon a chair. He spread his fingers over her derrière and then squeezed again. "I have to stretch to reach all your lovely curves. You're a compact woman I want to hoist over my shoulder and toss up onto the nearest bed."

"There's no bed to be had tonight, I'm afraid. Not here." Eugenia mimicked him, clutching his bum in her small hands. "But first, where's my kiss, sir?"

"Coming, at any moment." But it wasn't. Teddy was going to make her wait just a little longer. And if she'd thought he'd held back before, she was in for a rude shock when he did kiss her at last.

He backed her toward a low chair across the room. The perfect height, in his opinion, for lovemaking of any short duration in this room. He would seat her there and fall to his knees and do so many wicked things to her body before they had to part.

Eugenia sat on the edge and raised her skirts to her knees before leaning back to look up at him. Even in the dark, he could see the desire in her eyes and the expectation of pleasure from only him. He let his gaze trail down her body, pausing on her heaving chest and restless legs. There were red ribbons holding up her stockings tonight. A bold color for an equally bold lover. He reached out to trace around her slender leg and let his fingertip just happen to slip higher onto her bare skin.

Eugenia sucked in a sharp breath. "Where's my kiss?"

"I'll get to that. I promise."

Eugenia stirred, spreading her thighs a touch wider, though

her skirts still covered her sex from his view. She pouted suddenly. "Will you always make me wait?"

He smiled because that pout was so completely out of character for what he knew of her. "This passion of ours is not something to be hurried."

"What if someone comes?"

"Let's hope that they don't," he whispered. "I want only pleasure for you tonight, not a scandal."

Eugenia grabbed his coat by the lapels and pulled him down over her. "Enough talk."

He pretended to resist, taking time to position his hands close beside her hips. Then Teddy leaned down to steal a kiss. Then another, and another from her soft clinging lips. It was clear she wanted more and sooner than he was prepared to give yet. He would give her what she asked for in the end, though— all of his passion, all of his need, starting from tonight.

Eugenia's fingers rose to cup his throat, her tongue darted out to flick across his upper lip.

Teddy growled softly and sealed their lips together. She enthusiastically encouraged him to all but ravish her mouth and gave as good as she got. His need to be close had them rocking against each other within moments.

Teddy was burning up to strip her bare, but there really was no time for the sort of luxurious lovemaking he'd prefer. That would have to wait until he could bring her to his house when it was properly furnished, and he'd moved in.

He snuck his hands under her skirts and spread his fingers over her soft thighs. Eugenia let out a gasp as he moved his hands higher and higher.

"Dear God, but your skin is so warm," he whispered as he broke the kiss and pressed his head to hers.

"Your hands are rough. I like that," she hastened to add before licking his cheek. "I want them on me everywhere."

He moved his fingers up between her thighs until he could just touch her curls. She was wet. He jerked her to the edge of the chair and pushed her legs apart roughly. "I'll treat you well, I swear."

"I know. That's why I picked you out of all the distinguished rogues in London."

Teddy looked down at her lap, moving her skirts from view to reveal her pale thighs. His breath churned from anticipation and not a little lust. "That's why I'm here then. Because you chose me."

Teddy claimed her mouth in a hungry kiss, leaning over her as he grasped her hips to bring their bodies into closer alignment.

The touch of her quim against his groin made him groan with need. He'd be inside her tonight. He knew it, but he had to keep his head.

He had a sheath in his pocket, he always carried one just in case he became swept away by lust, and he'd heard they might interfere with conception, too. He broke free of her arms to grab it and toss his coat aside in the process. He set the condom on her lap for when he needed it and went to pull her back to him.

Eugenia had lifted it up to study it in the dim light from their window. After a moment, she shrugged. Clearly, she'd not expected him to be prepared or to wear one.

Teddy returned his hands to her thighs and slid them up until he touched her curls again. Her legs parted on a sigh, and she leaned against the chair back, willing, it seemed, to have him do with her as he liked.

So long as she was satisfied by the end that was fine with him.

Humbled by her trust and openness to heated passions, he teased his way through her damp curls until he discovered her wet folds. He parted her lower lips, intending to stimulate her until she moaned.

Teddy ducked his head down and kissed the curls above her sex, before dipping lower.

Above, a shocked gasp escaped her before she had her fingers in his hair, urging him to keep exploring her body. He was happy to oblige. He loved the taste of women inflamed by lust, and Eugenia was definitely excited tonight.

He ran his tongue back and forth through her folds, teasing her, kissing her, sucking on her clitoris, until her legs were stretched impossibly wide to give him unlimited access and her feet were high in the air. He brought one of her legs to rest upon his shoulder. The other she placed there herself.

This is what he loved. Giving pleasure to a woman because she wanted it. Needed it as much as he did. No pretense, no false modesty. Just two people with a burning need to feel.

It wasn't long before he could tell Eugenia was close to release. She was already rocking her pelvis into his face in search of that pinnacle of excitement. For all the speed of their coming together, he hadn't expected to be left behind. He hadn't even gotten his trousers lowered.

He lifted his head from her quim, loosened his trousers, and reached for the French letter. Eugenia helpfully tucked his shirt under his waistcoat while he rolled the length of gut onto his cock. Eugenia took hold of him then, drawing the tip down so he could tie the ribbons that would hold it firmly in place.

Clearly, she was familiar with their usage.

That made things easier, less awkward—and he firmly told himself not to think of the man who'd made love to her before him, or any who would after.

Suitably protected and aching to be inside her, he caught her face and kissed Eugenia hard with all the pent-up hunger their secret meetings and sly touches had excited in him. And as he carefully eased inside her warm depths, at last, he felt a small part of his soul roar with triumph.

He brought her face close to his, watching her react to his possession. This was the moment when lovers should be perfectly attuned.

He drew back and pumped his hips, unable to help himself. To be inside a woman was magic. That it was Eugenia was glorious. He would never wish this moment undone.

He clutched the back of the settee with one hand and her hip with the other. She had lost some of her passion, perhaps, but she'd have it back and more before they were through. He lowered his lips to her slender neck and nipped at the softness of her throat. Eugenia gasped and writhed beneath him, clearly enjoying their lovemaking.

Suddenly her hand slipped between them, clutching at his cock. After a moment, he realized he'd been in danger of sliding free of the protection he'd insisted upon wearing. He drew back to see that she'd caught hold of the ribbons and was trying to tighten them.

Teddy held still, cursing the ill-fitting thing under his breath. There was, of course, accidental displacement with condoms. But he could not continue if it was so loose that he might slip out while he was thrusting into her. He made sure he was completely protected again before he slid back inside her and held still there.

Teddy slid his fingers to Eugenia's clitoris and stroked her, teased her, brought her to the brink once more while he held still with only the squeeze of her depths to excite him. He pulsed his hips carefully, staying deep and hoping to find a place of sensitivity he'd read about in one of his erotic books.

Her fingers wrapped again around his cock tightened, and she fumbled about to stroke him around the base.

It wasn't enough alone, but then she kissed him and teased her tongue deep into his mouth to tangle with his, and he lost all sense of caution.

The thrill of her actions brought him closer to the brink, but he concentrated on securing her pleasure first. Thankfully, Eugenia shuddered and cried out a moment later. Her body clamped around his aching cock like a vise while he gritted his teeth and held still, not trusting his condom to do the job it was meant for.

When he could hold back no more, when her shuddering subsided, he pulled from her wet heat—condom dangling half off his cock. Eugenia slid it onto him again and then pumped his flesh fast and hard with her hand, and he came inside the sheath.

When he was spent, he fell forward onto her, settling his face between her breasts, and heaved a satisfied sigh. Eugenia was perfect for the pleasures of the night.

"Thank you," she whispered. "You do not disappoint."

He laughed and eased his face from the warm bower between her breasts, then dropped to kiss the tops of each one. "I hope not."

He started righting their clothes but paused when he caught her watching his face. "What is it?"

She leaned up and cupped his cheek before brushing her lips across his. "I was thinking I'd like to see you again like this."

He grinned and nuzzled her cheek with his lips. "We'll find a way. Soon."

"Good," she whispered back before bursting to her feet, straightening her gown and blowing him a kiss as she waltzed out the door.

Gods, he wanted to chase after her and drag her back for a second bout of lovemaking for that cheeky exit. Saucy didn't begin to describe a woman like Eugenia Hillcrest.

Chapter Eleven

Society was a fickle beast—one moment gracious and the next cold as snow. Eugenia glanced around at the wallflowers, all sitting forgotten on the sidelines at yet another ball, and hated to see it. Thaddeus had done his best, but his friends were once again dazzled by the heiresses and willing widows.

She understood that a lot of great families required an injection of new money at frequent intervals to remain solvent, but that did not mean they should ignore ladies without great fortunes who only hoped to be shown a little kindness and the occasional smile.

Worst of all was how wallflowers seemed to accept this was the way things were always meant to be. She shook her head. She had tried to convince them to be bolder, but habits of a lifetime were hard to break. Reputations were at stake, and the family's good name was all they had to trade upon.

Eugenia was on the sidelines, too, but she wasn't worried for herself. She had a lover, a handsome man watching even now from a distance and hopefully waiting for a chance to be alone with her again. Eugenia couldn't wait to touch Thaddeus again, either. To feel his hands on her thighs, his fingers teasing her quim to ecstasy.

She sighed. Soon but not yet.

Aurora came rushing back from the dance floor, face flushed, cheeks pink from an exuberant dance with young Lord Brandestock. "I swear I cannot keep a straight face when he tells me about his favorite horse anymore," she whispered into Eugenia's ear.

"Try," she warned. "We don't need anyone to enquire about what he said to you that was so amusing."

Aurora agreed and quickly sobered.

Eugenia patted her hand soothingly. It was hard for both of them to appear meek, mild, and dull around certain gentlemen. Her gaze fell on Scarsdale, watching her cousin from across the room. She clenched her jaw tight, hating how he hovered. She glared, wishing they'd never welcomed that man into their acquaintance. He seemed no longer to stutter which Eugenia now suspected was a ploy of some kind to get into their good graces.

Scarsdale finally looked away, then took himself off toward the card room. Eugenia smiled and turned to Aurora. "Are you thirsty?"

"Parched." Aurora linked their arms. "I don't have another dance until later, too."

"I'm glad that you're dancing tonight."

Aurora's brow furrowed. "What of you?"

"Never mind my dance card. I'm happy to know yours is filled. You look to be having a glorious night."

"I am. I am determined not to let anyone affect my peace of mind."

"Good for you."

They sauntered through the crowd, and Eugenia was pleased to see that Scarsdale gave them a wide berth when their paths unexpectedly crossed again. He headed back into the ballroom without acknowledging them.

There was a line of a few people waiting at the refreshment table, so they were forced to linger there longer than expected due to a shortage of punch. Eugenia spotted their dear friend Miss Waters at the table ahead of them, and waved to catch her attention when she glanced over her shoulder.

Their eyes met, and Charlotte grinned widely. She also allowed the woman between them to take her place at the front of the line so they could talk without rudely shouting around her.

"How lovely you look tonight," Eugenia whispered.

"Oh, thank you, Eugenia. You always say such nice things about my gowns, but I must say I am envious of yours. You look simply radiant. I must know your secret."

She felt radiant, too. She had felt a bubble of happiness growing inside her chest ever since Thaddeus' first touch and kiss. "I had the most wonderful sleep last night," she told her. Not strictly true. She had dreamed and remembered Thaddeus making love to her, becoming so feverish with lust all over again that she'd had to give herself relief.

Memories of trysts were good, but the real thing was far more satisfying and necessary. Eugenia looked about the chamber, hoping to spot Thaddeus lurking. Unfortunately, he seemed not to have followed her to the refreshment table.

With cups of punch finally secured, she and Aurora and Charlotte strolled toward the card room doorway and chose a spot where they could see into the chamber, and the ballroom as well.

Charlotte nudged her arm gently to gain her attention. "Do you think Brandestock is courting Miss Philips?"

Eugenia turned to look back into the ballroom, where the pair were just gliding past. Miss Phillips was plain but well-dowered. "Perhaps. I saw her standing with his mother a short time ago. They seemed on good terms."

"She's much too stiff for him."

Aurora laughed. "Shouldn't it be him that's stiff?"

Charlotte blushed at the question. "I didn't mean it that way," she protested, blushing even more. "But you are right. A future husband should be solidly erect around his future bride."

At that moment, Lord Hurlston wandered past, frowning at them, then shaking his head on the way into the ballroom. Eugenia thought he might have overheard their conversation, but clearly, he'd decided he must have misunderstood.

Miss Waters sighed. "Why does it have to be the most handsome men who get snapped up before we can even try to impress them?"

"Because they were handsome and rich before ever seeking a bride, I expect."

"They can have their pick, marrying with their heads rather than their hearts," Aurora warned, her usual disapproval clear.

"Mr. Berringer is different," Eugenia disagreed. "He's going to marry for love."

Two pairs of eyes fixed on her suddenly. "Where did you hear that?"

Eugenia blinked, startled that she'd let slip so delicate a confidence from him. She shrugged as if it was obvious. "He seems the type to me."

"His cousin waited years to be married for love," Miss Waters added helpfully. "I suppose he'll be under no pressure to please his family because of their example."

"Yes, I expect that's the case." And then her heart stopped, because he was standing across the room watching her talk with her friends again. She could not help the smile that burst over her face as he winked. All she could think about was feeling his lips against hers, his hands on her body, and his cock…

Well, she could almost swoon thinking about making love to him again.

She turned her attention to anywhere he was not standing and drew in a shuddering breath, trying to stem the tide of her excitement.

Thankfully, Sylvia and Lord Wharton were coming toward them, apparently done with the card room already.

"Cousin, my lord," she murmured as greetings were exchanged.

"I finally convinced your cousin to come away from the games and dance with me," Wharton teased. "But she wanted to see you pair first. And good evening to you, too, Miss Waters."

Charlotte had confessed to being a little afraid of embarrassing herself in front of the marquess and stammered out a mumbled reply.

Eugenia took in her cousin's pink cheeks and took charge of the conversation. "How much did you win tonight?"

"I lost. I seem to have no luck of late," Sylvia answered, without truly meeting her gaze.

But since Sylvia had an uncanny ability to win or lose any hand she chose. Eugenia did not believe luck had anything to do with the outcome. She raised a brow.

Sylvia held her gaze a moment and then had the grace to flush a little.

Eugenia frowned at the proof she was involved in another nefarious scheme concocted by her intended. No doubt another friend of Wharton's had fallen on hard times and needed his finances to be propped up with a short-term injection of funds miraculously won at cards to salvage his pride. Eugenia didn't approve of the way Wharton meddled with his friends' lives, but she had never really been asked her opinion, either.

She looked away and discovered to her delight that Thaddeus had moved nearer, speaking with Hurlston and a trio of rogues a few steps away. She supposed he'd find his way to her side soon enough, but she was sure it would feel too long.

Eugenia was pressed to follow her cousin Sylvia and Lord Wharton back into the ballroom, nursing her secret delight in her lover tight to her breast as she passed Thaddeus by with only bestowing a polite nod. No one could ever know how freeing it had felt to be entirely herself with a man at long last.

She hadn't felt that way in a very long time. There had been no selfish self-indulgence with his passion. He'd made her feel desperately needed there in the dark with him, desirable and irresistible.

She trailed along, greeting friends and new acquaintances on the way to the edge of the dance floor, but her mind remained fixed on a certain gentleman with rough hands somewhere in her wake.

Wharton twirled Sylvia away to dance, leaving the three of them to watch from the sidelines.

"They look so happy together," Charlotte said wistfully.

"Your turn will come soon, I'm sure," she promised, hoping

that was true. Charlotte was the nicest person, but she lacked that certain spark men found irresistible.

"I hope so. I'm practically bursting to be ruined," she blurted out.

The sound of a man starting to choke somewhere behind Eugenia made her turn around slowly, fearing the worst. Lord Hurlston and Thaddeus stood behind them, and Lord Hurlston was staring at Charlotte with truly frightened eyes. Thaddeus, however, was trying not to laugh.

Charlotte took one look at the pair and fled, a tiny wail of apology lingering in the air.

Eugenia decided the best course of action was to pretend not to acknowledge her friend's last shocking statement and forge on with a greeting instead. "Good evening, Lord Hurlston. Mr. Berringer. What a pleasure to see you both here tonight."

"Ladies," Thaddeus said, offering a short bow, but his grin remained on his utterly kissable lips.

He nudged Hurlston with his elbow. The poor earl was still staring after Charlotte with his mouth hanging half-open. "Oh, yes," he said quickly, recovering his lapse of composure. "Indeed. A lovely evening to be spent among friends."

"Have you been here long?" she asked of Hurlston.

"I have only just arrived," he managed to say, but she did not have his complete attention. He seemed to be looking after Charlotte still. She was afraid he was not going to forget what he'd overheard. She only hoped he didn't make the shy woman feel worse for expressing her need for passion.

They stood awkwardly together, but then Hurlston broke the silence. "Shouldn't someone make sure Miss Waters is all right and not hiding behind a potted palm somewhere?"

"I'll do that," Aurora offered and quickly slipped away.

Eugenia glanced at Thaddeus and then at Lord Hurlston. The pair were great friends, she had assumed, but she didn't really know very much about the earl or what he thought of spinsters desperately waiting for a husband. At least Thaddeus seemed unconcerned about Charlotte's comment now, so she caught

Hurlston's eye. "I hope you won't make my friend feel embarrassed when she comes back."

"I wouldn't dream of it."

Thaddeus nodded. "Neither would I. She's good fun, Miss Waters, but has a timid heart."

Eugenia looked at him curiously, and Hurlston gave him a suspicious side glance too, but then he nodded. "If you will excuse me," he said. "There is someone I must speak with tonight."

He strode off, leaving Thaddeus and Eugenia standing side by side. They watched Wharton and Sylvia dance past before turning to each other at the same moment and grinning. "What a thing to have said out loud," she murmured.

"I thought Hurlston would faint," Thaddeus confessed. "What do you think, E. Shall we take a turn about the room together?"

She noted the shortening of her name but let it pass for now. "Perhaps we could see what is keeping Aurora and Miss Waters."

"Not a bad idea."

Thaddeus did not offer his arm. They both perhaps felt the tension simmering inside them. They strolled side by side, nodding to acquaintances who noticed them together and acting as if nothing had really changed. She ached for him to touch her, but here, with so many around, there would be no chance it could go unnoticed.

They did not find Aurora or Miss Waters in the adjoining hallway or in the card room. So, they circled back toward the ballroom, crossing paths with Hurlston, who appeared to be searching for his someone, still.

She glanced up at Thaddeus when he was out of earshot. "Why did you call me E?"

"I don't know. Do you not like it?"

"Not particularly. I like my name. I'd rather hear it tumble from your lips than any nickname."

Thaddeus nodded. "Then I won't do it again, but I can't

promise I won't slip and call you something else more endearing."

She chuckled softly and drew a little closer to him. "I must confess that whenever I hear the Duke of Exeter address you as Teddy, I want to ask him to stop. Do you not think it childish of him?"

"The duke is older, and so he does as he pleases." Thaddeus smiled to show he was not concerned. "My mother always addressed me that way, so I don't really mind hearing it from him. He is the only family I have left, and we all make allowances for family and good friends, don't we?"

"Yes, but I think Teddy definitely sounds too young for what a woman my age would want you for," she whispered.

He laughed at that. "Then call me whatever feels right. I'll answer to anything, anywhere."

For an answer, she merely smiled and asked, "When might we meet again?"

He glanced about, checking who stood close. "Tonight," he whispered. "Like the first time we met, only this time it will not be by accident that I discover you alone taking the air. I'll be waiting…and hoping it's soon."

She grinned, but then Aurora and Charlotte returned. Charlotte looking a little embarrassed still as she finally met Thaddeus' curious gaze. "Shall we return to the ballroom together?" she said, somewhat more shy than normal.

"Not me. I must away," Thaddeus apologized.

"Oh, what a shame," Aurora complained, pouting a little as she looked up at him.

Eugenia moved smoothly between them. She couldn't have her cousin flirting with a man Eugenia was involved with anymore. "I'm sure we'll see him again soon enough."

Thaddeus bowed and made his escape.

They strolled back to the ballroom. Wharton and Sylvia were just leaving the dance floor by then. Wharton began to fan Sylvia to cool her red face and laughed. "Is that better?"

"Exhilarating," she gushed, looking up at Wharton with all the love in her heart.

"Truly." He handed back her fan. "Just wait till mother hears you persuaded me to three sets in one night. She'll be miffed not to have seen it so she could criticize me for drawing attention to us."

The pair laughed, and Sylvia hung on his arm. "I wish she could hear the music."

"If she was here for that, we would finally be married," he warned.

They continued their loving banter, wrapped up in their own little world. Aurora and Charlotte were whispering together. No one was really paying Eugenia any attention. Now would be the perfect time to slip away.

She took a step backward and then another, until she was at the threshold of the balcony. There was no way to know if Thaddeus had had enough time to slip outside and was lingering in wait for her, but she hoped he was as she spun and stepped out into the darkness.

Her hand was caught, and she was dragged far from the open doorway. She knew those hands and the dark shape towing her along.

Thaddeus spun about and placed his hands on either side of her face. "Hello, lovely."

He dropped a soft kiss upon her lips, then another.

Eugenia slipped her fingers into his hair and held him close for a deeper kiss. "I wanted to do that since the moment I saw you across the crowded ballroom."

"Did you now?"

She drew back. "Didn't you?"

"So much I considered bounding across the dance floor to sweep you into my arms and carrying you outside. You make me uncomfortably hot and hard in a room crowded with proper society."

She smiled as she tangled her fingers in his hair and lay her body against his. He was hard. She could feel his cock firm against her sex already. "I'm glad you waited, and I am relieved that no one knows about us."

"We'll keep us a secret for as long as we can, but I must warn you, you are really my sort of woman. Irresistible and equally keen."

Eugenia laughed softly, smiling up at him. "I wish I could stay out here all night with you, but my absence might already be missed."

"I don't want to get you into trouble. And I'm afraid I won't be able to see you for a few days. I have to leave Town tomorrow for an appointment of longstanding. Nearly forgot about it, but I cannot delay it even if I want to. It is the last trip away for some time to come, thank heavens."

"It's for the duke?"

He nodded. "It is a matter only I can handle, apparently. Tedious and boring, I fear, like so many others. But I will be back on Tuesday, and I will call at Wharton's that day if it's not too late."

"Come to me at Albemarle Street on Wednesday."

His breath caught. "Are you sure you want me visiting you there?"

She kissed him quickly. "I'm sure I want you everywhere. Be safe and hurry back to me."

"I will," he promised, then stole a deep, hungry kiss from her.

Eugenia patted her cheeks, which felt hot, and hurried back to the ballroom. When she slipped inside, Wharton noticed her return but said nothing about her disappearance. He only shrugged and turned his attention once more to his bride-to-be.

"Ooh, look, there he is again," Aurora whispered. "I wonder where Mr. Berringer disappeared to just then?"

A feeling of annoyance filled Eugenia at hearing Aurora talk about her lover and where he'd been. It wasn't unusual that they spoke of the comings and goings of the *ton's* gentlemen at society events. They frequently pondered who they favored or met with in secret all the time. But it was strange because Thaddeus had met with and kissed *her*, with great passion, just a moment ago.

Thaddeus was her lover and should not be her cousin's to contemplate.

But how was she to warn off her cousin and halt her pursuit of him, without giving herself away? She didn't know.

Eugenia glanced across the room and spied an old client of theirs, someone Aurora found irritating.

"Did you see that Lord Sullivan is here, Aurora, and with that same blonde woman on his arm again as we saw on Bond Street a month ago?"

"His cousin, Miss Smith," she said sourly.

"Do you think he's courting her?"

"Probably. But she's bound for a life of utter boredom with him if he proposes."

Eugenia clucked her tongue in disapproval. "That was too harsh, even for you."

Aurora sighed. "There's not an unpredictable bone in his body. How could that be with those good looks of his? He ought to be wicked, but he's not."

"Predictability has some benefit." For instance, she knew that Thaddeus would spend the next two dances circulating the ballroom before leaving to spend a certain amount of time in the card room. He wasn't addicted to cards like so many others were but likely believed showing an interest was expected of him. She lived the same way most of the time—doing what was expected and safe. Yet sometimes even that could lead to a most remarkable experience.

She would count the days and hours until she could be alone again with Thaddeus, and next time it would be in the privacy of her home and her soft bed. She felt secure in the knowledge that there would be many more trysts between them both. As he'd said, there was great reward in not rushing his kisses. His were to be savored rather than squandered, and she definitely looked forward to more in the weeks to come.

Chapter Twelve

TEDDY PEERED at the distant building, Wharton House, keen to attend a dinner he'd only just found he'd been invited to while he'd been away on the duke's business. He smiled, looking forward to seeing Eugenia again—and having her in his arms tomorrow.

He'd thought of her so often while he'd been away. Indulged in fantasies of what they might do together in the future.

His eagerness to be alone with a spinster was quite an unexpected yearning on his part. Time away from London hadn't curbed his appetites, and he couldn't seem to help the way his mind worked and his body behaved when he thought of her writhing beneath him in the throes of ecstasy. She was everything a man might hope for in a lover. Smart, wanton as hell, and content not to hear a proposal of marriage.

He tapped his knee, impatient to reach his destination.

To see her again.

To touch her hand.

He didn't know if she'd be even at this dinner, but he desperately hoped so.

The carriage finally stopped to deposit him at Lord Wharton's door. He bounded out without waiting for the grooms to put down the step, tugged down his waistcoat, and smoothed his hair before he looked up at the building.

He had to admit he'd dressed with more care tonight than usual in the hope of seeing Eugenia's smile of approval. She did like to watch him, and he liked to watch her, too. She had a lovely figure.

Wharton's door opened slowly, light spilling out down the stairs, and he started for it.

"Excuse me, my lord!" a man cried out behind him.

Teddy, who was not addressed as lord, continued on his way, but only made it as far as the bottom step when the man hailed him again—only much nearer.

"Sir, please, if you could wait a moment."

Teddy turned at the plea. A fellow, shorter than himself in a dark coat and rather dated hat, tugged on his sleeve.

Teddy brushed off that grasping touch immediately. "Can I help you?"

"Yes, I do hope that you can," the fellow said, puffing heavily. "I am looking for someone."

"I'm sorry, but I do not live in this square."

"I know. I've asked all around, and no one in the grand houses will help me."

Teddy frowned. He likely couldn't help the fellow, either. "And the name of the person you are looking for."

"Mrs. Robert Bagshaw."

Teddy shook his head. "There is no one known to me by that name."

The fellow chewed his lip. "She must be here somewhere."

"I'm sorry. I am acquainted with a great many women, and London is a large city, but no Mrs. Bagshaw that I recall. Can you describe her?"

"Dark hair, though it might be gray now, bookish tendencies. I suspect she might be using another name." The fellow smiled quickly. "She was expected in Dover and never arrived."

Something about this fellow's query did not sit right with Teddy. If the woman was using another name, no doubt there was a reason for it. She might be trying to hide from this man. "Why are you looking for her?"

"She's owed some money, and I must find her in order to give it to her. I need to find her as quickly as possible."

"Ah, well, I've not the faintest idea who she might be, but I wish you well in your endeavors. Do excuse me. I am late for dinner."

The fellow bowed deeply. "Thank you for your time, good sir," the fellow called as he turned away. "May fortune guide your steps."

Teddy hurried into Lord Wharton's home without further delay. The butler let him in, and from the entrance hall, he heard the murmur of men's voices raised in disagreement coming from the library. He passed off his hat to the butler and made his way to join his friends to see what was amiss.

At the doorway, he scanned the crowd for Eugenia but only saw gentlemen gathered about. He called out a greeting to anyone who might hear him over the din.

Lord Hurlston hurried over. "Were you accosted on the street, too?"

Teddy blinked. "I would not say accosted, but yes, I was approached by some fellow."

"Wharton, there's been another imposition," Hurlston called out.

"I wouldn't say it was an imposition," he hastened to assure his friends.

Wharton cursed under his breath anyway. "I'll have him arrested if he bothers one more of my visitors tonight."

Teddy drew close to Wharton, where a butler held a tray, and claimed a glass of red wine. "What's going on?"

"The same fellow that spoke to you is bothering everyone who comes to the square, it seems," Wharton explained, sounding none too happy about it. "Running up and down the pavement, accosting gentlemen, and ladies, too, no matter their station.

Teddy glanced toward the front windows. "He's looking for a woman, but he can hardly describe her appearance."

Wharton shook his head. "And is it any wonder she's gone to ground with such a fellow nipping at her heels," he complained.

"I assumed he was in a solicitor's employ trying to settle an inheritance on her."

"Or trying to rob her of it. Hurlston got the impression the fellow might be her husband, and he was first to be questioned. His story keeps changing. He told Scarsdale he was a friend of her brothers."

"Perhaps he's trying to garner cooperation by glossing over certain facts of their relationship." They walked to the window together to peer out. The man was nowhere to be seen now. "People are more inclined to be helpful when there is money involved."

"All too true, I'm afraid," Wharton grumbled. "He seems to be certain she is to be found in this square, though. Someone must know her."

"I do hope for her sake it's an inheritance and not a husband trying to drag her back home unwillingly." Teddy scratched his jaw, thinking over their conversation. "Did he mention to you the lady's first name, by chance?"

"I don't believe he did to me," Hurlston answered.

"Nor to anyone, I think," Wharton added. "Does that strike anyone else as odd?"

"Most definitely suspicious," Teddy agreed. "I wonder if he does not know it. He did say to me she might be living under an assumed name."

"Well, he'll never find her if she is."

Teddy peeked out the front window again. If the fellow was still out there, the night had swallowed him up. "If he was her husband, he certainly should know her first name. I wonder what he really wants from her."

"Haven't the slightest, but he should stop bothering my friends before I have him arrested for public nuisance," Wharton complained, then shrugged before he addressed the room. "Gentlemen, I'm afraid to inform you that the ladies of the house will not be joining us this evening for dinner."

"Oh, damn shame about that," Hurlston said. "We'll have to amuse ourselves somehow. We'll each need a tasty beverage to soften our disappointment."

"Make it an even dozen," Lord Sullivan suggested. "And brandy."

Although he laughed, Teddy was incredibly disappointed to hear the news that Eugenia wouldn't be seen tonight. His friends were all well and good, but he'd really hoped to speak with her instead.

"Mama is feverish, and the women will not leave her bedside," Wharton explained and then sighed. "I'm afraid we will have to amuse ourselves tonight with drink and conversation."

Scarsdale clapped an arm around the marquess' shoulders. "Just like old times. Who needs women anyway, eh?"

Teddy did. He'd thought of nothing but seeing Eugenia again for days. "I'm sure we'll manage."

The call to dinner was sounded, and they moved toward the dining room in pairs.

Scarsdale grinned at him. "At least it will stop Wharton from trying to make a match with one of us to the remaining Hillcrest cousins tonight."

Several laughed and held up their crossed fingers to ward off any such attempt.

Teddy moved toward Lord Hurlston and walked beside him to whisper, "I hadn't realized Wharton was doing that. Trying to marry them off, I mean."

Hurlston shrugged. "Only subtly. Wharton's never been one to show his cards all at once. They're unmarried, and so, of course, he'd encourage any good match that secured their futures."

He glanced around their friends discretely, trying and failing to picture any of them as Aurora's or Eugenia's husbands. "Has anyone seemed keen?"

"Not to me. I like them," Hurlston confessed, "but not enough to encourage any one of my friends to choose them over an heiress they might desperately need more."

Brandestock came upon Teddy's other side and leaned close. "The younger is jolly good fun, but the older sees right through a man," Brandestock complained. "Reminds me of my old nurse. Frightening stare."

The elder was perfect, in Teddy's opinion.

For everything but marrying one of his friends, that was. He was glad no one knew he'd taken a keen interest in Eugenia and had no intention of stopping anytime soon.

Without the lady's expected to join them, the dining table had been reset to a smaller proportion. They would not have to shout at each other to be heard tonight but likely would do just that anyway, as usually happened when the drink was in plentiful supply.

Teddy took a seat near Hurlston when Wharton suggested they sit where they pleased. He and Hurlston got along best out of all of them.

"Did anyone take note of the Duke of Montrose's return to Town?" Hurlston asked the gathering.

"My God, he's back?"

"Indeed. And he's married," Wharton informed them, directing the footmen to begin serving the first course.

"Dear God, who is the poor woman who took him on?" Brandestock joked and then dug into his first course with gusto.

Many laughed either at the question or how Brandestock always seemed to be starving for the first course of any dinner.

Hurlston grinned. "From what I understand, Montrose married his cousin's widow, so it's a family affair through and through."

There was silence at that, and Teddy did not know what to think. There was nothing illegal about marrying a cousin's widow. It had the benefit of returning any fortune, large or small, back to the family. But more than one widow had been persuaded against their own interests by well-meaning family members to agree to wed a cousin, even if they'd prefer to marry someone else instead.

Scarsdale sat forward. "Does anyone know her or the late cousin of Montrose?"

The whole table, including Teddy, murmured a negative.

"Montrose usually keeps his family far from London," Hurlston added. "The cousin I remember from school. Quite different to Montrose. Open-minded, friendly chap he was back then. I wonder if she was given any choice about the match."

Brandestock seemed aghast. "Surely, he wouldn't have forced her to marry him. I mean, that's low, even for him."

Wharton held up his hand. "By all accounts, she is lovely but is known to walk with a cane. Montrose is said to be very protective of her."

Brandestock drained his glass just as the servants filed in, their hands full of platters and dishes. "Has she any acquaintances in London who can confirm she was a willing party to the match?"

"Not that I'm aware of," Wharton murmured and then glanced toward Teddy. "Do you know if Montrose has been in contact with Exeter at all? I can think of no one else he'd call upon first with his new duchess."

"No, but I have been away for a few days, so I do not know if he's tried. I'll make inquiries."

"Please do. For the sake of harmony, it would be well for all of us to welcome the Duchess of Montrose to society. It is not her fault her husband is a humorless ass."

There was a murmur of agreement around the table. "Montrose has always been so damn prickly. We shouldn't hold that against his bride unless she's cut from the same cloth as him."

"The wife is an unknown indeed," Hurlston murmured. "Perhaps she'll have some luck at settling his temper."

"Only if she doesn't lock him out of her bedchamber," Scarsdale joked.

Hurlston threw a napkin at him. "You'd best hope your wife doesn't do that to you when you finally tie the knot."

The remarks from that point on became rather bawdy and political, too.

Teddy was well versed with the ways of society gossip. Before becoming known as the Duke of Exeter's heir, he'd followed his cousin around, pretending to be a footman. He had been privy to many such dinners between influential lords and wealthy gentlemen who had the power and conviction to bend society to their will, and see others lose favor. As far as architects of change went, Wharton's warnings to not be too quick to rush to judgment on the new duchess were at best only slightly self-serving. A happy Duke of Montrose meant that he was more likely to support proposals in the House of Lords. If he was in a bad mood, and that had been often, he always made things more difficult.

The dinner was lengthy, and Teddy found it utterly boring by the end. The same crude jokes, the same gossip, the same men voicing dissent to popular opinion sprung up time and again. He stood up as soon as the dinner ended, and cigars and port were brought out, intending to leave early. He peered down the long table as half the room lit cigars and puffed putrid smoke into the air. "Gentlemen, it has been a pleasure as usual."

"Oh, are you leaving so soon?" Brandestock complained, three sheets to the wind already.

"I'm afraid so," he apologized.

No one else voiced an intention to go, so he waved his goodbyes and let himself out of the dining room. But before he could call out for a servant to bring him his hat, a shape moved into the hall.

Eugenia.

He grinned and strode directly to her.

She grasped his hand and pulled him behind the drawing room door and wrapped her arms about his shoulders. She kissed him thoroughly, again and again, appearing ravenous for the taste of him.

Aware they could be discovered at any moment, he lowered his lips to her ear when they finally parted and spoke to her only in a whisper. "I feared I wouldn't see you tonight."

"You almost didn't. It is very late. Welcome back to Town."

"Thank you. It's good to come back to so warm a reception.

How is the marchioness now? Wharton said none of you would leave her."

"She became restless, moved too much, and started to bleed again. I stayed, not really for her, but for Sylvia. She'd started to cry."

Teddy squeezed Eugenia's head a little more firmly against his. "I'm sorry. It's such a difficult recovery, isn't it?"

Eugenia nodded. "How was your evening?"

"Dull without seeing you there at the table to distract me."

"That is so sweet." She kissed his cheek. "When can I see you?"

"You invited me to Albemarle Street. Is that still what you want?"

She looked into his eyes and kissed him softly. "Yes. Very much so. I will be there by two o'clock in the afternoon tomorrow."

He nodded. Tomorrow was his usual day to call upon Sophie, but with her color so much improved last week, he felt certain he could skip a visit. "What if you're not there? Should I wait? Where?"

"Inside." Eugenia pressed something warm and hard into his hand. A key, by the feel of it. "I'm trusting you not to steal my furnishings for your home to spare you the pain of making decisions on your own."

"I would never take something that didn't belong to me," he assured her, adding the key to his pocket. He slid his hand down to her rear and squeezed. "How is it I'm so lucky I get to touch you?"

"It's my choice to let you, not luck," she whispered, reminding him she was with him of her own free will with no expectations whatsoever.

Eugenia was as soft as he remembered. The scent of her skin, heavenly. He really didn't want to let her go tonight, but there was a roomful of lords nearby. One of them, possibly Wharton, might come out and find them alone together. Wharton would insist he had compromised Eugenia and owed her a marriage proposal.

He drew back from her, caught her fingers in his, and kissed the back of her bare hand. He wasn't ready for a marriage, but he would look forward to more secret trysts with Eugenia any day. "Until tomorrow."

"I cannot wait." Eugenia slipped away through the drawing room, escaping via a distant door so no one might see her ascend the main staircase.

He let himself out into the hall, woke the oblivious butler to ask for his hat, and then strode out into the night with a heart a great deal lighter than when he'd left the dining room, fearing he might not see Eugenia at all.

Chapter Thirteen

EUGENIA SETTLED on Sylvia's bed after receiving an answer to a knock at her door to come in. "You're awake early."

"I would be if I had been able to fall asleep yet," Sylvia complained with a heavy sigh. She was in bed but propped up by her many pillows. She had a lost look about her face as if she didn't know which way to turn or what to do.

Eugenia placed her hand on her cousin's brow and then her cheeks as well. She seemed in perfect health. But because of all their late nights sitting beside the marchioness, she looked like a worn-out rag today. "Poor Sylvia. Do you need a tonic to help you drift off?"

"No, I should like to keep my wits about me a while longer. The marchioness has finally fallen into a calmer rest. She might wake and need me again."

With the danger appearing to have passed, Sylvia ought to rest herself. "You need to sleep while you can. You can't wait up, expecting the worst. We left her maid behind in her chambers, and yours, as well. There's no more you can do for her."

"I know, but I am feeling frustrated and anxious. How much more of this can she endure?"

"Quite a lot, I'm sure, but she'd hate to hear you so cast down. Try to keep faith that she'll get better soon."

"I try, but some days…" Sylvia smiled sadly. "I'm sorry that we missed the dinner last night. I know you'd gone to some trouble with your appearance and were looking forward to a night of fun and good conversation. That was a very pretty gown you were wearing last night before you changed."

She had dressed to see Thaddeus, but there would be other

occasions to be with him, she knew. He had told her he would not leave London for any extended length for some time to come. He would go home to the Duke of Exeter's country estate at Christmas, no doubt. They had all the time between now and then to indulge in forbidden pleasures. She was nearly certain that by that time, the thrill of bedding each other might have eased. "The marchioness is more important than any dinner."

"She's the mother I never had."

"I know. And you're the daughter she wishes to keep near." Eugenia smoothed her cousin's hair back from her face. The marchioness had daughters of her own, but Wharton had sent them back to stay in the country to give his mother some peace and quiet. The pair were excitable girls and argued constantly. That was not welcome behavior in a sickroom. "From what I recall of your mother, those two would have gotten along quite well."

"Thank you for saying that. Sometimes I feel I betray her."

"It's not as if she were around to give you the advice you might need at this time in your life, or could she have. She had no experience of the *ton*." Eugenia chuckled softly. "I quite look forward to seeing you and the marchioness storm the *ton* when she's in better health."

Sylvia nibbled on the tip of a lock of hair. "I try not to think that far ahead. Wharton has his interests, and I have mine, which at the moment is keeping his mother alive."

"When she's better, and you're married, you do realize you'll be one of the most influential women in society. Wharton will make sure everyone knows it, too. He's already begun carving out your place in society by his side."

"All I care about is the happiness of the people I love." Sylvia glanced up at Eugenia and winced. "Am I keeping you and Aurora from having your own life?"

She was in a way, but it was nothing Eugenia would change. She was also needed by the marchioness to a degree, but mostly by Sylvia. She would not abandon her cousin when she was overwhelmed and afraid. And on the edge of exhaustion, too.

She cupped her cousin's cheek and leaned down to kiss her brow. "As you said, all that matters is the happiness of those we love. You're so tired right now and not thinking straight. I can help you in a small fashion." Eugenia went to fetch a small bottle of laudanum Sylvia kept tucked away in a drawer for emergencies. She measured out a tiny dose for her cousin and took it to her. "Here, drink this. No argument. It is just enough to help you drift off and rest for at least a few hours."

Sylvia sighed. "I suppose I will need it after all. Thank you."

"Good girl," Eugenia crooned.

Sylvia tossed it back and handed her the glass with a shudder. "What about you?"

"I shall visit Aurora and dole out the same remedy if she is still awake, too."

Aurora, though, had slept in a chair by the bed for an hour at a time last night. She was lucky that she could do that. Neither Sylvia nor Eugenia ever managed the feat.

"I'll see you in a few hours," Eugenia promised as she tucked her cousin into her bed, drew the drapes to darken the room and, upon a mumbled farewell from Sylvia, slipped out of the room.

Eugenia crossed the hall to her other cousin's room. She tapped quietly, then let herself in. Aurora was reclining on a chair, her head stuck in a book.

"I hoped you'd be asleep," she said. "The marchioness would remind you that reading novels like that will give you unrealistic expectations of marriage."

"I can tell the difference between fantasy and fact as well as you can." She set the book aside. "I thought you'd be asleep already, too."

"I was just putting Sylvia to bed."

"Laudanum again?"

Eugenia nodded solemnly. "She must rest unless she wishes to become ill herself."

"True. She'll worry herself to death the way she cares about people." Aurora stood, seemingly full of energy. "Are you getting enough rest yourself?"

"As much as I can. Why?"

"Oh, I don't know." Aurora twirled her finger in a lock of her hair. "I thought perhaps a certain rogue might be keeping you awake and trembling in anticipation of seeing him again."

Eugenia turned to meet her cousin's playful gaze in surprise at her suggestion. "What gentleman would that be?"

A smile curved her lips. "Must I name the fellow? Is future duke description enough? I am impressed you caught his eye. Lord help me, but I tried and failed to."

Eugenia pursed her lips. She had thought she'd been discreet, but Aurora had sharp eyes. There was no point in dissembling. "Who else suspects? Sylvia?"

Aurora shook her head. "Not that she's told me. She is too concerned with her own affairs at the moment to pay you and me much attention. Not that she needs to know. I'm certainly not going to spoil the surprise for her."

Well, that was a relief. Sylvia definitely had enough on her mind. "How did you discover us?"

Aurora drew close and placed her hand on Eugenia's shoulder. "A long look exchanged. A shared smile. The brush of his hand against yours when he passed you at a ball. Tell me, is he very romantic?"

Eugenia blushed. They had not been discreet enough at all, it seemed. "It is all very new between us, but yes, I feel treasured."

Aurora flopped on her back on her bed and sighed loudly. "I knew he'd be a man worth having. Have you?"

Aurora was an earthy sort. She liked to discuss seductions and lovers and all the interesting things they could do to a woman. Eugenia hesitated to share too much about Thaddeus with her, though. She would not like to describe all the aspects of their intimate relationship for fear that Aurora might try to tease him with that knowledge one day.

"I can guess by your silence that you have. I'm glad."

"What of you?"

"No one noteworthy. Not for a while, actually."

Eugenia moved to sit close to her cousin on her bed. Aurora

seemed sad. For a change, Aurora was the only one of them without a current beau. "I suppose that is because our circle of acquaintances has shrunk since the engagement."

"Yes, an endless parade of stuffy lords and reckless younger sons to pick from. What wouldn't I give for a truly wicked man to appear at our doorstep and sweep me off my feet and into a dark corner?"

"Be careful what you wish for, cousin. Fate is always listening."

"Then I will wish fate to smile upon you and deliver up a proposal."

She glanced at Aurora sharply. "Do not imagine more to my affair than there ever could be."

"Why do you say that? I think you're entirely worthy of becoming a duchess one day. I can see it now. You make a handsome couple, and any children would be well-favored, too."

Aurora always got ahead of herself. That's why her heart had been broken so many times in the past. "No, I most certainly am not meant for marriage or children. It is a fling and nothing more."

Aurora pouted and rolled onto her stomach, kicking her heels high in the air. "If Sylvia can win herself a marquess, I see no reason for you not to snare a duke."

"Future duke," she corrected before she mimicked her cousin, lying on the bed with her heels in the air. "Aurora, your fanciful imagination is running away from you again. It is an affair, not a courtship."

"Why couldn't it be more? You're smart and pretty. Clearly, he likes you more than anyone else he's met in society. He's had his pick from anyone and chosen wisely with you."

Did Aurora truly not understand? "Becoming his lover is not the same as becoming fated to be his duchess one day. He needs to marry his equal."

"You'd be his match in every way then," Aurora promised. "He puts on no grand airs or graces like lords do. He's a mere mister right now."

"And for many years to come, I hope," Eugenia laughed. "He'll grow into the expectation long before he takes the title. But he's changed since we first met him. He'll change again, I'm sure."

"Change together. Grow into the expectation together. I think he's worth pursuing for a husband." She grinned impishly. "You'd outrank Sylvia then."

Eugenia leaned hard into Aurora's shoulder. "Your dreams are always so grand for others, but please consider finding a husband for yourself first before you try your hand at matchmaking me."

"Oh, I do already consider it, but my imagination is vast. There is space enough to consider the happiness of many."

"Tell me again what you want in a husband," Eugenia whispered.

"Oh, that's easy. He must be funny and smart and possess just enough wealth to make him impervious to bribery or excess. But he must not be too impressed with himself." Aurora erupted into a fit of giggles. "Also, he must possess the most wicked tongue around me."

"For your sake, I hope you can meet such a remarkable man. Or have you already?"

Her brow furrowed. "I suppose not. It seems meeting a man who meets my high standards might mean I could be waiting a long time. Anyone who comes close ends up lacking in one area or another. Usually they lack passion."

"Perhaps you ought not to be so impatient. Not every man reveals their wicked side so readily."

Aurora's eyes suddenly grew wide. "You missed a chance to be with your lover last night. He was here, and we were with the marchioness. Oh, I'm so sorry."

Eugenia smiled impishly. "I found a way to see him, and as he likes to tell me, his kisses are worth the wait. I'm sure there'll be other opportunities and dinners, soon."

Aurora clutched her hands before her breasts and then pretended to swoon. "Now that was romantic. I'll have to help," Aurora mused aloud.

Eugenia stared at her cousin. "I beg your pardon?"

"You can count on me. Whatever you need—an excuse to go out, a distraction so you can slip away, an alibi for when you're late. I'm here for you, and for him, too."

Eugenia pushed up from the bed and smoothed her badly wrinkled gown. "You're incorrigible."

"I'm your best friend in the whole world," Aurora announced, and not for the first time in her life. Aurora *was* her best friend. But so, too, was Sylvia. "Yes, you are, and I may need your help one day. But not today." She yawned and rolled her shoulders. Sleep was calling for her. "If you're not going to sleep, can you keep an eye on the marchioness for Sylvia? I'm for bed, but not here. I'm going to spend a few hours at Albemarle Street, where it is definitely quieter."

"Pity it has to be an empty bed there." Aurora sat up with a grin. "Or will it be occupied?"

Her eyes lit up with excitement when Eugenia nodded slowly.

"When you see him, tell him that I know, and I will try to help you both meet whenever I can," Aurora offered.

Eugenia shushed her and let herself out of the room, shaking her head. Aurora was impulsive, romantic, and naturally devious. But she had been very useful in the past when conducting an affair. It was a weight off her chest to know that her younger cousin supported her choice of lover, but she was far off the mark when it came to her future as a wife.

Yet, she felt closer to Aurora today than ever before. She did dislike keeping secrets unless she absolutely had to. But she'd been stumped for how to announce she was secretly seeing a man her young cousin had been so obviously flirting with just a few days ago.

She had no doubt Aurora's offer of help was genuine and from the heart. She had always spoken very highly of Thaddeus Berringer's appeal. She was grateful Aurora harbored no great disappointment over Eugenia catching his eye. She was lucky to have her cousins at this time of her life, and to have formed such strong bonds of affection and support.

If Eugenia could help Aurora, in the same way, one day, she certainly would do all she could too. She would help her cousin marry for love and not a title, as she'd always vowed she would.

Eugenia retreated to her room, changed into a fresh gown and wide-brimmed bonnet, and slipped downstairs without encountering the Marquess of Wharton or any lingering servants.

She hailed a hack herself and directed them to Albemarle Street as quickly as they could get her there. She was at her old door in short order, breathless with anticipation for what was to come.

As she entered her old home, an odd prickling sensation ran down her spine, and she glanced over her shoulder.

There was no one in the street behind her, not even Thaddeus lurking about. Just the usual rush of pedestrians and the occasional carriage passing by.

When she closed the door, she turned to find Thaddeus standing a few feet away.

She quickly latched the door, then rushed to him and hugged him tightly. "You came."

"Not yet, but with a welcome like that, I'm sure to explode soon," he teased.

Eugenia looked up into his grinning face and laughed at his little joke. "That is why you're here, sir," she promised. "For my eager welcome."

She took him by the hand without another word and rushed him upstairs and into her old bedchamber. Even though no one was living in the house anymore, she shut and locked her bedchamber door, too. "There. Perfectly alone."

Thaddeus' long arms wrapped around her from behind, pulling her into his embrace. "I could hardly sleep last night thinking of you, of us, alone here like this." His lips grazed her cheek, his stubble cleanly shaved away. "Is this your old room?"

"Yes."

"That bed looks particularly comfortable."

She could feel his hard cock pressing insistently against her bottom already and grinned. Would they even make it as far as the bed? He had a wondrous body that had given her great pleasure last time. She hoped to have him more than once today. But she had to return home by five o'clock at the latest in order to dress for a ball tonight. She couldn't be completely carried away by passion and forget that she had made other promises, too. "It is. I miss this place so much."

"Then let's get you reacquainted with the delights of your home." They glided across the room together until they were forced to stop by running into her bed.

She grasped him by the lapels of his coat. "I want you."

"And I want you," he promised. "On your hands and knees on the bed, with my hands on your hips and my cock buried deep inside you as soon as possible."

Eugenia shuddered at his description and reached for the buttons on his breaches, then turned around to put her hands on the bed.

Chapter Fourteen

Dear God, Eugenia was wondrously agreeable. She'd followed his instructions to the letter but also flipped up her skirts as she'd crawled onto her bed. He slipped his fingers through the moisture he found between her legs, discovering her more than ready for a good hard tupping.

Surprisingly, since he'd really only kissed her and pressed his cock against her bottom through her skirts. "Have you been thinking about me?"

"Yes. Every day. Every night you were gone. Every moment since I woke this morning."

"I thought of you, too," he promised. His hand had worked extra hard last night to make sleep possible, but today his cock had hardened at the first sight of her wicked smile of welcome at the door downstairs.

And here in her townhouse, without servants or family expected to interrupt, they had leave to be however they chose. Loud and urgent, uncaring of discovery, or sweet and quiet, tender. He had a feeling that there would be great freedom and even more blunt honesty than when he'd bedded her the first time. Before, they had been somewhat restrained by the fear of discovery and the uncertainty of their coming together. Today, that was not the case.

It was just the two of them inside an empty house, knowing exactly what they could do with each other.

He took a moment to tease her folds before he slowly pressed his fingers inside her body. Eugenia's back arched, and a moan tumbled from her sweet lips. The sound made him harder still, and he set about to gently slide his fingers in and out of her heavenly hot sheath.

She was already on her hands and knees, and he pushed her slightly more forward, then bent down to kiss her nicely rounded arse. Her skin was peach rather than pale white. But the hair between her legs was dark and short, as if she trimmed it. While he stroked inside her with one hand, he explored all the folds and sensitive spots he could reach with the other.

He widened her stance and tipped up her hips even farther, allowing him a deeper penetration and more pleasure for her, he hoped. Eugenia's quim was now completely visible to him. He kissed her sex, loved her with his mouth while she panted and moaned, clearly loving every moment of wickedness. He slipped his fingers in and out while he lapped at her folds with his tongue at every opportunity. But he couldn't wait for when it was his cock taking her. The taste of her on his tongue made him want to be inside her soon.

"Thaddeus," she gasped, clearly on the brink of her first orgasm.

He straightened, eased his fingers from her body to halt her climax and moved to fit closely behind her, wrapping an arm about her waist. "It's all right. I've got you."

"I've never imagined a man's mouth and fingers could be so pleasurable together," she gasped out. "If I had stayed like that, I might have come."

"I have access to an extensive collection of erotic engravings for inspiration. That is but one way a daring couple might make love."

"I want to see them. The engravings," she whispered. "For inspiration."

He chuckled. "If you like, I can bring them next time and leave them for you to peruse at your leisure. There are some that can be indulged in while alone, too."

"Yes," she nearly moaned.

Teddy fitted his cock between her legs but did not seek immediate entry to her quim. He brought her legs closer together, trapping himself between the heaven of her hot thighs. He thrust and withdrew, sliding through the wetness dripping from her quim. "I must warn you, some of the positions require a great deal of stamina and flexibility to maintain," he admitted.

"I'm willing to try anything."

Teddy parted her thighs again, ending the exquisite torture as his cock wept at the idea of what he could do with Eugenia next time they were alone together. "Anything I want, you say? You might not like it all."

"I'm not about to fall to pieces if you push a dildo inside me, sir."

He pressed a kiss to her spine, panting at the thought of seeing her come undone in that fashion. "Have you done it before? Had a dildo inside you?"

"No, but I have heard they can heighten a woman's orgasm, and a man's, too."

He gulped, pushing down the image she'd painted. "Dildo's, floggers, and anal plugs feature heavily in the erotic engravings, and I've found them all arousing. I'll purchase a dildo especially for you tomorrow."

"I've never found the nerve to venture to that sort of shop myself, so thank you. I'll let you watch me pleasure myself with it," she gasped, pressing back against his aching cock. "It's only fair."

Teddy hadn't fully undressed already, but he ripped off his coat now as a flush of heat and excitement swept over his skin. The bold talk of pleasure toys and masturbation while he watched excited him unbearably. He discarded his waistcoat and then his cravat and shirt. He was burning up, desperate to have her, make her come, and never stop. He awkwardly removed his trousers and stockings until he was completely naked.

Eugenia peeked over her shoulder to look at him, and he flexed his arms so his muscles were revealed and waggled his hips so his stiff cock might appear to wave at her, too.

She moaned in response and sank low, leaving her bum in the air. "Heavenly."

Teddy admired her pert bottom and then below that to her dripping quim, waiting for him. The urge to slide inside her was great, but the thought of wearing a sheath that would mute all sensation of her body again halted him from rushing the moment.

He teased his fingers into her depths. Eugenia immediately pressed back against him and started to rock, making love to his fingers with an urgency he admired. It wasn't what he wanted. Wasn't all he needed from her, though.

He craved to be inside her in the worst way with nothing between them but the proof of their mutual desire slicking her passage. He folded over her, pressing against her back. "You're astonishingly liberated, my dear. Almost too much for a man who is trying to keep his head."

She moved, stretching an arm under herself to grasp his cock. Pumping him a few times until he groaned. Then she placed his tip against her damp folds. "I am also highly aware of my reproductive cycle. In a few days, my menses will begin. Conception today is unlikely to occur."

Teddy didn't waste another moment to consider the truth of her claim but surged in till he could go no further. The warmth of her walls was incredible around his cock; almost as incredible as the desperate wail that burst from her lips.

He sank his fingers into her hair, holding her in place as he pumped hard and fast, seeking friction and more moans from her.

He was not gentle; he was not lenient in any way. He was a man desperate to have his woman cry out before he could do the same.

Eugenia's climb toward her peak began slowly, her pants and cries escalating the harder and longer he fucked her. When she finally screamed out, he was unable to delay his own climax long enough to withdraw. He tumbled with her, rushing headlong toward bliss in a tangle of sweaty limbs and moans and mindless grunts. His seed filling her, mingling with her own juices.

In any other situation, with any other woman, he'd be slightly embarrassed by his urgency.

He collapsed over her, shocked, stunned…but elated.

Eugenia was unlike any other woman he'd ever made love to. So perfectly willing to do anything with him if it was wicked.

Aware he was likely crushing her, Teddy untangled them and tossed her aside on the mattress, where she lay sprawled. Soft, sated, and desirable. Her eyes were closed and her chest heaving as he lay down beside her on the bed.

"Eugenia," he whispered. "Love."

Her eyes opened slowly, her gaze unfocused, but then her smile slowly grew wider. "Can you do that to me again?"

He had to laugh at her question. He probably could. Certainly wanted to. He was bursting with energy, and even now his cock stirred, keen to join with her again soon. "I'll do my best," he promised, kissing the back of her hand.

Her gaze focused on his lips. She reached out to touch his mouth, and then her fingers swept down to rest upon his damp, heaving chest. "You are society's greatest secret. Well known, but constantly full of surprises."

Teddy laughed and slid strands of her dark, damp hair back from her face. "Don't tell anyone."

"Oh, I have no intention of sharing what I alone have only just discovered." She rose up to rest her head on her hand as she held his gaze. "I had no idea you were so naughty, sir."

He shrugged. "It's hardly something a man should advertise in polite circles. You seemed quite chaste on the surface but equally wicked of thought, I've been pleased to discover."

She collapsed back onto her bed, wriggling until she was comfortable. "Hmm, yes. Some might consider it a curse in a lady."

He reached out to trace around her breast, circling the nipple until it pebbled to a hard point under the material. "I think it one of your greatest unknown accomplishments."

She stilled his hand and met his gaze. "You flatter me, but I only ever aim to please myself."

He was sure she had. "You pleased me then without even trying." He glanced down at his cock, which had grown surprisingly firm as they'd talked. "Better than you can possibly imagine."

"I can imagine a lot with you between my legs," she teased him, cupping his cheek and sat up to fling off her clothes. They landed every which way about the chamber. "You've a wicked tongue, and I look forward to being lashed with it again and again." She must have noticed his face was warming up because she laughed. "Should I not say I enjoy a particular pleasure to the deliverer who brings such a powerful release?"

"You can tell me, but there will be consequences," he warned, as he trapped her under him. There was nothing he liked better than a naked woman under him. "We were quite loud, and I wish you could always be so, but we will have to be careful if we indulge in sex in places other than here. The shriek such as you made when you came today would be noticed anywhere beyond these walls."

"It's your own fault I was so loud," she teased, wrapping her legs about his hips. She rocked against his budding erection. "Your cock is quite delicious without that terrible condom distracting me."

He was fascinated by her open honesty concerning matters of desire and bent his head to nuzzle her ear. Eugenia couldn't seem to keep her hands still. Not that he was complaining. He liked that she enjoyed his body so well. Her kisses were moving slowly but determinedly lower down his throat. He eased up as she wriggled down the bed under him, kissing his chest, his nipples, his stomach, and the point of his hip. When he felt the brush of her fingers against his inner thigh, he rolled onto his back. But he had to ask, "What do you think you're doing?"

Eugenia repositioned herself to kneel between his spread legs. "I want to taste you."

But she didn't at first put him in her mouth. Her fingers slid around him, testing his size, the texture of his balls, before she pumped his length. To have a woman he'd only just bedded so keen for a second round was unexpected, but who was he to stop Eugenia.

She leaned down to kiss his cock at the same time her fingers strummed over his balls.

He let out a shockingly desperate grunt.

Eugenia chuckled. "Someone isn't entirely sated yet, I see."

"I can hardly explain it," he whispered. "It's your fault."

He curled upward to watch her descend toward his cock. He held his breath as she took him into her mouth and sucked while her skillful fingers worked to arouse him toward another complete erection. Hand and mouth slid over his cock and down his shaft in a rhythm that had his hips lifted in time. Hardening him to the point where joining with her again was all he could think about.

He pushed her onto her back, covered her completely with his body, and drove home once more.

"How have I lived without this for so long?" he whispered.

"How have I?"

"Never again. I'll make sure you're always satisfied," he promised.

"As will I, sir."

He put his back into it, driving steadily and surely toward their mutual second climaxes. Eugenia's fingers digging into his back and backside, always guiding him deep and true and harder, too. This time he saw her expression as she climaxed a second time under him. He vowed there would be many more occasions like this between them. So free, so perfectly attuned in desire.

He rose up on his elbows, even as Eugenia wrapped her long legs about his hips and lifted her lower half up to stay close to him. He was going to come. He couldn't stop himself. Again, he would tempt fate that she knew her imminent courses would prevent conception.

But even if there was still a risk, he wanted nothing more than to only ever have her this way.

He deliberately stilled himself, loving the way her body looked spread out before him like a feast. The rise and fall of her chest, the jiggle of her pretty breasts, and the sweat damping her brow. He toyed with her nipples a little and kissed one. Then the other, alternating and sucking on her nipples.

Eugenia's hips rocked against him, trying to urge him to move again. But he was not yet ready. There were other desires he wanted to fulfill this day. "Put your fingers between us and join me in pleasure again. I want to feel you squeeze me as you come."

She did as he asked, a sly smile in her eyes.

He positioned her so he could remain inside, feeling every clench of her inner walls, and see the brush of her fingers against her quim. He concentrated and flexed his cock inside her, teasing her with his length and size.

Her fingers quickened on her clitoris as her eyes fluttered shut. "Tell me about your engravings. What is your favorite?"

"My favorite is of a woman stretched out on a bed, her hands on her quim like this, with a cock and anal plug buried deep inside her."

Eugenia whimpered, and her body clenched around him.

Teddy answered by pressing a little harder into her sex. "In the engraving, she's wearing nothing but a smile like yours."

Teddy flicked the tip of her pert nipple with his finger, but on her gasp, he caught her breast in one hand. He continued to squeeze her breast and flick her nipple with his thumb. He rolled the tight bud between thumb and forefinger and then pinched.

"Move," Eugenia demanded, gasping. "I need you."

He couldn't have declined even if he wanted to. Knowing what she wanted from him drove Teddy wild, and he thrust into her as briskly as he could. As she climaxed, he couldn't stop his seed from pouring out a second time, and he howled like a barbarian.

Eugenia twisted and bucked on his length as she shuddered and climaxed much longer than she'd ever done before with him. But everything must end, and she collapsed back on the bed a second time, panting and gasping. "Oh my. Oh hell," she gasped out, struggling to breathe. "I never imagined…"

"Wicked indeed," he said, satisfied beyond belief.

Teddy remained over her, his weight supported by his arms, his lips grazing her throat as their passion cooled and their breathing slowed.

Eugenia's fingers danced down his side. "No lover I will ever have in the future could match this."

"No," he agreed. "You are without compare."

Her fingers settled on his back, and she let out a weary sigh. "I think I will envy your next lover and wife and all the pleasure they'll have from you. Jealousy is such an unpleasant character trait in anyone, especially so in myself."

"Marriage is very far in my future." They separated to lie on their backs side by side. He laughed softly and reached for her hand. "Don't think I won't be jealous of your future lover and his good fortune, either."

"What should we do?"

"I suppose the sensible thing would be to marry each other and let everyone be jealous of *our* passion," Teddy suggested—then his face heated with shock at his own words. Three delightful fucks were not the basis to begin any marriage.

Eugenia started to laugh. "Suggestions made in the heat of the moment and just after good sex are never wise, Thaddeus Berringer. I swear, I would never hold you to such a preposterous suggestion. Besides, you said you were not marrying until next season at the earliest, least of all to someone like me. I intend to hold you to that."

Thank God. He tried to hide his relief, but given the way Eugenia still grinned, it meant she already knew he had immediately regretted his unthinking suggestion that they wed each other. He slid away from her, distancing himself further from his impulsive words. "Kind of you to release me from any obligation. I was only imagining the satisfaction of bedtime encounters with you and spoke without thought."

"It would never be a duty with you for any woman," she promised, then sat up in bed to look around. "I am suddenly starving."

Their clothes were scattered about the room.

"Wait here a moment," Teddy said quickly before she could rise and rushed out the door naked.

He retrieved the picnic basket he'd brought with him and presented it to her with a flourish and a deep bow. "I didn't think you'd mind me bringing a little something to nibble upon, other than myself, of course."

He came closer and spread out the contents between them on the bed. There was plenty to feed two hungry lovers. He'd even brought wine, since he wasn't sure what remained in the cellar here, if anything. He offered her a piece of chicken to eat from his fingers.

"Hmm, just what I needed. Thank you."

He repositioned to settle beside her and pulled a blanket around his hips, since there was a chill in the air. Not surprising since a fire hadn't been lit here in some time.

Eugenia snuggled close, the bedding wrapped tight over her breasts now, and then glanced up at him. "Never worry that I'll hold you to any promise, sir. This changed nothing for me. I am exactly where I want to be and need no commitment to welcome you back again."

He hugged his lover close. At least his unthinking suggestion of them marrying and then a withdrawal from the proposal hadn't soured her opinion of him. He fed her more portions of chicken from his fingers and offered cake, too, as the next hour ticked on.

And then Eugenia fell fast asleep in his arms. He listened and watched her as she rested, finding even that a pleasure. But... even if his proposal had been a mistake, and refused by her, he couldn't stop thinking about it. Surely a marriage to a lusty lady wouldn't be all bad—especially not one whose hand even in sleep had slipped onto his thigh under the covers to arouse him.

Chapter Fifteen

THERE WAS nothing more satisfying for a woman than to have frequent orgasms. She and Thaddeus had managed to meet again, and for the last week at Albemarle Street, at odd hours. Her courses had come and gone on schedule and she'd reveled in his wickedness ever since.

Last night, they'd even managed to spend the night here together rather than her returning to Wharton House and him to Grafton House. No one at home had batted an eye that she'd planned to stay the night here. She'd promised to return early enough to still attend a picnic with her cousins.

But there were disappointments to be faced today. Eugenia would return to Wharton House, and regret that she had to.

Eugenia glanced over her shoulder as her bed shook under her. Thaddeus was finally stirring after a satisfying night beneath her sheets. She'd managed to sleep for a little while and now felt quite satisfied.

Or she would be, if he was not preparing to go. She hated this part of an affair, the re-dressing, the moments before separation even if it was entirely necessary. Eugenia was only his lover. An honor she relished and would enjoy while these exquisite moments of lust lasted.

While she'd much rather stay in his arms for another hour or two, she really did have to return to her cousins. There was only so much time Aurora could distract everyone if she was wanted at home.

She sat up and wrapped her arms around her knees. They'd been lucky that their affair remained a secret still. Thaddeus had been adamant from the beginning that no one could know about them and, with the exception of Aurora figuring it out on her own, she wanted that too.

When he stood, Eugenia climbed out of bed, crossed the room, and went to stir the fire. It had died down during the night, and she stroked it until a nice blaze burned again, warming the chill from her room. There had been no need to hide the fact she was here last night, after all.

When she straightened up and turned, Thaddeus was staring at her with a look that held a great deal of heat for so early in the day.

She had forgotten to even throw on a robe, after all, which she had noticed he seemed to like her to do.

Eugenia crossed the room and stretched out on her side on top of the coverlet. She held his gaze and smiled knowingly. "Is there something the matter, lover?"

He blinked and shook his head. "Not from where I'm standing."

Eugenia rolled onto her back and ran her hands down her body, starting with a lingering grope of her own breasts, then down to her thighs. She sighed. There was no point stirring him up too far, or herself, if he was going, but damn if what they were doing didn't feel liberating. Though all good things must end.

She burrowed back under the coverlet, covering herself.

Thaddeus paused beside the bed, trousers half on, his torso bare and beautifully broad, but a frown marred his handsome face. "Is something the matter?"

"No," she promised him. He could go, and she might even fall back asleep for a while before returning to Wharton House. She sighed and rolled over onto her stomach.

Wharton House. Eugenia was not looking forward to going back there today, even if her beloved cousins were expecting her.

Teddy's fingers teased lightly across her shoulder. "I only ask because you didn't speak to me at the Piermont luncheon yesterday."

She had seen Thaddeus, watched on as he'd paid court to an heiress and a widow, and hadn't liked the feelings that had assailed her. Those women could openly seek to attract him to their side, and even though she was his lover, she had felt the sting of exclusion and not a little jealousy. She had no right to think that he belonged to her in any way. "I had nothing new to say yesterday, or nothing fit to be overheard by others."

"You can always talk to me."

Eugenia rolled over to look at him. They already talked a lot. But in public, she knew she had to go on as if they were still near strangers. "I know that."

He frowned again. "Is this secret of ours becoming a burden?"

"Goodness, no. Why ever would you think so?"

"I don't know," he smoothed her hair back from her face gently. "I just have this nagging feeling that I've disappointed you in some way."

Eugenia got to her knees and crawled toward him. "You never have. You never could."

He came closer, drew her against his chest, and kissed her soundly.

Hoping to distract him from wondering what she thought of their affair, Eugenia slipped her tongue into his mouth. She enjoyed him a little too much than she probably should. She was always excited to see him, sad when their wicked interludes were over. They were always too short.

Eugenia slid her hand down his body to fondle his cock.

Thaddeus drew back, laughing slightly. "Enough of that. I have to go."

"I know." She grinned impishly. "I just wanted you to remember me after you're gone."

"How could I forget? You're in my thoughts always." He cleared his throat. "Speaking of remembering…"

She thought she knew what was coming but acted surprised as he dug inside his coat pocket. She'd felt a bulge there when she'd helped him undress when he'd first arrived.

She sat back on her heels, watching him produce a handkerchief. She wasn't sure how to refuse the gift, but of course she must. She wasn't in the habit of accepting tokens of appreciation from her lovers. No money or jewels should ever change hands for pleasure. "Thaddeus, you shouldn't have. I can't—"

"Don't say no until after I show you what I found. I thought very hard about this," he warned. "Of course, you could not openly wear jewelry from me. Your cousins would question you, and no doubt Wharton would hear of it."

He revealed a fine gold chain, unusually long, with a small charm attached to one loop. It wasn't what she'd expected from him at all.

"I long for any occasion to see you wear this in private for me." He held his fingers wide in front of her, showing her the charm in closer detail. The tiny gold disk was fashioned in the shape of a heart with the initials EH engraved on one side. The other side was blank.

He lowered his hands to her waist and hugged her close. "And I hope that occasionally you might wear it beneath your gown in public, and whisper to me that it's there."

When he pulled back, the chain encircled her waist, fitting snugly above her hips.

She was stunned, and also delighted with him. He'd made a good choice. But the question was, could she keep it? It wasn't diamonds or rubies, but something simple and from his heart. And it was engraved with only her initials. "Oh, Thad, you shouldn't have, but…thank you. It's beautiful."

"I wanted to give you a token of my affection but be discreet about it."

She nodded. She could keep this one gift from him for now. She'd wear it all the time until their affair was over, and then she would hand it back. Her eyes suddenly stung with the threat of tears, and she lowered her head to hide them.

Thaddeus slipped his finger under her chin and raised her face. He frowned at her tears and then smiled softly. "None of that now," he chided. "It's just the beginning."

She drew back and placed her hands protectively over the

chain. "It's a perfect gift for a secret lover, and I want nothing more from you."

Eugenia hurried off her bed and rushed for the mirror. A naked woman wearing a simple chain about her waist seemed more decadent than one opening wearing costly gems. Eugenia had to admit, she was looking forward to wearing it out and telling him about it to see his reaction.

Gift admired, she rushed back to Thaddeus and embraced him. "You really shouldn't have spoiled me so, but I appreciate that you wanted to."

Thaddeus' arms tightened around her only briefly before he stepped back again. "I wish I could stay, but the duke—"

Eugenia rushed to press a finger to his lips.

The duke quite depended on his heir. She understood. She knew he always would come first. The duke took precedence over everything and everyone. Thaddeus had to leave, and she wouldn't pout or protest. There was no need. "Meet me here tomorrow night if you can."

"I would try very hard to," he promised. "Except, are we not both attending Lady Bisley's party, too?"

"Oh, I'd forgotten. Likely I won't be able to avoid it now." She winced. "Perhaps we can meet the next night."

She finished buttoning her lover's waistcoat, smoothed her hand over his wide chest, then pressed a quick peck of a kiss to his stubbled cheek.

She could not expect him to come every time she suggested it. He had his own key to Albemarle Street and could come and go from her bed as he needed to.

He left, clearly reluctant, and blew her a kiss from her bedchamber door. Eugenia listened carefully until she could no longer hear him moving through the house, then hurried to the slightly parted drapes to peer out to the street. Thaddeus' carriage was already waiting to take him away, and he disappeared around the corner without a wave of goodbye.

Eugenia let the drape fall and returned to the mirror. Thaddeus was too generous for his own good to be already spoiling her. She left the chain around her waist as she dressed herself to return to Wharton House.

Eugenia threw a cloak over her gown and quietly slipped out onto Albemarle Street. At this hour, the streets were largely deserted, and she walked the short distance to Bond Street, where she hailed a hack to return her home to Wharton's House.

The butler didn't smile as he let her in.

In fact, he was doing everything he could not to look at her at all.

She held out her cloak for him to take. "Is everything all right with the marchioness, sir?"

"Yes, indeed," the man promised. "She passed a good night, but," he paused and glanced around before continuing, "the marquess is looking for you, and he is most unhappy."

She craned her neck to look around. The library door was closed, but the drawing room doors were open and the room empty. "I wonder what that could be about? I'll go to him after I've said good morning to my cousins and partaken of breakfast."

After the exertions of last night, she was ravenous.

Eugenia slipped up the stairs and along to her room. Once inside, she washed her face and chose a new gown for the day.

Aurora slipped into her chamber. "You're already changed?"

"As you see," she agreed, as she added a shawl around her shoulders. "I swear I may have to dismantle my bed and move it here."

"Is it the bed or the company?"

"Possibly both."

Aurora curled up in a chair. "I'm glad you have someone," Aurora whispered.

Eugenia sat too. "Thank you."

Aurora sighed. "But it's not fair."

"What is?"

"You and Sylvia with your beaus, while I have no one special."

"You will." Aurora was meant to be a wife. The prettiest of them, and the most accomplished, deserved just the right man to come along and sweep her off her feet. She'd gotten wrapped up in her affair that she'd forgotten that Aurora needed a husband. She'd make it up to her by going out with her today, and tonight they would prowl Lady Bisley's route together and hope she caught the eye of someone tall, dark, and unknown to them both.

Eugenia frowned as a rapid tap was beaten on her door. "Come in."

Mr. Bloom appeared, and not with the breakfast she had expected. "What is it?"

"The marquess requests you come immediately," he glanced toward Aurora, "and alone."

Aurora sat up quickly at hearing that. "Oh, dear, that is never good."

"I'm sure it's nothing important," Eugenia promised and then nodded to Mr. Bloom. "Please tell him I'll be down directly."

Mr. Bloom departed, a look of concern on his features, almost the same expression that the butler had worn upon her return to Wharton House. The marquess must be more vexed with her overnight stay at Albemarle Street than he'd originally let on. "Was Wharton out of sorts about me spending another night unchaperoned at our old home?"

"Not that I noticed," Aurora promised. "But I left him and Sylvia seducing each other in the drawing room and went to bed early last night."

"I suppose he'll insist I take servants with me next time."

"That wouldn't be a good idea," Aurora teased, grinning.

"No. They might report back to him about my midnight visitor." She laughed softly and stood.

Aurora grasped her hand. "Do you want me to come with you?"

"You're aware you're still in your nightgown. I can handle Wharton." She shoved her feet into her slippers and waved. "I'll return shortly. Don't eat my breakfast when it arrives. Order your own, and we'll eat together when I get back."

Aurora waved her off. "Don't lose your temper with him for simply being protective of your reputation!"

Wharton house was usually quiet at this hour and warmed by fires lit hours ago. Even so, Eugenia shivered as she went down the staircase.

The butler materialized and pointed her down the hall. "He is waiting for you in the study, madam."

Eugenia hurried there, keen to have any discussion over so she could return to her room and breakfast tray.

She knocked and barged right in. "You wished to speak with me, my lord?"

"Indeed."

Wharton appeared rather untidy. His cravat was badly tied and his coat absent. He looked like he hadn't combed his hair that day. "You need to find a mirror, my lord."

He turned furious eyes on her. "Do not pretend to care about me or anyone else, madam."

"I beg your pardon," she replied, taken aback by his hostility. Obviously, he'd confused her with someone else. He'd referred to her as madam, too. "It is *miss* or *Eugenia*. I've already given you leave to use my given name."

He blinked at her, and then he set his jaw as his face grew red. *"Miss?"*

Never had she seen him so furious. Oh, she disagreed with him on occasion, and they'd had some heated debates before moving in, but they'd been getting along just fine until now.

He jabbed a finger in her direction. "I always knew you were keeping something from me."

Eugenia blinked. Dear God, Wharton had found out about her affair with Thaddeus Berringer. "It wasn't important for you to know."

He blinked several times. "Not important? Madam, there is a vast deal of things in life I consider important. The secret you've been keeping changes everything."

Eugenia closed her eyes briefly. Wharton was going to make trouble for her, and for Thaddeus, too. He'd force them to wed unless she could make him see just how bad that idea was. She squared her shoulders and looked him in the eye. "I knew what I was doing. I suggest we sit down, you and I, to discuss this matter rationally. There's no need to involve anyone else, is there."

"Are you suggesting we cover it up?"

She nodded. "It's the best thing to do, really. There'll be a scandal otherwise."

Wharton was suddenly in front of her. "I'll want more details later, but it is beyond my understanding. I heard you confided everything to your cousins, and them to you."

Aurora, of course, knew, but Sylvia… She gulped. "I would have. Eventually."

That didn't seem to please him, either. "Well, you won't be able to hide the truth now."

"What do you mean?"

Wharton pulled a sour face. "You have a visitor, and I guess you won't need an introduction or a chaperone to be alone with him—nor any gentleman ever again, either."

Wharton shook his head, still clearly upset with her, and she was at a loss to understand what her affair with Thaddeus had to do with chaperones. But he suddenly caught her by the elbow and marched her to the drawing room, despite her protests that he was hurting her.

He did ease his grip at the drawing room door. He opened it and led her in at a slower pace.

She looked up and saw a drab, rounded man across the room jump to his feet and bow.

"At last," the man cried before hurrying toward them.

Eugenia recoiled. "I beg your pardon?"

The fellow stopped, hands clenching at his waist. "I'm not surprised by your reaction. It has been many a year, hasn't it?"

Eugenia would have taken a step back if Wharton hadn't been holding her in place. She looked up at him. "I don't know this gentleman."

Wharton's jaw worked. "Only now do I understand why

you've always denied the need for a chaperone," Wharton muttered. He shook his head. "Look at him again. Look closely."

"My cousins are my chaperones," she murmured, but she did glance at the man again.

A look of profound adoration lit up his face as their eyes met. His were a murky green, like her own. The stranger was a little over her height, portly, and in need of a new waistcoat to contain his girth. His hair brown hair was thin and peppered with gray at the temples. He had a scar on his chin as if he'd tangled with the wrong man some time ago…

…or a clumsy woman with a garden hoe.

A memory of another man with the very same scar teased her mind, and she squinted at the stranger a little harder. Only in her memory, the scar had been just starting to turn from red to pink as it healed.

"Do you remember me now, blossom?"

Blossom? That nickname on the stranger's lips sent her pulse roaring in her ears.

The scar…

A wound she'd made to a man she'd once loved…and married…and then lost forever.

"No!" She reached for Wharton's arm to support herself. "It cannot be."

Chapter Sixteen

"*Devil take it*, it's true," Wharton cursed, shaking off her grip to walk away from her.

"It's not possible," she whispered, staring after him.

Wharton spun about, his eyes ablaze with anger. "But you *do* know this man."

"Have a care how you speak to my lady, my lord," the stranger warned, clearly believing he had the right to defend her. "I won't have anyone shouting at my *wife*."

"Be quiet, sir," Wharton ground out. "I will have the truth from her own lips. Well, Eugenia? Do you know this man or not?"

Eugenia studied the stranger. "Perhaps, but…"

"Well, there is no doubt in my mind that you do recognize his face, and also clearly do not want to admit it," Wharton said in a deathly cold voice. "How could you not tell us that you were married, Eugenia?"

"Because Robert is dead!" she cried as she stumbled back, tripping over her own feet in her haste. She fell hard and cried out in shock, aghast at her own clumsiness in front of a stranger.

Aurora burst into the room just as the man bearing the passing resemblance to her late husband, Robert Bagshaw, reached for her hands.

Eugenia slapped him away. "Don't you dare touch me!"

"I only want to look after you, blossom."

Aurora helped her stand.

"And don't call me blossom, either. Ever."

"Yes, my dear," he said, lowering his head but smiling softly. "Anything you say, my love."

Submissiveness had not been the nature of the Robert Bagshaw Eugenia had known and married years ago. He had changed.

She stared at the man she felt was a stranger, confused by him. If they'd passed on the street, she'd never have looked at him twice.

Aurora smoothed a hand down her back. "What happened?"

"I tripped over my own skirts," Eugenia admitted to her cousin. "I am not hurt."

"I apologize if my outburst of temper had anything to do with your fall," Wharton said quietly. "I did not mean to seem so intimidating that you might fear I'd strike you."

"Forgiven, my lord," she promised, because she felt he really meant it. He was in as much shock as she. He might shout out his opinions sometimes, but he'd never struck her as a violent man.

The stranger looked on, wearing Robert's face, albeit looking more than four years older than when she'd last seen him, and smiling as if all was perfectly normal for him to have returned from the grave.

But it wasn't. Her husband could not be alive and be so changed.

Aurora turned her away from the men to whisper, "I heard it all from the hall. Why did you not tell us?"

"It's a long story," Eugenia muttered, embarrassed by her fall and the fact that her cousin had discovered her long-held secret. Her greatest disappointment and loss.

How had it taken her so long to recognize the stranger as Robert? Did she really remember the man she'd fallen in love with and impulsively married so little after all these years?

But it *was* impossible to her that he could be Robert, back from the dead. She'd been told of his demise from a reliable source she'd never doubted. "I need to sit."

Aurora guided her to a chair, warning off the stranger who came forward to solicitously be of service to the woman he seemed to think was his wife.

Wharton held the stranger back, murmuring for the man to be patient.

"My dear, you shouldn't upset yourself that you didn't recognize me," the fellow started, then fell silent as she glared daggers at him for daring to speak with her. "Too much excitement is not good for your nerves."

The warning also rang false in her head. Robert had *liked* her excited. He'd have laughed and encouraged her to exert herself when he'd been alive. Even the day she'd nicked his chin in her frustration with her overgrown garden, he'd laughed off the injury and told her to try again. Although he had stepped back much farther than the first time she'd swung the scythe.

Whoever this man was, he was no one she'd ever met before.

"Summon the watch, my lord. This man is an *imposter.*"

Sylvia burst into the chamber then, looking frantic. "What's going on?"

Eugenia stared between her cousins, still at a loss for words to explain that she'd once had a husband and that he'd died.

Wharton came close to his future bride and placed a gentle hand on Sylvia's shoulder. "It appears your cousin is a married woman."

"No!" Sylvia's eyes were wide with shock when they locked on Eugenia's face, and she felt very small and terrible for not having told the truth long ago. Why hadn't she?

"Not to him," Eugenia promised. "I was married, but he died. Drowned."

"I'm hardly dead now, am I, my dear," the stranger murmured. An oily smile she didn't trust appeared on the stranger's face as he approached Sylvia with his hand outstretched. "Mr. Robert Bagshaw, of Dover."

Eugenia closed her eyes. Robbie had come from Dover, too. "You lie," she insisted.

"Now, now. Let us not quarrel at our reunion after so many years apart. I've returned to do my duty as I promised in my letters. I've kept all of yours by my side all these years. His lordship has them as proof of our intimate connection."

Sylvia gasped. "You really were married?"

Eugenia winced, ducking her head a little. "A long time ago."

"I will require additional proof," Wharton announced, his jaw set in a hard line.

"I've given you everything necessary," the fellow answered. "The love letters, proof of the marriage. She is my wife, and no man may come between us, or so the church and law promise."

Wharton seemed to pause. "Indeed, it does."

Eugenia gripped the arm of the chair for support—and for reassurance that she wasn't trapped in the most dreadful dream. He had her love letters to Robert and the marriage license, but she *couldn't* be married to such a man.

Aurora's arm slipped around her back and was too familiar to doubt she was in anything but a waking nightmare. She put her head in her hand to hide her flaming face. "That cannot be my Robbie."

"Yet he swears he is. You recognize him, don't you?" Sylvia whispered as she crowded close to her side.

"A similar face," she argued. "While I admit a resemblance is there, my husband died."

Sylvia exhaled slowly. "When were you married?"

Eugenia met her cousin's gaze. "Just before you wrote to me, suggesting we pool our resources and live together."

"A happy day our marriage was for both of us, eh, Mrs. Bagshaw?" the imposter interrupted. "We were both so impatient for the banns to be called and, of course, to have our wedding night. I remember… Well, that is best for us to talk about another time."

Eugenia shuddered at the thought of being a wife to a man she barely recognized.

Sylvia, in uncommonly firm fashion, spoke to the stranger. "If you don't mind, sir, I am speaking with my cousin. Kindly do not interrupt us again."

Wharton took that as a sign to draw the imposter away from them.

"Thank you," Sylvia said to Wharton. Then she grasped

Eugenia's hand tightly and whispered, "I wrote when I heard your brother had died. Did he know Mr. Bagshaw?"

"No. We met a little after his death. I was three and twenty, and alone, but suddenly found myself very much in love."

"To Mr. Robert Bagshaw?" Aurora queried, as she seemed to study the man now speaking with Wharton across the room and craning his neck to see them still. "Do you love Robert still?"

"I have always felt so much sadness for what might have been," she promised. But as Eugenia searched her feelings, the deepest recesses of her heart, she found no bright spark of recognition or yearning in her for the gentleman standing across the chamber claiming to be her spouse. "He might wear my beloved's face, but I do not love that man."

"That is good enough for me," Aurora promised. "You have always been guided by your intuition, and it has never failed you before."

"Perhaps you've merely forgotten your feelings," Sylvia murmured, but there was an edge to her tone that she suggested she disbelieved her own words.

"I forget nothing." Eugenia had never forgotten the bright moment of love she'd experienced as a young woman in Hastings when a dashing young man had charmed his way into her heart, despite her grief for her brother's passing. Her first and only true love. Her secret loss all these years. She'd been swept off her feet and agreed to a marriage almost immediately with Robbie Bagshaw from far off Dover. Back then, he'd seemed almost worldly compared to her.

But now, looking at a man who resembled her departed love, albeit wearing an older version of the face she'd once thought so handsome, she keenly felt the absence of any tender feeling.

Robbie was gone. Dead nearly four years.

The man claiming to be Robert Bagshaw had no effect on her emotions other than revulsion for the charade he was perpetuating.

The imposter suddenly bowed to Eugenia and abruptly took

his leave of them, robbing her of the chance to question him further.

Wharton waited a beat to make sure he was gone before he rushed to join them. He pulled a chair closer, so they all sat in a circle. "Bagshaw will return tomorrow. I convinced him that his arrival has been a great shock to you, Eugenia, and that you need time to compose yourself before speaking with him again."

"Shock doesn't begin to explain my feelings," she warned. "I'm outraged that creature is masquerading as my late husband. It isn't right!"

Wharton pulled papers from his pocket. "He gave me these, claiming to have written them to his mother. And I did try to confirm the handwriting was his, but he's broken a bone in his arm since and now uses his other arm. Barely understood a word he wrote."

One was a letter from her old parish in Hastings, confirming that there had been a marriage between herself and Robert James Bagshaw. It had been a small wedding, the few who'd attended had been elderly neighbors of hers. There were also letters in her hand, letters written during her brief courtship with Robert. Back then, she'd been a woman overwhelmed by love. At her age, well beyond the first flush of youth and beauty, she'd nearly given up on love and marriage and having a family. Children, too.

Another letter was written in Robert's bold hand. She ran her finger over his penmanship, remembering the thrill of finding similar notes had been slipped under her front door overnight during their courtship.

But she blinked back tears as she read the words on the page. In this, as in so many others, Robert spoke of his love but repeated his promise to return to her as soon as he could.

That was meant to be four years ago…not now.

She glanced at the page from Robert again. "I never saw this before. It is not franked."

"Yes, I noticed that too," Wharton murmured. "Odd, that."

She took a deep breath. "I will not deny that I was married

once. The vicar who signed the letter is the same man that married me to Robert."

"Then you are married still," Wharton insisted.

"I am a widow of Robert Bagshaw," she repeated. "That man is *not* him."

"But you have never been known as a wife or widow by your own family," Wharton chided. "Tell us about that? Why did you keep it from us? Did you think he would be an embarrassment to your wider family?"

"No." Eugenia exhaled angrily. "I married Robbie Bagshaw, a rushed decision perhaps. I had little to recommend me, no fortune or connections in the district. I was alone, and I was smitten with him from the moment we met."

"He took advantage of you?"

"No, I will never believe that. The day after we wed, my husband left by packet ship to return to his mother, whose health had been delicate. I'd known of his plan to break the news to her in person from the day the banns had been called, and arranged passage with an honest ship's captain who I knew working out of Hastings. Since he was sailing to Dover and back on the same ship, he should have returned within a month. But two weeks after his departure, the captain came to see me and gave me the news Robert was dead. He was very sorry for me. I grieved for Robert like any wife would."

"Did you see his body?"

"The ship was closer to Dover than Hastings. He was buried there. Miles and miles from me. I couldn't stomach looking at the sea from that day on."

Sylvia and Aurora grasped her hands tightly.

"And so, you just decided to forget you were married?"

"I did not mean to." She winced. "When Sylvia's letter came out of the blue, proposing we live together, I was grieving for two men—my brother and a husband she didn't yet know about. I had nothing to stay in Hastings for. Afraid every moment for how I would go on alone."

"You answered my letter as Miss Hillcrest, not as Mrs. Bagshaw," Sylvia whispered.

"I must have automatically written my maiden name in the reply and not realized. I never even noticed until the moment you introduced me to your friends as Miss Hillcrest. I wasn't myself. I decided not to correct you." She sighed. "I had only lived with my husband for one night, after all. It seemed easier to make a fresh start rather than revisit so brief and tragic a past."

She glanced down at her bare fingers. "I didn't even have a ring or a copy of the marriage license as proof of it. Robbie had taken the latter with him to show his mother."

"If you married Robbie at three and twenty, and you're just turned seven and twenty years now, where has he been these past four years?" Sylvia asked.

Aurora snorted. "That is a good question, and I wish he was still here to answer it now."

"His absence seems odd," Sylvia agreed. "Did he offer any explanation for why he didn't return to her, Alexander?"

"I asked about that, and he said he would only explain to his wife and seek her forgiveness in private later, when they were alone." Wharton sighed.

"Don't leave me alone with him. I might scratch out his eyes and his lying tongue," she warned.

"I will need to hear those answers myself before I am comfortable with settling any funds on you."

Eugenia glanced at Wharton sharply. "*Don't.* What need do I have for a dowry if I'm supposed to be already married?"

That gave Wharton pause, but he recovered quickly. "But I could not in good conscience allow you to leave this house without knowing your husband can keep you in the style you deserve. If he cannot, I will settle funds on you."

"No amount of funds will ever make living with him comfortable." Eugenia's stomach churned with dread at the thought. "You cannot expect me to go off and live with a man I barely recognize."

"Talk to him tomorrow. Find out where he's been all these years," Wharton suggested.

"Pretending not to be married, by the way, too," Aurora noted harshly and folded her arms across her chest as she glared at Wharton. "It's hardly Eugenia's fault that she pretended not to be married when he has done the same for years. I say he's an imposter."

Wharton held up his hands, palms out. "I did not say I am comfortable with the notion that he might be playing us false, Aurora. Did you quarrel with Robert, Eugenia?"

Eugenia shook her head. "We were not married long enough for that."

"Quarreling can happen before marriage," Wharton muttered, glancing sideways at Sylvia with a wry smile.

"I'm sure that is true for some, but not in our case," she said. "I fell in love with him and he with me. We were happy, and he was excited to come and live in Hastings. He'd planned to close his shop in Dover and open one and resume his trade in Hastings. He was a cabinet maker."

"Yes, that fellow said he was born with sawdust in his veins," Wharton said slowly. "I look forward to hearing his excuses as to why he abandoned his lawful wife when he comes back. There might be legal grounds to pursue in a claim for your upkeep as well."

All three of them stared at Wharton in shock, but it was Sylvia who looked at her future husband as if she'd never seen him before. "You would extort funds from my cousin's false husband for her upkeep?"

"Well, if he is playing us false, it is unlikely he'd pay up. A demand of compensation due might just send an imposter packing," Wharton reasoned and then reached for Sylvia's hand. "Never fear, my love, I'd never go through with the threat in truth. It's just a ploy to judge this fellow's attachment to the scheme to take Eugenia off with him."

"He had better go off alone, and fast too," Aurora added sourly.

Eugenia stared at Wharton. He was usually a good judge of character. Surely, he could see through the fellow's lies. "What do you think of him?"

"If he is your husband, then I imagine I would eventually think well of him for choosing to marry you," he said carefully.

"And if he's proved an imposter?"

"I hope you'll grant me the pleasure of dealing with him *for* you." A vicious smile appeared on Wharton's face and then disappeared just as quickly. Wharton put his hands on his knees and stood. "We'll hear what he has to say for himself tomorrow. Excuse me, I'll leave you ladies to talk amongst yourselves."

He kissed Sylvia's cheek and rushed off, disappearing toward his study.

Sylvia leaned against Eugenia when he was gone. "I hope he's about to arrange for Mr. Bagshaw to be thoroughly investigated."

Eugenia put her head back into her hand. "This is intolerable."

Her cousins rubbed her back. "You could have told us."

"And what would you have done? Looked upon me with pity for becoming a widow so soon after I married?"

"Gracious no," Aurora promised, giving her a little shake. "But think of all we could have accomplished with our widowed cousin as our chaperone these past years."

"I would have been a severe chaperone," Eugenia warned, though she saw little amusing in the discussion.

"Many things would have been very different, I imagine," Sylvia murmured. "You could have taken discreet lovers and worn tokens of affection from them proudly," she suggested.

Eugenia put her hand to her waist over Thaddeus' gift of a chain as she studied her cousins in turn. They were taking the news of her marriage well. Better than she'd ever dreamed they might. She had feared they would be angry instead of accepting. But how would Thaddeus feel? If she was married, she couldn't be his lover anymore. It wouldn't be fair to him. Not to her, either.

I can't lose Thaddeus! Not when I'm falling for him!

She gulped back her despair at the realization. Thaddeus was very much against participating in adultery, and she might just be guilty of that same immoral sin. He might never want anything to do with her again. She flicked her fingers over the chain, encountering the charm with her initials engraved upon it. She'd have to give it back now. "I never accepted a gift from a lover before today."

"Today?" Sylvia frowned and drew back. "Was that what you were doing last night? Meeting a lover?"

She nodded sadly. "Probably for the last time unless I can prove the imposter a liar."

Sylvia gaped and then stared hard at Aurora. "Have you one, too?"

"A lover?" Aurora shrugged. "Not right now, but I'm always hopeful of inquiries."

Sylvia wet her lips, frowning at them. "We really are good at keeping secrets from each other. I had no idea you were sneaking off to meet someone special."

"She's exceptionally good unless we admire the same man," Aurora noted and then laughed. "We really should decide if we will ever trust each other *not* to keep secrets from each other after all this is settled."

"I do trust you both, but we've had a lot on our minds and little time to talk frankly of late, especially here. I swear to you both now, that man is not my husband," Eugenia insisted again because it was comforting to say it out loud. "I know this in my heart, because I don't want to be intimate with him. The very idea is revolting. I couldn't wait for Robbie to touch me when he was alive, before I even knew what I craved was natural and right. So, it cannot be him, can it? It just can't."

Sylvia hugged her. "We believe you. He's not your husband, but however are we to prove it before word spreads? That's the man who's been banging on all doors in Cavendish Square looking for his missing woman.

Aurora gasped. "But remember, his story was always different depending on whom he spoke to."

"I never even saw him." Eugenia blinked. "I cannot live as that man's wife. I'd rather die than give up my life."

Aurora gasped. "He could claim all your funds as his own. Move into Albemarle Street and sleep in your bed."

"Wharton leases Albemarle Street for us now," she reminded Aurora.

"That man could force you to share your bed anywhere," Sylvia whispered in a horrified tone.

Eugenia considered casting up her accounts then and there.

Chapter Seventeen

Teddy strolled along Bond Street, inspecting the wares on display for purchase in shop windows with a spring in his step. It was a sunny day, and he appreciated the improved weather enormously. It matched the happy feeling around his heart. He was alone; he'd left his men behind at Grafton House, though they were none too pleased about it.

For the first time in quite a while, he felt on top of the world. Eugenia had been overwhelmed by the small gift of a chain and charm and that he'd placed about her waist so no one might notice. A mere first token of his affection, but there would be others. The woman deserved diamonds adorning her throat, to be sure, but that smacked too much of branding her his mistress and she'd claimed not to want that.

He felt a certain way about Eugenia. He wasn't sure what that way was yet, but he felt sure they would be together for some time to come. They were only just beginning to explore the depths of their attraction and mutual lust.

And explore it they would. As far and as naughtily as needed until they were sated.

That was why he was shopping for her today. He knew what he wanted to buy to add to their bedchamber frolics. He surveyed those strolling Bond Street in search of familiar faces so he could avoid them. He wanted to be sure there were no witnesses to his visit to an establishment that sold rather risqué implements to enhance sexual pleasure.

As sure as he could be that no one who knew him was around, he reached for the door handle of the shop. The jangle of the little bell that announced his presence had him slamming the door shut very promptly.

He paused to look around. This particular apothecary shop was a tidy establishment catering to a vast assortment of ailments but was also crammed full of wicked and also practical implements. He'd found this shop once before on his own wanderings when he'd first come to London and had been astonished by the wide variety of devices available for pleasure inside.

Before coming to live with the Duke of Exeter, he'd never have imagined such things existed. However, the window display barely hinted at the items on offer here that a pleasure-seeking gentleman, or lady, might acquire if they'd the funds.

And he had plenty to spend now.

Today, he was after something particular. A dildo to please his new lover. Eugenia had promised to let him watch her use it on herself.

He couldn't wait to see her again. She had not appeared at Lady Bisley's last night. None of them had attended, actually, though they'd all been expected to put in an appearance. With the marchioness still in her sickbed, it wasn't unheard of that they'd send no apologies to the hostess for changing their plans at the last minute.

Today he seemed to be the only customer in the shop, so he felt less uncomfortable than he might normally be if he was overheard asking questions.

He approached a glass-topped cabinet. There were all sorts of lengths and thicknesses of dildo inside. Some made from wood, others ivory, and behind the counter for the wealthier clientele, polished quartz, and even Jade, too. He studied them all, tapping his finger over each one as he considered and rejected each.

When he stopped tapping, the proprietor burst out of the rear room, face wreathed in smiles of welcome. "May I be of some assistance?"

"Yes, I came for a dildo, but..." he began as he glanced around. His eye caught on a mask in plum silk and embroidered in gold thread, and he thought it might suit Eugenia very well. There would eventually be a masquerade ball that they could both attend together. He would love to spend an evening with Eugenia on his arm in public, but with their identities hidden to protect her reputation. He could whisper his desires in her ear all night until she begged for a release he'd be only too happy to give in some shadowed corner. "I'm not sure if that is all I want for now, though."

"Birches and floggers are over that side of the shop," the proprietor said, pointing out his wares. "Restraints and masks to the right. Feathers and ticklers upfront. Unless you're wanting a poultice made special. You'll have to ask for that."

"Not a poultice," he murmured.

A set of ropes strung from the ceiling above the proprietor's head caught his eye next, complete with metal cuffs at each end. There had been an engraving he'd seen of a similar device, stung up on a bed frame with a lover bound to it. But he'd been certain the cuffs had been leather, not metal in the engraving. The one on offer here seemed…almost painful.

He passed it by, deciding to stick with what he had come for in the first place. He perused the dildo collection again and chose one in smooth black marble, two inches wide at the base, nine from tip to base in length.

He returned to the masks and chose the one that had caught his eye, along with a short feather tickler that was small enough it could be tucked into his coat pocket.

He couldn't wait to use them all with Eugenia, who seemed just as interested in exploring erotic bedroom experiences as he was.

She would never claim him boring in bed, like she had hinted a previous lover had been. Or was it lovers? He wasn't sure how many men had come before him, but they didn't matter. He had Eugenia now, and they didn't. He didn't plan to end things with her anytime soon.

They'd be together tomorrow or the next day, if he could arrange to casually run into her at Lord Wharton's residence that afternoon when he called unannounced and suggest another rendezvous.

He paid for his purchases with coin rather than put them on credit and tucked the discreetly wrapped parcel—brown paper and twine—under his arms before strolling out to the street, hoping to see no one he recognized.

Of course, he ran headfirst into a friend.

"Berringer," Lord Hurlston exclaimed as he glanced past Teddy's shoulder to the shop he had just exited. A smile curved his lips. "Excellent dinner the other night. A pity you had to dash off early."

"Hurlston!" Teddy gulped and shuffled away from the door a few steps, his parcel wedged firmly under his arm, while Hurlston moved more toward it. "It was a good dinner, wasn't it?"

Hurlston nodded. "Did you receive an invitation to Sullivan's for dinner next week?"

"Not as yet," he added, still hoping for a quick escape. "I'm afraid—"

"Mine came this morning," Hurlston said, seemingly determined to keep him talking. "I'm sure you'll find one waiting for you when you return home today. Sullivan does set a good table, so you should certainly accept."

"I'm on my way home now," he promised, glancing down the street. A trio of ladies he knew was walking in their direction. Miss Waters, Miss Draven and Miss Long. The paper-wrapped parcel under his arm crackled, and he tensed.

Teddy nearly groaned when Hurlston's eyes dipped to it.

"I'll see you later," he promised his friend.

"Yes, don't let me keep you if you have somewhere pressing to be." Hurlston seemed to be biting his lip, and then he laughed as Teddy brushed past him to go. "Do enjoy yourself with that, Berringer," he called out loudly.

Bastard!

Face flaming with embarrassment, Teddy didn't dare stop again until he found a place where he could hail a hack for the journey home.

Teddy hoped to hell that the next time he met his friend, Hurlston would not want to discuss his satisfaction with his purchases. The earl had the oddest sense of humor.

Once safely returned to Exeter's townhouse, he was surprised to find the house a bustle of unexpected activity. He passed off his hat to the butler and asked, "What's amiss?"

"The duke and duchess have returned."

Teddy groaned at the bad timing. Sinclair and Kitty were not supposed to be back for days yet. "If either asks, I'll be right back down."

"Why wait?" the duke said right behind his back.

Teddy winced and turned around. "Cousin, when did you get home?"

"While you were gone, obviously." Sinclair came close and embraced him. "How have you been?"

"Very well. I thought you'd be gone another week or more still."

The duke grunted. "Kitty invited a guest to stay with us without telling me until after we were just about to leave the Baxter's estate. She's derailed all my plans to spoil her with an extended trip away from Town."

"Oh, I am sorry."

"None more so than me." Sinclair urged Teddy into the library and shut the doors. "This is not what I'd intended, and I am sorry."

"Why be sorry?"

Sinclair winced. "Kitty invited Miss Felicity Hunter to stay with us."

But Teddy grinned. "When does she arrive?"

"She's here now," the duke grumbled. "And her father came, too."

Now, Teddy *did* wince. The duchess' brother, Mr. Hunter, tended to make a mess…along with having the dangerous habit of blowing things up, too.

"I hope you don't mind," the duke asked.

"Why would I mind?"

"Well, Felicity will need you to escort her occasionally. Can't possibly take her father anywhere with breakables. He's agreed to confine his experiments to this house, though, so it should be relatively safe." Sinclair smiled. "Dance with her a bit and help us keep an eye out for scoundrels lurking about."

"She did well more or less on her own last Christmas," Teddy reminded his cousin.

"That was different," Sinclair went on. "They were our friends' sons whispering to her. Here in London, with her pretty looks, they'll eat her up for breakfast."

"I'll have a word with my friends. We can all keep our eyes peeled for trouble concerning her and any scoundrels."

"I'd appreciate that." The duke sank into a chair with a groan. "So, what have you done with yourself while we were away?"

"This and that," he said, evading any clear answer. "Have you seen today's mail?"

"Not yet. Why?"

"I ran into Hurlston, and he mentioned I might have an invitation to dine with Lord Sullivan."

The duke studied him. "Sullivan has a widowed cousin."

"I am aware of that. Mrs. Smith." He pulled a face. "She winked at me when I was following you about society two years ago while still a married woman."

"Ah, so not at all interested."

"She's already tried to lure me into adultery once. I certainly won't be the victim of it as a man married to her." He smiled. "Since I wasn't expecting you back for a week, I'm afraid I've not planned your welcome back dinner yet."

"Kitty will arrange something for tomorrow night with Felicity's help. Is there anyone special you wish to have attend?"

The duchess did occasionally invite Sylvia Hillcrest to dinner. Her cousins, Eugenia and Aurora, did not always attend with her, though. He wanted to see Eugenia very much and having her here could be fun. He knew all the best hiding spots in this house. Places perfect for lovers to exchange a kiss or more.

"Wallingham and Pinner are still in Town and always enjoy emptying your decanters."

"Yes, I have noticed that tendency. I'll ask Kitty to include them, too, and find a few other women to join us to keep the numbers even."

"She could always simply invite all the Hillcrests on the one invitation."

"That's not a bad idea," the duke mused. "With the middle one's future set, Kitty mentioned she'd like to see the others find suitable husbands, too."

"Pinner might be good company for the younger Miss Hillcrest at the dinner," he murmured. The pair had been exchanging speculative glances at the last ball they'd attended together. If Kitty placed them together, he might just be seated beside Eugenia. Of course, he could ask for that, but if he did, he'd be alerting the duchess—and his cousin—where his interests lie.

Teddy pushed himself up from his chair, but he put his hand down on the package at his side.

The crackling paper drew the duke's attention immediately. "What is that?"

"Nothing," Teddy gulped, fighting to keep a telling blush from his face. "I should put this away and change before I see Miss Felicity."

The duke's eyes narrowed on the package in his hand, and then his brows shot up high on his face. "Yes, that is probably a good idea if that is what I think it is."

Teddy strode from the room as fast as he could.

He changed and strolled along to the chambers the duchess used most days. At his knock, she urged him to enter.

"There you are at last," she cried.

"I missed you too, Kitty," he promised, kissing the back of her outstretched hand. "Did Sinclair give you any trouble while you were away?"

"Only the usual kind. He never wants to get out of bed in the morning," she complained, but laughed. Sinclair had become slightly more inclined to sleeping late since his marriage to Kitty. That was only fair and good. Teddy had felt the same way the last time he was leaving Eugenia's bed actually.

"So, I hear we have a pair of guests?"

"Don't worry, my brother has gone out. We're all completely safe from his experiments for the afternoon."

Teddy did feel a bit easier, but there would be dangers to avoid tomorrow, most likely. He'd have to keep his wits about him.

The door burst open, and a young woman rushed into the room. "Aunt, you'll never guess what occurred to me..." She skidded to a stop and curtsied. "Mr. Berringer."

Teddy stood and bowed to her. "Miss Felicity. How wonderful to see you again."

The duchess' niece was young and pretty, and she grinned impishly. "I bet you think it's too soon since we last met."

He winced and glanced about with exaggerated suspicion. "I trust one of your new friends isn't hiding behind another curtain somewhere."

Felicity scowled. "Oh, I definitely left the pea-goose behind —the nerve of trying to compromise herself with you. You're so old," she teased.

Teddy sighed dramatically. Several of Felicity's new young friends had tried their hand at flirting with him. He'd learned to be polite but always ready to flee. "It is a curse indeed to be so ancient."

The duchess laughed. "Don't let his grace hear you despair your age. He'll tell you to hurry up and find yourself a wife again."

"More than he does now? Is that even possible?"

"He wants you to be happy."

"I assure you, I am."

He turned his attention back to the duchess' niece. She'd grown up in London but had never moved in the same circles with the duke. He hoped she'd find her feet quicker than Teddy had. Rogues and scoundrels would find her fresh face and smile much too intriguing. "I won't ask how your father is. I assume I'd have already heard if he'd blow off a limb or another finger."

"My brother has gone off to visit old haunts, Teddy."

"Aunt, may I be excused for a moment?"

"Of course. Hurry back, my dear."

Felicity fled the room, and the duchess sighed. "If only her enthusiasm for being in London wasn't so evident in her speed through the house."

"She's young."

"As are you, sir. Do not listen to my niece declare you decrepit."

He laughed. "I'm glad she thinks me too old for herself and her friends. It means I do not need to worry about entrapment when she's around."

"Has there been an incident while we were away?"

"No. But I am always taking precautions to avoid wives and spinsters."

Well, he normally avoided spinsters. Of Eugenia, he couldn't see her enough.

In fact, he was starting to think he might always like to see her…

"I've already had a note delivered from Lady Starling. She hinted that you'd turned your eye on her daughter."

"Not true," he vowed.

"Lady Norris also claimed an attachment was in the wind between you and Miss Waters."

"I can promise you, I have no attachment to either lady, but I did enjoy speaking with Miss Waters at a ball."

The duchess worried her lip a moment. "It is said, too, that you and Lady Fuller had parted on bad terms."

"Parted?"

"Must I come out and say it?"

Teddy blinked. "We were never involved."

"And you made a fuss over Miss Waters to make her jealous."

"Good grief, the gossips have it all wrong. Lady Fuller was rude to Miss Waters, who I was promised to dance with." He heaved a sigh. "Miss Waters is a friend of my friends, Wharton and the Hillcrest ladies. I was merely helping her be seen away from the company of wallflowers, as you might have wanted me to do of anyone."

"So, you don't mind that a man with red hair has been calling on her."

"I am overjoyed to hear it," he promised. "I introduced a young man with red hair to Miss Water's at the very same ball. He's an acquaintance."

The duchess heaved a sigh of relief. "I like Miss Waters very much but not so much her absentminded parents."

"You've nothing to fear. I'll not make a match without consideration of your feelings, or my cousins, too."

The duchess poured him a cup of tea, and Miss Felicity returned. She was wearing a different dress now, prettier and more suited to having company come to call. He glanced at the duchess, then saw that there were more cups than people. "Expecting friends?"

"Lady Darrow is coming."

"Then I ought to slip away while I still can and allow you the privacy of a ladies' gathering."

"You are welcome to stay."

"A discussion of hats and bows interests me very little, your grace."

"That is not all we talk about."

"Well, whatever the topic, it is likely not for my ears," he muttered. Lady Willa was engaged in a years-long affair with the Duke of Baxter—a married man. Something he disapproved of, and they all knew it, except perhaps young Felicity.

He offered a bow and hurried out before Lady Willa could arrive.

He went into the library and shut the door behind him.

Teddy found Sinclair, standing at a lectern placed beside the window, squinting at a book wearing his new glasses.

Teddy cleared his throat. "Having trouble again?"

The duke made an uncharacteristically angry sound and slammed the book shut.

He stormed off toward his study. Teddy waited for a beat and then followed after him.

The duke's eyes had started giving him trouble some months ago, not that he would admit to any impairment. He simply hated wearing spectacles.

Teddy poured himself a drink and then waved the decanter at Sinclair, since he had a glass on his study desk already. "A refill?"

The duke shook his head.

Teddy moved about the chamber, studying the spines of the duke's many books, biding his time till his grace was not quite so uncomfortable. "I see what you mean about Felicity. She's even prettier than at Christmas."

For an answer, the duke only grunted.

"Come now, cousin, no thorn in your side is ever so bad you cannot talk to me about it in confidence."

"I don't like getting old," the duke finally grumbled.

"No one does. Please don't start laying boiled onion on your face twice a day to stave off the odd wrinkle."

"Who did that?"

"My father."

That, at least, made Sinclair laugh.

"He also took baths in mud and turmeric and was regularly bled," Teddy confided. "My father's last years were devoted to preserving himself for a long reign as the next Duke of Exeter."

"That explains why he was always in such a bad mood," the duke muttered.

"And stank of onions constantly." Teddy smiled. "You look half the age he was when he died, and you were older by three years. *He* walked with a cane."

"To make himself feel important," the duke said ruefully. "Ah, Teddy. I don't want to get old and die."

"No one does," Teddy promised. "But you won't die anytime soon. You're going to live till one hundred and three, so you're old enough to see my children make a marriage."

"A duke, forever, I think not," he chided.

"I'm in no hurry to lose you, as I've said before."

The duke stared at his desk. "Baxter was telling me only yesterday he doubts his son's love for him."

"That can be the case. There's no love lost between Pinner and his uncle, either."

"Why is it different for us?"

"Because we possess a compatible sense of humor." Teddy smiled. "We could fight, too, if you'd like us to."

The duke shook his head. "I think it impossible for me to fight with you. I love you too well."

"Then stop your worrying."

"I'd be happier if…"

Teddy rolled his eyes. "I will not marry just in case you're about to die."

Yet, when he imagined making a marriage today he suddenly thought of Eugenia with a yearning heart. He would likely need to tell the duke of the affair, because he'd always made a habit of confiding everything important to his cousin eventually. And Sinclair's eyes were sharp, despite his recent trouble with small print in books. "I've begun thinking of furnishing the house you gifted me."

The duke frowned. "You're not leaving because of Felicity being here, are you?"

"Not at all. I started thinking about it, and it gives me something to do every now and then."

"You're always welcome to live here," Sinclair promised.

"An empty house is a sad house," he said. "If I furnish it, it could be leased, and I could put the extra funds aside or invest in something worthwhile."

"Well, whatever you decide, I'll accept. Just don't ever think I don't want you here."

The duke's London townhouse was large enough for the present family. But Teddy really had no space here of his own. No privacy. Nowhere to take his lover. He wouldn't mind a study of his own and a place to put up his feet uninterrupted, as he might at Clifford Street, or even at Albemarle Street, where he'd grown very fond of visiting.

The door burst open, and Hurlston appeared, eyes wild without the usual footman accompanying him to see if the duke was free.

Hurlston apologized profusely to the duke for the interruption but charged over to Teddy. "I had to come and share the news I just heard."

"What news?"

"It seems Eugenia Hillcrest is a married woman! She's the Mrs. Bagshaw that fellow was asking about outside Wharton's the other week!"

"No…" Teddy whispered.

Hurlston nodded profusely. "Do you remember how he bothered us all that night? Well, that's her husband. Imagine! He's come to reclaim her and take her home to Dover. I called at Wharton's, and he let it slip. He's not taking it well."

Teddy was sure the ground under him shifted…and not in a good way.

Chapter Eighteen

EUGENIA WAS WALLOWING in bed three days after her husband's return when she heard the distinct sound of someone opening her bedchamber door. She quickly wiped her eyes, embarrassed to have been caught feeling sorry for herself. Although she considered raising her head to see who it was, she didn't want to face her cousins yet. She assumed it was one of them coming to check on her yet again.

The imposter came back, day after day, only to be sent away after an hour of awkward conversation with her. That was all she could bear before misery started to get the better of her good sense. She felt nothing of her former love when she was with the man. He kept talking about them living together and her skin crawled.

But she would have to face him again soon—face everyone not connected to this house, too, eventually. Her cousins understood her reticence to show her face to the world and hadn't pressed her to be at home to anyone. They promised Wharton understood, as well. She hadn't been brave enough to face the marchioness or Thaddeus yet…not that he had even bothered to call to see how she fared under a cloud of such scandal.

She was sure he must have heard by now. His silence was nigh on deafening. After what they had shared in recent weeks, what he must have heard from gossip, she was sure she'd shocked him into not liking her anymore.

An odd creaking sound drew closer, together with the halting footsteps of someone trying to be quiet.

The creaking stopped, and the footsteps scurried from the room.

Eugenia sat up and found herself face to face with the Marchioness of Wharton. The older woman was a tiny figure in her invalid chair—pale as a sheet, her cheeks hollow and her eyes sad. This was the first time she'd ventured from her room, to Eugenia's knowledge.

"My lady."

"Well?" she said, eyes narrowing. "What have you to say for yourself?"

"Good morning," she said quickly, brushing her hair away from her face and into some semblance of order, sitting up fully to smile at the older woman. The marchioness had insisted she be kept informed of all matters pertaining to the family and society at large, despite her slow recovery. Sylvia would have informed the marchioness of Eugenia's changed situation—her husband's return from the grave.

"You are not in your best looks to attempt that smile, so do not try." The marchioness' eyes narrowed even more. "You are not pleased."

"No." Eugenia shook her head. "I couldn't sleep."

"I am familiar with that difficulty, along with many other maladies. But I would never let a husband deprive me of my rest."

The marchioness had a dry wit that usually made her smile. However, today she was beyond cheering up. "I have been trying to reconcile my memory of Robbie Bagshaw with the stranger that appeared in the drawing room, to no avail. They could not be the same man, and yet the similarities are there to see. He knows facts about me only my husband could know. Plans we made to meet in secret before we married."

The marchioness winced as she moved in her chair, leaning a little closer. "Similarities are common in families. Did your husband have a brother? A cousin?"

"He did not mention anyone besides his mother. He was all she had in the world, he'd said."

"There must be a purpose for your husband coming to claim you now."

"He's not my husband," Eugenia snapped at her, then instantly regretted the outburst. "Do forgive me, my lady."

However, a pleased smile creased the marchioness' weary face. "Hold tight to your belief he's an imposter, child. Misery does not become you. Your resolve will be tested in the days to come, I'm sure. Test him." She gasped suddenly and quickly rang a bell that had been hidden by her hands in her lap. "Find out where's been all these years," she gasped.

The marchioness' maid rushed in and, upon seeing the marchioness in distress, carefully turned the invalid chair to face the door. But the marchioness' hand suddenly rose to halt her exit. "Eugenia, be as shrewish as you can when you question him. Play the part of an unhappy wife to the hilt, and give him every reason to reconsider his ploy. If he was never dead, then your husband abandoned you for four years. Never let him forget his failing as your provider and protector. Question his honor every chance you get."

The marchioness chuckled, but it turned quickly into a gasp of pain. "As a start," she croaked, "go out with your cousin and purchase something exceedingly expensive and useless and hand him the bill to pay."

"If I cannot afford to pay for extravagances from my own pocket, I would not ever do such a thing," Eugenia reminded the older woman, who sometimes forgot the Hillcrest family were not as well off as the Whartons were.

"Would an imposter know that about you?"

"Robbie would have."

"That's what I thought. Wharton will pay whatever trifling amount you consider extravagant, my dear," Lizzy promised. "He will hardly notice the loss in his pocket, I assure you."

"I could always return the item when the point has been made that he couldn't afford a wife," Eugenia mused.

"Do whatever you feel is right, dear. You always do."

The maid wheeled the marchioness away slowly at her

command, being careful not to jostle the woman any more than necessary.

Aurora darted into the room almost immediately. "Was that the marchioness out of bed?"

"Indeed, it was. I thought she must finally be feeling better in herself, but I think she just misses ordering me about."

Aurora shushed her. "Sylvia will be so relieved to hear she got up. What did she want?"

Eugenia smiled. "The marchioness is a remarkably determined and clever woman. She sees things from a unique perspective I might never have thought of myself."

"I am almost afraid to hear what she suggests be done," Aurora said as she climbed on the bed as if waiting for a good tale, rubbing her hands together. "So tell me."

"One of the things Lizzy suggested is that I shop extravagantly, and hand my would-be husband the bill of sale to pay."

"Oh, my," Aurora said with a wicked laugh, clearly exciting with the idea. "That could be painful for him if you let me help you."

"Indeed, it could be," Eugenia agreed. She wouldn't have to be truly extravagant at first. She could work up to that, taunt him with the ongoing expenses a wife might incur for a London season. Eugenia knew that stranger wasn't her husband, but she couldn't prove it still unless he forgot himself. "I've been wrestling with the problem for days, but I can't wait for Wharton's investigator to report back. The marchioness has delivered the lightning rod to stir me to rid myself of him once and for all."

"I want to help!" Aurora cried. "I'll go and change to go out with you."

"Thank you," she called after her cousin, grateful for her unfailing support.

If Eugenia had been abandoned by Robbie, she'd have every right to be furious with him. She'd married him, given him her innocence, and what little funds she'd saved—fifty pounds—had gone with him upon their marriage. To her, those funds had been a fortune. It still was, too. When the imposter dared complain about her high spending today, she could demand to know what had become of her money…and any past pin money that should have been paid to her over the years he'd been gone.

Eugenia rushed to her wardrobe, but only drab colors and dark tones greeted her. Not that she'd deliberately chosen to mourn Robbie by wearing mourning for all these years. She'd believed the dark colors had suited her complexion better than pale gowns. But now, if this stranger claimed she was a wife, well, she had every right to desire a completely new wardrobe of bright new clothes in any color she fancied.

She changed into her prettiest gown for her early morning shopping spree and then went to her dressing table, where she saw Teddy's gift sitting in her drawer. She picked it up, and her heart longed for him as she admired it anew.

So perfect a secret gift, but their affair was likely over now.

Aurora returned, dressed to go out, smiling and eager to be underway. But she stared at Eugenia, sitting before her mirror. "Please tell me you are not primping to impress him?"

"Don't be ridiculous." On impulse, she decided to wear Teddy's gift around her neck instead of her waist from now on. The gold chain and charm fell down her bodice, and she quite liked the way she looked wearing the token of her lover's affection.

She hoped not for the first time that she hadn't lost him.

Aurora came closer, frowning at the necklace. "Is that from *him*? From Teddy,"

"Yes. I had intended to give it back when we were over, but I can't give it up yet."

"I don't blame you. I'd want to keep him, too," Aurora confessed.

Eugenia nodded slowly. The one thing she'd accepted in the past few days is that she did not just like Thaddeus for passion. *She loved him.* What hurt the most was knowing she'd lost him before she was ready to let him go.

Eugenia and Aurora stumbled up the stairs of Wharton House four hours later, utterly exhausted and laughing, with their footman Mr. Bloom and a groom from the carriage bringing up the rear, both with their arms full. All the years Eugenia had scrimped and saved every shilling to make ends meet had repressed her desire for any personal extravagance. It had come to a screeching halt today in the very best way imaginable.

Eugenia had found, once given a good excuse, she had quite expensive tastes after all.

Aurora had had a glorious time pointing out items for her consideration. Eugenia now owned so many pairs of dancing slippers she didn't truly need that she'd felt a pinch of shame at the likely tally at day's end.

But she was trying to make a point to her husband's imposter that he couldn't afford her—or to continue his little game another day longer.

The butler took their hats and whispered, "He's returned."

Eugenia liked that the butler did not refer to the stranger as Robert Bagshaw, a man lost and mourned. "Thank you. Where might I find him?"

"In the library with Lord Wharton."

When other footmen tried to relieve Mr. Bloom of his packages and take them upstairs, she asked them instead to stack her purchases on the round table in the center of the front hall. "Mr. Bloom, do you happen to have the bills of sale for all this?"

"I do," he promised.

Eugenia had admitted her plan to him at the start of their shopping trip in a bid to unmask the imposter. To say he was supportive was an understatement. He believed her straight off. Said he'd not liked the look of that pestersome fellow who kept coming round the grand houses in the square.

"Be a dear man and interrupt Lord Wharton to deliver the bills of sale to the gentlemen pretending to be my husband in the library. I'm sure Wharton will not mind."

While she waited for Mr. Bloom's return, Eugenia flittered around the vast pile, showing Aurora her purchases again and, once or twice, roping in the butler for his opinion, too.

"Lovely," he muttered, looking perplexed by her behavior.

She didn't want everyone to think she'd become a pea-goose without wit or intelligence. She slipped him a vale. "The marchioness suggested a shopping spree would improve my mood and sour the imposter's."

The butler chuckled softly. "Ah, that explains your," he searched for the right word, "transformation."

The imposter burst from the library, practically breathing fire, and the butler wisely backed away. "What is the meaning of this, woman?"

"Just a trifling few things I needed," Eugenia said in the most air-headed tone she could manage upon seeing him. "I knew you'd happily take care of it all."

He shook the papers at her. "Are you trying to bankrupt me? I'll not pay for one half of this. Take them back."

"I couldn't possibly do that. It would take all day and break those poor shopkeepers' hearts," she said with a shrug of unconcern. "After all the years I've done without, surely you can understand why I'm anxious to turn heads now. Everyone believes I was an abandoned bride. This will prove I'm not, and help improve society's opinion of me."

The imposter ground his teeth. She heard them gnashing before his oily smile appeared. "Of course, my dear. Buy whatever makes you happy. Everyone in high society lives on credit anyway."

Wharton had followed and looked on curiously. "Women are expensive creatures, Bagshaw," he warned. "Satisfy one need and another soon arises. I should probably deliver to you her other bills now, and discuss a settlement of the past expenses and the upkeep I've endured on her behalf. Be grateful she has no love of horses or fine carriages, or you'd have the expense of stabling to bear, too.

"There's really no sense me holding on to her bills when

she's a perfectly good husband to settle her accounts all over Town now. It shouldn't take very long, if you have a moment to sort through the pile that's much larger than those," Wharton promised, gesturing vaguely to her purchases. "Mr. Bloom, attend to all this, just as you have the others in the past."

"Yes, my lord." Mr. Bloom nodded.

The butler came forward. "Shall I have a bottle of that French champagne you liked so much when the Prince Regent called last time served with luncheon today?"

"Oh, please, my lord," Eugenia gushed, holding her hands at her chest. "It would make me so happy, but we will need three bottles I'm sure."

"Whatever you like, my dear," Wharton promised. "Only the best for my future wife's relations."

"Oh, you are a dear man indeed," Eugenia gushed. "It is just the thing to revive our energies before we go out again shopping this afternoon."

The imposter's eyes kept growing wider and wider as she gushed and fibbed about her plans, but his mouth remained firmly shut. She'd have to try harder to aggravate him.

"I am looking forward to going out to tonight's amusements."

That loosened his tongue. "Out?! Where?"

"The Duchess of Baxter is hosting a charity dinner to raise funds for the poor orphans. I'm sure there'll be a bidding war over who gets the first dance with her son, too. Last time, he attracted a winning bid of five hundred pounds. I'll do better this year and beat everyone."

Bagshaw's eyes bulged. "Do you have five hundred pounds to waste on a dance?"

"Oh, gracious no. No money ever really changes hands at these things. Far too gauche. I simply promise to pay, and it all works out in the end."

"I paid last year," Wharton lied, since Eugenia hadn't known him then, nor lived under his roof at that time. "But of course,

I'm happy to step aside so you can have the honor of footing the bill all for yourself."

Wharton walked away, covering his mouth to hide a grin, and returned promptly, hands full of papers. "I haven't had time to sort it all out yet, but I'm sure you'll manage admirably without my help. It should only be a few thousand pounds this quarter. I'll get the rest to you tomorrow, or the next day at the latest."

The imposter stared at the papers and then at her as if she were a live snake. "I can see that the sooner we return home to Dover, the better. London has corrupted the sweet lass I fell in love with so many years ago."

"Sweet?" Eugenia frowned at him. No one had ever described her as sweet. Especially not Robbie. "And where were *you* for all those years, might I ask?"

"We'll discuss that later." He glanced down at the paperwork. "After I deal with this." He turned a glare on the butler. "Well, don't just stand there. Fetch my hat, man."

Wharton stepped forward. "Are we not going to settle her debts now?"

"No. I'm afraid I have an important engagement that I am late for. I'll return tomorrow," the imposter claimed. "And I expect you to not be late again."

Wharton nodded to the butler to go for the hat, but his eyes remained fixed on Bagshaw's openly hostile form.

Eugenia pasted a smile of unconcern on her face as she watched her would-be husband struggle to control his temper. For added irritation, she twirled her skirts. Appearing vacuous and foolish, but what did she care if he thought ill of her? He obviously took her for a fool who would meekly fall into line and do as he demanded.

Robbie would never have behaved like this man. He'd been a gentleman. Respectful to those above him and below. She would have felt ashamed of nearly bankrupting her late husband if he'd been here, instead of the stranger standing in his place.

Bagshaw turned to her. She saw the exact moment when he

noticed the appeal of her body. His nostrils flared as he approached, hand outstretched. "Wear that pretty smile for me again tomorrow, wife, and all will be well between us."

But her smile had been for Robbie…not a scoundrel wearing his face.

She held her ground, determined not to respond to his entreaty to place her hand in his. She did not want his hands anywhere upon her. Yet, he came closer anyway and wrested her hand into his. His touch was repellant, even with his fingers encased in gloves. He gripped her hand tight, and his eyes locked on hers.

Then he did something that nearly buckled her legs. He stroked his thumb over the back of her hand, the way Robbie had done to charm her when they'd first met.

The way she still did occasionally to muddle gentlemen.

She jerked her hand back from him. Appalled that he knew even that trick, too.

The imposter smiled. "Perhaps tomorrow you'll be in a more loving frame of mind, wife."

"Never," she hissed, letting all trace of vacuous stupidity fall away.

The man's eyes dipped to her cleavage. "Indeed, I have stayed away from the delights of my wife too long. Never fear, I will not leave you alone again, wife. Into my arms first, and then home to bed." He said it all softly and with a degree of certainty that made her want to shiver.

Wharton drew closer, clearly trying to hear what was being whispered to her. He shook his head, apparently missing the threat but not the change in atmosphere between her and the imposter.

He was suddenly at her side, standing closer to Eugenia than he normally would. "Do you have a home, sir? Where is it?"

"It's a charming property on Albemarle Street. I asked around and I'm told it is leased to my wife, though now it belongs to her husband," he taunted, smiling his oily smile.

Eugenia nearly threw herself at him to scratch out his eyes, but Wharton caught her hand instead and held her firmly in place. "Don't you dare," she hissed at him.

"*Our* home now. All I need is a key or a locksmith." The imposter smiled, clearly pleased with himself. "I'll return for my wife tomorrow."

Eugenia waited until he was gone before she turned on Wharton. "How could you tell him about Albemarle Street?"

"I never said a word to him about the place. That means he's either followed you there or has been asking around." Wharton shrugged. "Not to worry. The men following Bagshaw will report any incursions into the townhouse and expedite his eviction. The lease is in *my* name, not yours. If he goes there, he's trespassing."

"But my belongings are there. I need to know that he's not going there now to take possession. He could take everything I value away with him and claim it's his right."

Wharton nodded. "I'll send a few servants to stay there and report back to you, but you absolutely must promise me you will not go there alone anymore."

"He wouldn't hurt me."

Wharton turned astonished eyes on her. "How would you know that if he's a stranger? The way he looked at you just now concerns me greatly. A woman alone cannot hope to defend herself against a much stronger man bent on ravishment. And since he claims to be your husband, no court on earth can stop him taking you whenever he likes. You will take Mr. Bloom and another footman whenever you leave this house, and that is final."

Eugenia shivered and, on longer consideration, agreed to Wharton's sensible demand. "You know, Robbie would never have forced me into his bed. He never had to."

"I suspect you are dealing with a far different creature. An imposter, or perhaps a man changed by the years apart from you. But make no mistake, he is determined to cling like a barnacle to your skirts."

"What more has he said to you that you haven't told me?"

"It's not so much what he said but the way he questions how

we live and where we go. I suspect he's planning to include himself on the basis of being family to my future bride."

Eugenia winced. "I'm sorry."

"We will adapt if we must."

Eugenia vowed there would be no need for anyone to adapt at all.

Shoving her shopping spree in his face hadn't had the effect she'd intended. She'd meant to anger him, show him she was too good for him, not put herself up on a platter for him to devour with his eyes. She would have to remember she wasn't dealing with a gentleman. She was faced with a man with no conscience and no qualms about impersonating a dead man.

She longed for Thaddeus, and his arms wrapped tightly about her body. "Did anyone come to visit today?"

"Not today. It has been blessedly quiet save for Bagshaw demanding breakfast again while he waited for you. Were you expecting someone in particular?"

"No." It had been four days now since she'd last seen Thaddeus. Last touched. Last kissed. It wasn't a comfortable feeling, not knowing what he thought of her.

She had to talk to him, and nothing short of a face-to-face discussion would do.

Chapter Nineteen

NOTES *COULD* BE IGNORED. Teddy *might* have pretended not to have received Eugenia's politely worded summons to meet with her at Lord Wharton's home that day. It would be impolitic, brazen even, to call on a married woman when he'd had vigorous sex with her in the same house.

Her husband was probably in that house again today!

Teddy sank lower in the carriage. He'd seen the man, her husband, coming and going from Wharton House on his way past, hopelessly confused by the situation he'd found himself in.

Teddy had fallen in love with a married woman—and she'd never know, now.

He couldn't imagine meeting with her would change anything, but he wanted one last moment alone with her so he could end their affair.

He grimaced at the word: *affair.*

Adultery.

He'd fallen into the very type of relationship he'd absolutely intended to avoid. Blindly. Completely. He had committed adultery and, to his shame, had enjoyed it.

And Eugenia had said nothing to warn him away. She knew his distaste for scandalous liaisons with married women. He'd specifically told her he would never be an adulterer.

He remembered she'd been pleased with his decision.

And yet…

Teddy's carriage drew to a halt before Wharton House, and he tightened his fist, determined to see this encounter through to the inevitable end. He handed the waiting butler his card.

"Lord Wharton is not at home, sir."

"I would like to speak with Miss Hillc— That is to say, Mrs. Bagshaw. She's expecting me."

Another footman appeared, nodding his ginger head vigorously. "If you will come with me, Mr. Berringer. I'll take you to her now."

Teddy nodded and followed after the servant up the stairs to the same long gallery where Eugenia had tempted him with bold suggestions, soft lips, and a promise not to expect a marriage proposal.

Of course, she couldn't have married him if he'd even offered or if they'd been found together like that.

So now everything he'd believed about Eugenia was proved false. Eugenia Hillcrest was Mrs. Bagshaw. Mrs. Bagshaw was a wife. And those lovers she'd spoken of…her husband and other adulterers like him, most likely.

He steeled himself for the coming interview with her as the footman announced him.

At the door, he looked up slowly, and her wary gaze met his across the span of the chamber.

But in that moment, too, his heart—his stupid, traitorous heart—yearned for her still. However, she wasn't alone. Her younger cousin Aurora was at her side.

The footman backed from the room, and Teddy just stood there—frozen with indecision. Was there even anything more to say between them? His lover was a married woman.

Aurora smiled warmly, but Mrs. Bagshaw did not.

She whispered to her cousin, "Could you give us privacy?"

"Of course." Aurora slipped across the chamber and disappeared behind a connecting door.

His feet unlocked, and he was somehow standing before Eugenia the next moment, staring down into her beloved's face. "You're married?"

"It's not true," she promised, but then winced. "I mean, I *was* married, and I am a widow."

Teddy kept his hands by his sides, wanting to shake her because she would not speak the truth to his face. She had a husband still. He was here, somewhere about most likely. He came to see her every day, and soon, no doubt, she'd go away with him.

In the depths of his soul, he'd held out hope that it was all a grave misunderstanding. That she might yet be the wicked spinster he'd fallen in love with.

But no. Eugenia, the wife, was no one Teddy should have intimate knowledge of. He couldn't continue with her the same way. Her admission changed everything between them. Forever. They had to stop.

Now.

He took a deep breath, accepting that this was the end of them. But his heart hurt. Every fiber of his being rebelled, even as he inhaled to say what needed to be said. To end things and go. He bowed to her. "Thank you for your time, Mrs. Bagshaw."

"He's not my husband," she promised.

"In the eyes of the law, he is."

"I do not believe it!" she cried. "He may resemble my lost love in a certain light, but he is not the Robert Bagshaw I married all those years ago."

He reeled back. Married *years*, and still not willing to admit it. "Your name is Mrs. Bagshaw. Not Miss Hillcrest, as you have let me believe since our first introduction."

She gulped. "I can explain."

He stared at her. It mattered not to him why, but she had lied to him from the beginning. She'd made a fool of him, as well made him an adulterer. He closed his eyes. "There is nothing more I need to know. You are Mrs. Bagshaw."

"So, what do we do?"

"We say goodbye and make no plans to see each other. I will not bother you."

"But we *will* still see each other," she promised him. "It's impossible not to."

"True." He sighed heavily. He owed her the truth. "A wife with a living, breathing husband is the type of woman I avoid. I will tell you this and go: I have loved every moment of our time together, but now… I have to stay away from you."

"No!" she cried, attempting to grab hold of his hands and keep them. Eugenia's were cold against his bare skin. "This changes nothing of how I feel for you."

His heart squeezed to hear her confession because he felt the same. He did love her. He'd not meant to fall, but he couldn't ignore the truth. He loved her and still had to let her go. And he was dying inside thinking of her with someone else.

He disengaged from her grip gently. "I will relish every moment I stand in the same room with you, madam, but I will not show it. I will not seek you out, though I will not deliberately try to avoid you either."

"So, you just expect me to go along with this and become Mrs. Bagshaw? I can't give you up," she whispered. "I love you."

His heart slammed against his chest at her words, but what good would it do to admit the same? He ached with the unfairness of their situation. But she was a married woman and, as such, belonged in someone else's life, not his. Their hopeless love had nothing to do with her marriage.

He took a pace forward and impulsively pressed a chaste kiss on her brow. One last brush of his lips across her skin, then he drew back even farther. "What you do is not for me to have an opinion on anymore."

Eugenia whipped around, showing him her back and crossing her arms over her chest. "Go then."

"Eugenia, please," he begged. "Don't be angry with me because I want to do the right thing."

She wiped her cheeks with an angry brush of her hand. "Just leave. If you don't believe me, you cannot help me escape my fate, either."

He shut his eyes, wishing with all his heart that he could do something to soothe the pain in her voice. But she was married to a man clearly still alive and very much determined to be known as her husband.

To remain involved with Eugenia was morally wrong. At least

they'd managed to keep their affair a secret from all but Aurora. He was sure she would not tattle to Eugenia's husband and make her life difficult.

He opened his eyes and then bowed deeply to her, even though Eugenia's back was still turned. He let himself out of the chamber without another word.

Aurora was in the hall, and she smiled sadly as he passed her on the way to the staircase to leave. But putting his feelings away was not at all easy.

He was a few feet along the entrance of the hall when he heard the voice of a man he did not immediately recognize coming from the dining room.

"Tell me, is this what you normally serve the marquess and my wife?"

"Yes, sir," another man, probably a servant, answered. "Of course."

"Very good. Quite good. You may serve me another portion."

There was a long pause, and then, "More wine, too, Mr. Bagshaw?"

"Indeed, yes," Bagshaw said. "Then you may go and inform my wife that her husband is growing impatient with her tardiness."

The husband was a pompous prig to make demands in Lord Wharton's home.

Clipped footsteps came his way, and one of Wharton's servants slipped into the hall. The fellow pulled a face at the door he was closing, then noticed Teddy standing a few feet away. The man quickly plastered a polite smile on his face, and when Teddy silently waved him off, he scurried away, carrying a tray stacked high with empty dishes.

Curious about Eugenia's husband, Teddy moved to the dining room doorway that had failed to close properly and peeked inside.

The short, blubbery-looking fellow who had accosted him on the street outside sat at Wharton's dining table alone, shoveling food into his mouth as if he were sitting at a pig's trough. He grasped his wine glass and gulped the lot down in one large swallow.

Clearly, Eugenia hadn't married a man possessed of any table manners.

Teddy kept watching him. Watching the rival for Eugenia's affections, and couldn't see how she would have chosen this man to marry in the first place. He was slovenly, while Eugenia was neat and always elegant in her dark-hued gowns.

Perhaps Bagshaw had changed in the years they were apart.

Or was he as she claimed…an imposter?

The fellow stood, leaned over the table, and grasped a silver candlestick. He pinched out the candle flame and tested the weight in his hand, dripping hot wax on the polished mahogany, then settled it back on the table.

He stood and began to prowl the room, seemingly admiring everything not nailed down.

Wharton would be livid if he saw this himself.

When Bagshaw passed close to the table again, Teddy clearly saw him pocket a dirty silver spoon. He continued to pace the chamber as if he'd not done anything amiss, then went to a window to admire the view of the street.

Teddy drew back in disgust. Eugenia's husband was not an honest man.

Husband or imposter, it seemed impossible that she could know about his habits…or was that why she had hidden her marriage?

He shook his head. Her life now was none of his business. He would not tattle on Bagshaw to Lord Wharton, but nor would he remain to watch the man take advantage of her connections and profit from them.

Yet at the front door, his feet became stuck to the floor again. He didn't want to leave Eugenia to be married to that other man and caught unawares. She'd be humiliated and could fall out with her family if Bagshaw continued to steal from the marquess.

He couldn't leave without at least trying to warn her about what he had just seen, so she could protect herself.

He slipped back upstairs silently, headed back to the long gallery, where he'd left Eugenia. He still cared about her. Too much to utterly abandon her. He cared about protecting her reputation still.

At the door, he overheard Aurora talking to Eugenia again. "He's become testy with the servants and your delay. Will you even speak with him today?"

He peeked inside in time to watch Eugenia dry her eyes. "No. I've nothing to say to the bounder pretending to be my husband."

His heart yearned to believe her. To comfort her and dry her tears, tell her of his love, even if he might cause them both more pain to say it out loud. They had no future. No chance of happiness, only shame and disgrace.

He hadn't wanted to end their affair. Except, it hadn't felt like an affair *or* scandalous while they'd been together. It had begun to feel right to be with her, any time of the day or night.

"If only he'd not shown us proof of a marriage," Aurora was saying. "Wharton would have tossed him out long ago. Do you really not have proof of his death?"

"No. The captain said everyone onboard saw him drown and could do nothing to save him. A dozen witnesses onboard saw his body recovered from the sea, lifeless and cold, and put into a skiff to be taken into Dover for burial," Eugenia whispered. "If there was any proof at all, the captain never gave it to me. I have nothing but my word against his, and that means nothing. Less than nothing, apparently. Not even Thaddeus believes me. I cannot forget the way he looked at me like I was a stranger to him now. Even when I told him of my feelings, he said nothing."

Teddy closed his eyes. Ashamed that he had hurt her by keeping silent.

"I am sure he cares for you more than he can admit," Aurora promised. "I saw his face as he was leaving. A more disappointed man there never was."

Yes!

But there was silence inside, then a sob. Teddy peeked into

the room as Aurora comforted her cousin, who was crying against her shoulder because he'd failed to convey what she'd begun to mean to him.

"If we'd known of the marriage from the start, we would have been better prepared."

"What good would it have done to be so pitied by everyone?" Eugenia spat out, spinning out of Aurora's arms. "The marriage had barely begun before it was over. He was *dead*. I had no reason to doubt that. None at all," Eugenia nearly shrieked as she threw up her arms.

The pain in her voice cut Teddy to the quick.

"It's not *him* that I married, though they might seem similar today."

"Are you sure he did not have a brother or a cousin?"

"Not that I recall."

Even Teddy knew that not everyone spoke of their family members, especially when they were on the outs. But his own opinion was clouded by suspicion, which wasn't surprising, since he was being displaced by a rival with a prior claim on Eugenia's heart.

His only consolation was that she did not sound pleased to have her husband come back to life. She appeared to loathe the man, not love him.

She viewed him with the same suspicion that he did.

Teddy couldn't stand idly by while Eugenia harbored any doubt about the man's identity.

He quietly walked back into the chamber without bothering to knock. "There has to be proof that the man downstairs is who he claims to be," he told the pair.

Eugenia met his gaze, and her whole body seemed to sag. "I have nothing."

Aurora suddenly snapped her finger. "Is his mother still alive?"

Eugenia's eyes widened. "The imposter hasn't mentioned her yet...but Robbie always talked about his mother before we married. I assumed her dead and never thought to inquire when she died. She wasn't a well woman when I married Robbie."

Teddy approached Eugenia slowly. If there was a mother still living, he wanted to find her and discover once and for all if Bagshaw was who he claimed to be. Only then could he walk away from the woman he loved. "I can search for her on your behalf, bring her to you if she still lives to prove his identity one way or the other."

"No. I'll find her myself," she insisted. "This is my problem to solve."

Teddy nodded slowly but his mind raced. "You *should* go. His mother might not want to talk to someone not immediately connected to her family. Any stranger saying he was acting for a woman claiming to be her dead son's wife might have a difficult time convincing her. Only you can ask the right questions, and answer *hers* about her son, and be believed."

"Bagshaw is not just going to let my cousin traipse halfway across the country to prove him an imposter. He comes every day, waiting for my cousin to show her face so he can threaten to take her away from us again," Aurora warned.

Although Eugenia shuddered, she shook her head. "He can't stop me if he doesn't realize I'm gone. I could slip away tonight with none the wiser."

Teddy nodded, thinking through an escape plan for Eugenia that would allow speed and safety for her reputation. He could provide the carriage and men guaranteed to hold their tongues. All that was needed was her agreement to let him help her reach Dover, and to decide upon a meeting place. "The fewer people involved, the better."

Aurora nodded quickly. "And the fewer people who know who might try to stop her going, too."

"I absolutely cannot confide in Wharton," Eugenia said, even as he thought the same thing. "Or Sylvia. She'd tell the marchioness, who would worry. Lizzy might demand Wharton fetch me back."

Aurora was nodding, seemingly committed to supporting her

cousin in any endeavor. "But how will you travel so far? Surely not on the mail coach?"

"I can make a carriage and men available to you for a long journey," he said quickly. "No one would ever suspect my involvement."

No one would suspect she'd have a personal protector on her journey, either. Aurora wouldn't need to know he intended to go along with Eugenia, to see this through to the end.

Eugenia exhaled. "Thank you. That is exactly what I needed to hear. A carriage, a team of fast horses, and to slip away."

"You'd best leave before first light tomorrow. I need some time tonight, to make arrangements for the carriage and men to meet you by then. But they will take you anywhere you wish to go. Protect you and return you to London when you have your proof in hand."

"I'll find it," she declared. "I will not be bound to that man in unholy matrimony."

He admired her determination as he considered where she should meet the carriage. "First light tomorrow, in Vere Street, which is not far from here."

"I will be there."

"I'll take her myself," Aurora promised.

Teddy winced. He'd prefer not to involve Aurora more than he had to.

Eugenia approached her cousin and clasped her hand. "And how will you return home without being found out?"

"I'll take Mr. Bloom into my confidence. He's been of great assistance with keeping Bagshaw fed and distracted so far. A little dawn walk for me will not be of any great note to anyone else in the house if he's by my side. I'm sure he'll want to help you, too. He doesn't care for Bagshaw in the least."

Teddy nodded. Carriage, men, and Eugenia safe, as well as her cousin. All that remained was to gain her freedom, if that was possible. "Good. Make your preparations. The carriage will be well-stocked with food and funds for the journey, so only carry essentials. There'll be quite a fuss kicked up when you're discovered missing. I suspect everyone in the household will be questioned."

"I can manage a delay until late afternoon," Aurora assured him. "No one will know how long she's really been gone. She's avoided Bagshaw before and claimed to be unwell, too. Wharton hasn't minded that she hasn't shown her face around."

Eugenia hugged her cousin, then held out her hand to him. "Thank you. You are a kind man."

He clasped her hand and resisted the urge to pull her into his arms. What remained between them was more than simple kindness or compassion. He feared he might be hers, no matter what they discovered in Dover.

What mattered most to him was her happiness. She was not happy now, but perhaps she could be so again, when her fears were laid to rest.

But first, they had to find the elder Mrs. Bagshaw, if she lived, and discover the truth of her son. And then…

And then?

He did not dare to consider what might come after.

He released Eugenia's hand, knowing he could not presume there could be more to come for them. Not yet. Not until Bagshaw was unmasked as an imposter.

Chapter Twenty

Eugenia hurried out through a rear servants' entrance at Wharton House, following Mr. Bloom and Aurora, bundled up in a heavy cloak. Mr. Bloom carried an old and tattered bag that no one would miss containing only a few bare essentials to carry with her on her journey to the coast.

It was still night; the sun hadn't even lit Cavendish Square properly yet or the surrounding streets. The houses were still bathed in deep shadows, and not a soul stirred.

She chose a roundabout way to her destination, determined to avoid her would-be husband who'd taken up haunting Cavendish Square at dawn. She would not be dragged to Albemarle Street, where the imposter intended for them to live as husband and wife.

Never that.

By the time her absence was discovered, Eugenia intended to be long gone from the city of London, and with only three people aware of where she'd gone, Bagshaw should search in vain.

Eugenia would not warn Aurora of her decision that if she could not find Mrs. Bagshaw or her husband's grave, she was not returning to London. Though it would break her heart completely, she had packed every bit of wealth she possessed and would run away if she must be free. It was only thanks to Thaddeus' generosity that she had the means and a head start.

No one besides him, Aurora, or Mr. Bloom would ever have to deny they knew her whereabouts, if they even knew to question him.

Eugenia caught Aurora's hand as they rushed along the empty streets, side by side, trying not to be too obvious about it. She feared she was late and that the promised carriage might not still be there. It was hard enough to believe Thaddeus had offered it without also offering to come with her. But she supposed he felt he couldn't. She was married in his eyes, after all.

Aurora suddenly grinned at her. "I cannot believe we got out without waking anyone."

"Neither am I, but I'm glad that we did. Don't stop now. Sylvia might wake early and seek us out. She'd only argue about my going or try to come with me. The marchioness needs her more." She glanced over her shoulder, but there was no one behind yet. "Are you sure you don't mind lying for me?"

"I'll not stand between you and true love," Aurora said, smiling as they darted down a side street.

Magnificent mansions rose above them, dormant but for a few servants going about their early morning work. Eugenia kept her chin down and urged Aurora to do the same. "I do not love Bagshaw. It's absurd to suggest I could feel anything for such a man."

"I meant Thaddeus Berringer."

Eugenia stopped to stare at her cousin, causing Mr. Bloom to nearly run into them.

He went ahead at Aurora's urging.

Aurora grinned. "Why else would I be willing to rise this early? He loves you, I'm sure of it. My heart is breaking that you could be separated."

"That was always our fate. He's to become a duke." Eugenia started walking again but briskly now, trying to run from a thought that had troubled her of late. She might love Thaddeus, but there was no possibility he'd ever marry a woman like her. Not now with this scandal tarnishing her reputation. She wasn't rich or particularly accomplished. She had none of the important connections a future duke needed. He was kind to help her but that was as far as his interest in her went. She was to rendezvous with his carriage and go on alone—without him.

She looked back over her shoulder to the empty pathway, reassuring herself that no one followed them still.

They crossed a street and hurried down a narrow lane. They broke out onto Vere Street to see a black traveling carriage, four horses, and six men waiting idly ahead.

Thaddeus was not standing nearby to bid her goodbye, but at the sight of Eugenia arriving, the grooms sprang to life and made ready to get underway.

Eugenia turned to hug her cousin again. "I love you. Wish me luck."

"Luck and love. Always and forever, Eugenia. If the search goes on too long, write to me at Lady Bisley's address to relieve my mind that you are still well and in pursuit of the truth."

She hugged her cousin one last time and whispered, "I promise I will."

Eugenia took her small trunk from Mr. Bloom. He looked worried as he handed it over. "Are you sure you'll be all right traveling alone, miss? I could come with you."

"I'll be safe with these fine fellows guarding me." She glanced at Aurora one more time. She hated goodbyes and turned back to Nigel before she cried. "Take good care watching over my cousin while I'm gone, sir. See her safe back to Lord Wharton's home and hold my secret as long as you can."

"Forever. I'll always do my best for you, Miss Hillcrest."

Eugenia nearly wept at the use of what she considered her true name. Mrs. Bagshaw was someone she'd never really been. Her marriage a brief dream—almost entirely forgotten.

She hurried across the cobblestones, keeping her steps light and quiet. A groom wearing no discernible livery held open a door and ushered her into the darkened interior.

Because the sun was not yet up and the carriage so dark, she did not immediately realize she wasn't alone. But when she did, she jumped, and a hand shot out of the dark to steady her.

"I could not let you travel all that way alone, Eugenia," Thaddeus whispered.

Eugenia threw herself into Thaddeus' arms and hugged him tightly. "I wanted to ask you to come with me so badly, but I didn't know how my request would be received."

"I was always coming with you. I just didn't want your cousin to know I was." Thaddeus cupped her face in his warm hands. "You could have asked, but I'm glad of the deception we managed. Now Aurora doesn't have to lie about my being with you."

She hugged him again. "Won't the duke realize you're gone?"

"I've gone to Hastings to inspect a mill, which he mentioned a need to see yesterday. Thankfully it is more or less in the direction you wish to go, too. South out of Town. I'll give the grooms new directions along the way," Thaddeus promised her, setting her back on her seat on the opposite side as the carriage got underway. "I hinted I might not return straight away. Exeter won't be worried unless I'm away longer than a week."

Eugenia nodded. "I hope that's enough time."

Thaddeus stared at her. "We'll be traveling as if we were brother and married sister. I'll secure separate chambers each night at the posting inns on our way south."

She nodded again. "If you feel we must."

"I definitely do. Until we find the mother, we should go on as if you were indeed a married woman and take pains to protect your reputation. But I also think we should use different surnames rather than our own."

"Is that really necessary? No one but Aurora and Mr. Bloom knows that I'm headed out of London."

"I think it is for the best to take all possible precautions. Wharton has a long reach. Even if Aurora holds her tongue, it is likely he'll send runners to every inn along all major traveling routes within a day's ride from London in search of you, once he discovers you gone and not with the imposter or friends. Let's not leave him an easy trail to follow."

"Oh, dear. Is he really so skilled at finding people who don't want to be found?" She gulped when Thaddeus nodded. "He hasn't found one single detail about the man pretending to be my husband yet."

"The lack of any information to find is telling in itself. There is nothing Wharton won't do or pay to uncover a secret, and," Thaddeus winced, "he thinks of you like family."

Eugenia worried her lip. If Aurora's plan to distract everyone from her whereabouts failed before nightfall, then they could expect to have Wharton's men hard on their heels tomorrow. And Wharton would not be happy about Thaddeus spiriting her from London, even if it was for support and her protection. Having them come to blows or worse was something she'd like to avoid. She nodded quickly, agreeing to his precautions. "So, a new name and a very discreet trip to Dover. Who shall I be?"

"Pick any surname you like, and we can practice addressing each other as such along the way. Don't worry about the grooms being surprised. They're familiar with my habit of traveling under an assumed name. My cousin taught me to do it all the time to avoid matchmakers."

"Smith," she suggested. "There's dozens of those in every town."

"And I'll be traveling as Mr. Fleming. The town drunk where I grew up," he grinned. "A man with six cousins of fearsome tempers."

She noticed the rising sun revealed they'd have good weather for the start of their journey.

"Where was it you grew up, Mr. Newton?"

"Mostly to the west, Mrs. Smith." He sighed, opening up his side of the carriage to look out, too. "My father had only taken up residence in Cornwell during the last years of his life."

"You don't sound fond of him," she murmured, setting her head back upon the squabs to watch the fleeting light dance over Thaddeus Berringer's handsome face.

"There wasn't much to be fond of." He looked down at his hands and clenched his fist. "He lived in expectation of inheriting the ducal title until the day he died. Lorded that fact over everyone."

"And then you became the duke's heir after he was gone."

"I ran away from my father's creditors banging on our door

day and night, and from the title I'd come to loathe as my eventual fate, since the duke had still not married by that time."

"You don't feel that way anymore, do you, about the title?"

"No. Sinclair has been a great help to me understanding the burdens and delights that will one day be mine and has shown me more kindness than my own papa ever could."

"I'm glad. It's obvious he means a great deal to you."

Thaddeus shrugged. "He's impossible at times, but I love him dearly. We became friends very quickly."

"And now that he's married?"

"He and his wife are my family, and both are dear to me. Almost the parents I never had growing up and full of wise advice," he said with a laugh. "Don't drink or gamble to excess, get enough sleep, and don't fall into the bed of a married woman because it will only lead to heartbreak."

"Sorry," she whispered, wincing.

"According to you, you're a widow, and we're on our way to prove that," he declared.

"I hope we can. It was such a long time ago. She might be dead."

He leaned across the carriage, caught her hand in his, and squeezed. "Let us hope not, and if she is deceased, we will question her neighbors and try to find out where Robert Bagshaw might be buried."

Eugenia sighed. "I would like to know where he rests so I can pay my respects. He was a good and honest man."

"The fellow we left behind stole silverware from Wharton's table yesterday." Thaddeus suddenly shifted to sit at her side. "I won't rest until we find your answers."

She looked up at him, saw that he was unhappy. She had caused that without meaning to. It would be days at least before she found any resolution to her questions, and he likely knew there might not be good to come of their journey. And even if they found Mrs. Bagshaw, there was still a slim chance Eugenia might be proven wrong about Robbie. If that happened, if her memory of Robbie was in error and she was truly married to that horrible man she'd left behind in London, she'd likely never be alone with Thaddeus like this again.

She didn't want to waste a moment of their cozy isolation in the carriage. She ought to ask Thaddeus all the questions she could imagine asking in case she might never have the chance again. But first, she had a particular thank you to utter to him. One more scandal to discuss, and only then could she pretend to be his sister. "I wanted to thank you for the time we spent together. I will treasure the memory of our trysts for the rest of my life."

A wry smile twisted his lips, and he nodded. "As will I."

She shook her head. She must stop thinking about their past passions now and focus on what was only possible between them in the future. She wanted to be his friend still. To know everything there was to know about him. "Tell me about your earliest memory of a birthday."

He looked surprised by her question. "My birthday. Why?"

"I'm curious, and it is easier to speak of the past before we met and not the present or the future."

He drew in a breath and let it out slowly. "Our cook always baked a custard on my birthday."

"I like custard."

He bumped her shoulder. "Now your turn. It's a long way to our first stop to change the horses. Tell me about your birthdays?"

"My older brother gave me a new dress when I turned seventeen. White muslin with sweet little bows across the bodice."

"I've never seen you in a pale color," he murmured.

She shrugged. "It doesn't suit my complexion."

"It isn't because you're a widow?"

"No. I've worn darker shades all my adult life. They wear better and don't show marks of age as easily. I once had a carriage fly past and splatter my pretty white gown with mud that stained. After that, I dyed those pale gowns a darker color and only had new gowns made for me in darker hues."

He nodded and then smiled. "I never had a brother myself. What did you like most about yours?"

"He was tall. So tall he used to hook his arm about my waist and lift me over muddy puddles so I wouldn't ruin my shoes. Brothers have many unexpected uses like that."

"I'll have to remember that one if it is raining when we stop to change horses, little sister," he teased as he looked down on her, smiling broadly.

Although he called her little sister, that smile made her want to burrow into his arms. But she couldn't do that anymore. He'd said he didn't approve of dalliances with married women. And for now, proven or not, she was one in his eyes. It wasn't fair that she could not be with the man she loved. Their affair had ended far too soon.

She inched toward the window away from him and looked out at the passing fields.

"Eugenia, what's wrong?"

"Nothing," she promised, feeling herself on the verge of tears. Determined not to reveal her upset, she kept her gaze on the view.

He set his hand on her shoulder. "It's not easy to be strangers again, is it?"

A tear spilled down her cheek, and she wiped it away angrily. If she didn't find Robbie's mother, she'd belong to another man forever. The thought was unbearable. She had to win freedom. "No, it is not. I like you. So very much, and I could use a hug for reassurance that everything will be all right."

"Brother's hug their sisters when they are upset, don't they?"

"Mine did."

He groaned, and she was dragged into Thaddeus' arms at last, and inhaled his cologne and felt his warmth and strength surround her. "It will be all right. I cannot believe otherwise."

She clung to his chest. "I couldn't live with him. I'm going to run away."

Thaddeus' lips pressed against her brow. "I won't lose you."

She laughed bitterly. "I will go away, somewhere he'd never find me."

"I'd find you. I wouldn't rest until you're safe in my arms again."

"I'd want you to find me, but never him." Eugenia burst into tears, ugly ones. Expressing all of the fear of losing her freedom that she'd repressed since the imposter had appeared at her door. She'd accepted she'd lose Thaddeus to a wife, but it wasn't fair that she might lose him to a husband of her own and a marriage she no longer recognized.

Chapter Twenty-One

AT LAST, the carriage rolled to a stop before another in a long line of splendid posting houses. Teddy's backside could use the release of getting out and walking about. Even though their long journey of togetherness was almost at an end, he would be grateful when it was over. He'd had quite enough of playing brother, too.

Even though he might have to give her up.

Forever.

Teddy did not think he could anymore.

He helped Eugenia from the carriage, concerned by her soft moan. She'd kept up a brave face over the last days of their journey, but she couldn't hide her worry from him.

Even though they'd been traveling at reckless speed, reaching Dover was taking longer than he'd anticipated. The more time spent in her company, the harder he thought their separation would be in the end. Yet he wished to stay with her to know what her future might be…and therefore his, as well. Hopefully, before Wharton found them together.

The innkeeper welcomed them like long-lost friends, directing them inside to a private parlor where they could refresh themselves.

Eugenia declined the invitation. "I should like to stretch my legs first, sir. Could you point me toward a pretty vista? I feel the need for a long walk."

"You go that way past the cobbler's and then turn left until you see the river. The mill is a pretty spot for a lady to walk to and not far at all."

"Thank you," she murmured and turned away.

Teddy quickly paid for their lodgings, paying above normal charges to ensure Eugenia's comfort, and sent his men and carriage off to be stabled for the night.

Although not invited to go with her, Teddy hurried to follow Eugenia. He did not know this village, and a lady alone on the cusp of nightfall might not remain unmolested by unsavory characters.

He caught up with her just as the river came into view.

She turned that way with a heavy sigh.

He tried to catch a glimpse of her face, but her bonnet shielded her from his view. "Are you sad again?"

"I cannot seem to help it. Tomorrow seems so far away still."

"We've made excellent time today, but the men need rest before we can go on."

"I do understand," she promised. "And I apologize for my impatience. I don't mean to be demanding or ungrateful."

She could have taken the mail coach, he supposed, and been there already. Bruised, battered and alone. Wharton might have expected that. Their slower journey, with stops each night, added to his anxiety. He forced himself not to appear worried, though. Being caught together was the least of her concerns. Teddy caught her hand and wound her arm through his. "Try not to think about tomorrow."

"There's nothing to distract me here." She looked about the little village. "This place reminds me too much of where I grew up."

"Mine, too." He pointed upward to a nearby empty hill. "That could almost be where my father's home still stands."

"Who lives there now?"

"I've not the faintest idea. I've always found looking back difficult, so I have not returned."

"That's all I seem to do now. Look back, doubt, and wish I haven't had my life turned inside out and upside down," she said and then sucked in a breath. "Do you see that small cottage far down the road? My brother's home was placed in a similar situation. I ran everywhere as a girl, from one end of the village to the other, and always arrived with my hair a mess."

"I like it when your hair is in disorder from my hands running through it," he whispered. He laughed at himself. Still flirting, even knowing he shouldn't. He looked for something else to talk about. "I had a pony as a boy, at least until my father sold it to pay off one of his debtors."

"He was in a bad way? Financially?"

He raked his hand through his hair. "He wasted money trying to impress people, to seem more important than he was, wasted his life waiting for something that would never be his."

"Do you feel that way too?"

"No. Never," he promised. "The duke allows me to come and go and learn from him. I'm grateful for his patience and the sharing of his vast knowledge. I couldn't imagine how I'd get on if I was denied his confidences. I'd be floundering for years, and the estate and tenants would likely suffer. And let's not imagine what might have happened should I have sat in the House of Lords unprepared."

"Inheritances can cause all sorts of trouble in a family," she murmured. "You are lucky to have such a peaceful existence."

"Hmm, that is true. I am on good terms with Sinclair's nephew and niece and their spouses, but Sinclair's main concern is that we'll fall out if he lives too long."

"How ridiculous."

"Not to him, though I try always to reassure him," Teddy shook his head. "He sees how it goes in other families where sons wait impatiently for their turn, and their wives whisper suspicions and schemes to speed a father's demise or curry favor with rivals into their ears. My father couldn't wait to claim the title."

She clucked her tongue. "If there is anything I know for a fact about you, it is that you'd never marry someone so shallow or mean-spirited toward your cousin."

"I'll try not to." Teddy studied Eugenia. She would not resent Sinclair if he continued to live as duke for a very long and happy time to come. But many ladies married with an eye on the next title their future husbands would inherit. At present, he hadn't a title. He remembered Lady Fuller very clearly as she lamented that he'd never possess a title until Sinclair passed away, and then asked after his health in the next breath. But titles were important markers of status and influenced precedence in so many things. A duke's daughter, used to leading most women at a dinner, would not easily come last because she'd chosen to take a mere mister for a husband—even if they had a bright future.

They paused by the river, and they both inhaled deeply. The view was lovely and soothing. The wind kicked up and tugged on loose tendrils of Eugenia's hair, blowing them about and making her seem ethereal in the failing light of day.

He could lose her to another man—a situation he found ever more intolerable as the days wore on.

He put his hand on her upper back, and she slid sideways into his arms to be embraced. They were good together—a perfect fit in attitude and background.

If only it were possible to remain together when all was said and done.

If not for Bagshaw's untimely arrival, he might have proposed to Eugenia already.

He glanced down, startled, at the woman in his arms and drew her closer against him. Letting the new idea that had come to him settle in his mind. Eugenia had said she loved him, and he'd not wanted to think of that before. He'd fallen for her, too. Would they have been happily married?

He imagined they might have been.

But with her having a husband in London, he'd never know now.

He released her slowly, cursing that fate might yet rip Eugenia from his life. Yes, he might marry her if he could. But that decision was yet another thing that must wait for tomorrow.

By mutual agreement, they walked slowly back to the inn side by side. An arm's length apart. There they would pose as brother and sister again for another evening, dining together, and then retire to their respective rooms alone until dawn.

He absolutely resented his displacement, but what could he do?

Nothing.

At the inn, the innkeeper's wife bobbed a curtsy and gushed over Eugenia's pretty pelisse and shawl as she took them from her, promising to take them straight up to Eugenia's room.

"The dining room is ready if you are at all peckish."

Eugenia glanced sideways at him. "I am indeed."

Teddy heard the longing in her voice and stiffened…everywhere.

He quickly removed his hat from his head and placed it strategically before his groin. Certain phrases and looks from Eugenia seemed always destined to torture him. He was fairly sure she didn't do it deliberately though.

He followed her into the dining room and requested a pot of tea for Eugenia and ale for himself. He could have gone to the taproom, and he might still.

The first night's stay of their journey had been hard, and he expected to miss her even more this evening when they went their separate ways. They had spent the entire journey talking and getting to know each other. So much more than might have been shared if he was ever to openly court her.

For instance, she abhorred dogs but loved sheep. On a farm, such as the duke possessed, there were plenty of both. When he had mentioned that, she'd claimed to have perfected shepherding without the use of dogs. That was something that could never have been uttered in polite society.

Since separation was still a few hours away, he decided to seek her counsel about a matter that was very much on his mind of late. And he suspected she might like the distraction of a subject quite removed from her own situation, too.

"I wonder if I might appeal to you for an opinion on a situation I find myself in, sister dear," he murmured after the maid laid out tea and ale on the dining table.

"I can try," she promised, pouring herself a cup, sugaring, and adding cream.

He took a sip of his ale and discovered it quite good. "I am glad for the changes in my life. I never would have amounted to very much if the duke hadn't found me." He sighed. "And because of my improved situation, I am able to do good for others now, too."

She nodded approvingly. "Which charities do you patronize most?"

"Not a great many yet, but my first was a family."

Her brow lifted in surprise, and she set her cup down. "Oh."

"Last year, I happened upon a group of children begging on the street."

"Homeless orphans are everywhere in London," she murmured.

"Very nearly every street corner or square," he agreed. "In this case, their mother was gravely ill, and my heart was touched by their desperate plight. I began to support them while ensuring she recovered, and continue doing so to this day."

Eugenia frowned. "Has she been unwell all this time?"

"She promises to be improving upon each visit."

Her brow furrowed even more. "How often do you visit her and the children?"

"I try to call every week, but that is not always possible with the demands on my time. They have servants and a house, etcetera, that I pay for."

"It is quite a commitment for a bachelor to take on a widow and her children." She paused and searched his face. "Forgive me for being blunt, but how committed to the woman are you?"

"Not in any way that affects us," he promised. "She is an ill woman and has no one else to help her. The children are a little rowdy at times, as all siblings can be, I understand, but utterly delightful. Smart and well-mannered usually to me. I'm determined not to let the family sink into poverty. I'll see to the boys' education, the girls' too, and clothe them all."

"I do hope the lady is suitably grateful," she said finally with a wide smile. "There are not many who would do half so much for their own family. You are most unusual in that."

"Perhaps it is the fault of not having siblings of my own. We are of a similar age. Sophie always tells me she appreciates my support and looks forward to my next visit very much."

"Sophie? Not Mrs." Her brow arched at his informality.

"I address her as Mrs. Darling usually. I only used Sophie for you. I assure you, nothing improper is going on between us and never will."

Eugenia mulled that over. "Hmm, if you give too much attention to the lady you are aware it might give rise to an expectation in the poor woman that she can always rely upon you. Forever."

"Nonsense."

"Then, in what way might I offer an opinion on the situation?"

He moved to sit closer to Eugenia. "I wondered how to gently broach the subject of her future without her feeling like I want to be rid of her. Making a second marriage will afford her a level of protection she currently lacks, and that I cannot forever offer."

"You do not need to make all her decisions, Thaddeus. She'll marry when she's asked, when she is feeling stronger. Have you considered that she'd have to go out to meet a suitor and be introduced to them by mutual acquaintances? Does she have many good friends, people of her class, who could do that for her?"

"I'm not sure. She did mention a friend had taken the children out for air the last time I saw her." He bit his lip. "I never thought to enquire about her other friendships when she's always so ill."

"Perhaps that is where you ought to start if you feel she has improved, thanks to your aid. You don't have to support her all of her life, or her children, either, to ensure they prosper. But it is good of you to worry about her so much. Many would have turned away from so desperate a family after the initial fear for her life was in the past."

Teddy brushed aside her praise. He'd done what he'd considered right at the time. Helping a family out of compassion for the children's likely suffering was a goodness his cousin had teased him about too. But he would do it again in a heartbeat and likely would many times over in the years to come. He threw a shy smile her way. "You called me by my first name just now."

"You use mine all the time without ever having to ask my leave," she teased. "Do you not like your full name?"

"I like everything of mine on your lips," he said without thought, then rolled his eyes at himself for starting up a flirtation yet again. He kept falling into that trap on their journey. They both did, and both of them took pains to try to act as if they hadn't afterward. It was deucedly wearying, but he might have a need to stick a pin in his tongue to keep it under control around her in the future. He sighed in exasperation. "It seems natural to speak plainly with you, along with so many other things we've done together."

She nodded. "I've become a corrupting influence on a very proper gentleman. Who would have thought it possible that the Duke of Exeter's heir could have his head turned by a spinster?"

"A widow and a wildflower," he corrected softly, "I've loved every moment of your wicked little heart's cravings." He stood, strode to the window, and leaned against the frame, pretending to be interested in the view. But it was no good. He turned to find her watching him, as he always wanted her to. Gods, this was sheer torture, ending things with her. "I wish only *you* to know my deepest secrets, and if I had my way, I'd want you to corrupt me forever," he whispered.

She laughed dismissively at his suggestion, but he was entirely in earnest. If he had a chance, he would marry Eugenia. But he might not be granted that wish tomorrow.

If she was married, he had to leave her alone.

Because there was a maid expected to return with dinner, Teddy excused himself to confirm all was in order with their rooms above in the inn, and then he'd check on the men, horses, and carriage in the stables, too. Anything to distract himself from thinking of the future he might miss out on with Eugenia.

His chamber was a narrow room at the top of the staircase, but he'd requested the largest room for Eugenia, which was supposed to be next to his.

He took the stairs two at a time and found his door easily enough. His luggage had already arrived. One of his grooms was acting as valet again tonight, and was lurking about the fire. A maid from the inn was supposed to be available to Eugenia whenever she had need of one.

He spied a connecting door between the chambers and frowned at it. That was something he'd not considered might exist in this inn. The innkeeper at the last inn had set their rooms farther apart than just one door. He went to the doorway, tested the door handle, and found it locked.

That relieved him.

His valet paused in the act of turning back his bedding. "If you want the key to that door, sir, I warn you it connects to Mrs. Smith's chamber. You'll have to apply to her to let you in."

"No. I won't need the key tonight." Best not to give in to temptation now. So far, he'd acted honorably and left her alone at night. But they still had miles to travel tomorrow before he found out if he could resume their affair, or whether he really had to let the woman he loved more each day go back to her husband.

Chapter Twenty-Two

Eugenia accepted Thaddeus' assistance to alight from the carriage late on the following afternoon. They'd halted at the bottom of a steep, narrow lane. She glanced around, noting the squalor of the neighborhood and the air of decay of all the narrow cottages. Beneath that she could smell the sea. She refused to look at it. "Are you sure your men found the right place?"

"I'm sure." Thaddeus moved closer to her, his touch light on her back. "Did you believe Bagshaw was a wealthier man?"

She glanced around, seeing nothing that reminded her of anything Robbie might once have described to her. "No, but I assumed his family was from a better neighborhood than this."

"It's been years," Thaddeus warned. "Perhaps they've fallen on hard times since?"

She nodded and tried not to worry even more about what she might find here.

Thaddeus tipped his hat to a local who had come out to stare at them from one of the houses. Their traveling carriage would draw even more attention the longer they remained.

Eugenia shivered and drew her shawl tighter about her shoulders.

"Take my arm," Thaddeus asked. "Stay close to me."

Eugenia nodded and slipped her arm through his. She was familiar with the dangers of traversing an area on foot where money was in short supply. While not rich herself, she might just be better off than anyone who lived here. Thaddeus' grooms fanned out before them, and some fell behind. Those in front knocked on doors and asked if anyone knew a Mrs. Bagshaw, along with the exact location of her home.

The first people they spoke to claimed not to know her and shut the door in their faces. But she caught glimpses of children running up the steep hill, jumping fences as they ran ahead.

"She must be here," she whispered. "Surely they can see we're harmless."

"We're strangers, and my men all carry pistols for our protection, but they won't use them unless we're in any danger," Thaddeus whispered. "Give them a chance to find the right house."

Eugenia squeezed his arm a little tighter. With Thaddeus so determined to remain by her side, help her discover the truth, she would never stop.

A groom knocked on a faded blue door halfway along the row. The door opened a crack, and someone inside spoke to one of his grooms. And then the door opened wider, and a tiny old lady appeared on the stoop. She raised her hand to shield her old eyes as she peered at them down the street. And then her hand went to her throat.

Eugenia prayed it was her and rushed forward to meet the woman. "Mrs. Bagshaw, mother of Robert Bagshaw?"

The woman drew herself up as tall as her five feet, if that, would allow. "I am. What do you want with me?"

She had fretted about how to introduce herself. The old woman may not even have known about her existence. After so long, she couldn't recall if Robert had written to his mother about her or had just planned to tell her after the marriage. She had decided to be honest from the beginning and hold nothing back. "I am Mrs. Robert Bagshaw. Eugenia. Formerly of Hastings."

The old lady's eyes widened. "It cannot be."

She reached for her reticule and the only proof that she had to verify she'd known the woman's son. "I have a letter your son gave me. If you would spare a moment of your time, I'd be very grateful if you would look at it."

The old lady glanced around suddenly. The neighbors were all standing in front of their cottages, doing little to hide they were watching. "You'd best come inside. Not much happens around here that others don't want to know about."

Eugenia exchanged a hopeful glance with Thaddeus and followed the tiny woman into a sparsely furnished cottage. It was only as wide as one room on the ground floor and likely the same above. There was a threadbare rug upon the front room floor where Mrs. Bagshaw led them and only a few pieces of hardwood furniture to be seen. But the cottage was lovingly kept. Neat and clean. The old woman went to sit by the fire on the only upholstered chair in the room, leaving two stools for them to sit on.

Eugenia moved her stool closer to the woman. "How do you do, madam?"

"Very well," she said, inclining her head toward her. But then her eyes flickered to Thaddeus.

"This is my…"

"Thaddeus Berringer," he said, apparently deciding that disguising his name was not necessary anymore. "I represent the Duke of Exeter."

"A duke," the old woman exclaimed and then stared at Eugenia in surprise. "What do you want with me? I don't have any money."

"Please, I want to know everything you can tell me about my husband?"

The woman huffed. "There's not much to tell."

"And his family," Thaddeus added. "Mrs. Bagshaw's memory of the time she lived as Bagshaw's wife is patchy at best. I hope her request is not too difficult."

The old woman glared at him. "Do you think my memory of my son could be flawed?"

Eugenia studied the woman. From here, she could sense no malice, but defiance. Pride, too. They could dance around the subject for an hour, and Eugenia would likely come away with no more knowledge than she'd arrived with if she didn't win the woman's cooperation quickly. It might be easier all around to come straight to the point with this lady. If she was her husband's mother, they were family.

"I met Robbie when I was three and twenty. It was just after my brother had died. He swept me off my feet, and he proposed the very next day. We were married a month later by banns, but he had to leave to return to you. He left very early the morning after we wed to travel by packet boat to Dover."

"You said you'd show me a letter."

"Yes, this is what I found he'd left on the hearth mantel after he was gone." She passed the letter over, and the old woman squinted at the folded paper. She stood and moved to the front window, squinting still to read the faded words of her son, who would have died the very next day by drowning, if what Eugenia had been told was true.

And then a sob tore from the old lady's throat. "He said he'd met a girl he wanted to marry and I could hardly believe it. But I always wondered what happened to you."

The old woman suddenly rushed away into an adjoining chamber.

She and Thaddeus exchanged a long look. They could both hear the rummaging around in the other room very clearly. A moment later, Mrs. Bagshaw returned with a second yellowed paper clutched in her hand. The paper appeared the same size and shape as Eugenia's letter from Robbie. As old, too, perhaps.

"He wrote to me before you must have married."

Eugenia took the note she was given and read it where she sat, but turned toward the light as well. Thaddeus likely couldn't see the words but was probably as eager to know what that letter contained as she was.

Eugenia cleared her throat and read it out loud.

My Dearest Mama,

It will no doubt surprise you to learn I intend to be married before I return home to you. I have met the most gracious and charming woman in Hastings that I find I cannot do without. Mama, I am sure you will grow to love her as I have, and at last, I will be able to make good on my promise to get you away from Dover for a quieter life where I can continue my profession in peace. My future wife has a home large enough for us all to live in, too. We might all be very comfortable and never bothered again. Make ready for your journey, dearest Mama. I shall come for you within a week of my marriage, and finally, you will be free of embarrassment.

Your loving son,

R. J. B.

"Robert James Bagshaw," Eugenia whispered as she wiped away the tear that had slipped down her cheek. She had forgotten until now that Robbie even had a middle name, but seeing the initials written down brought the knowledge rushing back.

She could understand Robbie wanting to move his mother out of this part of town. But Robbie had not told her that Mrs. Bagshaw should have come to live with them.

If only she'd known, they might not be the strangers they were today, and both their lives might have been very different indeed.

She took one last look at the letter, then folded it and handed it back to her mama-in-law.

She looked across at the older woman, who was clutching her letter, and Eugenia's, too, to her chest and did not ask for it back.

Thaddeus cleared his throat. "May I see both letters?"

Eugenia passed them over when Mrs. Bagshaw finally gave them up. Thaddeus spread both out upon his knees, comparing the handwriting in both. "Identical penmanship in every way," he murmured.

"Of course they are. I'd recognize my son's handwriting anywhere."

"Would you recognize him, too, even now?"

"What sort of a question is that?"

Thaddeus nodded slowly. "Madam, would you be willing to make a journey to London?"

The old woman stared at Thaddeus, eyes wide. "What do you expect me to do in London?"

Thaddeus glanced Eugenia's way, and she knew what he was about to say. "A man has recently come to London claiming to be Eugenia's husband, your son Robert Bagshaw, but she was assured that he drowned before he could reach Dover."

"My Robert *did* drown." Mrs. Bagshaw swallowed. "I buried him."

Eugenia rocked forward, nearly shedding tears in relief to hear those words spoken out loud. Robbie had not deserted her, and the man in London *was* an imposter.

"Not to be rude, but are you certain it was your son you buried?"

The old woman paled. "A mother knows her own flesh and blood when it is laid out for burial in her own parlor."

Thaddeus turned to Eugenia. "Then who is it parading about London, I wonder? You say he looks just like Robbie."

"Similar, but an imposter, obviously. Just as I said he was from the start." She gulped through. "A very convincing imposter in possession of my late husband's papers."

Thaddeus turned back to Mrs. Bagshaw. "Did Robert have a cousin who favored him in appearance? Or a friend that could pass for him who might know intimate details of his courtship of Eugenia?"

The old woman's eyes had narrowed, turning as hard as the sea. "His bastard half-brother could pass for him in poor light."

"A half-brother?"

"My husband's bastard comes around from time to time. Snooping and tormenting me with his face, so similar to my lost boy."

"Snooping?"

"Found him here six months ago. Cursed him to hell and back as he scampered away like the gutter rat he's always been. Hasn't returned since, but he stole from me. I thought it was just another way to hurt me because I won't have anything to do with the likes of him. If only Robbie had lived long enough for us to have met, I would have escaped him to live in Hastings with you and never had to deal with him again."

"What is your husband's son's name?"

"Calls himself Regis *Bagshaw*," Mrs. Bagshaw supplied with a grimace of distaste. "Not that he has the right to the surname."

"What sort of man is Regis truly?"

"Useless, good for nothing but scraping muck from the hull of a stinking whaler and stealing into places he doesn't belong. He is nothing like my son. My Robert was a good lad. Honest and kind. He never spoke harshly to anyone, except for that Regis."

"So Regis came here and took…how many letters did your son write to you?"

"Plenty. My son was smart and wrote to his mother every week he was away on business."

"And then so armed with your son's letters from here, knowing his life history and Eugenia's name, he must have decided to reinvent himself as Robert Bagshaw," Thaddeus whispered, disgust evident in his tone.

"But how did he get the marriage license? Robbie had that and the captain never returned any of his possessions to me." She looked at her mama-in-law. "Did you have our marriage license?"

"No. But Regis was following along from the dock when my son's body was brought to me. He had…" the old woman scowled. "He was carrying Robbie's trunk, but I never saw it again after that day."

"So he stole everything he needed," Eugenia sat back, appalled. "He might have even gone to Hastings. It's where Robbie and I married, and from there discovered where I'd gone to from the vicar or even an old neighbor," Eugenia mused.

"It's a fair conclusion," Thaddeus murmured. "Do you write to anyone in Hastings still?"

"Yes. A neighbor. I wrote and told them about Sylvia's

engagement to the Marquess of Wharton, but that was only last week."

Thaddeus rubbed his jaw. "He *could* have acquired the Albemarle Street address from someone in Hastings, come to London and learned you'd recently moved, and possibly followed you or your cousins back to Lord Wharton's abode."

She shuddered.

"I ought to give that weasel a piece of my mind for meddling with my daughter-in-law," the old lady complained suddenly.

"Could you come with us?" Eugenia spun to face the old woman. "Right now, Regis is making a nuisance of himself in London. We need to expose his lies and make it clear that I was never married to him."

The old lady nodded. "I would be glad to."

"We will see to your every comfort on the journey there and back," Thaddeus promised.

The old lady looked at Thaddeus. "This Duke of Exeter must be very fond of my daughter-in-law?"

"His whole family is," Thaddeus promised.

Eugenia put her hands over her belly. "If my memory of Robbie hadn't weakened over time," she said. "I would have remembered how often he wrote letters to you and come to you sooner. Regis claimed an injury of his hand had changed his penmanship when Lord Wharton made him write out his name for comparison to the license."

"I should have come to you, just like my boy wanted," Mrs. Bagshaw apologized. "But I couldn't leave Dover with him so recently buried here."

"I would have liked to have met you sooner." Eugenia smiled and looked up at Thaddeus, who had stood. "What more can we need to prove he's an imposter?"

"Well," Thaddeus sat down again, facing Mrs. Bagshaw. "Aside from taking this dear lady to London, I'm sure we can clear up any doubt about his good character, given he could be in possession of stolen property of Wharton's."

The old lady grinned evilly. "He won't be happy to see me.

I'm responsible for him breaking his arm when I caught him trespassing just after burying Robbie. He fell out the upper window, clutching his ill-gotten gains in his grubby hands. Dropped half of it before the neighbors chased him off."

"A career criminal. All the better." Teddy smiled in delight. "A confrontation involving Mrs. Bagshaw senior should unsettle him enough to reveal the true man behind the disguise. Would you happen to know if anyone in these parts remembers him well?"

"The local magistrate will."

"I wonder if he could be persuaded to travel to London to answer a summons from the Duke of Exeter. All expenses paid, of course."

The old woman's eyes were lit with excitement now. "I'll hit him again if it helps, too."

"Let's hope violence is not called for, but between you and me, I'd enjoy planting him a facer myself after his charade," Thaddeus confessed.

The old woman looked around suddenly. "What about my things?"

"I can leave a groom behind to watch over your possessions while you're gone. I can assure you everything will be as it is now upon your return. I'd like to leave tomorrow at dawn if that suits you both."

Mrs. Bagshaw nodded and then turned to Eugenia, her eyes pleading.

Eugenia glanced at Thaddeus. "Could we have a moment alone, sir?"

"Of course. I'll wait outside. Take all the time that you need."

As soon as Thaddeus was gone, the old woman smiled. "You've fallen in with important people since my Robbie died. I'm glad you had someone to look after you."

But Mrs. Bagshaw had no one. She'd been left to the uncaring and grasping attentions of her husband's bastard son. "My cousin, Sylvia, is to marry a marquess soon. My other cousin, Aurora and I, reside with them in a grand mansion in Mayfair."

"And who is this formidable duke Mr. Berringer speaks of?"

"His cousin. A friend, and a fine man for all that he's titled."

"Married?"

"The duke? Yes, to his childhood sweetheart."

"And what of this Mr. Berringer attending you? He seems quite invested in discovering the truth with you."

Eugenia had never been asked that question before. He was her friend and lover, but she could not tell her mother-in-law that upon their first conversation. "He is a man who seeks to right a wrong being done to me. He offered his help, carriage, and men, to find you. I could not have done without him."

"He's a good man then, and has my thanks for uniting us at last. Robbie would be glad you have so many who care about you."

Eugenia inched her chair closer to her mama-in-law. "I can't tell you how very satisfying it is to meet you at last."

"You must have thought the worst of my son after Regis' pretense. Imagined he'd not died after all, and he'd used and deserted you."

"Not for a moment," Eugenia promised. "When I looked in Regis' eyes, I saw a man I had never loved or ever could."

"My Robert would be glad to hear it. He was too often mistaken for Regis as a lad." The older woman's eyes fixed on her.

"Perhaps that's where Regis got the idea to become him," Eugenia mused. And she'd stop him as soon as possible. She stood and reached for her mama-in-law's hand.

Mrs. Bagshaw gripped her hand tight. "Did you have his child? My Robbie's?"

Eugenia winced. "No. We were together one night and then he was gone. It wasn't to be."

"I'm so sorry to hear it," Mrs. Bagshaw whispered, all the life draining from her. "There's nothing sadder than a woman without her children."

Eugenia swallowed a sudden lump that had formed in her throat. "Yes."

She'd never had a chance for a family. Love did not come along every day, nor did children if a lady took precautions. She regretted that was how it had to be. It might be nice to sit by a fire and have children playing at her feet, and to have a husband who loved her no matter what sitting in a window looking on. *Teddy.* She nodded. "Well. Until tomorrow, Mrs. Bagshaw."

"Until dawn, Mrs. Bagshaw." The old lady stood and escorted Eugenia to the door and beyond.

Thaddeus, the man she loved, was waiting on the cobblestone street in the company of his men, who were waiting to escort them down the steep slope to the carriage.

A pair of his men introduced themselves to Mrs. Bagshaw and promised to return before dawn to take charge of her house in her absence.

Eugenia waved goodbye to her mama-in-law and started down, holding tightly to Thaddeus' strong arm.

"I'm not married," she whispered.

"You're a widow, Mrs. Bagshaw," Thaddeus whispered back.

She winced at the name she'd never really thought of as her own for so long, but there was no escaping it now. She would have to adjust to it, answering to the name for the first time in four years. The elder Mrs. Bagshaw would certainly use it when she came to London with them, and so would everyone else eventually, too. "At least now I am able to always go about without a chaperone."

"What a lovely development for me," Thaddeus murmured as he helped her into the carriage. He spoke to the driver and then joined her in the intimately darkened confines.

Chapter Twenty-Three

Teddy had never known such happiness in his life. Eugenia was a widow, not a wife. The minute they were underway, he scooped her up from her seat and placed her firmly on his lap, straddling him, laughing as she squawked in surprise. He wrapped his arms tight about her and bent his head to rest against hers. "I feared I'd never hold you again."

She wriggled on his lap to loop her arms about his neck and clung to him. "I was right," she cried out softly. "I was right. He was not the man I loved and married. I'm free. I'm saved."

Teddy crushed her to him even tighter. "Thank God!"

She kissed his cheek. "I really can do as I please now."

The carriage curtains were still down from when they'd arrived and the intimate atmosphere was now charged with relief, and something more, too. "Are you all mine tonight, madam?"

"Most certainly, sir," she promised. "Do anything and I'll likely beg for more."

Teddy's fingers caressed her cheek and then dropped down to cup her breast. "I'll kiss you all over if you let me."

Eugenia silenced him with a passionate kiss, seemingly more than ready to return to the way things had been between them for yet another scandalous night. And then there would be many more after that. Nothing would stop them being together now.

She broke the kiss suddenly. "We'll need to wake early tomorrow and get that imposter out of my life forever, though. I dread to think what he's accomplished, strutting around using Robbie's name while we've been gone."

Teddy rubbed her back and then set his fingers to encircle her middle. The gift he'd given her was fastened about her waist. That made him smile. "We cannot travel at a reckless pace with Mrs. Bagshaw in the carriage tomorrow. But I agree, we should waste no time returning to London."

Teddy eagerly awaited the moment when Wharton set his foot to Bagshaw's backside and propelled him back to the gutter where he belonged. But Teddy also wished he could be the one who got the honor. If he could be there to see the imposter get his comeuppance, that would be enough.

Eugenia moaned as the carriage rocked her sex against his hardening cock. He tightened his grip on her hips to incite her passions higher.

However, Eugenia seemed distracted and flicked a curtain back briefly to look outside at the passing houses. They had already reached a better class of neighborhood. "Where are we bound?"

"To an expensive inn. To celebrate," he promised with a smile.

"To make love?" she asked with a shy smile.

"We will have to be somewhat circumspect there," he warned.

She pouted. "Surely we will not have to pretend to be brother and sister again."

"No. I have another idea for tonight," he swore to her. "A Mr. and Mrs. Hais will break their journey at this inn."

"Hais?" Eugenia climbed off him and resumed a seat on the opposite side of the carriage. "I thought we were done with disguises?"

"Not quite," he admitted. "I've learned to use a vast assortment of false names when I travel. I posed as a groom on my own carriage just last month to avoid a matchmaking mama cornering me. The groom wearing my clothes had a good laugh when she found him instead of me sitting in the carriage with his feet up on the seat."

"Ingenious." Eugenia laughed but then quickly sobered. "I *am* sorry Robbie died, you know."

"I know, and I'm sure Mrs. Bagshaw understands that, too,"

he hastened to assure, leaning forward to take her hands in his again. "But he died a long time ago and you've no cause to feel guilty over his death. He had your love, and that is a precious thing indeed."

Eugenia stared at their joined hands a moment before looking up. "Robbie never told me of his plans to bring his mother to live with us."

"Given what we both just saw of where she lives, it's understandable he'd want to. They'd have both had a very different life in Hastings with you."

"They'd have been away from Regis," Eugenia whispered. "I think she's afraid of what Regis might do if he returns to Dover after the unmasking."

Teddy sat back. "If all goes well, he won't have a chance to bother her again."

"He's been a nuisance all his life and he might just try to punish her for helping me escape a marriage with him, and the riches he must think he could claim through my connection with Lord Wharton." She looked up at Teddy. "I'm going to help her move somewhere Regis can never bother her. She is family, after all."

It was an admirable ambition but helping others was not always easy. "Get to know her first. I suspect Mrs. Bagshaw senior will not find it as easy becoming accustomed to living in higher society as you have."

She looked at him in surprise. "Who says I'm comfortable in society?"

"You fit there as well as I do," he promised with a wink.

To him, Eugenia seemed a natural part of the tapestry of London. Not a leader by any means but an accepted part. The longer she moved in society, the more she would belong. Just like he would.

"She could live at Albemarle Street."

"Regis could easily discover her there alone," Teddy warned.

"I'll go with her."

He drew in a sharp breath. "Would you really leave Wharton's protection, and your cousins, too?"

"I have considered it for a while now," she admitted. "I also thought it would be more discreet for us to meet there instead of slipping away together and running the risk of being caught kissing in the closets."

"I worry about that, too." Teddy huffed. "But you'd miss your cousins, surely?"

"After this past week, I know I'd miss you more if I couldn't see you," she promised. "You could call on me there, at Albemarle Street, without having to pretend you just happened to bump into me."

Teddy nodded. "I want to be with you whenever I can, but I also do not want you to do anything you would regret."

"I assure you, I regret nothing about you, sir, or ever could."

It hadn't ever been easy to see Eugenia. His busy schedule of travel would continue. They'd been lucky so far to sneak off together at some events, but that wouldn't always be the case. He didn't want to lose their intimate connection, but he also didn't want to be without her company in society, either. If she left Wharton House and there was an enduring scandal over Regis' claims and her pretense of being a spinster, Eugenia's name might be dropped from any number of hostess guest lists.

Of course, marrying her would prevent that from happening.

The carriage rolled to a stop outside a prosperous-looking inn and Teddy alighted to secure their best pair of rooms. The name Mr. and Mrs. Berringer rolled off his tongue instead of the lie he'd originally intended to tell of their names here.

Once spoken, though, he couldn't change it. Here, they would be known as husband and wife. Here, he would make love to a woman who said she didn't want to be a wife to him or anyone.

But did she feel differently now?

He was sure of his own feelings on Eugenia's place in his life. He loved her and wanted marriage now. Yet, not too long ago,

Teddy had intended to spend this one season without committing himself to any woman.

But somehow, he *was* committed. His happiness had become wrapped up in Eugenia's completely.

He led her inside, fighting a smile, and upstairs to a pair of pleasant rooms. Eugenia frowned as the innkeeper's wife addressed her as Mrs. Berringer, but requested dinner be served to them in two hours, here in their chambers instead of below in a private dining room.

When the doors closed, he stood rooted to the spot.

Eugenia's gaze rose slowly to meet his.

It felt like an eternity since they'd been alone in the same room when it was only days, really. He didn't quite know how to start again.

But Eugenia must have, because she rushed across the room and flung herself into his arms.

"My love," he whispered.

Eugenia pulled his face to hers and kissed him soundly. "My darling man. How I have missed you touching me!"

With her fingers already in his hair, her body rubbing against his, Teddy decided that discussion of the future could wait until after they'd made love—if he really needed to say anything more. They belonged together, and he would not deny his attraction to her.

Teddy wrapped his arms about her body, ran his hands up and down her spine as they kissed with increasing urgency. As ever, they seemed in perfect harmony in matters of pleasure. Eugenia whipped his cravat away, just as he started on the buttons of her gown.

He peeled the fabric from her shoulders roughly, and her gown fell to the floor under their feet. He shrugged off his coat and waistcoat with her help and kicked off his lower garments, too as she removed her undergarments in a hurry.

Eugenia stepped back until she hit the wall. Her eyes were full of mischief and desire as she waited for him to follow.

Damn if seeing her standing there wearing nothing more

than his gift of a chain about her waist didn't decide him on how they'd make love. This was not the time to worry about the niceties of lovemaking and foreplay.

"Beautiful, as ever." He wanted her now.

"Come here and take me in your arms again," she said with a husky edge to her voice.

He crossed the distance between them in two long strides and swept her up against him, so her feet no longer touched the floor. Her slim legs wrapped around his hips immediately.

"You're so soft and warm against my skin," he told her.

Eugenia looped her arms about his shoulders and tousled his hair. "You're hard where it counts," she whispered, dropping her eyes to where his eager cock already nudged against her curls.

Teddy framed her face. "I want you just like this. Here against the wall."

A slow smile twisted her lips as she adjusted her position. The tip of his cock came to rest against her warmth. He'd denied himself the pleasure of this on the journey to Dover, but now he had no reason to hold back.

With one slow thrust, they were as one again.

Eugenia let out a gasp, *yes,* as he reached her limit and drew back, only to thrust again.

Teddy closed his eyes, buried his face in her neck and got lost in the wonder of her passionate responses.

Eugenia gasped as she crawled toward the pillow on the large bed, her body damp and trembling from exertion. "Sir, you go too far."

"You goaded me to do it, and you enjoyed every wicked kiss, I'm sure."

"Yes," she admitted sheepishly. She collapsed, wrung out from yet another explosive orgasm thanks to her lover's wicked tongue. Except she had never imagined his licking her bottom would drive her so quickly toward her second peek. "I need a moment."

His lips brushed the base of her spine. "I agree."

Thaddeus rose from the bed, and Eugenia rose to watch his muscled form retreat to the washbasin. He lathered his hands, soaped his face, and then rinsed his skin clean. When he finally returned to the bed, swaggering across the bare boards naked, swinging his cock suggestively, she couldn't help but laugh at his antics. "You are impossible."

He dropped a kiss on her shoulder. "I am a man in love. Utterly without shame, too."

While Eugenia blinked and tried to accept his claim of love, he climbed onto the bed, over the top of her, and flopped down onto what she was already considering his side. He was an expressive man. He hid nothing of his desires or his feelings, it seemed, when they were alone. But it was difficult to believe he had fallen in love with her, too.

"You said you loved me," she whispered.

"I do."

"Are you certain?"

"Absolutely. I wanted to tell you before, but then at the same time, I learned about Bagshaw."

She turned to look at him. "You thought you shouldn't love me?"

"Yes." He struggled to get under the covers and then pulled her tight against his side. "I wanted to shout out my joy when Mrs. Bagshaw declared you a widow and not a wife. Thought it would have been bad form and cruel to be happy to know her son's demise was in fact true."

"I'm glad as well."

But that felt wrong to say out loud. Meeting Mrs. Bagshaw had reminded her of what she'd almost had so many years ago. A chance to have a home and a family of her own. Children. To be loved and adored and worshiped, and always respectable.

She didn't need all of those things, but to be free to love again was a heady joy. To be loved by someone, too, well...she'd not expected that at all yet. But she did have such strong feelings for Thaddeus. She just wasn't sure if she should repeat them when she was quite unsuitable to be his wife now she was scandalous. She was hardly a proper candidate to become a duchess if he even wanted to ask her to marry him one day.

Which he hadn't hinted at, save for that one time when they'd talked about how well-matched they were in passion.

She rubbed herself against him now and earned a chuckle and a kiss.

"Can you be ready to leave before six o'clock tomorrow morning?"

"Yes. I suppose you're eager to get on with your errand for the duke, too."

"The duke can wait. It never was urgent that I go there. But I wanted to give you a good reason to accept my assistance out of London, so you wouldn't refuse my company. It was a long way to travel alone, and I couldn't bear the idea of further separation. And what if Regis had followed you all the way to Mrs. Bagshaw's house? If he's as cunning as your mama-in-law makes out, you'd better be prepared and well-defended when you see him next. He could be dangerous."

"He wouldn't touch me," she replied.

"A husband has the right to do anything he wants with his wife, short of murdering her, which some men have gotten away with." He glanced down. "What would have been his if we couldn't have disproved his identity? What would he have taken from you?"

"Albemarle Street is leased in Wharton's name, but my possessions there would have passed to him, and the little money I had saved up." She sighed. "And Wharton has mentioned a desire to settle a dowry on Aurora, and me, too, though I have fought against the idea all along."

"I hadn't heard that you had a dowry."

"It seemed unnecessary. I wasn't looking for a husband myself. I'd hoped to see Aurora make a match first."

He nodded. "Did you inherit property from Robert?"

"I don't know. I suppose Mrs. Bagshaw's house might be mine unless there's another male relative somewhere who takes precedence. Nothing, of course, can go to an illegitimate brother. I'll enquire about any estate when I know her better. She might not like the question asked too soon. She's a proud woman, and Regis has already taken so much from her. I've no interest in taking from her, too. She's already lost her son."

"I'm glad you found her."

"So am I," Eugenia said and then shuddered. "Imagine if she'd been left to be pestered by that scoundrel Regis."

"We'll deal with him together," Thaddeus promised.

"Wharton could have him charged or insist upon some other punishment for his crimes of theft."

"Given what we heard of him, that is possible, too," Thaddeus agreed, kicking his feet out of the blankets. "Pretending to be someone else speaks ill of his honesty and character."

Eugenia sat up, face flaming. "I am ashamed of myself. I was wrong to forget Robbie. He was a good man, and I loved him with all my heart once. I should have been his widow proudly instead of pretending I'd never met him."

Thaddeus was silent behind her. She turned to look at him. He smiled and moved a tendril of her hair from her cheek. "You didn't mean to do it, and I believe that."

She shook her head. "I hid his existence from my cousins. It has taken me too long, but I must embrace who I really am. Eugenia Bagshaw, a wicked widow. I need to look forward again, but also remember the past."

Thaddeus rolled to his side and resting his head on his hand. "What will you look forward to?"

She sighed. "Endless parties, maneuvering to curry favor, dull dinners with too many handsome bachelors who know I'd never expect a marriage proposal if they seduce me."

"Widow's do have more freedom, Eugenia. There will be parties, but perhaps the kind of invitations you'll get now might never have come the way of a Miss Hillcrest. Maneuvering to slip away with a lover after dinner for a stolen kiss or caress will be a great deal easier, and highly desired by many men. I'll have my work cut out for me keeping my place in the front of the line."

"You've nothing to fear," she teased. And then took a steadying breath before announcing, "Loving you has been the highlight of my life."

His eyes lit up with surprise. "You've been mine, too."

A blush suddenly warmed her cheeks, and she looked away. Admitting her feelings a second time for Thaddeus had not been as hard as she'd feared it might be. Now that was done, they could go back to their affair again.

Thaddeus suddenly rolled out of bed to pour a glass of water for himself. He came to the end of the bed with it, his face serious again. "I have to leave you behind early tomorrow morning. I should not travel back to London with you in the carriage, so I'll ride on horseback and go ahead. There's no telling where Wharton might have positioned men upon the road, and I have my errand for the duke to explain where I am coming from."

"I feared you would decide to do that," she told him. "But I do understand why you wish to avoid any scandal that might force a marriage between us."

"Better to decide to marry than to have the decision made for us. I will be at Wharton's at three o'clock on Sunday, which is approximately when I hope your carriage might arrive back in Town. I'll speak to the coachman and make sure he knows what is expected of him to time the arrival perfectly. No diversions. No delays for any reason. I want to be there with you when you face Regis again."

"I want you there, too. We've come so far together."

"Thank you. I want to be there for other reasons as well. It could be an ugly confrontation, given all we heard yesterday from Mrs. Bagshaw about Regis."

He went to his traveling trunk, where he rummaged around. He returned with another delicate object glittering in his hand. "A chain for your ankle, to match your necklace."

She smiled in surprise. "It's beautiful. Where did you get it?"

"From the same merchant where I bought the longer chain."

"Is there more to come?"

His eyes narrowed, but he was smiling. "There might be. I'm not sure I should tell you about the others just yet."

She admired the chain about her ankle and the one around her waist. By wearing Thaddeus' gifts there, hidden beneath her clothes, she would always have a token of his regard and secret love.

She caught his face and kissed him soundly. "Tell me about the others when you're ready."

He nodded. "When Regis is well and truly out of your life once and for all."

Thaddeus dove back onto the bed and placed a kiss on her ankle over the chain he'd just given her. When he continued kissing, moving higher with each one, and she didn't ask him to stop. His kisses always aroused her and left her wanting so many more. She'd set aside her desires for the man she'd come to love once and wouldn't do without him again.

She guided his head between her legs, trembling at the first lick of his tongue across her quim. The most wonderful thing about her lover is that he did just that.

He loved her…and she never wanted their affair to end.

Chapter Twenty-Four

TEDDY ARRIVED BACK in London the evening before Eugenia was due to arrive in the slower-moving carriage, exhausted and mud splattered. His first port of call the next morning, though, was to visit Mrs. Sophie Darling and her children in Duke Street, and check that all was well.

He was days late in checking on her, thanks to his trip with Eugenia, though he felt no guilt over that. He regretted nothing of that trip to Dover. He was completely and utterly in love and knew what should come next in his life, once the drama surrounding Eugenia had subsided and Regis Bagshaw was put in his proper place.

He drew his horse to a halt before the townhouse he'd leased for Sophie and dismounted, staggering a bit as his legs adjusted to his weight again. The hard ride back to London had left him aching and in need of rest. Getting back on his horse this morning had been a painful experience, but as he'd rode, he gradually had grown more comfortable.

There was a hitching post outside Mrs. Darling's home and, as usual, a willing urchin appeared out of nowhere to watch over his horse for the price of a shilling.

He glanced around the street, surprised to hear the sound of feminine peals of laughter echoing off the townhouses. Someone was having a remarkably good morning.

He struggled up the stairs to knock on Mrs. Darling's home.

The butler he'd hired appeared, but the man seemed uncertain about letting him in. "Is there a problem?"

"No sir, but…"

It was then that he realized the laughter was coming from

inside Mrs. Darling's home. Concerned a visitor might be taking advantage of Sophie's weakened state, he barged past the butler and burst into the parlor, intending to ask the woman to moderate her tone.

But there was no stranger, only Sophie, sitting across a gentleman's knee.

And Mrs. Darling was not just laughing with the man, she was kissing him, too!

He averted his eyes quickly and cleared his throat repeatedly.

"Oh! Good lord, sir," Sophie cried out, jumping off the man's lap. "I wasn't expecting you to call today."

He heard the rustle of fabric and a whispered demand from the strange gentleman she'd been on top of to explain who "he" is. *He* being Teddy.

"It's only my landlord."

Given that Teddy funded Sophie and her family completely, and had done so for so many months, he was highly offended by her reply. "Landlord? I suppose you could put it that way."

The old fellow frowned. "I thought you said he was old and walked with a limp."

He stared at Sophie, incredulous about that description. She had the sense to look guilty for a moment, but it only lasted a moment before her smile reappeared. "I didn't want you to get the wrong impression, Commodore." She turned that smile on Teddy. "Sir, I'm so happy to see you've finally come about the rent."

"Rent?"

What the devil was she talking about? She paid no rent. He paid the lease out of his own pocket for her.

"I'll settle the bill now, Commodore, and be right back. If you'll just come this way, sir." Sophie took hold of his arm and propelled him into a nearby chamber and firmly shut the door. She turned swiftly, frowning. "Ooh, you're going to spoil a perfect day," she complained.

Teddy folded his arms over his chest and glared at her. "What game are you playing with that poor fellow, madam?"

"Nothing that concerns you, sir."

"It bloody well does concern me what goes on under this roof," he nearly shouted. He quickly regained hold of his temper but continued to glare at the woman who he'd expected to find alone or ill. "I won't have that fellow coming round and taking advantage of you in your weakened state."

She pinched the bridge of her nose. "Oh, are all men blind? Your toplofty ways were the reason I couldn't take you into my confidence. A more proper man has never lived than the heir to the Exeter estates." She moved to sit on the window seat, and Teddy followed, annoyed.

"I had no idea you despised my aid."

She huffed. "How would you know, when you never stay more than a few minutes at a time? The commodore was aboard my husband's vessel. He had a soft spot for me while my husband was alive—but I never encouraged him, I'll have you know. Now I'm widowed, and he is too, he's been coming round to check on me. If I'd told the commodore I was squared away because of your aid, he'd have never kept coming back so often."

There was a strange sort of logic to her words, but Teddy still didn't like being misrepresented. "So, your plan is to…what?"

"Marry him as soon as can be." She waved her hand at him, where a thin gold band now adorned her ring finger. "The commodore has just made me an offer, and I accepted. I am the happiest woman in all of England!"

"Congratulations, madam," he said dryly. But then he peered at her. "Is it my imagination, or are you in perfect health?"

She waved her hand about airily. "My malady comes and goes."

"That is not what you told me at any time that I called," he ground out.

"If I'd gotten better too quick, you'd have withdrawn your support, and I couldn't be sure of the commodore until he proposed today."

He gaped. "What manner of woman are you?"

Sophie pouted. "A lady who'd never have lifted her skirts without a marriage proposal first, not even for a duke's heir."

"I wasn't going to ask you to," he hastened to declare. "Ever."

She glared at him, and he glared back, and then her anger faded from her face. "You didn't have to say it that way."

Teddy rolled his eyes. "*Devil take it!* Did you really believe I was waiting for your health to improve so I could seduce you?"

She twirled a lock of hair around her finger. "Well, I am very pretty."

"Not enough to tempt me."

Her gaze grew definitely frosty. "The commodore likes the way I look just fine," she announced and shrugged. "I'd best return to my commodore before he gets jealous that we're all alone."

Teddy shook his head. He'd been played for a fool by the widow, and she was still intent on using him to further her hold on the poor commodore. "He's no reason to think I'd want you that way unless you suggested it," he said with more spite in his voice than he probably should have.

"You don't have to take that tone with me, Mr. I'll-one-day-be-a-duke-Berringer." Sophie smiled tightly. "Don't you dare ruin this one chance for my children and me to have a settled life with a good man. I love him."

Teddy squared his shoulders to respond but before he worked out what to say next, she flounced out of the room.

He should by rights warn the commodore that he'd been lied to about Sophie's arrangement with him here, but…what good would that serve? Teddy had hoped one day that Sophie would find herself a husband and a good life elsewhere, hadn't he? She claimed to be in love, and the commodore had liked her enough to propose. It could be a good match for all he knew.

He followed Sophie back to the sitting room where the commodore was sipping port, despite the early hour of the day. Several of the children were there now, too, and after being greeted by them, they went off to their own games somewhere in the house as if he didn't matter to them anymore.

He felt a pang of loss, but it lasted only a moment.

He'd just been a means of survival for all of them.

Sophie slipped from the room shortly after a period of awkwardness, promising to return in several moments with a fresh glass for Teddy.

After her steps could no longer be heard, the commodore cleared his throat. "You mustn't think badly of her."

"For what?"

"Pretending her generous young patron didn't exist. I knew she'd fallen on hard times and that someone had to be paying her way," he murmured.

"She was near death when I met her," Teddy warned him.

"Yes, her oldest boy told me how you charged in to save her life, fed them all, and moved them to better lodgings here. I am beyond grateful for your intervention while I was away, but if you don't mind, I'd like to be Sophie's hero from now on."

Teddy studied the fellow. There was apparently no reason to warn the commodore. He'd already seen through Sophie's lies and still wanted to marry her. It was only Sophie who believed continuing her deceptions were necessary. "I have no objection so long as you treat her well, and the children, too."

The man nodded, sipping his port. "The eldest wants to go for the navy like his father did, so I've found him a place with my old ship."

"Mad for the navy, he's been. He'll be grateful, I'm sure," Teddy mused, remembering their trip to the docks only a month ago and the boy's excitement. The boy had known everything that there was to know about the vessels docked alongside. Teddy had learned a lot from the boy that day. "I was going to see if I could help him gain a commission… Well, none of that matters now, I suppose."

The commodore pursed his lips. "My Sophie treated you ill, sir, but you have my undying thanks for being a good and decent man who only wanted the best for her and the children."

Teddy nodded and decided not to waste another moment here. Sophie and her children would be adequately cared for by the commodore. "If you don't mind my asking, where will you all live when you are married?"

"Dover. I'm retired now, been staying at a hotel not far away so I could be close to Sophie. I gave up my commission when I set out to find her, you see," the commodore confessed. "Got a nice pension from the navy, and we'll do all right living with my old mama. Going to leave this place by week's end, by the by, and move in together there. Servants are keen to come with her, so you needn't worry about their wages anymore."

Teddy nodded. It seemed that his aid was no longer needed for anything but ending the lease when Sophie and the children had moved out. The cunning Sophie had certainly fallen on her feet.

Since she hadn't returned, and it never took this long to find a fresh glass even in a mansion, he realized she wanted to avoid speaking with him again. It was the perfect time to make his own escape. He had nothing more to say or do here anyway.

He nodded to the commodore, "If you'll give my apologies to Mrs. Darling when she comes back. Tell her I wish her all the best in her new life."

The commodore frowned at the far door to which Sophie had disappeared through, clearly disappointed not to see her return, but then he shrugged. "Thank you, sir. She'll be sorry to have missed your leaving."

No, she probably wouldn't be.

Teddy saw himself out.

It was only when he was stumbling down the front stairs to retrieve his horse that he realized he'd never actually been introduced to the commodore by name, or the commodore to him, either. He shrugged away the slight and turned for Mayfair and home.

The first person he saw there was Exeter.

"I heard you were back," he cried, jumping to his feet in the library and rushing over. "Why didn't you wake us?"

"You were sleeping," Teddy reminded him. He glanced down

at his clothes. He wanted a bath, and then a change of clothes before meeting Eugenia at Lord Wharton's house.

"How was your journey?" Exeter asked, offering him a sherry.

Teddy declined. "Good and bad. I never actually made it as far as the estate you wanted me to inspect."

"Nothing wrong with you, I trust?"

"No. Nothing at all." He glanced at the duke, hating that he'd have to lie to the man. But it was impossible to tell him the truth about Eugenia yet. "I, um, holed up in an inn for a few days with a lovely distraction on the way south."

The duke blinked, and then a slow smile crossed his face as he sat down. "Happens to all of us at some point."

"You're not angry I didn't get to see the estate for you?"

The duke patted the empty cushion beside him. "Your life shouldn't be all work and no play, Teddy. The estate purchase wasn't urgent."

"I'm glad." He sat and stretched out his legs with a groan. "I should go and catch up on some sleep. I left the carriage behind to ride for the return."

The duke chuckled. "Tell me about your lovely distraction."

Teddy laughed. "Beautiful and smart."

The duke nodded. "Those are excellent qualities to look for in a wife."

"I agree with you."

The duke sipped his drink and stared straight ahead. "Are you in love with her?"

"Yes."

The duke sucked in a breath. "Will it pass?"

"No."

The duke exhaled. "I am happy for you, but also…"

"Don't be worried. I know what I'm doing," he promised, as he slapped the duke on the knee.

"Everyone thinks so, usually until it goes horribly wrong." The duke pulled a face. "If it really is love, don't let her get away."

"I have no intention of letting that happen."

The duke grinned. "When do you plan to see her next?"

"Today."

"So, she's now back in London, too." The duke raised a brow. "Will I eventually meet her?"

Teddy put his hand on the duke's shoulder as he raised himself back up to his feet. If he sat still for too long, he was afraid he might nod off sitting upright. "You already have."

The duke gaped. "Really? Imagine that. Well, well, well."

"You've introduced me to a lot of women, Sinclair, and she's definitely not the woman you're thinking of."

Teddy poured himself a drink from a crystal water pitcher.

"Never thought you'd look at any of my suggestions twice. Miss Waters?"

Teddy tossed down the contents of his water glass and refilled it. "No, not even close. I've always said you are quite terrible at guessing games, cousin."

The duke grimaced. "Impertinent pup."

"Grumpy old duke," he replied, smiling.

Sinclair, despite being called grumpy and old, laughed. He ought not to tease Sinclair about so important a subject, but he couldn't seem to help himself. He was in too much of a good mood, despite his tiredness.

He was going to ask Eugenia to marry him as soon as her scandal was taken care of.

"It is no one you might imagine I would pick, but she will be perfect for me and, like me, will also expect you to live to a ripe old age of eight and one hundred years."

"Ripe?!"

Teddy laughed softly. "Perhaps I could have phrased that better."

"Indeed, you should have," he said, bristling a little. "I do not smell, sir."

His grace, the Duke of Exeter, took control of his body odors very seriously. He bathed frequently and applied cologne in strict moderation. Teddy wished other lords would adopt his good example, especially when they were all crowded together.

"Don't think I didn't notice you've increased the age I must live to by another five years."

"That's just for starters," Teddy promised.

The duke suddenly beamed. "When can we expect to host a dinner in her honor?"

"When the time is right and not a moment before. I haven't asked her to marry me yet."

The duke made an unhappy sound.

"Don't be concerned. She knows I love her."

"Then what is the holdup?"

Teddy tried not to grin. He'd be having this same discussion with Sinclair until the day he announced his engagement, most likely. Sinclair would continue to pester him, and Teddy would do his best to evade giving an actual answer. It would be interesting to see if Sinclair ever guessed correctly, though. "Where is her grace today?"

"Visiting Lady Wharton to see if there is anything we can do." The duke's eyes widened. "Oh, do you even know the fuss that's gone on while you were away."

"What fuss?"

The duke leaned forward. "Sylvia Hillcrest's cousin has disappeared. Poof. Gone in the dead of night."

He pretended to be shocked. "No! Which one?"

"The smart one? The eldest."

"Miss Eugenia Hillcrest," he murmured, suddenly missing her very much. It had been a whole two days since he'd stood in the same room with her. Leaving her to travel alone had been hard, but she'd had the company of her mother-in-law to amuse her along the way.

"No, it's Mrs. Bagshaw now. I thought you were here for that development."

"Yes, of course, I was, but it slipped my mind while I was away."

The duke refilled his glass. "So, the lady has been pretending to be a spinster when she was a married woman all along. And then one night without warning, she was suddenly gone. No one knows where or how. Wharton is furious. So is her husband."

"What's been done to recover her?"

"Runners were sent out, but Wharton is said to have suspected the husband of abducting her. It was a vile confrontation between them, I hear."

Teddy winced. "Did they come to blows?"

"No. The husband accused Wharton of spiriting her away. Wharton denied any such thing. Many expected Wharton to call him out for the suggestion of interference in the marriage, but he didn't."

"Wharton doing nothing is impossible to imagine. What *did* he do?"

"Called off his search entirely, saying that Bagshaw could look for his wife himself and pay the bill for it. Personally, I think Wharton is waiting."

"For what?"

"For Eugenia to return with proof the fellow is an imposter. She's claimed all along apparently that the man couldn't be her husband."

Wharton was a smart man. That explains why he'd noticed no sign of pursuit on the way back from Dover. He wondered if Aurora had told Wharton the truth of where Eugenia had gone and why, or if he'd figured out her intentions for himself. "An imposter? I don't believe it!"

"You really do need to keep an open mind in matters of the heart, cousin. Before she disappeared, Mrs. Bagshaw did admit to being a wife but insisted that the man claiming to be her husband was an imposter. Public opinion sways to and fro on whether to side with her or him at this point. Either way, after this, I doubt she'd ever be welcomed in society very often."

Teddy straightened, alarmed by the news. "Surely you would not give her the cut, too, cousin?"

"No, most likely not, but I am only one man. It is the hostesses who will remove her from any invitation lists. They can be quite vicious when a lady fails to meet their high standards."

Most of the hostesses were married, and many conducted illicit affairs. Hell, he'd been propositioned by quite a few just in the last month because he was a duke's heir. They had no moral high ground to stand on with him. If they cut Eugenia over Regis Bagshaw, he'd give them the cut direct, too. "I would believe Eugenia any day. If he turns out to be an imposter, that is hardly her fault."

"Yes, true. But," the duke said with a smile, "these are the thorny problems I happily leave in my wife's capable hands nowadays."

The Duchess of Exeter, a woman from a common country upbringing rather than descending from a regal family, would likely welcome Eugenia into her home. And when they were known to be married, everything would be quickly smoothed over.

But that might not be soon.

It all depended on Eugenia's wishes for the future. He hoped she could see the way forward as he did. Always together.

Chapter Twenty-Five

Eugenia was tired. Tired of waiting to take back her life. The journey from Dover to London had seemed interminable. The only bright spark had been spending so many hours getting to know her late husband's mother. Jeanne Bagshaw was a proud woman. Devoted to her son's memory and furious with Regis Bagshaw's deception.

So angry that Eugenia had enlisted one of Thaddeus' groom to follow them inside Lord Wharton's home, to make sure she didn't commit murder upon the first sight of Regis. He would pay for his crimes but at the hands of the authorities only.

Mrs. Bagshaw clutched her old and worn reticule tight. Everything about the woman was that way. She'd suffered hardships the likes of which Eugenia could never imagine during her long life. She had sold most of what she owned to survive this long. Taken in boarders, strangers, some of whom had used her ill and stolen from her, too.

Although Thaddeus had left a man behind to guard her home, Eugenia hoped to convince Mrs. Bagshaw not to go back to Dover. They were family, and the lady was in need of comfort and protection in her twilight years. If she could be persuaded to consider the idea, Eugenia hoped to convince her to remain in London with her at Albemarle Street.

The carriage turned into Cavendish Square, and she soon saw the grand residence of the Marquess of Wharton.

No one there knew that she was coming home today, but she would waste no time freeing herself from her unwanted marriage that had never been real.

The carriage drew to a halt, and Mrs. Bagshaw looked out

and up at the facade of the mansion. She squinted at the building and then nodded. "Is this it?"

"Yes. My cousins reside here. I cannot wait for you to meet them."

"I look forward to that, too," she promised. "And you're sure that villain will be here?"

"If he's not, Wharton will send for him when I ask him to." Eugenia drew in a steadying breath. "Regis wants me, and what little money I have and the connections I've cultivated. I cannot imagine he'd have left London emptyhanded," she promised.

But she hoped he had gone while she was away. She wanted never to see him again after today, if he'd not. She wished he'd never come and dug up her sad past. Her consolation was that her family would rally around her. Her cousins had believed her, but without proof, no one else would have.

And Thaddeus loved her, too.

A groom put down a step and helped her out, then turned to help Mrs. Bagshaw. She looked left and right, hoping that Thaddeus had already arrived before them. She wanted him to see Bagshaw get his comeuppance.

Eugenia took up Mrs. Bagshaw's hand to guide her up the front steps. A groom had already knocked to alert the butler of her return. She murmured her thanks to the groom as she passed him, knowing he'd disappear with the carriage as soon as he possibly could.

Wharton's butler beamed at the sight of her. "Miss Eugenia, the marchioness and your family will be overjoyed to see you safely returned!"

"Thank you, sir. Rest assured, I was never in harm's way. Please assure everyone in the household that I am the picture of health and happiness."

"I speak for the entire household staff when I say we are delighted to hear it."

Eugenia gestured to her mother-in-law. "This is a very special guest of mine. For the moment, I will not give you her name, but she will be staying with us for an indeterminate length of time."

"A pleasure to meet you, madam. I will have a chamber close to yours prepared within the hour." He nodded and smiled at Mrs. Bagshaw, who was currently gaping up at the high painted ceilings as if she'd never seen such a thing before. She may well not have, too.

"Well, isn't this fancy," Jeanne finally muttered to herself.

Eugenia had gotten used to her improved surroundings, but that would never mean she wanted to live in a rarified world such as this all her life. She longed for her quiet home, and for Thaddeus to be there with her, too.

The butler smiled. "The marquess indicated he was very eager to speak to you upon your return."

She nodded. Wharton was no doubt livid with her for running away without leaving a note of her whereabouts behind. But he was not her brother, who could give her orders that she had to obey. She would remind him of that when they spoke if he gave her any trouble. "We should like to wash our faces before speaking with him, though."

"Of course. The morning room is presently unoccupied."

"Good." Given the increase of women in the house, the purpose of that chamber had been restored to regular use from being a smoking room. The morning room was also connected to the lower retiring room, where ladies freshened themselves up and fixed their hair. Eugenia led her mother-in-law there, explained the plumbing of a water closet, and left her there to splash some water on her face at a basin. She smoothed her hair back into some semblance of neatness.

Mr. Bloom rushed in tea and little sandwiches on a silver tray and wore a beaming smile of welcome.

"Here you are," he promised, "just the way you like it best, and a bit to eat as well."

"That was very kind, Mr. Bloom. Thank you."

He stood back and bowed. "My pleasure. Always."

He backed away when Jeanne emerged, although it was clear he'd hoped to talk with her further.

Jeanne's face lit up when she saw a tea service and plate of sandwiches waiting. But then she startled when Aurora and Sylvia burst into the room and rushed to embrace Eugenia.

She was enveloped in the warmest welcome of her life from both of them. "I found proof," she whispered. "I'm free."

Each of her cousins fought to hug her tight again.

Aurora whispered, "I haven't slept a whole night through since you've been gone; I was so worried. Mr. Berringer and several others arrived half an hour ago."

"None of us have slept," Sylvia promised.

She faced Sylvia, worried that she'd be angry about being left out. "How is he?"

"Wharton? Worried about you, of course."

"I meant the imposter. Regis Bagshaw, my late husband's illegitimate brother."

The pair gaped.

"That explains the similarity of his face," Aurora murmured. "Regis Bagshaw is eating well while pretending to care about your disappearance. He comes each day and makes demands that Wharton trot you out, but only after eating a seven-course luncheon," Aurora added.

"He tried to stay here overnight once, wanted to search the house for you, too, but Wharton nearly knocked his block off for the insult that he might be complicit in your disappearance," Sylvia murmured. "He's here again now, consulting maps of London in the library with Wharton. He did not see you return, but Wharton surely will know you are back."

Mrs. Bagshaw rattled a teacup and saucer somewhere behind Eugenia's back.

Eugenia turned quickly. "Forgive us, madam. Might I make my cousins known to you?"

Mrs. Bagshaw inclined her head as regally as the marchioness was prone to do.

"This is my cousin Sylvia Hillcrest, who is to marry the Marquess of Wharton in the near future. And second but never truly second to anyone is my other cousin, Aurora Hillcrest.

Ladies, I have the honor of introducing to you my mother-in-law, Mrs. Jeanne Bagshaw of Dover."

Both dipped deep curtsies. "It is an honor to finally meet you."

"And you. Beauty I see runs in your family, Mrs. Bagshaw."

"It does," Eugenia promised, her heart so full of happiness at being with her cousins again that she was nearly in tears. She glanced at the door. "Do you want to see the imposter thrown out on his ear?" she asked her cousins.

"Wild horses couldn't drag us away from the spectacle," Aurora promised.

Sylvia moved to the door and held up one finger. "Let me go and check that everything is ready. Just wait here a moment longer."

Aurora went with her, so Eugenia sat beside her mama-in-law, drank some of her tea, took a few bites of the sandwiches, and felt better for it.

Jeanne smiled sadly. "You're lucky to have a loving family."

"There's always room for one more. Will you stay with me after Regis is taken care of?"

Jeanne looked around the chamber, seeming to shrink into herself. "I don't know if I could. I'm almost afraid to breathe in this rarified air."

"My cousins and I used to live in Albemarle Street, some distance away. Our home was much less grand, but it was cozy and warm. I had thought to return there when my cousin married, and the marchioness' health had improved."

"All by yourself?"

"Aurora might have come, but I wouldn't have pressured her to. I'm sure you and I could be just as comfortable there as anywhere."

Jeanne looked around again. Clearly she was considering it, but hadn't made up her mind yet.

A tap sounded on the door, and Mr. Bloom appeared. "Lord Wharton wishes me to inform you that he and Mr. Bagshaw are ready to speak with you in the library."

"Thank you." She turned to her mother-in-law. "Ready?"

Jeanne grasped her faded old parasol and brandished it as a weapon. "Death to the imposter!"

"Well, perhaps not death. I wouldn't want his blood spoiling the floor rugs in this mansion."

Jeanne glanced down and winced. "Probably a good idea. They are too lovely to have soiled by his blood."

"Follow me so we can surprise him." Eugenia went first through the door, Mrs. Bagshaw's steps following close behind. The doors to the library were flanked by two footmen, who grinned to see her and opened them smartly.

The first thing she saw was Wharton. His face was a masterpiece of inscrutability. She had no idea if he was angry or relieved to see her, so she moved into the chamber and waited for his explosion. Bagshaw had been standing with his back to the door, speaking with Sylvia as they studied the map.

Regis Bagshaw suddenly turned, saw her standing there, and then rushed toward her, hands outstretched as he cried, "Darling, where have you been?"

But he never reached her. Never got within six feet actually, because Jeanne Bagshaw stepped directly into his path, parasol pointed at his gut. "Grubby little no-good urchin! How dare you come near my daughter!"

Time slowed for Eugenia as Bagshaw tried to avoid being skewered by the furious old woman. His body arched away from the point, and he stumbled backward. "Mama!"

"Don't mama me, you greedy pretender. You were never good enough to lick the mud off my Robert's boots!"

He glanced around, eyes pleading. "But I am your son, Mama. Don't you recognize your own little Robbie anymore?"

Mrs. Bagshaw turned. "Didn't I say he'd suggest I was losing my mind?"

"He is very predictable, isn't he?"

"Never did have much of an imagination. Always did copy my Robert."

The marquess stepped forward and placed a restraining hand on the parasol. "Who is he?"

"My husband's *other* son. Regis Bagshaw. A bastard he got on a whore down by the port. Everyone there knows his face. A certain magistrate from Dover is eager to become reacquainted with him upon his arrival in London."

"So it's true this Regis character looks similar to your son, Robert?"

"Not to me. Same color eyes but my Robert's tilted up more at the corners. He was a happy boy, my Robert. Always good to his mother," she said, and then scowled. "But this one would sooner spit on me than pay me the courtesy of taking himself away."

"And how does he know about Eugenia?"

"Stole the letters I kept from Robert describing meeting Eugenia from my home six months ago."

"Those were my letters! I diligently wrote to you whenever I was away. I showed you some as proof, my lord."

Eugenia moved up to stand beside her mother-in-law. "He didn't show you all of them, my lord. What of the last letter?"

Mrs. Bagshaw lifted her chin. "The one where my son made me promises he would have kept."

"I…" It was clear to see Regis was floundering now. He snapped his fingers. "Let me see the letter to refresh my memory," he said. "And then, of course, I will happily fulfill every promise I ever made you both if it's in my power."

Wharton held out his hand. "Madam, if you'd be so kind as to show *me* that letter first."

Eugenia encouraged her mother-in-law to share. "You can trust the marquess."

Mrs. Bagshaw pulled the much-folded last letter from her bodice and reluctantly passed it over.

Wharton read, and his eyes widened. "Now that is generous indeed."

Regis hurried to Warton, attempting to read over his shoulder. "What does it say!"

Wharton moved away from him, squinted at the lettering. "Appears genuine and very much in the style of past correspondence from Robert Bagshaw. How do you still have it, madam?"

"I keep it with me always." She pointed to her chest. "Here, where it couldn't ever be lost."

Wharton folded the sheet and promptly handed it back, and the letter disappeared down Mrs. Bagshaw's bodice very quickly.

Regis Bagshaw grimaced, deciding not to pursue the object.

Wharton stood back, and his eyes narrowed on a distant door. He nodded, and from an adjoining room, a half dozen lords Eugenia knew well spilled into the room, Thaddeus included.

She was so relieved to see him she almost ran to his arms.

"So now, gentleman, we are faced with a conundrum. This fellow doesn't recall what's in the letter he was supposed to have written to his mother. I think it unlikely he could have written it and forgotten. And yet, it was a long time ago."

"I am truly sorry to have the matter slip my mind."

"My Robbie would never have forgotten any promise he made to his mother."

Lord Hurlston smoothly stepped between Jeanne and the imposter. "Was it jewels, a new shawl, or a bigger house, perhaps? Only the real Robert Bagshaw would know."

"A new shawl for her to wear to church on Sundays and a pin for her best dress," Bagshaw exclaimed. "That must be it. I was always bringing her back pretty trinkets from distant parts."

Eugenia smiled. "Not even close, Regis."

He glared at her, his jaw firming. "Be quiet, wife!"

Teddy was suddenly at her side. "Have a care how you speak to her, sir. You are not standing in some low dockside brothel in Dover anymore."

Wharton held up his hand for silence. "On the one hand, we have written proof that Mr. Robert Bagshaw was deeply in love with his new wife, Eugenia, and on the other, you claim you'd quarreled with her, leading to an abandonment of the marriage."

Regis' jaw set into a hard, mulish line. "It doesn't matter what happened then. She is trying to escape her vows now, when the law says she's to do her duty to her husband."

Wharton grinned. "That letter actually promised that Robert and his mother were finally going to escape *you* by moving away to Hastings."

"The hell it did! Robbie would never abandon his own flesh and blood."

Eugenia smiled. Regis had just described Robert as a separate person to himself.

Mrs. Bagshaw slipped around Lord Hurlston, finger raised and pointing at Regis. "My Robbie was tired of your grasping ways, spoiling his friendships and always begging for a handout. And when he died, you kept up your begging with *me*, pleading with me to take you in. Poor Regis lost his big, wealthy brother. But I had already caught you stealing things that belonged to your dead father, claiming you had the right to take them when you don't even have a right to bear his name! I wouldn't have you in the house."

"He was my father, too," Regis growled. "My brother. They loved me."

And there was further proof of his deception, right from his own lips.

"Robbie was ashamed of you. Always grasping after something you didn't deserve." Mrs. Bagshaw gestured toward Eugenia. "Like her. She's too fine to be your wife."

"I'd treat her well."

"Robert Bagshaw was twice the man you'll ever pretend to be," Eugenia said quietly. "You could never take his place in my heart."

He came forward, hand raised to slap her, but Thaddeus was faster and blocked the attempt. He twisted the man's arm, forcing him to bend low. "I wouldn't do that if I were you."

When Thaddeus released Regis, he drew back, but he was captured by a pair of burly footmen. They gave him no choice in staying as they dragged him from the room.

"I appreciate your intervention, Berringer." Wharton nodded, pulling down his waistcoat. "And you too, Hurlston. I was not expecting violence. Thank you."

"Anytime."

"But now I must ask you to leave. My betrothed's cousin has had an eventful day and is in need of rest."

"I'm not tired," Eugenia protested.

"Good, then we will speak about your disappearance." Wharton nodded to Thaddeus and the others. "Sir, gentlemen, this is a family matter now, and the least number of ears to hear what I say next, the better. Please show yourselves out."

Eugenia could protest Thaddeus had been an integral part of her disappearance, but that would raise eyebrows. For now, he had to leave, but she hoped he would return soon. They were not done with each other by any stretch of her considerable imagination.

She bid him goodbye, easily seeing his reluctance to go.

But he nodded and left her to her family.

"Come with me," Wharton started, turning on his heel and striding off—clearly expecting her to obey and follow. She considered rebelling, but he had the housing of her, and very generously too.

"Go with him," Sylvia whispered. "It will only take a minute. Mrs. Bagshaw and I can become better acquainted while we wait."

She supposed she owed Wharton a version of the truth. "All right."

She found Wharton pacing his study. "Shut the door," he demanded.

Eugenia frowned, worried by that. Nothing she could say to him was so very private from her cousins that a door had to be shut.

"Please," he asked again.

"All right." She shut the door and moved to the center of the room.

Wharton rushed across the chamber and hugged her. "Don't

you ever run away from us again!" He released her just as quickly and moved back a few feet.

Eugenia, who'd never had much to do with Wharton, stared at him in shock. The man raked a hand through his hair, making it stand up on end. "Are you well, my lord?"

"Eugenia, you worried me half to death!"

"I was only gone a few days."

"Too many days," he complained.

She exhaled. "I had to prove I was right."

"I know. I didn't like it, but I always knew deep down you'd come back when you found something or someone to contradict him."

"From what Mrs. Bagshaw tells me, he has been trading off my late husband's identity all his life. I had to stop him."

"The magistrate and I will deal with him from now on, Mrs. Bagshaw."

Eugenia winced. "I suppose I must be that woman now. But on the bright side, you need never worry about having a chaperone for Sylvia or Aurora, if I'm with them."

He scowled. "There is that, but I fear you'll find yourself in the center of a whirlwind, now you're back. The word is already spreading that another Hillcrest has angered me."

"How is my widowed state something to be angry about?"

"Well, I've been introducing you, along with your cousins, as unmarried women. Potential wives. Gentlemen need to know they can count on me speaking the truth."

Eugenia shook her head. "I never asked for you to do that. I can find my own husband if I should ever want one."

"Your cousin did," he warned. "Sylvia is of the belief that both her cousins should have their own households."

"I do already. Albemarle Street."

Wharton sucked in a sharp breath. "You cannot move back there alone. I forbid it."

Eugenia waited for the marquess to consider the impact of his words before she answered him. "I am going to choose to believe you said that, in that tone, out of a desire for my cousins and I to stay together."

"That is how I meant it."

"And I do want to remain close to them. However, I have another concern now. Mrs. Bagshaw is my family, too, and she is not suited to living here. Not yet anyway. I want her to remain with me, but I think she will not fit in here in this grand house. So, I am moving us, Mrs. Bagshaw and I, back to Albemarle Street to live for the foreseeable future. Aurora will make her own choice about where she stays, but I am certain she will agree to remain with Sylvia to protect her reputation until you marry."

Wharton appeared aghast at her plan. "There's room here for another woman."

"It is not in my mother-in-law's nature to enjoy the excesses of society. Do not fear, Wharton, for I am sure you will see quite enough of me in the weeks and years ahead."

"But Sylvia—"

"I will make her understand my decision," she promised. Sylvia wouldn't like it, but her heart was here with the marquess and marchioness now. Had been for many months. She stood. "Try not to worry, my lord. There are no more skeletons in my closet to upset you."

"Next time, come to me for help first."

She smiled serenely. "Wharton, you are forever trying to fix things."

"I want you to be happy."

"I am," she promised, heading for the door. "More than you'll ever know."

She was a widow, a daughter-in-law, and she supposed a secret mistress now, too. She could openly wear the gifts Thaddeus had given her about her throat, and few would care or question where they came from. She had the best situation possible. Happiness without restriction. Love without end—and a lover with an equally wicked mind to hers.

What more could she possibly want in her life?

Chapter Twenty-Six

TEDDY FLICKED the summons he'd received from Wharton across his thumb the next morning, puzzled by the summons from his friend. He'd been invited to arrive at ten o'clock, when he hoped to discover how Eugenia and her mother-in-law had fared last night at Wharton House. He quite hated that he'd been sent away yesterday, but how could he complain he'd a right to stay?

Not that he truly had any rights where Eugenia was concerned yet. But he had been instrumental in saving her from a marriage to an imposter.

He was not quite sure his involvement had gone completely unnoticed, either. It was his carriage and his men who had delivered Eugenia back to Wharton House after all.

He peeked across Cavendish Square from his carriage, a little worried, to be honest, about what sort of reception he might receive. But he noticed a string of carriages lined up to drop off their passengers.

Feeling somewhat relieved to not have to face Wharton alone, he gave his driver instructions to deposit him at Wharton's door as soon as possible.

He received a warm welcome from Wharton, who was pacing the front hall upon his arrival.

"Good to see you," Wharton said as he rushed to shake his hand. "No hard feelings about driving you off yesterday?"

"None at all."

"Good. Well, it seems everyone has answered my summons to discuss the latest development. We're in the library."

"What development?"

"I'll not repeat myself," Wharton warned, and left him to follow behind.

Teddy feigned nonchalance as he strolled inside Wharton's library, but quaked when he saw quite a crowd had been gathered. There were all of his friends and a number of ladies, too.

Miss White was present, sitting on a chaise beside Aurora and Sylvia Hillcrest at the front of the room, but Eugenia was nowhere to be seen.

He found that troubling.

He took a seat at the back of the chamber and crossed his arms over his chest, worried about where she was hiding herself. If Wharton had thrown Eugenia out over hiding her married name or the imposter that had tried to take her away, there would be trouble.

It was probably time he started asserting himself in society. Even if the idea of it sat ill with him.

"Thank you all for coming," Wharton began, calling everyone to order. "I consider you all good friends who deserve to hear the truth from me directly, rather than from nasty gossips later."

"That would be appreciated, Lord Wharton," the elderly Lady Bisley declared, looking around. "I hardly get out of bed for anyone at this hour."

Wharton cleared his throat. "Not long ago, a man came to my door claiming to be married to Eugenia Hillcrest."

A hiss of shock swept through the crowd, although most would have heard something by now. The rumor mill ran at full power during the season.

"Now, while it is true that Eugenia was married once, she believed the man dead and buried four years ago."

"She must have been very young indeed," Lady Bisley observed.

"She married at three and twenty, and I'm sure you could do the mathematics to decide her age now."

Teddy did, discovering Eugenia was slightly older than him. How had they managed not to have discussed their ages?

Wharton continued, "Her relationship with her late husband amounted to a brief courtship and one night as a wife before a separation. She was informed from all reliable sources of the death of her husband by drowning two weeks after the marriage. She never had cause to question the information she was given.

"She went about her life trying to put that brief happiness and loss behind her, moved to be nearer to her cousins, but due to her grief clouding her judgment, she continued to describe herself as a spinster, possibly out of embarrassment that her too brief romance hadn't lasted."

"What a foolish thing to do. My best days were always as a widow, not a wife," Lady Bisley said out loud, causing the room to erupt with laughter.

"It was never with malicious intent that she kept the truth from her relations or from society," Wharton promised. "It is a mistake she regrets very much."

A murmur of disapproval swept the chamber.

Wharton held up his hand for silence. "Now, I know what you're thinking, and I want to apologize to any man who is inconvenienced if they thought Miss Eugenia Hillcrest was an innocent. I know you'd likely preferred to have known she was a widow all along, but it is probably best for our friendship that I never had to call one of you scoundrels out."

More laugher, but of the nervous kind, could be heard. Wharton played his audience well.

"Mrs. Bagshaw was always in the company of her cousins or my mother here, and to my knowledge, never developed a tender for any one of you, or you for her, I suspect."

"I always found her quite charming and a model of maidenly decorum." Lady Bisley peered about the chamber at all the rogues. "I should hope none of you have any cause to regret not seducing one more widow."

A burst of laughter swept the room.

Wharton huffed. "Eugenia is and always will be dear to my mother and me."

Hurlston raised his hand. "What happened to the fellow who claimed to be her husband? Is he in custody or will he escape the consequences?"

"Since Mr. Robert Bagshaw is quite deceased, and *Regis Bagshaw* has been pretending to be him for some time, he remains in custody until such time that a particular magistrate who traveled all the way from Dover can be heard. Robert Bagshaw's elderly mother has confirmed she buried her son, and that it was her husband's bastard son parading about using his name. It was an offensive masquerade, and I intend to see him prosecuted for every offense possible."

Lord Sullivan slowly raised his hand. "Where is Miss Eugenia Hillcrest now?"

"In disproving Regis Bagshaw's ruse, Eugenia has, at last, made the acquaintance of her mother-in-law. The elder Mrs. Bagshaw is now in need of a home and loving family to care for her. They have removed to Albemarle Street until such time as Mrs. Bagshaw senior has become accustomed to life in the city and greater society."

"Was that her idea or yours?" Teddy asked, pretending to be learning all of this only now like everyone else.

"Entirely hers," Wharton promised with his hand over his heart. "She considered it a kindness for Mrs. Bagshaw, who was ill at ease here in our home after just a few hours. I did try to talk her out of going," he promised.

The room erupted in more laughter. "Easier to part the sea than change a woman's mind," someone called out.

"Not an easy feat," Lord Sullivan mused out loud. "The former Miss Hillcrest has always been a woman of decidedly firm opinions."

"As I have discovered. Stubbornness is possibly a Hillcrest character flaw, too? What do you say, my love?" Wharton asked as he smiled down on his future bride sitting in the front row.

Sylvia protested, "We are no more difficult than a certain marquess."

He laughed at that and turned back to address the gathering. "Now I understand there'll be some talk of a falling out between the two families, as happened once before, but I assure you, I consider Eugenia to be part of my family already. Under my protection still, if not my own roof. I will take offense if I hear any ridiculous assertions of strife or disrespect—and don't any one of you think to seduce her. You may circulate that threat to any and all who care to keep their health."

There were more laugher and other questions, but Teddy tuned them out. He should have guessed that Eugenia would return to her home immediately. She'd thrown out enough hints about missing being mistress of her own abode.

As the gathering broke up and people started to disperse, Aurora approached him. "Sir. Might I speak with you a moment?"

He inclined his head. "Miss Hillcrest. Of course."

"Did you know she would leave us?"

"I had a feeling. You did not want to go with her?"

"One of us must stay with Sylvia to prevent tongues wagging even more than they must be already about our living arrangements."

"Everyone is aware of Sylvia's devotion to the marchioness, and the marchioness' dire need for Sylvia," he promised. "I'm sure you made the right decision, but it cannot have been an easy one."

"It's only been a few hours since she left, but I miss having Eugenia here already." She suddenly looked behind her.

Scarsdale was watching. She flicked her fingers at the man, and he stalked off in a huff.

Aurora sighed. "He's such a pest. I'll have to speak to Wharton about his lurking today."

Teddy nodded, glad to hear it. "I'm sure he'll take care of the problem for you, but remember you still have Sylvia here."

"She's often preoccupied, and will be even more so when she's finally wed. When she does marry, I'll almost be alone, I suppose."

"You'd be welcome no matter where Eugenia lived," Teddy promised and then winced as Aurora's eyes lit up with excitement. "And I'm sure you'll always be wanted by Sylvia, too. I don't know what to advise other than patience and trust that everything will work out."

"Hmm, I suppose you're right. You've always been so easy to talk to, Mr. Berringer, but I just worry about the sort of men who might call upon my cousin when I'm not there. She's a widow now, you know. Are you going to call on her today? I'm sure she's missing you."

He glanced at Eugenia's cousin and saw a hint of teasing in her expression. The woman was aware of their affair and clearly approved of it continuing. "I'm not sure if it's the right time."

"You should go today before someone else tries to take your place," she warned. "As a spinster without funds, she was popular enough for conversation, but imagine how the line of scoundrels will form once the word spreads that she's actually a widow. Even with Wharton's threats."

Teddy inhaled sharply as he realized Aurora was probably right. He pressed his lips together. His heart was already entwined with Eugenia's. There hadn't truly been enough time to talk about their future yet, but there would be one. He wasn't about to let the perfect woman slip through his fingers. "It is fortunate that I have my foot in the door, so to speak."

"I'd suggest you speed your feet to her door as a matter of urgency today, sir. I clearly heard someone here mention calling on her just now. You wouldn't like to be pushed out of the running from someone with a larger foot or a heavier purse."

"How is it that you understand your cousin so little?" he whispered. "A sense of humor, a trim figure, and a wicked imagination are what Eugenia's heart desires. Apparently, I possess all three, so no one stands a chance."

"I hope that's true." Aurora linked her arm through his, and they took a turn about the room together. "Tell me more about this wicked imagination of yours."

Teddy laughed. "Not in this room and not without Eugenia present."

Aurora pouted. "So unfair."

"Stop flirting with me. There is only room in my heart for one Hillcrest, and it is not you, I'm afraid." And since he knew a thing or two about how close the cousins were, he added, "You can ask Eugenia about me, and she'll answer if she decides she wants to share the details or not."

Wharton approached. "We're going out."

Aurora clapped her hands. "Where are we going?"

"Never you mind," Wharton chided. "This is a gentlemen-only outing."

"Oh, you men have all the fun," Aurora said before she flounced off and disappeared out the door.

Aurora Hillcrest was incorrigible. "Where are you going?"

"The club, Madam Bradshaw's, and other places where gossips gather. I want to stay ahead of the rumor mill this time."

Teddy considered going along to help with that, but he wanted to see Eugenia more. The hours of their separation weighed on his mind—along with his need to learn her plans for the immediate future from her own lips. "I have an appointment."

Wharton nodded. "Very well. I will see you another day, then. Please ensure anyone you speak to has the right story, especially his grace."

"I'll make sure I tell him everything he needs to know."

Teddy headed for the door and accepted his hat from the butler on his way out. He'd sent his carriage away and might have had a long walk ahead of him to Albemarle Street. But he hailed a hack and settled back to think. The journey gave him time to consider all he'd heard today.

Despite Wharton's views on the subject, Eugenia likely wouldn't return to live under his roof anytime soon, which would make calling upon her at Albemarle Street easier, and also more noticeable if he did it too often.

And if his activities were commented upon, word would spread back to Wharton, and Exeter, too. He hadn't told his cousin who he'd fallen in love with yet. He'd also been quite clear with Eugenia that he hadn't been ready for marriage when they'd started up.

If he didn't propose immediately, or she wasn't keen on the idea at first, they would have to be extremely careful continuing their affair. But their relationship had changed. They could never be occasional lovers again, or even mistress and protector as Aurora assumed he might want to be.

No, they were at the start of something that would last a great deal longer than a few nights of mutual pleasure.

All he needed to do was make it clear that Eugenia was the woman for him.

Nothing less than marriage would do. He needed her to have no great fortune or experience of society. Like him, she could learn what she needed to know over the coming years of their marriage. Teddy watched the passing parade of grand houses as the carriage continued south with a feeling of excitement growing inside him. If they were married soon, whenever he turned around, she'd be somewhere nearby, and whenever she desired to see him, too, she could.

He wasn't so foolish as to assume she'd readily agree to wed in haste, of course. She had a mother-in-law to think of now, and becoming a duchess one day was probably as frightening to her as becoming a duke had been for him in the beginning.

If they spoke of their fears with each other, as they'd already been doing so far, he could avoid the marriage mart completely but probably not a courtship. Eugenia deserved to be singled out for attention like any other woman.

But in full awareness that his intentions for his life had dramatically changed because of her.

He found himself at her door and out of breath all too soon. Why not propose to her today and let her know he was here to stay? He'd already found his match in bed. He liked Eugenia's stubborn streak, and they had many similar friends and experiences. Loved her passion and wit. She was clever. One day, she would become a formidable duchess, he suspected. Which had never been his first consideration when it came to picking a wife but was likely a good idea.

He could even see them growing old together, surrounded by their children, and having his cousin Sinclair and Kitty watching on in their old age.

Teddy rapped on Eugenia's door, smiling broadly. When it opened, he was surprised to find she now had a butler he recognized.

He hastily reached for his card and presented it with a flourish to the ginger-headed footman who'd accompanied Eugenia to his carriage several days ago. "I should like to speak with Mrs. Bagshaw. The younger," he added quickly, for clarity.

"I'm afraid she has a gentleman caller at the moment and is not to be disturbed, Mr. Berringer."

That took him aback. It hadn't taken very long for the scoundrels to come calling. He put his foot in the doorway and stepped inside. "I will wait."

"Very good, sir. May I show you to the drawing room?"

He heard a burst of Eugenia's laughter and a deep-throated male response and bristled with not a little jealousy. Clearly, whoever was with Eugenia possessed a sense of humor. Teddy hoped to God the fellow was portly and dull in every other sense, rather than some libertine trying to take his place. "Yes, please do."

Chapter Twenty-Seven

Eugenia laughed in delight. "I'm so happy to hear you say that, my lord."

Lord Sullivan offered a wry grin from his chair in the library in Albemarle Street. "You were right all along. All I needed was more time."

She topped up his teacup, pleased with all she'd heard in the last quarter hour since his unexpected arrival. "Now, if you're determined upon making a good marriage this season, I suggest you waste no time surveying the marriage mart candidates. There is no time to waste in the season, as marriage announcements are on the rise. I think there are but three heiresses left to be swept off their feet."

"I won't need to venture to the marriage mart to make my choice, nor do I need an heiress, though my family might not agree," he told her with a blush.

Eugenia beamed at the change in Lord Sullivan. Gone was the man wracked by guilt as he contemplated remarriage after losing a wife he'd loved deeply and the son he'd longed for. In that place was a man ready for a challenge and excited by the promise of a new future with someone else. "Don't tell me you've already chosen?"

He took a sip of tea. "I have, but I still have some preparations to make before I put myself forward."

"I've always said marriage should never be rushed into, and I'm glad you feel the same. Do you still fear whoever you choose will not be good enough to please your family? You've mentioned before that they've been impossible."

"I've decided to please myself, not them."

Eugenia sipped her tea, smiling in approval at his determined attitude. Too many men try to please their families when they took a wife. They considered the greatness of the match first rather than remembering that they are the ones who have to live with the woman. "Then what do you fear? Does your lady not return your regard?"

Sullivan peered at her before shrugging. "She may not, in fact, like me enough right now, but I hope to convince her of my suitability for her hand when we are better acquainted."

Eugenia did not ask who it was, but it did not sound very promising. It was not her place to play matchmaker with academy clients. She was here to wave Lord Sullivan off on his journey, not hold his hand for the duration. "Your family name is well regarded in society, and you are much admired yourself. You can be sure that is in your favor. She could find no fault with you, and if she does, she must need spectacles. Be firm that you wish to win her hand in marriage, but also make it plain what you want from the match, too. Respect, honesty, and affection are paramount, in my opinion. Women always know what we want and when. But sometimes, we hesitate to ask for it."

"I shall make my interest quite clear and hope to hear from her what more I can do to win her favor," Lord Sullivan said, just as they heard the front door open and close, and the heavy footfalls of another caller being directed into the drawing room to wait. "I see I'm not the only gentleman keen to know if your door is open again to clients. I had best not monopolize your time today, so I might call again another. I do hope we might have occasion to see each other very soon, Mrs. Bagshaw."

Eugenia had decided to resume her business immediately. Her part in the matter of Regis Bagshaw had been more or less resolved yesterday, but two clients in one day were more than she dreamed possible starting out on her own. She would be the sole tutor for gentlemen who needed to practice courtship. Sylvia was much too busy now with the marchioness and Lord Wharton. And Aurora had decided it best she remains near their cousin for propriety's sake.

"Well, then. My door is always open to you, my lord. Do drop by and let me know how your pursuit is coming along from time to time."

"You'll be one of the first to learn of my good fortune, I'm sure," he promised with a wide smile.

As was the custom here, he dropped a small pouch of coins as payment on the corner of her desk on his way out the door. She didn't bother to count the coins before locking them in her desk drawer because Lord Sullivan had always paid fairly before. The academy never asked for a particular sum from any man as payment, only asked to be paid the fee the client thought they deserved. But that was when Sylvia and Aurora had worked alongside her in this room. Now it was just her, and she ought to have far fewer expenses each month.

She saw Lord Sullivan out and then turned to Mr. Bloom, her new butler in training, who was patiently waiting for her attention. "Did I hear another client arrive?"

He handed over a card. "I put him in the drawing room, as you requested, Mrs. Bagshaw."

Eugenia glanced at the card, and a flood of excitement swept over her. Thaddeus had come. She'd been desperate to see him since the happy moment yesterday when Regis Bagshaw had been unveiled as an imposter and taken away to be charged.

With all that had happened yesterday, including the private celebrations with the ladies of the house in the marchioness' room, she'd missed sending him a note of thanks last night.

She'd not been able to send word to Thaddeus about her change of residence yet today, either. Her mother-in-law was keen to talk and bridge the gulf of years and experience of the world between them.

Eugenia slipped into her drawing room, eager to be in Thaddeus' arms once more.

He was standing facing the doorway, hands on his hips and looking cross. "Who was that?"

"Never you mind, sir." She rushed to him and pressed her body against his and raised her face for a kiss that never came.

Thaddeus studied her instead, through narrowed eyes. "Have you had offers of protection from other men already?"

"Gracious no!" She pointed to the door behind her. "That was a client. Where did you get such an absurd idea that I would even consider having a protector?"

His cheeks started to redden.

She shook her head at him, sorely disappointed. "Have you been speaking with my cousins?"

"Aurora," he admitted sheepishly, scrubbing at his head. "Clearly, I won't ever again. I apologize that I jumped to the wrong conclusion, but when I heard you say you looked forward to seeing the other man, I feared I was too late to stake my claim."

She clucked her tongue, but she was also secretly pleased by his reaction. It was good that Thaddeus did not take her affections for granted. Part of her wanted him to be a little possessive about her, but only every now and then. She patted his chest soothingly. He had nothing to fear from other men. None could ever replace him in her affections anytime soon. "I have a mother-in-law to support, sir," she reminded him. "I'll not take another penny from Wharton if I can avoid it, either, so I must earn a living."

He looked around the newly dusted chamber. "So, you *did* reopen the academy?"

"Just today. Do you disapprove?"

"I have no opinion yet." He smiled quickly and stole a kiss from her lips. "Tell me, where is Mrs. Bagshaw now? What does she think of all this?"

"My mama-in-law is resting in Sylvia's old bedchamber upstairs—which have become hers now, since Sylvia will not be back. And my mama believes it a sensible scheme that we ladies support ourselves however we can."

As soon as she finished speaking, Thaddeus bent to steal another kiss, a long and searing one that eased her loneliness and brought forth cravings for pleasures only he could satisfy. He drew back eventually and pulled her to sit on a chaise beside him.

He toyed with her fingers and brought them to his lips to kiss her knuckles. "Are you sure about this? Moving here?"

"Indeed I am. This is where I belong," she promised. "A simple life is all I require for my happiness."

He squeezed her fingers and kissed them again. "What if you're meant to live somewhere else? Later in your life, I mean."

She frowned. "I have no looking glass into the future."

"What if you must already know one path you might take, but it scares you witless to contemplate? What if it's not a simple life you could have, but as complicated as it gets?" He smiled sheepishly. "What if I did ask you to marry me?"

She snorted. "You're not ready for matrimony yet, sir. Neither am I."

He smoothed her hair back from her face and smiled softly. "I cannot think of another woman I'd consider undertaking it with, if not you."

"In time, you would have other choices available to you," Eugenia said with a heavy sigh. "As I was just telling my client, there are three heiresses left on the marriage mart. More are sure to appear next year and beyond."

"What if we reached an agreement? Say, to enjoy a long and secret engagement first? Would that change your answer? An engagement while we decide if marriage to each other is what you want."

She stared at him. "You suggest we become engaged and not tell our families?"

"Until we have to or want to, yes. I know it might seem a sudden proposal and quite foolish to keep it a secret, but I am committing myself to you here and now. There will be no misunderstandings, no other women, no cause for concern that my affections have waned. I will always be busy going about the duke's business. He could keep introducing me to more young women, though I've told him I'm in love, but not with whom now.

"And you have a business to run here, and your family, too." He twined their fingers together. "I do love you, Eugenia. More than I thought I could love anyone, and yet, marriage is not perhaps an immediate desire for either one of us yet. You've just reclaimed your independence. Your married name, too, and with a new mama-in-law to get to know, I can understand why making a marriage with me is the last thing on your mind."

"And you have a house to furnish," she suggested, nodding to all he'd said so far. "Marriage is a big step."

"Indeed, it is. The furnishing of my house isn't important. I'll not bother with the redecoration anymore. I think my wife might want to have a say in that. I'm not concerned about staying with my cousin and his wife still, either. I love them dearly, and I suspect, too, that when I do embark on a marriage, they agree that I should have my own home. We will need somewhere that is just ours. I'd like it to be here instead of Clifford Street."

"I have missed my work and this house," she whispered. "And I have missed you these past days, too. The business will keep me occupied and well-funded most of the time, but not all year or forever." She glanced sideways at him. "It was Lord Sullivan who called upon me as soon as he heard I'd come back to live here. He was a client before and wanted to know I was all right, given what Wharton had told you all earlier."

"I imagine other gents will do the same," he suggested and then grinned. "Call on you to see if you're in need of a protector, too."

"Sullivan never offered. He came to speak on a matter we've discussed many times before—his need to make a second marriage," she admitted. "Talking to him has reaffirmed my wish to keep my career, offering instruction to uncertain gentlemen. I stopped only because Wharton disapproved."

"I've no quarrel with your need to work or what you do here. A life of idleness has sat ill on my shoulders as well."

"What will you do if we don't marry?"

"Keep an eye on my cousin and future concerns, and extend my knowledge of the woman I adore until she realizes she cannot live without me, either."

She smiled up at him and leaned into him a little harder. "A statement like that warms my heart. You'll do well when the time comes to make a proper proposal."

"A smile like yours always warms certain parts of me." He frowned, though. "What exactly constitutes a proper proposal? I've never been sure of that."

"An admittance of feelings, a promise to always be there for the other person no matter what they do or decide in years to come…"

She suddenly gaped at him, realizing he'd already done all of that for her, and more.

Thaddeus pressed his lips to her brow. "I'm already yours, heart and soul. My wings clipped. My desires mirror yours when it comes to life and the pleasures of the night. Haven't I already proved my devotion to your cause? Will you have me, Eugenia?"

"Can it really be so easy?" Eugenia met his gaze, lifting her hands to cup his face. Eugenia had never imagined she'd marry again, or have to decide so suddenly. She'd been content to be alone except for a string of easily discarded lovers.

Affairs always end. Sometimes painfully. But when she looked into Thaddeus' eyes, she only saw a challenging future with him, not something to fear.

She loved him, and he loved her. They could be together forever until death parted them.

She had even known Thaddeus longer and more deeply than she had Robbie Bagshaw, and she hadn't hesitated to wed him. "Yes, it could be."

He broke free of her hands to nuzzle her neck. "Was that a yes to my proposal, my love?"

Her heart softened, allowing her to admit to herself that she'd dreaded losing Thaddeus to another. "It is a yes to everything you might ever suggest, sir." She slid her fingers between the buttons of his waistcoat, rested them against a warm heart that beat fast with hope and expectation of their love. "I want to be with you."

"And I with you. Now." He drew out the ring to match her chains and slipped it upon the first finger it fit on her left hand.

There would be other jewels in the future she supposed, but nothing proved his devotion more than the perfect gift of him. He brought her fingers to his lips to kiss and then hurried to lock the door, so they could begin to celebrate their love.

Eugenia laughed as he lay her down on the settee, and she moaned as softly as she could to everything else he did to her… forever after.

Epilogue

TEDDY LEANED toward Eugenia as she twirled a simple gold ring around the third finger on her right hand and whispered. "What do you think are our chances of escaping this?"

"Highly unlikely now."

"A pity. I suddenly thought of us at that inn in Dover, of having you up against the wall."

She settled the ring that matched her chains upon her finger and stared at it in the moonlight. She'd done that every day since Thaddeus had offered it to her two months ago. A happy day it had been, too, when she'd agreed to take his name for her own one day. Only he hadn't expected to receive another from him so soon.

She wore a second, gem studded ring around her finger now too. Trying to become accustomed to the costly ring on her finger was going to be harder than wearing the first. "Perhaps we could do that tomorrow night, on our way to Grafton Park."

"I'd already planned to." Thaddeus grinned. "His grace will come after us if we delay much longer. You remember how pleased he seemed when we told him our news earlier? Well, when we were alone after, he practically danced a jig across the library floor. He cannot wait to share the good news of our upcoming marriage with everyone." Teddy squared his shoulders. "We'd better get this over with then?"

Eugenia laughed nervously, stealing a peek inside Lady Bisley's ballroom before drawing back. "Please remember, you brought this down upon your own head when you asked me to marry you."

He laughed. "How was I to know you couldn't keep our secret betrothal an actual secret for more than two months?"

"It was that dreadful Lady Fuller. She had her filthy paws on my future husband, and I was so angry at her presumption that it just came rushing out," she said with a grimace.

"I don't mind. I'm glad to end the deception." He caught her hands and brought them to his lips and kissed each of her knuckles. Her hands were a little cold tonight, nervousness perhaps brought about by their upcoming introduction as a betrothed couple. "We'll stumble through this together, yes?"

She sighed. "Neither one of us wanted the fuss of a grand wedding, but I suppose the duke is making plans?"

"He's certainly trying, though we could always elope. Sinclair and Kitty cannot really complain if we follow in their esteemed footsteps."

"They will be large shoes to fill, indeed," Eugenia whispered and then laughed. "Oh, look at us, Thaddeus. Paralyzed by fear over announcing to the ton what we feel for each other. It's not as if we've suddenly become titled. We're just marrying each other."

He glanced down at her twisting hands with one brow raised. "Imagine their shock when they learn you are increasing already, too."

"Might be," she warned. She placed her hands protectively over her belly where once his gift of a long chain had hidden beneath her gown, but which now appeared to be suddenly too small to fit her waistline. Eugenia's courses were late, which was unusual for her, too. However, their two months of being secretly engaged hadn't diminished their mutual lust for each other, so it was entirely possible they'd be parents after Christmas.

And after what they'd been through together to reach this point, he hoped for a child to come as soon as possible.

"Do we really need to say anything? Couldn't everyone just find out when my stomach swells round enough not to be able to hide it?"

"Exeter won't be able to keep his lips shut once he learns,"

Teddy warned. "Our child will be spoiled before he even draws his first breath."

Eugenia arched a brow. "He?"

Teddy caressed her cheek. "A figure of speech, my love, though for the duke's sake, I hope for a son. Sinclair worries about the succession even when he has me."

"He worries too much about that, but at least he has the peace of mind now that you are doing all you can to expand your family by at least marrying someone."

"Not just anyone." Teddy pulled her close against his body. "I love you with all my heart."

"I know, and that was the reason I accepted. I'd be entirely satisfied spending my whole life slipping away with you if only we could get away with it that long."

"I am so glad we chose to wed each other and end the speculation of who I would choose. It will likely be a long time before we are titled. Until then, we are Mr. And Mrs. Berringer. A husband and wife with an expectation of riches and great responsibilities to fall upon us sometime in the future."

"A very distant future, it had better be." She looked inside through the curtain. "Oh dear, I can see his grace. He's consulting his pocket watch again. No. Now his foot is tapping, too, and he's beginning to look cross. We had better go in."

Eugenia started forward, but Teddy captured her hand and held her in the shadows with him a little longer. He inhaled deeply as he looked down upon her slender neck. "Do you remember?"

She glanced over her shoulder at him. "How could I not? This is how you first kissed me."

He nodded. "Do you know what I've been thinking since?"

"No. What?"

"That I should have done a more thorough job of it that first time." He turned her around to face him, drawing her away from the brink of joining society, and pressed her back against the wall.

"Oh, Thaddeus," she whispered. "I've never been

disappointed in your first kiss. They all have been worth the wait."

"Darling Eugenia, all I thought I had that night was a willing partner to indulge in the pleasures of the night. What I needed more than nights was the days too, and all the hours in between."

"You will have them," she whispered. "Always."

Teddy placed his lips beside Eugenia's, teasing her with the idea of a kiss without stealing one. There was so much more to love than just pleasure. There was yearning for the next stolen moment and scandalous kisses, too. Afternoons spent reading together, dancing at balls, knowing how much they meant to each other, and finding countless ways to increase their intimacy.

Teddy stole a kiss and then another, knowing he never wanted to stop. But duty called. He took Eugenia's hand firmly in his, giving it a squeeze to calm his own nerves more than hers, before leading his future wife into the ballroom to continue their happy pairing in public.

Thank you reading PLEASURES OF THE NIGHT! I hope you enjoyed Teddy and Eugenia's romance.

Distinguished Rogues Series

Book 1: Chills (FREE READ)
The rogue she can't have is the only one she wants.

Book 2: Broken
His wicked ways could be the best hope for her future.

Book 3: Charity
Reclaiming the love of his life is bound to break a few rules.

Book 4: An Accidental Affair
Being good was a damned nuisance!

Book 5: Keepsake
The runaway bride is back to cause trouble!

Book 6: An Improper Proposal
Educating the innocent might have been a mistake.

Book 7: Reason to Wed
Duty is the last thing on his mind once they kiss.

Book 8: The Trouble with Love
Keeping a promise has never been harder!

Book 9: Married by Moonlight
The marriage mart is murder!

Book 10: Lord of Sin

In the battle between love and duty, the heart has the most to lose...

Book 11: The Duke's Heart

He's looking for love...just not for himself!

Book 12: Romancing the Earl

Can a broken heart be won?

Book 13: One Enchanted Christmas

He's betting on love...

Book 14: Desire by Design

It's the quiet ones that bear watching...

Book 15: His Perfect Bride

Accept no substitute when it comes to love...

Book 16: Pleasures of the Night

Even spinsters have imaginations...

More Regency Romance...

Wild Randalls Series
Book 1: Engaging the Enemy
Book 2: Forsaking the Prize
Book 3: Guarding the Spoils
Book 4: Hunting the Hero

Saints and Sinners Series
Book 1: The Duke and I
Book 2: A Gentleman's Vow
Book 3: An Earl of Her Own
Book 4: The Lady Tamed

Rebel Hearts Series
Book 1: The Wedding Affair
Book 2: An Affair of Honor
Book 3: The Christmas Affair
Book 4: An Affair so Right

Miss Mayhem Series
Book 1: Miss Watson's First Scandal
Book 2: Miss George's Second Chance
Book 3: Miss Radley's Third Dare
Book 4: Miss Merton's Last Hope

...and many more

About Heather Boyd

USA Today Bestselling Author Heather Boyd believes every character she creates deserves their own happily-ever-after—no matter how much trouble she puts them through. With that goal in mind, she writes steamy romances that skirt the boundaries of propriety to keep readers enthralled until the wee hours of the morning. Heather has published over 40 regency romance novels and shorter works full of daring seductions and distinguished rogues. She lives north of Sydney, Australia, with her trio of rogues and pair of four-legged overlords.

Let's be friends! Find Heather at:
Heather-Boyd.com

facebook.com/HeatherBoydRomanceAuthor

twitter.com/Heather_Boyd

instagram.com/iheatherboyd

bookbub.com/authors/heather-boyd

goodreads.com/Heather_Boyd